Whispers OF THE past

I0738038

BOOK ONE

Whispers of the Past

BY OWEN CLOUGH

weka
ficton

WEKA FICTION
owencloughbooks.com

No part of this book may be reproduced, stored in a retrieval system, or transmitted by any means, electronic, mechanical, photocopying recording, or otherwise without written permission from the author.

Copyright @ Owen Clough 2016.

All rights reserved.

The right of Owen Clough to be identified as author of the work has been asserted by him in accordance with the New Zealand Copyright Act 1994.

Cover design by Tania Hassounia of Drawer Full of Giants.

National Library of New Zealand Cataloguing-in-Publication Data.

ISBN IngramSpark Edition: 978-0473-45552-1

Published in New Zealand

A catalogue record for this book is available from the National Library of New Zealand.
Kei te pātengi raraunga o Te Puna Mātauranga o Aotearoa te whakarārangi o tēnei pukapuka.

This book is dedicated to
my wife Kaye, our daughter Tania,
our son Brent and our granddaughter Sofia.

AUTHOR'S NOTE

This book is a work of fiction. All persons, places and events in this story are a product of the author's imagination, and any similarity to real people, places, events and organisation is coincidental. Although some mention is made of historical events they are there to enhance authenticity, they are not intended to be fact, or to describe or portray any real world person, tactics, beliefs or policies.

> *'Study the past if you would define the future.'*
> \- Confucius

ACKNOWLEDGEMENTS

Writing any book, as always there are many people to thank. In my case, I have been very lucky to have some wonderful women to do the hard yards in making this become a reality.

My wife Kaye, who tirelessly, went over every chapter correcting grammar changing the flow of the story so it would make sense to the reader. I would never have been able to get to this stage if it had not been for her.

My daughter Tania who designed the cover of the book, a dedicated graphic designer illustrator. I was pleased as punch to have another family member involved in the production of the book

My Cousin an author from Australia, Kylie Price who was instrumental in starting me on this journey, to her my sincere thanks. Pointing me in the right direction when I was unsure.

To all those too numerous to mention for their help, encouragement and helpful suggestions my sincere thanks.

GLOSSARY

Haera Ra – Goodbye.
Hangi - Oven in the earth.
Hongi - Greeting nose to nose.
Hui - Gathering/Meeting.
Hapu - Clan.

Kai - Food.
Kainga – Unfortified village.
Kai Pai – Good.
Kawakawa – Tree Leaf for medical purposes.
Kereru - Wood Pigeon.
Kete - Flax bag.
Kumara – Sweet potato.
Kupapa - Maori who fought on the side of the English.

Marae - Gathering space in front of meeting house.
Mere - Short broad blade weapon made from Greenstone.
Moko - Tattoo face/body marking.

Pa - Fortified Maori village.
Pakeha - White person/European.
Porangi - Mad
Putu - Short broad blade weapon mainly of stone.

Ruru - Owl.
Rangitira – Leader.

Taiaha - Fighting staff.
Taihoa - Wait.
Tamariki – Child/Children.
Taniwha - Mythical creature.
Tao - Short spear.
Tapu - Sacred.
Taupa - Percussion double barrel shotgun.
Ti Kouka - Cabbage Tree
Tohonga - Priest/Healer, expert practitioner of any skill.

Utu - Revenge

Wahine - Woman/Female
Whaeo - Mother
Whanua - Family
Whare - House

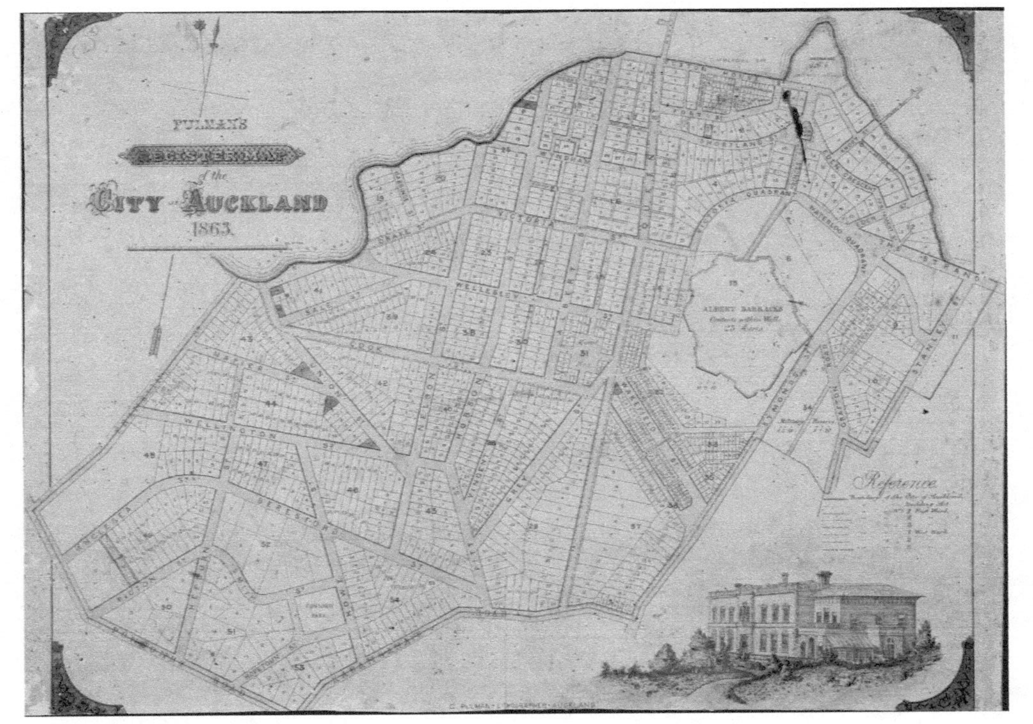

FULMAN'S
REGISTER MAP
of the
CITY of AUCKLAND
1863
ALBERT BARRACKS
Reference
VICTORIA
WELLESLEY
COOK
WELLINGTON
BERESFORD
NELSON
HOBSON
VINCENT
STANLEY ST
WATERLOO QUADRANT
SYMONDS ST

CHAPTER ONE

Looking back on what happened to me and my mates, I'm still in a bit of a daze. Where do you start? How do you put it down on paper? I'm not a writer, but I need to categorise what cropped up over the last twenty months or so. Not to tell the world as such but try to and clear my own head about the things that went on up there in the Tongariro National Park. I have kept it quiet well, the government told me to and anyway who the hell will believe my story, it's so unbelievable. However, it did happen, and I need to put it down in writing so even I can understand it. Officially, the government will take a dim view of me if it got out; they would come down on me like a ton of bricks, they said. Nevertheless, I need to get the story down on paper for my sake and bugger the consequences.

My name is Bob Kydd, thirty-one-year-old ex-air force, driver by trade, a keen tramper. I enjoy history, the bush, mountains, music and half a degree in history. My two mates: Shane Langford thirty-year-old ex-army, overseas service in Timor, motor mechanic, he can put his hand to anything; and Samuel McInnes, thirty-year-old ex-army, he works for the Department of Conservation 'DOC', with a degree in conservation. Three blokes from different backgrounds with a common love of being in our national parks of New Zealand, close as mates can be. Furthermore, we all have a passion for music. Sam can play about five instruments, a pretty talented individual. It was funny how we met. We were all in the services at the time, stationed at Linton Military camp on a driver's course. We ended up in the same hut; we were even assigned the same truck, and just hit if off. They called me Brilly or Brill, an old air-force sling off from the Second World War, 'Brill cream boy', so Brilly or Brill stuck. Shane was Grunt army slang for soldier. He scared the hell out of me for a man of his size, creeping around without being seen or heard whilst blending into the surrounding bush. It might be because of his Māori heritage a good man to have on your side. I only saw him as a bloke with an all-year tan, light at that. My eyesight was really excellent, and he could still get close before I could catch a sign of him; yes definitely best to have him on your side. Then, there was Samuel: 'Sam' was the hunter, as good as – or even better than – Grunt in the bush. He is skilled with a gun, an excellent tracker, and he could read the bush and the weather by just looking at the sky. A natural bushman. A quiet man, deep. All big men seem to have these characteristics. Both blokes were far better than me in the bush, though I enjoyed the tramps, the mountains, and fresh air on my face. Shooting a rifle was natural for me as I had an air-force marksman badge for the effort, though that didn't cut the mustard with my mates, they just seemed to have this perfection with any type of weapon. I was the shortest of the bunch;

the other two were about the same height, just over two metres, six feet five inches I'm about one point seven metres, five feet six inches. Now, and again, they would call me 'runt'. On the rugby field, it was a different kettle of fish I could tackle those blokes with ease. It was always nice to drop them to the ground. Big blokes cannot run without legs, and I used to get them every time. We played rugby while at Linton, to fill in when their team was short, another way of bonding I suppose. We also played a bit of club stuff while in the Manawatu. I even played against them a few times, gaining their respect, because a little fella like me could drop them like a sack of spuds, and that was enjoyable. Shane thought he was quick, but down he would go when I got to his legs. Our love of the outdoors, quiet nights in the bush, listening to the night sounds made us close, more like brothers. We were together for over six months and when we left to wherever we always kept in touch as much as possible.

Eventually, we all left the services. We made a pact to stay in touch and do at least one good tramp a year together. We have every year since, in fact, and we can get in a couple if we are lucky. We all have an input on our next tramp. We have done a few tramps now: Fiordland, Mount Aspiring, Able Tasman, Waikaremoana, and so on.

This time it was Sam's pick. He suggested Tongariro, he thought; it might be good to include some pig shooting in at the same time. As a DOC employee, they were getting worried about the number of porkers in the National Park. He said it would be a good tramp with a bit of hunting.

He would arrange for a chopper to lift out the dead-uns, as long as we brought them back to a pickup point of his making. We were all for that, humping Captain Cookers out of the bush is hard work. Captain James Cook brought pigs with him to New Zealand, gifting them to local Māori, and of course, they bred. They occasionally escaped into the bush and formed the wild populations that we have today. As a result, feral pigs in New Zealand are often referred to as Captain Cookers. These wild ones look quite different than most domestic breeds. They have a distinctive shape. Large shoulders, smaller rear quarters, larger snouts and tusks, with a straight tail, a hairier body, more than the domestic ones. Don't give them any leeway as they will turn on you as quick as a wink. We decided to take an extra few weeks off work, and on top of the holidays, that gave us six weeks out there in the wide-open space of the Tongariro Plateau

Living in the South Island, I was working on the Christchurch rebuild, after the devastating earthquakes they had from 2010 to 2012. Plenty of work for drivers, big machine stuff, and making good money. None of us being married was a bonus. Shane was living in Petone, Wellington, working for Ford; all his family were from the far north. Sam was a rover for DOC, so he could be anywhere, though his family home of Dunedin was in the deep south of New Zealand. He was a cunning sod actually, choosing the Tongariro area, as he would incorporate this tramp into his job and so did not have to take leave. Lucky bugger, I envied his job sometimes. Not so much in winter though. So we had a good old chinwag on Skype, decisions were made, and we picked a date the middle of February to head out. Getting holidays was not too hard, which we pencilled in. We talked about what we needed to take: six weeks in the bush, you really have to prepare. Then I started to write lists.

Everything had to pack in, pack out, so a lot of thought was required. We should be okay for meat, we would live off the land, and there were plenty of pigs. I mean, that's what we were going to cull, but also deer, goat, and possum. People cannot get their head around eating possum. It tastes just like chicken, though some say it can be tough depending on how it is cooked. It can be gamey and it's an acquired taste, but nothing wrong with it – cook it for three hours and the meat just falls off the bone. The possum is a curious animal, not afraid of human scent. Make a noise and they will be up a tree looking down at you, so easy to knock off. You just have to have to be careful, as they can carry TB. As long as there are no white spots in the liver, they are good as gold to eat. Therefore, meat will be plentiful. Just the other basics we would have to think about for the whole period, and that was regularly left to me. I was also the first aider, even though we all were competent. The other blokes still had army first-aid packs – war zone stuff. So we were lucky in that respect, perks of the job eh! Those army packs were the serious stuff. Bandages, tape; all types of wound dressings, Atropine injection syringes, and intravenous equipment. The list went on and on. You had to have a bit of an idea as to how to use it all. We all had some training. Really, they were only there if needed, and we hoped they would not be used. So we thought. Legal, probably not, as they had things in those packs, drugs and the such-like that we were not supposed to have. Hell, some rules are meant to be broken, and if they helped us when something went wrong, that's good, isn't it? We would be in contact at every opportunity until we leave, and it's a good chance to catch up with my mates' families as well. We were safety conscious, and the families needed to be kept in the loop. They would know where we will be at any given time, well, up to a point. No cell phone towers where we were going.

Shane's parents were really great. His mum was a quarter or an eighth Māori, his dad's a retired a builder now. Grunt had a good handle on the building trade as well, an all-rounder. His mother loved to talk about her family. I enjoy her stories. Not as though she lived the Māori life, or spoke the language – she just made sure her children learned a bit about their Māori background, so they could remember who and where they were from. I had a Māori third-great-aunt way back, listening to Grunt's mum talk about her family conjured up warm feelings of my dad talking about the early days of our family in New Zealand. It would be great to find this aunt of mine on my family tree.

We would catch up with his parents in Wellington as they were down visiting. I would pick up Shane there, so it would all tie in. I was looking forward to it. Sam's folks were so different to him: his Dad an accountant, his mother a teacher. The apple couldn't fall further from the tree. To have a son as a hunter was a bit unusual, but they were proud of him, and he did have his degree. His mum would say, 'Oh our son lives in the bush or mountains.' They were from Dunedin, with ancestors from Scotland. He said his third-great-grandparents were from Falkirk. Sam's mum was really keen for him to meet a girl. Whenever he went home, there was a young lady around for dinner. Sam joked about it to us. 'Mum and her horseflesh. I'm always interested to see whom she has jacked up this time. I feel sorry for the girls.' He would say, 'We have nothing in common, but mum would still insist I take them home. So as soon as we are out of the place, we would go down to the pub for a few drinks and a laugh. She would tell me all about how she was manipulated into coming.' Nice girls, but like us, he's not ready to get tied down. Me, well, I might have been a disappointment to my dad. He was a fisherman out of Riverton, at the bottom of the South Island. Funny, I'm bloody useless in any type of boat, I puke in a bathtub which left Dad horrified. They tried every medication, including witchcraft, to stop me being sick but nothing worked. I use to love the boat, the smell of the sea, but once out in it, I would feed the fishes. Therefore, to be a driver was a bit of a let-down to him, though he never showed it. My sister took over for me. She was the perfect skipper, loved the sea, the rougher the better; she was the apple of dad's eye. Dad was the only one of his family to move from the North Island, born in Auckland, went south as a young man on the oyster boats and stayed. He went home on holiday, met mum up in Whangarei; they married, and then went to live in Invercargill the bottom of New Zealand. Both my sister and I were born down there in the deep south.

So there we were three average blokes, planning a nice six weeks away from the hustle and bustle of work, no worries in the world, looking forward to the mountains and freedom of the wide-open spaces. Things were coming together pretty well by the end of January. I had most of the provisions list worked out and also had booked the mountain radios. We never go anywhere without them on any tramp. They can be life or death. I have spoken to the boys quite a few times, making sure that at least one of us had a GPS phone. I'm still old-fashioned. My phone can only text, and that's it. The others will take their phones with them. They are good cameras, as well as nice and light. Sam also wanted a record of how many pigs we culled. The phone was ideal for that. I would take my very small, slimline camera that would fit into my top pocket. It takes photos good enough for me. I also found in Dick Smith's shop a multi-function USB solar panel for thirty dollars that was light and easy to slip into the pack. So we can keep our phones charged, a bit of a bonus. Ammo was also a big thing. Six weeks is a long time, we had to make sure that we had enough to last. There was no point firing away willy-nilly, without hitting a thing, so every shot had to count. Even if you are a good shot, things out of your control can happen. You could wound, or even miss what you are shooting at. We had done a bit of shooting together and have a pretty good routine. Sam and Shane lock on to one animal. One covers the shot, usually, it goes down, but if not, the second bloke is there to make the kill. I am the backup. I'm down on the beast like a bolt out of hell after we don't see movement, to cut its throat, or to finish it off if need be. Now and again I do the firing if it's a clean shot. I don't mind playing second fiddle to them as they are better than I am, but I do have good eyes and can pick up movement up to one thousand metres, so they look to me as their human binoculars. It works well, up until now, we have had a ninety-nine percent kill rate; only once we all cocked it up and the bloody pig turned on us. Three bullets in him and he came for us in a rage. Shit on a blanket, I have never climbed a tree so quickly in all my life. I beat the other two buggers. I was up into the leaves before them, giving them encouragement where the old boar was in relation to their arse. It was funny to see calm, cool Grunt and Sam climbing over each other, as they tore up the tree – I wish I'd had one of their phones then.

This was the once and we sure learnt from it, so we made very sure that the animal is dead as a dodo before we moved. We worked as a team; I did the spotting, the others did the killing. We only killed for food usually, but if we went into an area where there were a lot of animals, we would shoot as many as we could. All this stuff has been detrimental to our bush. New Zealand is a land of birds, but since all the mammals have been introduced, they have sure ruined our native bush. They have no protection and are fair game. This hunt was going to be a bit different. Everyone will shoot as much as possible; this was a cull not for food as such. So I was looking forward to having my fair share of culling.

Sam rang to have a yarn and to tell me he had arranged a chopper to drop us in, which would save us the hike. It was a hard day's walk into the hut. This would be a bonus, good old DOC. He went on to say they have a hut where we were going, which could be used as a base camp for the duration. From there we could branch out in any direction for any length of time that was required. If the weather turned bad, we would have a dry roof over our heads to go back to. He asked me to pass the news on to Shane. Furthermore, he arranged to leave our vehicle at the army camp at Waiouru. I was over the moon about this, as it's always a worry when you go out to leave your vehicle unattended for any length of time. So things were coming together well. All I had to do now is make sure my rifle was okay. I had an old 303 which was my great-grandfather Thomas' gun, from WWII, a Lee-Enfield with a ten-round magazine. How he got away by not handing it in after the war, goodness knows. It was passed down to the oldest son of each generation, so now it was mine and properly registered with the police. Well, I was. The only change I had done with this gun was to add telescopic sites to it, which made all the difference. It was a fine gun. It made me feel part of history and in contact with my forbearers. I was only three when my great-grandfather died. With me being keen on history and genealogy, anything to do with our past, I'm all ears.

In the meantime, things were moving in the right direction. The boat crossing was arranged for a couple of days earlier than necessary. There was enough time to be had with Shane in Wellington. His parents were staying with him, and I wanted to ask his mum some questions about Northland. I hoped she could remember something. Talking to his parents brought their stories of family alive and evoked memories of my own mum's family in the far north. Furthermore, I wanted to ask his parents if their family ever heard of a relation of mine, this third-Great-Aunt Mary Tilly née Hohepa, who married my third-Great-Uncle David Tilly, in Kaitaia about 1891. It was a long shot, but I was really interested in finding out about this part of my family and had had no luck to date. A phone call home to my folks. Dad had booked my Surf Wagon over on the ferry as he was a member of the motor club and had gotten a good discount. Then he posted me his card ID number, proof that it was him. Saying, 'Well, I belong to the club and have not had much time to use my card, the family should get something out of it.' Anything for a discount, I'm all for it. So I was booked on Bluebridge for a ten am sailing from Picton to Wellington. I would be at Shane's for a late lunch, about two pm and then out for tea with Shane and his folks. Last-minute preparations the next day; then north we would head.

Sam had popped home for a couple of days also. I got

a phone call to say he would catch me in Christchurch and travel up with me, which ended up bloody good. We would all be together in Wellington before we head north. I rang Shane again. 'G'day mate. Sam will be with me, put up the bunk for him as well.' 'Good as gold Brill, see you about two p.m. Saturday.' Mrs. Langford will be in her element with us being there. She had a couple of daughters who were not married, and Sam reckons she was trying to palm them off onto us. They didn't have their kids until they were in their mid-thirties. Lizzy, was twenty-nine now, Carolyn twenty-eight, Shane was coming up thirty-one while we were away. With only his parents there to say happy birthday, his sisters who lived in Auckland would phone no doubt before we left. I have to admit Carolyn and Liz are great ladies, but whenever we meet we just talked, had a few drinks, and it didn't move on from there. Their brother, my mate Shane, is a shy bloke around a woman. He clams up, but out with us gets him going, and you have to smother him to shut him up. I remember his mum saying that when he finds the right woman, he'll be gone in a day. Yeah right, I thought. So it was time to go. I locked up the flat. Mrs. Hill next door will look after the key and mail. Any bills, well, I would worry about that when I got back. Power off and the fridge emptied. Pack full at about forty kilograms, was a bit on the heavy side, just under half my weight. We were going for six weeks so we needed as many supplies as possible to carry in. I had sent the food requirements to the boys, so they would get the supplies we agreed to. We'll sort our packs out together before we head off, making sure everything was fairly shared with food, etc. That way, if someone loses their pack, or it drowns in a river, we have food in the other two packs. It works for us. I took one last good look around as Sam came around the corner in a cab. 'Cut that fine,' he said with a big grin on his face. 'Shit, it's good to see you, Brill,' slapping me on the back, which just about took my breath away.'Bugger me, Sam; you have got bigger,' I spluttered, 'what's with the no-neck look, Oh! You're a prop, hoping to get selected for the Highlanders mate.'He looked at me with a funny smile. 'Never told you or Grunt, but I did try out for Otago, but my job was too important, So I said no.' Well, you could have knocked me over with a feather. I would have given my left nut to be asked to play with a provincial club. Old Sam turned it down. I could not believe it. 'Wouldn't be able to keep my job mate. You of all people know how much I like the outdoors. I'm happy Bob. It was nice of them to offer though.' 'Shit, you must have got better over the years Sam, how did you fit it in, not even a whisper that you were playing?' 'Oh, I played a couple of matches for King Country last winter, and they told the Otago coach to look out for me, so while I was home I had a couple of trials, and they offered me a contract. It came right out of the blue. It took me all day to think about it, but in the end, I said no, my job is important, and it's what I do.' 'Shane is going to be bug-eyed, mate,' I said grinning at him. 'He always thought he was the bee's knees on the field. He was good, but he was a fraction too slow for a flanker. I used to get him every time when I played against him, remember.' Sam grinned. 'You sure did mate, me as well, but to tell you the truth; those blokes work their bodies hard, so really for the money, they earn it. No, I'm happy.' 'It would have been nice to tell people that my friend is a celebrity in his own lunchtime, but now I'll have to be happy that my friend is a Grizzly Adams,' I replied. Looking at my watch, 'We'd better get a move on; the boat won't wait for us. Hope it's a smooth sailing mate. I have had my sick pills, should be okay in the Sounds, and just need it to be calm in Cooks Strait.' We jumped into my Toyota 4x4 Surf and headed out into the wild blue yonder. Little did we know that in a few short weeks, things would never be the same again.

CHAPTER TWO

I love the early mornings. Leaving at 5 am on a new day is always to my way of thinking a brand-new start. The day we left for Wellington was one of those days. A few white puffy clouds across the sky, the expanse of blue, no breeze and hardly any traffic on the road. We settled down, heading north on State Highway One to our breakfast stop along the Kaikoura coast.

February is a good month to holiday. Schools are back and so is uni, only the tourists are about, the country is not as crowded like in January. The weather is really starting to settle down all over New Zealand, a great time for tramping. As we drove Sam would be humming along with the radio. Then we would both get into the song and beat it out. Life sure is for living, on days like this. Passing Parnassus, I said to Sam, 'My great-great-grandfather was a stockman here. This was the rail terminus from Christchurch, with just a shingle road to Picton. It must have been back in the 1930s. Later he up and tramped the Haast Pass before the road was in from Wanaka to Greymouth. No one around then, mate, wilderness stuff.' We yarned as you do, and came off the Hunderlee Hills to the vast expanse of the

Pacific Ocean. It always takes my breath away, the deep blue going on forever. The waves were silky and smooth, no power in them this day, just lazily pushing up the beach to die quietly before the froth slowly drained back into the sea, followed by the next limp wave. I have seen the waves here come up over the road. This was a special day, made for me, as if it knew that I had to get onto a boat and cross the Strait, good old King Neptune has calmed it all down for the trip over. I have my fingers, toes and all loose bits crossed, with a few prayers as well.

Sam was looking for a place to pull over for breakfast. We found a good parking area jutting out into the sea. We pulled in and parked. You could smell the seals as soon as you got out of the Toyota Surf. They are New Zealand fur seals, brought back from the brink of extinction, now fully protected and coming back in good numbers. They were returning to the rocks to bask and clean themselves after feeding. There is lots of kelp on this coast. We watched, as it lazily swayed in the ebb and flow of the water with some young seals playing in the pools below us. We found ourselves a good possie to sit. I had made some ham, tomato, lettuce and cheese sandwiches, big thick ones as we both liked our tucker. Sam got the camp stove going, boiled up the billy and made tea for himself and a cup of coffee for me. We sat down to watch the antics of the seals. You are good as gold, as long as you don't get between them and the sea. Just keep your distance. With a mouth full of food, he said, 'Neat mate, this is perfect. I'm honestly looking forward to the next month or so if

it's going to be like this. It seriously is going to be special.'
Little did we know.

Behind us, arising out of the sea are the Kaikoura
Mountains, from sea level to two thousand six hundred
metres. There are not that many places around the world
where you can swim, fish and ski in a matter of hours on
the same day. The mountains still had snow on the tops.
We will follow them all the way until they head inland
toward Nelson. We have tramped these mountains before,
and you have to be fit. This was really picture post-card
stuff, silky seals, blue ocean and snow-capped mountains.
It just couldn't get better than this. Sam said, looking at
his watch, 'We'd better move, Brill, as much as I'm quite
happy to stay, we don't want to miss the boat.' 'Okay,
mate,' I said while trying to shoo a wayward young seal
from under the vehicle. 'You drive, and I'll get some pics.'
With reluctance, we pulled out and headed north. The
traffic was still light at only six-thirty in the morning as
we drove through the town of Kaikoura. Whale watching
here is the big drawcard, with sperm whales less than a
kilometre off the beach. The Kaikoura Trench drops 1200
metres and is sixty kilometres long. The whales feed there
all year round, as well as big pods of dolphins, and other
sea and bird life. It is a nice place to visit out of the tourist
season. You might have guessed by now, that we do like
the quiet places. I have seen a pod of one hundred and
fifty odd dolphins off the beach. Just an amazing place! I
took some nice photos of the road up the coast north of
Kaikoura, and then we turned away from the coast and

headed inland. Seddon was a pee stop. These poor buggers had earthquakes last year as well just like Christchurch. There were a few buildings with fences around them, to keep the rubberneckers out, in case they fell on them. I have had enough of earthquakes, so was pleased to move on to Blenheim. We took our time. It was just after eight-thirty, so we decided to have a McDonald's breaky. I did say we liked our tucker. The drive from Blenheim to Picton would only take about thirty minutes, so in we went, had a feed, read the paper, and we were back on the road just before nine a.m. We are supposed to be there an hour ahead of departure, but I have found that thirty minutes is plenty, that way we have less waiting around.

Coming off the hills into Picton with the Marlborough Sounds spread out in front of us, I felt a little apprehensive, as we still had the crossing to do. Sam joked that I should take a bucket with me, just in case, later he recounted all the vomit stories he could think of. At the end of all the banter, he said, 'You will be fine, mate, it's as calm as a mill pond.' We drove into the vehicle holding area for the ferry, showed our tickets, received our boarding passes, then drove straight onto the boat. Bluebridge is a private company. I have always used them. I find the crew really good. I haven't travelled over on the Interislander for years. We drove on and parked in the designated area. I rang Shane to give him the update that we were on the boat and should be on time. The weather was still perfect, and it looked as though it would be with us for the next week, which was a blessing. I don't mind bad weather when I'm out in the bush; but on a boat, it has to be perfect. We settled down for the three and a half hour crossing.

The Sounds always have a magical feeling for me, deep green as the hills drop straight into the water. There is lots of farming here now, mussel, salmon and good fishing. It is the place where I can fish in a boat when it's calm; well, for a couple of hours anyway. Anyone who takes me out knows they will only be there a short time. We made ourselves comfy, put the seats back and dropped off to sleep. We came out of the Sounds just over an hour or so later, and right on time I woke up. I could see Cook Strait widen as we swung into the strait proper, heading south before turning north to go into Wellington's harbour. I held my breath, trying to keep my mind off my stomach. There was no rolling, flat as a pancake Right, I'm getting a coffee. I was feeling good with myself. Bloody Sam was just about into snore mode, but I got him a tea as well to celebrate a no-vomit day. I woke the bugger, out of spite, and celebrated a good crossing. We still had a couple of hours to go, but I was confident that I was going to be okay.

Slowly, as we got closer to the North Island, Wellington's harbour opened up. You could see the city with its high-rises and houses on the hills. It's the capital of New Zealand. This is where Sam said all the hot air is bottled and is one of the reasons why it gets so much wind. Yeah, right! After we drove off the boat, we headed up to Petone. Sam was on the phone to Grunt, just to keep him in the picture.

I was feeling peckish. I had had no food since Blenheim, and I was hoping that Shane had a lunch set aside for us. I hadn't eaten on the boat, just in case, I was crook. Out of the goodness of his heart, neither did Sam. He was talking about how he could eat a horse. So he found some lollies I had in the glove compartment, stuffed his face and offered me one.

It was only a fifteen-minute drive from the boat to Shane's in South Street, Petone. We both were getting a bit excited as Sam was talking away fifty to the dozen. When he was like this, I knew he was a happy chappie. I was feeling pretty good also, no troubles on the way up and crossed the strait with no sickness, we had a nice sunny summer day and we both felt on top of the world. A few minutes more and we would be able to catch up with Grunt. We pulled into his drive, he has a nice white 1930s bungalow that he bought about five years ago. He was left a bit of a legacy from his granddad Langford, enough for his deposit. He told me it was the best thing he could have done with the money he inherited as he bought the bungalow at a good price, and now it's worth twice as much. It reminded me of the crib, I have down home in Kawakaputa Bay, Southland. I picked it up for a song. Who wants to be there with a southerly coming off Foveaux Strait, in the middle of winter? It's bloody cold, and the trees grow at forty-five degrees. Well, I do. I have missed the place since I have been up north working in Christchurch. It's rented out to a fisherman mate, Ron, for a hundred and fifty a week while I'm away. It is a nice little earner, as I don't have a mortgage. Sam has been interested in looking at a place down south for an investment. I've been on the lookout for him. I have even been thinking he could buy into my place if he wanted to. However, that's another story. We had arrived, we are sitting in his driveway, out came Shane, ambling like a big old shaggy dog. Hell, he is tall, with a black beard, hair down past his collar, black tee shirt, and old rugby shorts. He grabs my hand in his bloody great paw and just about rips my arm off. He hasn't changed a bit. It's been six months since we have all been together. We were just pleased to be brothers again. Sam came around the car, with a mouth full of my lollies and grabbed Shane around the neck in a brotherly love thing. I stayed well clear until they have quietened down. Next Grunt turns and grabbed me, chucked me over his shoulder and proceeded to walk inside, with me looking like a sack of spuds. He dumped me on the floor and stuck out a hand to help me up. All this time Sam is looking for food. 'Oh, mate, where is the tucker?' True to his word, the dining room had a table full of meat, salads and fruit, enough for six people. We were feeling really hungry by this time, so we just stopped talking and ate. I asked Grunt where his parents were. He said they would be back by about 6 pm. They did not want to interrupt us. We would all get together with a catch-up later.

We sat down with a beer, after we polished off the food and yarned the rest of the afternoon away. Sam was explaining that the tramp-come-cull had been given official sanction. They will not let trampers, or day walkers, into the areas where we will be shooting for the next six weeks. I looked at Sam, a quarter of the National Park is ours, for six weeks, with no one there to bother us, 'Holy shit!' This was all good. He went on to say that the chopper was ours for the duration, as well. All meat would be checked by MAF – the Ministry of Agriculture and Forestry. The meat would then be given to the local marae for a big hui near Taupo. They were having a "do" at the end of March, though after saying that, there will be some choice bits that would not make it out of the area. Sam said, looking at us with a grin. Grunt and I were pretty excited about this. Shane turned to me. 'Did you know about this?' 'Nah,' I said. 'He kept it all close to his chest. I mean, a National Park to ourselves with our own chopper.' We would also be able to be transported to any area of the shoot without the longish tramp. It was coming to be more of an army exercise than a walk through the park. We didn't mind though, this was much better than we expected, and we were as keen as mustard. I had to ask how he got permission for us to be on the cull; there are plenty of DOC workers to choose from. Sam went on to say, 'I wanted you both; as far as I was concerned, we are all good bushmen. We have been together for a long time, trustworthy and dependable.' Then they looked at our service records, and I suppose that did it. Shane had always kept it quiet that he got the NZBM (New Zealand Bravery Award) for saving half a dozen East Timor children from a firefight. Sam and I were at the ceremony in Wellington. We were proud of our mate, but typical of Shane, he never acknowledged that what he did was brave. He said anyone would have done it, those kids needed to be protected, and he was the bloke on the spot. Sam had done some good work in Afghanistan, which he would not talk about. He had a few medals to his name, very secret stuff. I did try to get him to open up, but all he said was, 'If I told you, I would have to kill you.' So we dropped the subject. I was awarded a civil one for plucking a boy out of the bush in a howling gale on the Routeburn track. The crew members of the chopper also got medals. They were the brave ones, flying in that weather. They gave me one for just winching down and picking up the poor little bloke. So they looked at the records, decided we were upright citizens and let Sam make the decision. We were tickled pink. I thought what good bloody mates these blokes are. Not often in your life, you get a good mate, and I'm so lucky to have two.

We will head up to Waiouru the day-after-tomorrow. Giving us a day to get our packs sorted, guns checked and all the little bits and pieces done. Furthermore, Sam sprang it on us that all food will be supplied by DOC, and they would supply a cook as well. So we could just concentrate on what needed to be done. Bloody hell! It just gets better and better. Shane beamed, 'I hated your cooking anyway, Brill.' This was complete bullshit, as he was the one with the longest tongue, who always licked the bottom of the pan. Cooking for Sam was really hard because it was never enough. The hut was going to be our headquarters. We will be out every day and overnight if we are on a roll If not, we would be in for the night with great meals. It's better than a hotel. I wish, though, that Sam had told me earlier, as we all had bought a lot of food. He did apologise; he was only told the day before yesterday himself. We would make use of the extra food, and it won't go to waste. We will take it with us if we camp out overnight. If it's not needed the cook would incorporate it into the daily rations. Whatever way you looked at it, this sounded like six weeks of bliss. We decided to take it all; knowing us, we would eat the lot anyway. Sam was a walk-in kitchen tidy, just stand on his foot and his mouth dropped open. He was talking about all sorts of meat with sauces and even desserts. 'Hell!' I remarked. We only finished lunch. So we yarned until there was a knock on the door and in walked Shane's parents.

David and Mona Langford were chalk and cheese. David was shorter than Shane but the same build strong handgrip, grey hair, just a bit of tummy fat, but if I looked like him when I was sixty-six, I would be happy. Mona, a short woman about my height had a big smile, all teeth, and light brown complexion which Shane took from her; quite slim for her sixty-five years. Big brown eyes and a wonderful disposition, we all looked to her as our second mum. When she talked, we all listened. David like Shane was a quiet man, played rugby for Northland in the sixties; a flanker, who Shane took after. I was really wanting to talk to them. I only had tonight, which was going to be difficult, or first thing in the morning as they were heading off back home to Kaitaia, with a stop in Auckland to see their girls. Sam was chatting away to them, and everyone was talking at once when Shane said he had booked a table at the Valentines restaurant in Lower Hutt. We have to be there at 8 pm. That would give us about an hour and a half to get dressed and talk at the same time. David was saying they would leave about midday tomorrow, and make Taupo for the night, but if he couldn't do that, they might just stay at Taihape whatever way they would play it by ear. I said to Shane that I'll use the shower first as I'm the shortest, and I don't need to use as much water as they do. I got a Tupperware bowl in the back of the head for that remark. So off I trotted, hoping that Mrs. Langford would be dressed by the time I was out and was ready for a talk. None of us have much good gear with us for dining out, as we're going bush. I had a pair of jeans not too old, and a t-shirt, with sandals. I'm ready. We don't shave from now on, that's a task we would all worry about when we came home, though Shane already had a cracker beard, it goes with his shaggy dog look. Sam normally shaved, but this time he was going to give it a miss. I think because he was with us, not sure, as sometimes he goes into his own world. Though I don't think he shaved when he was overseas. I went into the lounge, and Mona was sitting on the couch. 'G'day again, Mrs. Langford.' She held up her hand and spoke. 'Please, call me Mona, heck you're over thirty, you're a big boy now.' It's hard to say no to her. I have always called her Mrs. Langford. It felt uncomfortable calling her by her first name. 'Okay, Mona, can I pick your brains? I've been wanting to for a while. It's about your family. Do you know your family tree? The reason is, you know I'm into genealogy. I thought I might try to work out your tree, as a future birthday present for Shane. I'll get it printed, and he can put it up on his wall.' She responded, 'I know a little, and that is a nice gesture Bobby, what can I help you with?' I had my notebook out of my pack and said, 'Great, well, can you tell me anything about your dad's family, places of birth, death, marriages.' Oops. I saw her frown. I thought, oh shit asking too much. I went on quickly, 'Or if that's too hard, any story that you can think of would be fine with me. I can do research when I get back, so the only things you think you might be sure of in your own mind. Rumours, anything like that.' I didn't want to lose her. I'm a bugger when I'm doing this, asking for too much information at once seems to clam people up. Softly, softly Bob for god's sake. 'No,' she added. 'I was just thinking. I can give you my parents and grandparents and a little bit about the great-greats. However, I can only give you information as much as I can remember.

There is a story about some people helping my third great grandfather's family in the New Zealand wars. Just stories, with no collaboration, have been passed down. No doubt it has expanded to something completely different after one hundred and fifty years.' Heck, I was intrigued by this. 'Can you remember any of it?' 'Well,' she continued, 'I think his name was Watene or something like that. As you know, Māori genealogy is quite hard to trace. The records did not start until around nineteen hundred and eleven, I think, so registrations were not recorded. Tribes would remember their own births, though a tohunga, or talking stick or some such thing. As you know, I have not had much contact with that side of my family, but my sister is a bit more clued up. I can give you her phone number, and you can make contact when you get back from your little adventure. She lives in Russell."Will she be okay with that?' 'I'm sure she will' she replied. 'She has also been interested in family history.' 'Okay, that's good, are there any other rumours or stories that you can remember off-hand? It doesn't matter if they are far-fetched or silly, you never know in this game, anything helps.' She stopped for a moment with a faraway look. I thought, oh shit, there I go again. I'm pushing her too hard. That's my problem: always too keen to get information, without thinking about the person giving it. She eventually said, 'There was more about this story, that I just mentioned, it is really quite unbelievable, so it must be a fable or something, but it has been around all these years. , You cannot tell where the truth is and fallacy ends.' She paused to think for a moment, and I wasn't going to make a bloody noise, just in case I spoil her train of thought. 'It was told by my grandfather, and it was passed down from his granddad, so we are talking about the 1860s. It's all a bit strange. I spoke to David about it, but have at no time passed on the full story to the kids. Well, in saying that, Shane knows a bit more, though he has never shown any interest. He just didn't think it was that important, being so long ago. The relevance doesn't seem to warrant much thought. To you, Bob, it might be the bee's knees. It's over one hundred and fifty years ago, the story no doubt has changed so much from the first telling, who is to say it's real or not. I was intrigued. 'Would you tell me?' I asked, fingers and toes crossed. 'Okay, Bob,' she said, 'But no smirking, as I feel it's a bit silly really.'

She began. 'This relation of mine went by the name of Watene. I think that's right, though not sure, I'll stick with that. From the Waikato in the 1860s. His wife could have been called Tui, but I'm vague on that as well. I cannot remember when the war started in the Waikato, but it must have been around that time. The story goes that Watene and his family tribe were planting or digging up kumara. 'This was a farming village away from the main pa but still within its protection. Out of the blue, they were attacked by English soldiers. The numbers have been lost in time … there was only Watene and another warrior, the rest were women and children and some old men who were digging, so the story goes. It wasn't really a battle; they charged in and shot the men, including Watene, though he gave as much back as he could, I gather there were too many of them, and he was shot. The soldiers then tried to rape the women and older girls. 'Now this is where it all turns weird, out of the bush come these black-face men, they charge into the English. They lay into them until they were all on the ground. I don't know if they were killed or anything like that, the story goes, they were laid out. Not a shot was fired, strange! 'Then one went into a whare, where I think, this woman Tui was about to be raped. The black man hits the soldier on the head with his fist so hard that he falls out through the wall. They tie him up with all the others. One of the black men helps Tui up. He spoke some Māori. Her husband was shot though was still alive, and they bought him inside, where they checked him out. Watene then just fell asleep,

I think that's how it goes. She thought for a minute and went on, he is raised on the third day. There is mentioned the light of God, lines hanging from bodies. Faces with cloth around them. Sharp steel needles, and light from the mouths of black-and-white men. Hands inside bodies, weird. These Maori people were Christians, all had been christened by the missionaries in the 1830s and 40s, they believed in what they saw – or thought they did. Then when Watene was raised, they took them to a new place to save them from the English. The children were healed as well. They believed that God had sent his angels down to help their people in a time of need. Later on, one returns with his woman, not sure about that though,' She stopped, frowned, and said, 'I think that's it, Bob, a bit far-fetched, don't you think?' I was sitting with an open mouth. 'You'll catch flies if you don't shut your mouth, Bobby.' 'Bloody hell Mona, what a story. I am certainly going to run with this. While we are away, do you think you could write it down, and I'll have a crack at it when we get back?' She smiled. 'Funny, out of everyone I knew you would be the only one interested. I'll certainly do that for you, as long as you make sure you take care of your mates.' 'I always do, and they take care of me as well, we are a good team.' I said through a grin. Neat story, I thought, love, to get my eye teeth into that; even so, this was for later, time to focus on the tramp and cull.

David walked into the room. Mona turns around and said, 'Just telling Bobby about the family story. He was keen to learn about our whanau.' He grinned. 'Yeah, it's weird, Bob. I would like to know the truth, but after all these years, everything gets distorted. You never know though, one day the truth might come out.' I never did get around to ask Mona if she knew about my family, her story sounded so interesting I forgot my purpose for asking her completely. Shane and Sam came in saying we had better get going. Sam was saying he could eat a horse. We had just had a late lunch; bugger me, he could eat. On the way out I said to Shane, 'Did Sam tell you about the contract he turned down to play for Otago?' Shane just about tripping over his bottom lip. It was nice for me to walk away with Shane pumping Sam about his defunct rugby career.

A good night out, a pleasant meal and a couple of beers at the end back at Shane's place. Mona headed off to bed and Shane's dad, with the three of us, had a nice quiet yarn. Then I announced I was off to bed; it's been a long day. Tomorrow there's last-minute stuff to do before we head out the day after. I said goodnight to David, who followed me out of the room. I undressed, piled into the pit. I could hear the waves, in the distance, lapping against the shore; they lulled me to sleep as I was thinking of the story Mona told me.

CHAPTER THREE

I awoke to the sound of the southerly pelting the rain against the windowpane and spilling out over the guttering. Bugger, it's pissing down, so much for the fine forecast. The house was quiet as I shuffled down to the toilet. I was first up, which meant I get the shower before everyone. It was going to be another long day. I was thinking: I hope this weather eases off for David and Mona as they have a wee way to travel. Not that far, fortunately, but it's hard driving when it's raining like this. I showered then went into the kitchen. It was quiet, though the rain was still heavy, the wind had dropped. I cranked up the computer to check the weather. It will be clearing by early morning. Well, fingers crossed.

The house started to come alive. Sam came out looking as dozy as hell. 'What's for breakfast Brill' he asked. 'Don't know mate, you will have to ask Grunt, he's still in night-night land.' He looked at me with gummy eyes. 'Can't have that, mate.' and proceeded down to Shane's bedroom. He didn't yell or say a word, just stood at the end of the bed staring at the prone figure of Shane fast asleep. Within minutes he woke up, 'What the hell!' 'What's for breakfast,

Grunt?' Sam asked. He got a pillow in his face, with some comment of, 'Look in the fridge and cupboard, help yourself you dozy bugger.'Later we heard Shane ambling down the corridor for a pee. Sam and I got to work on breakfast, eggs, bacon, snarlers, tomatoes, baked beans, toast, a jar of jam and a big pot of tea. We had polished it off in no time. We had just finished eating when Shane's parents walked in. Shane got up to make another pot of tea. Turning to Shane's parents, I said 'What would you like?' They were looking at the table with all the empty plates and smiled, knowing full well what had come before it. Mona replied 'Toast and jam would be fine, we don't have big meals in the morning now.' Sam jumped up and put the bread into the toaster. I cleared all the dishes off the table, then moved out of the way, so they could sit down. 'This weather is going to pass quickly. It's supposed to be over by early morning. So by the time you have had breakfast, showered, and packed all your stuff into the car, the front will have moved off. At least it will be a bit cooler travelling,' I said.

While they were eating, Sam shot off for a shower and Shane and I cleaned up. 'We have a bit to do, Brill,' Shane said. '. If you move your Surf out of the driveway, I'll get mum and dad's car out, then you can back it up and hook up the trailer. That way the folks can just drive straight out.' 'Good-oho mate, I'll do it now. Rain seems to have eased off a bit,' I replied. It didn't take long, Sam came out and said 'Grunt, the shower's free. I'll help Brill, you go and get wet.' We moved the vehicles around and I backed the Surf up to the trailer. This was so much better than piling all the stuff into the boot. Shane had a good hard-top trailer. It would take everything and leave us plenty of room in the Surf. It's not too far to Waiouru, about a three-hour drive. My mates, being big men, need a lot of space, so the trailer will work out that much better. With it done and dusted, we popped back inside, helped Shane's parents with their bags, and packed them into their car. The weather was starting to clear. Shane arrived with dripping wet hair, rubbing it furiously with the smallest towel in the world. David came in, saying, 'Son, I think we will hit the road a bit earlier than we intended. You boys have a lot to do. The weather is getting better and I think we will make Taupo today and be in Auckland tomorrow. We will have a quick shower and another cuppa. Then we will be off.'

Sam went to the kitchen to make the tea, while they showered. We talked in the lounge waiting for his parents to return. When they came back, he was ready with the pot, we poured ourselves a cuppa and sat back. David leaned forward and from behind his back, he produced a small parcel, which he handed to Shane. 'Happy birthday, son. We won't be with you on Monday, so this is an early present from us both.' Shane had that schoolboy look on his face as he examined the gift in one big paw. 'Aw Mum, Dad, I hope you haven't gone to too much expense. Just you coming down to see me was all the present I wanted.' Even as he said it, in his eyes you could tell he was really interested in seeing what they had got him. Grunt is not delicate opening prezzies. He ripped the wrapping off and gingerly removed the tissue paper. There sitting in his lap was this awesome Bowie Knife. It had a six hundred and thirty-five millimetre blade (25-inch) with a sturdy handle and hand guard. The blade had a half-moon curve at the end. I'm not into knives as such, but this was a deadly fighting weapon. It had a hard Indian pouch to slip it into, which could be threaded onto his belt. I could see this big smile on my mate's face. 'You know your mum is not happy with this knife. As far as she is concerned, it should be locked away, but I want you to have it. It's part of our family. You know the story.' He turned to Sam and me. 'My grandfather was wounded in France in World War I and was expatriated back to New Zealand. The ship stopped off in New York, and the walking wounded were allowed off for a couple of days. Granddad and a couple of his mates got into a poker game and he won this knife in the process. He passed it on to my dad, who like Shane loved the bush, and then he passed it on to me. I used it a bit at your age, but it's been in the cupboard for a few years now, and it's time it came to you, Shane. I thought since you are going out on this hunt, you will need a good knife, and this one is the best.' Shane was speechless. This knife was well over one hundred years old. Turning it in his hands he noticed the engravings on the blade JL. 'Those are my grandfather's initials,' David said. 'Yours are there too on the other side, I, err … we thought it would be nice to have your initials on it.' Shane turned it over again. The new engraving was there: SL. He was certainly taken aback. His eyes were a bit watery as he went over to his Dad and hugged him. 'This was a wonderful present and I will treasure it for the rest my life,' he told his dad. He turned to his mother and hugged her, 'Mum, I will be careful; this is only for skinning and cutting. I'll never need it for anything else so you don't have to worry. We are all sensible blokes.' He released her and looked into her eyes. There was something there, a worried look as though she knew what was going to happen. She took his face in her hands, dragging his forehead down to her lips and kissed him hard. 'I love you, Shane. Always remember that.' He passed the knife around for us to look at. It was a bit big for me, but Sam could handle it okay, and it had fitted nicely into Shane's hand. 'This must be worth a bit today,' I asked. David, who was talking to Mona, turned around and said, 'Not as much as you think, although I did price it in Auckland and they thought it might fetch about five dollars at an auction. I think it could be due to the design of the moon-crescent blade. It is never going to be sold anyway.'

Looking at his watch, David said 'Time is slipping by, honey, I think it's time we got going. These blokes have a lot to do and we are going to be in the way if we hang about any longer.' Shane was making all the noises of a good son. 'No, Dad, that's fine, you are never in the road.' 'Bullshit kiddo, time for us to leave and let you all get on with it.' We wandered out with them to the car. Mona came up to me with a hug and a kiss. 'Take care Bobby, keep an eye on my only son for me. I'll write out the story we talked about last night, while you are away, and post it down to you, so it will be there when you return. I'll give you my sister's phone number as well. Take care and keep safe.' She grabbed Sam and did the same. 'You are all my boys, look after yourselves.' She turned and got into the car with a tear in her eye. Quite honestly, I have never seen her like this before. It was as though she had lost a child or something. David came around and shook our hands. 'Good luck on the cull, and if possible, I would like some pork or venison. 'We might be able to get it sent up to Auckland,' Sam replied. 'Liz or Carolyn could pick it up from Whenuapai. I'll work on it. A little bit of coaxing with the Airforce crew might be the order of the day.' David got into their car and reversed down the drive with Shane walking beside them. One last goodbye, we were all waving as they turned and headed for the northern motorway.

While we traipsed inside I thought I would ring my parents. Sam was already on his cell phone talking to his. 'Shane's parents have just left, sent their love to you and dad, they hope to catch up when they are down south in June,' I told mum. 'They are going skiing with one of the girls, well, just watching really, and hope to call in while they are there. Mona said she would ring well in advance. 'She also said they hoped to catch up with Sam's folks at the same time. Would be nice if we could all get together, your place is pretty big, have them all come for a few nights, make a big do out of it.' I know my mum. She likes to have people around her and she jumped at the idea. As she is from Northland, it was a chance to talk with someone who knows a few of our family members. 'What a good idea Bobby,' she said. 'I'll work on that with your dad.' We talked for a while longer. 'I have to go, Mum,' I eventually said; we had things to do. 'Don't forget to get in touch with Sam's parents well in advance, they are always quite busy. Give my love to dad and Sasha.' They were out somewhere in the deep south fishing. 'I'll be in touch at the end of each week to give you an update, as long as the phone connection is okay. Don't be worried if it's not, we will be in some remote areas, and I'll get word to you when I can.' 'Okay, love,' she said. 'Love to Sam and Shane, take care, and enjoy yourself. Love you'. I said the same and hung up. Sam just ended his call as well. 'I think my mum is going to get in touch with your mum and dad, mate,' I informed him. 'Looks as though Mona and David will be down south in June and mum would like them all to come to her place to stay for a few days if they have the time.' Sam smiled. 'mum would like that,' he said. 'Though Shane's parents will feel the cold down where we come from mate.' 'Yeah you're right there,' I said. 'But it will be nice to have everyone together.' Shane came in with a couple of parcels left by the courier, which looked interesting. 'From my sisters,' he said. 'Must have bought me presents. Do I take them with me and open them on the day or now?' 'Open them now, mate,' Sam piped up. 'You can leave them here if they are not suited for this tramp.' 'Good thought,' Grunt replied, so we sat down to watch him open the two parcels sent by Liz and Carolyn. Liz had bought him Native American moccasins when she was in the States. They were so good; the leather must have been properly cured in order to pass through customs. He put them on. They were a perfect fit. 'I wondered what she was up to when she was down last time to visit, wanting to trace my foot because these are just the right size and they are really comfy,' Grunt said. Carolyn's present was quite flat; he opened it up to find a small solar powered unit for charging phones and cameras on the tramp. 'Well bugger me,' he said. 'Those sisters of mine sure know their brother. This is superb fellas, we can at least have one of our phones on charge each day, as long as the sun is shining. It is very lightweight, which is great.' We pulled out our phones and cords to try them out, plugged them into the socket and bingo, worked a treat. I tried my small camera and that worked also. 'Great presents,' Sam said. I have to agree, these are really practical for our purpose. The solar panel would be a great addition with the one I have. 'Well boys,' Shane said, getting up. 'We need to get organised.' It was ten a.m. and the morning was slipping by. The sun was now out, though it was only about fifteen degrees. The first task was to box all the food. We didn't need to carry it in our packs, only the daily stuff, and extra for overnight if required. The hut was going to be used as our base. What a pleasure it was to be able to take it all out of our packs. Sam labelled each box. As he was a real foodie, he liked to have his finger on the pulse and know where his beloved tucker was stashed. This done, we talked about our guns and how much ammo we would need. I had the old 303 Lee-Enfield; I carried a spare magazine of ten rounds and ten on the gun, and I would carry another twenty extra each day and the rest I would leave at base and top up daily. All my cleaning gear I take; the old rifle had a compartment at the base of the stock to store webbing and to hold the pull through. So I was set.

My mates had modern rifles. Shane had brought a Savage Scout rifle, with a nice dark blue barrel, not the latest you can buy, but she was a nice looking gun. It had a Leupold scope as well, which I gather is one of the top scopes you can buy. It only weighed three point two kilograms unloaded. The magazine held five or ten rounds of 308 ammo, slightly heavier than my 303. So like me, Shane would carry an extra twenty rounds in his pack and leave the excess back at the hut. Shane said, 'If I cannot kill anything with forty rounds, I'm leaving to join a religious ministry.' The only thing missing was the bipod. The newer models have one. Shane had purchased his gun before the latest one had come out. He was a bit disappointed with this. The bipod gives the gun more stability when you are lying on the ground for any length of time. Unbeknown to Shane, Sam and I had bought him one as a birthday gift, and a bloody big chocolate cake which we were wondering how to transport up there. Now with us not having to pack in, we boxed it; it will go nicely in the chopper. Sam, who's been in the bush more than us, had a Howa rifle, 308 ammo, short blue barrel, with a Leupold scope, and fully load weighed less than four kilograms. He was deadly accurate with this. I have seen him bring down a deer at eight hundred metres, which is getting to the edge of its range. Even without the scope, he has this uncanny skill of drilling anything on the button at five hundred metres. He's cool, calm and collected. Sam never gets rattled at all;

I wish I had his temperament. Though get up his nose and he is a terrier, and of course, on the rugby field, he takes no prisoners. We all had knives which complemented the Rambo look. Shane with his family's Bowie; Sam and I had a Kershaw roughneck thirty-centimetre blade, good for skinning; and of course my trusty Swiss army knife. I never go anywhere on tramps without it. We took everything out of the packs and repacked them. With no food to carry, they were much lighter, leaving plenty of room for extras. We checked our maps, mountain radios, made sure the phones are fully charged, solar panels packed and filled the water bottles. All our personal items from clothes – both winter and summer – to toothbrushes were ticked off. In New Zealand, the weather can change so quickly that people can be caught out on our mountain ranges. Hypothermia sets in quickly and you die. It's as simple as that. Once we had finished repacking, we all checked each other's packs to make sure we had not missed anything. It is amazing how you can miss a little item that someone else will pick up. Lastly, we checked torches, wet weather matches and the first aid kits which I checked, to make sure they were okay. We would not need everything in the kits, but we were not going to break them up for anyone; I would rather have them than not. 'Keep the kits out of sight of the military, fellas,' I said. 'We don't want the sods taking them off us.' We also had ex-army wet weather gear and both warm and cool, camouflage shirts and longs. At the bottom of Sam's pack, I came across a couple of tubes of black camouflage cream. 'Are we going to war mate?' 'Oh. I forgot about them, just leave them there Brill,' Sam said. 'If we are out in the evening, it would be ideal for covering your face and hands, as you know, your skin can shine in the moonlight, and can be seen by the wildlife.' He chuckled. 'Though in Shane's case, with that bloody beard he has, we cannot see any skin on his face, even in daylight.' So I left them in the bottom of the pack. I looked at the time. It was now four thirty p.m. We had worked through most of the day without stopping and I was wondering why I was feeling hungry. I hadn't heard a peep out of Sam. Usually, when it comes to food, he is the alarm clock. I turned to the boys. 'Let's get a pub meal,' I said. 'I cannot be blowed cooking tonight. Shane, you must know of a good place to go?' 'Yeah, there is one just up the road, about a kilometre. They start serving about five p.m, so we have time to wash up and be up there for the early sitting. They have a fouteen dollar roasts with a beer thrown in.' That suited all of us. Wash, shit, and clean our teeth and we're off.

The Hutt Arms is a cool little pub, dating back to about nineteen hundred, and the owners have kept the ambiance of the place. We were one of the first diners in, so there were plenty of empty tables. We sat down and ordered the roast of the day, which was pork. Shane implied 'I think we will see a bit more of this meat in the weeks to come.' They brought us our beers, and we sat quietly yarning until the food arrived. They were big plates, it filled me, but old Sam ordered another one. They were so surprised that they gave it to him for half price. I quite honestly don't know where the hell he puts it; I think he has hollow legs.

We had a couple more beers when we got home. Feeling pretty content, I got out my guitar and started to twang away; Sam playing his harmonica joined in. Shane, tapping his foot on the back of the chair, went and picked up his ukulele. So there we were, making all sorts of noise, hoping the neighbours didn't complain. I sling off at our music, but in actual fact, we play pretty well and complement each other. So it wasn't too bad. Shane's got a good voice as well and we all joined in. Time just flies when you are having fun. Looking at my watch I realised the time. 'I'm off to bed fellas,' I announced. 'I'm really looking forward to tomorrow. I think we need to be up a bit early to give the place a quick tidy. We don't want Shane coming back to a pigsty.' We were coming back to his place for a couple of days when it was all over, before heading home. 'So what do you think of five am?' 'Yeah okay, Brill, that's fine. five a.m. it is.' Sam agreed. 'If we get away about seven, or seven thirty am, we should be in Waiouru about eleven-thirty, or a bit earlier. We have to meet the CO at one pm, also the aircrew who will be with us for the duration.' 'Settled mate, I'm off to bed then, catch you two in the morning.' Muttering, I said, 'I'm looking forward to the sounds of the bush tomorrow night,' as I walked out of the room. 'Yeah,' said Sam, 'and the bastard possums on the roof.'
I heard the blokes also head off to bed not long after. The house went quiet, no sounds of the sea tonight. The southerly had died a natural death. I thought about what was in store for us in the next few weeks. I was excited and really looking forward to it as I drifted off to sleep.

CHAPTER FOUR

I awoke to the bed being shaken violently. I instantly thought, earthquake. My eyes slowly focused on Sam at the end of the bed, shaking it like hell. 'You shit,' I bellowed. 'I thought it was another quake.' Grinning, he said, 'Time to get up mate, it's just after five.' I climbed out of bed while chucking a few choice expletives at him. I was talking to his back as he turned and walked into the kitchen.

The day was going to be a real cracker. As I headed for the bathroom, I could hear the radio in the kitchen saying it had settled all over the country, and our high would be twenty-five for the day. We will get an inland country forecast when we reach Waiouru. I passed Grunt coming out of the bathroom. 'G'day Brill. You have about five minutes, Sam has breakfast nearly ready. He was on the ball this morning.' 'Okay mate, quick as I can.' I was out in four minutes and heading for the kitchen when Sam yelled, 'Breaky is ready you blokes.' We sat down to what is a normal breakfast for Sam: bacon, eggs, tomatoes; like yesterday really. I must admit it goes down a treat with a cup of coffee. I asked, 'Shane do you want us to pull the sheets off the bed and throw them in the wash?' 'Nah,' he replied. 'Don't forget you mugs are both coming back here before you head home, so you can do it then mate.' Sam piped up, 'Getting old Brill, forgetting stuff?' 'Habit, Sam,.' I drawled with a smile. 'Well, since garbage guts made breakfast, I'll do the vacuuming. At least, we can come home to a tidy place.' 'Yeah and I'll get the dishes done,' nodded Shane. 'Sam? If we put all our packs into the kitchen, you can pack them into the trailer.' 'Good as gold,' answered Sam. We all had our jobs. 'You were up a bit early Sam, couldn't sleep?' I asked. 'You're right mate, woke at four am. I was a bit excited actually, like a bloody kid at Christmas. I wasn't going to get back to sleep, so I thought I might as well get up make breakfast for us all.' 'Well, it sure has hell saved us a bit of time,' I replied. I went into my bedroom, finished packing my pack, made the bed, and headed into the kitchen. I stored my pack with Shane's. We could hear Sam down in his room singing 'Boney Fingers.' I think it's a leftover thing from his parents' teens; I still like mum and dad's songs of the mid 70s and 80s. They are easy to sing to and good for road trips. So I have a stack of CDs in the Surf that I only break open when I travel.

I took out the vacuum. It didn't take long to whiz around the house. Shane had finished the dishes and was moving around the place making sure everything was closed and locked. Sam put the last of the gear into the trailer. Just about set to go when there was a knock on the door, it was Shane's neighbour, Tom. He came over to pick up the key. He was to keep an eye on the place while Shane is away.

Passing the key over to the old bloke, Tom said, 'Don't you worry about a thing mate, I'll clear your mail. If anything goes wrong, I'll fix it. You can reimburse me if necessary when you get back. I know you will be out of contact. You go and have a good time, don't worry she'll be right.' Shane replied, 'That's good of you, Tom. I have left mum and dad's phone number on the table, also my sisters' in Auckland. So, if there is anything major, get on to them. Oh, don't forget the young bloke up the road will be down to do the lawns. So you may hear the mower going occasionally.' Shane introduced us. We all shook hands, and Tom headed out. 'Catch you blokes later.' We took a last look around, locked the door, and checked around the outside for good measure. Then into the Surf and we were off.

Shane was talking to us both, saying, 'You know he's eighty-odd.' 'What, Tom?! Looks pretty good for his age.' I paused. 'Did your sisters make contact?' I pulled into the street and turned south towards the Northern Motorway. It sounds a bit Mickey Mouse, but we had to travel south to head north. 'Yeah,' Shane replied. 'Just as I was getting into bed last night, they both rang within five minutes of each other. It was nice to hear from them. I love those girls. I thanked them for their presents. They asked after you both, and sent their love.' I was turning onto the Northern Motorway as Sam was going through the CDs. I thought it was a shame that I didn't quite click with Carolyn. Both Shane's sisters were lovely women. Poor old Mona, still none of her children married and no grandchildren.

I think she was getting desperate. Sam has a very young sister. His mum fell pregnant in her mid-forties, so there's a big gap in their ages. Sam really loves his wee sister Mary; she will be eleven this year.

It must be our generation. My parents still have no grandchildren. Sasha doesn't have a bloke. I reckon when we all get together in June, the olds will put something in the water. My old man says we are bloody useless. Time will tell.

We arrived in Levin for a quick pee and a cuppa about an hour or so after leaving. 'Will you drive this leg Sam?' I asked. 'When we turn into the base, they are expecting you and your name will be on the list.' 'Yeah, good-oh,' he said. 'I wonder whether they will put a meal on for us.' Shane just rolled his eyes and laughed. 'Hell, mate, I hope they have enough food in the camp for you.' We all had a laugh. I jumped into the back so Shane could stretch out in the front for the last part. He said the way things are going, we would arrive about eleven-is. We climbed up to the plateau from Taihape, with anticipation and excitement ready for the next six weeks as, Mount Ruapehu came into view. She's an active volcano that last erupted six years ago. This area was the first National Park of New Zealand. Not as big as a few others we have in New Zealand, but different. There are three major volcanoes clustered together: Mount Ngauruhoe, Tongariro and Ruapehu. There are a couple more besides, though not as well known. There are tracks around and over them. Most trampers do the Tongariro circuit track, and a lot head up to the crater. You can do it in a day. We were going to the northern end of the National Park, between Ngauruhoe and Tongariro. The bush down there is very thick, with fast running streams, springs, and hot mud pools. You always get that smell of sulphur in this park. As long as we are aware of our environment, we will be okay. Just don't turn your back on nature.

I was surprised to see no snow on the tops. In the South Island, the Southern Alps have snow all year. Even so, she looked impressive. We passed the Waiouru Army Museum on the right and turned into the camp proper. As we pulled up at the gate, a corporal came out with a clipboard in his hand. 'Can I help you, sir?' he said to Sam. 'Yes, I hope so mate,' said Sam. 'My name is Samuel McInnes. We are the DOC culling team, reporting to the base commander. He should be expecting us.' The corporal checked his board. 'Yep,' he responded. 'All here. He is in his office, waiting for you. He's been there all day. Just drive to the end of the road and turn left. You cannot miss his office. Flag's out the front.' 'Thanks, Corp,' Sam said. 'We'll catch you later.' The corporal stood back and raised the barrier arm. I thought he was going to salute, but he waved us through. 'Have a good day, sir,' he said as we drove past. I nearly died. 'Sir, bloody hell. Sam, you have come up in the world.' Sam laughed, 'Brings back memories eh.' We followed the corporal's instructions, saw the flag and pulled into the parking space side on. We still had our trailer attached so it stuck out a bit. We hopped out of the Surf, stretched, and headed for the door.

I left the services in 2008, Shane a year later, and Sam in 2010. We were bound to run into some people here that we knew. Once out though, I never went back, even for a reunion; past is past, you move on. I must admit it felt like coming home though; getting to the dizzying heights of rank didn't really happen to any of us. I was an Acting Sergeant when flying winch-man on the choppers, but reverted to LAC when back on the ground, mainly aircraft refueling. You had to wait for someone to die to be promoted. There were no incentives to stay on. Sam was a Lance Corporal, and Shane was a Grunt. I mean, Sam was a Grunt as well, but it would have made my life hell calling out 'Grunt,' and have them both answering. So Sam was Sam, never Mac, only sometimes, like if I was pissed off with him, or I was in a bitch or even unsure of things, then he would step quietly around me. Well, they both did. It didn't happen often. As we walked in Sam said, 'Bloody hell, Captain Flanagan.'

'Not any more, Sam.' He rose from his desk and came around to meet us. 'Colonel now, after that stuff in Afghanistan in oh-nine. You will remember it. I was promoted very quickly. They must have thought I was a pretty good bloke. So here I am, the CO of Waiouru.' The CO was a big man, nearly as tall as Shane and Sam, early forties and fit-looking. You could tell he was no pushover. A soldier's soldier. He was talking to Sam. 'Remember that game of rugby we had against the Aussies in Kabul? I can still remember you ploughing over for a try with about four blokes trying to tackle you. Marvellous stuff.' 'You were not bad either, Colonel, for a lock,' Sam replied. 'They used to call you "Tiny." Do they still call you that?' 'Yes, but it's spoken behind my back, as a kind of matey thing. You understand; well, I bloody well hope so.' 'I reckon this bloke beside me,' Sam pointed to me, 'could lower you if he had a mind to.' They did this banter for a while, and then Sam turned to us, 'Sorry fellas, I should introduce you both. Colonel, this is my mate Shane Langford, and my other mate, Bob Kydd.' The CO turned to us. 'Nice to meet you, fellas. I remember reading about you, Shane. It is a privilege to meet you at last. Wonderful work in Timor, a credit to the forces. You also Robert or Bob?' 'Bob, boss,' I said, dropping back into the old speech habits. 'That was brave hanging out of that chopper picking up that kid.' I was about to say it was the crew, when he put up his hand and said, 'Credit where credit is due. We could do with you blokes back in the services.' I grinned. 'Not enough money in the world would get me back boss, too independent, but Sam might. We cannot afford to feed him. He really needs a government subsidy.' The CO was a nice bloke, most I have served with over the years were pretty good. You can count on one hand the amount of arseholes, but you have to have them to appreciate the good ones. It was interesting, though. In all the years, we have known Sam, this was the first mention of anything to do with the army. The stuff he did overseas must have been secret squirrel stuff. 'Well, it's nearly lunch time,' the CO declared, 'I have arranged for you all to mess with me. The air force boys will be there, so it's a good opportunity to get to know everyone in a relaxed environment.' Was I hearing right, eating in the officers' mess? Sure enough, he piled us into his car and drove to the officers' mess. 'We look bloody awful to eat in your mess, Colonel,' What with rough beards, long hair, and old tramping clothes.' 'Not at all,' he reasoned. 'The SAS boys look worse than you, ask Sam.' Ah, I thought, another bit of info on old Sammy. We walked into the mess and were shown to the table by a young female steward. There were two air force officers seated waiting for us, they rose when we got to the table. The CO introduced us all. The taller one was flight lieutenant, Don Price, and the younger bloke was pilot officer, Tony Lovell. We all shook hands and sat down. The steward handed out the menu for the day. 'Not many in today, Colonel?' I asked. 'There never is on a Sunday. Most come in for dinner. I don't usually mess here on the weekends, only on special occasions, and that's you lot.'

Our food came, and Sam's eyes lit up. Steak was one of his favourites. He asked the air force
blokes, between mouthfuls, 'Do you ever fly to Auckland?' 'Yes,' they informed him. 'About once a fortnight. The air force alternates the aircraft, as they keep a few up there for search and rescue, and also to work with the navy.' 'That's great,' beamed Sam. 'If I give you some wild pork, would it be possible to take it up to Whenuapai where my sisters will pick it up? In return, my mates in MAF will take some of the porkers we are going to cull and pop them into the freezer at the officers' mess at Ohakea for you. Only if the chopper is empty; I don't want anyone getting into trouble.' The flight lieutenant grinned. 'You're

not listening, Colonel, are you?' 'No, I have gone deaf,' he said. 'Okay Sam, that will be fine. It has to be at the end of the cull, and the pork must have the health certificate from MAF.' 'Oh, it will be all above-board Tony. I don't piss around with tainted meat.' 'Then that's fine,' Tony replied. Sam continued, 'You'll meet the MAF blokes in Taupo when we start dropping those buggers into their lap. A nice bunch of fellas.' The conversation came around to when we would leave. 'I should think,' said Tony, 'at about 1530 to 1600 hours. We need to load the old girl up with your stuff, park your vehicle, do the checks and flight clearance. Does that suit you all?' It suited the boys and me. It looks like there won't be any shooting today so I mentioned tomorrow. The colonel disagreed. 'It might be the next day, as it would be advisable to get yourselves sorted up at the hut before you head out on the cull.' DOC had supplied a cook, who was already up there, and the army had sent a steward as well to help out. The hut was a big one. It has forty beds, with four separate bedrooms. It had solar power lighting and a composting toilet. The gas it produces is used for cooking and heating. With a big fireplace, double-glazed windows, insulation and all the bells and whistles. Being in a thermal area, the DOC staff had tapped into a hot spring, which is used for unlimited boiling water. It is more like a hotel for us. This hut is a prototype for things to come. With our own cook, we sure were going to be pampered. No dishes to wash, only if we are out overnight. I was wondering if I would earn my keep, but I was doing this for nothing. Shane and I were the only ones not being paid. Therefore, we will make the free the most of food and lodging Oh, by the way, did any of you bring a 22 rifle?' the colonel asked. 'If not, I have one, you can borrow. You all have firearm licenses, so that will not be a problem. It would be silly to waste your heavy ammo on possums.' 'That's pretty decent of you, Colonel,' remarked Shane. 'I was going to bring mine, but thought, too much stuff and our main job is to depopulate the feral pigs. Those possums are a bloody menace. So a night shot, even around the hut, would be a good idea.' 'Bit more meat as well for the pot,' Sam drawled. With all the talking and eating, it was getting on to two pm. The air force boys said, 'We need to get cracking, as we have a bit to do.' The colonel remarked, 'The fly boys will take you over to the chopper to load, and I'll drive Bob back to get your truck. He can meet you all there at the airstrip. It's on the other side of the base. So I'll catch up with you all later.' Tony had the use of an air force van for all their gear. They will be staying on camp most of the time, but sometimes will stay with us at the hut, depending how many pigs we get in a day. When I was in his car, the CO stated. 'I'll drop you back at your Surf, but I'll swing by the transport pool so you know where it is. I have arranged for you to leave your Surf and trailer there. The transport boys will look after it, just leave the keys with the duty driver. He will take you back to the aircraft.' 'Thanks Colonel,' I said. 'It's good to know our vehicles will be safe.' 'To get to the strip, head the same way we came,' he informed me. 'When you get to the T-junction, turn right. I'll see you all before you leave. I had better pop home, and let the wife know I'm still alive and kicking.' He smiled, 'see you about 1600.' He dropped me at the Surf, with a 'see you later'. He grinned and laughed, 'I think I've had too much for lunch. I'll walk home.' He parked up the car and got out. It only took about five minutes to get to the strip. The boys were waiting. The chopper had the rear ramp down, and the young pilot officer was there to tell us where to stack our stuff. Don, the flight lieutenant, took the van to register a flight plan. We unloaded the trailer into the kite and strapped everything down to Tony's satisfaction. 'I will take the wagon back to the transport section,' I said. Tony came over. 'Would you drop me at the officers' mess on the way?' he queried. He needed to pick up his flight gear and asked if I would pick him up on my return, once I had parked the Surf. 'Just ask the DD,' he said. 'Swing by, I'll be waiting for you.' 'Fine by me.' I responded. As he was getting out at the mess, I asked him for a favour. I explained that it will be Shane's birthday tomorrow. It was not usual for us to drink on a tramp, but this was a special occasion. Will he buy me a slab of beer, Speight's, Shane's favourite beer? He really would be doing me a great favour. 'Also if you don't mind bringing it up to the hut when you fly in? Tomorrow that would be fine, whatever suits you.' 'That's fine,' he replied, then went on to say he would do it tomorrow when the canteen was open. It might be a bit cheaper as well. 'We are staying tomorrow night in the hut.' This was turning out really perfect for us. 'We have a bloody big chocolate cake for him,' I said, 'so you and your mate will be able to help us polish it off with a couple of beers.' Nice bloke, Tony. It will be a memorable night for Shane's thirty-first, so I gave him forty dollars, dropped him off, and headed for the transport section. I parked in the yard, and the duty driver came out saying, 'You must be the bloke from DOC.' 'Yeah,' I confirmed. 'Thanks for looking after my baby. I've had her a few years, and I don't want to part with her.' 'No worries,' he replied. 'I'll put it in the shed over there with the trailer beside it. I'll take you back to the chopper. Don't worry about a thing. She'll be right with us.' When we got into his van, I asked, 'Can we go via the officers' mess to pick up the pilot?' 'No worries,' he said again as he swung out of the yard onto the road. Tony was waiting outside the officer's mess as we pulled up. 'Thanks, driver,' he said, and threw his gear into the back. We were at the airstrip in no time. 'See you when you get back,' the driver remarked. 'Good luck! Good hunting! If any meat falls off the back of the chopper, I'm appreciative.' We shook hands. 'I'll see what I can do,' I whispered to him. I cannot think of his name now, a nice bloke, oh yes, last name was Kapene.

The chopper was a new one, an NH90. Stubby nose, sits on three wheels, four blades, a rear ramp for easy access and two sliding doors for grunts to jump in and out of on both sides. I was surprised at the room. 'She will hold twenty, seated, and a dozen stretchers for evacuations,' Tony explained. 'It can mount a couple of nice big guns at the doors, with a couple of rocket launchers in the deal. Good for air to ground fighting. She was also quite a strong little beast, could lift about ten tonnes. Sling a hook under her with a net, and she will lift the old porkers easy as pie.' Don was just arriving with his flight plan. 'Well gentlemen, if you are ready, we will get going.' The CO turned up to give us the heads-up on what will happen with them over the next six weeks. 'As DOC have closed part of the park down, we have permission to conduct a few exercises in the area. So, I'll come up at the end of the week for a night. You can lay out your shooting schedule. We will keep right out of your way. We might even use the hut as a base camp if I decide it's appropriate. Big area, so you most likely will never see our blokes.' 'That's fine, Colonel,' replied Sam. 'I have got the areas in mind, so that's easy. It will be nice to catch up with you again, up on the tops.' 'Okay, boys,' Don called. 'Flight checks done and we are about to rotate.' We shook hands with the CO, thumbs up, as we all piled aboard the chopper. Tony gave us all headsets, so we could talk to the pilots. The trip would only take about fifteen minutes. It saves us a day's hike. Tony applied throttle, then lift. The chopper rose into the air like a hovering bird, left rudder, nose down, and we were away. We kept below the summit of Ruapehu as we flew to our destination. She is quiet at the moment, with no smoke or fumes coming from the crater. 'I wouldn't want to be here if she decided to blow,' I claimed. Nods all around. Great view from up here, with the vista of all three volcanoes in view. We headed north then circled to the left when we passed Ruapehu, keeping the other two mountains on our right. Turning again, we passed Tongariro. When we flew over Blue Lake, our destination came into view just past Sulphur Lagoon. Steam was floating out over the water in lazy wisps. The hut was further down, nearly on the edge of the bush line.

We could see a person standing by it, looking up, as we came into the drop zone. Don hovered for a few minutes so Tony could make sure there were no hidden obstacles before landing. They had checked it all out before, but these blokes were ultra-cautious. With an aircraft worth millions, I suppose you have to be. We were slowly sinking to the ground. She just kissed it lightly, and we were down. We all looked at each other as the rotors slowly came to a stop. Then quietness, with only the slight hiss of the motor cooling. We sat there for a minute taking in the solitude. This was it. We are here. You could smell the sulphur, but we will get used to it. We were all elated. Time to start. Let the culling begin.

CHAPTER FIVE

Tony slid the door open as we were hanging up the headphones and gathering up our gear. A voice from outside yelled. 'G'day fellas, I'm Margaret. I heard the chopper coming so I have a pot of tea ready for you all. Come on up to the hut.' I wondered … a woman up here with us for six weeks. She's a bit game, but as we traipsed after her, I could see she was much older than the rest of us, late fifties, a bit hippy and stocky, but she still had a spring in her step. 'Chuck your gear by the door and sit down over there by the window, while I get the tea.' There are two big old wooden tables, which seated at least ten people each. The view was spectacular; the cones of Tongariro and Ngauruhoe stood out against the skyline. To our left, you could look down to the start of the bush line. There is a knoll about four hundred metres on our left, that will give us a good panoramic view of the whole area in which we will be tramping. 'Oh, this is really bloody neat,' Shane burst out, as he sipped his tea. 'I'm surely looking forward to the next six weeks,' Sam replied. 'We will have to make the most of the good weather, you blokes. They can get over two thousand millimetres of rain up here a year, so we will need to use the fine days to our advantage. We will be out every day, as long as the weather isn't too bad. The flyboys are restricted with their flying in bad weather, so it's important that we get a good start and give them something to do. Otherwise, they will be sitting on their bums reading magazines.' We had a laugh. Margaret came back with some bickies 'Help yourself,' she broke in. 'Thanks,' we all said.

'I had better introduce myself properly,' Margaret stated. 'I've been doing this cooking thing for years off and on. Mostly with the shearing gangs, but DOC advertised for a cook for six weeks, and here I am. I'm a widow; my husband died ten years ago, in a work's accident. His quad bike rolled on top of him when we were shearing in the Manawatu, so I've been by myself ever since. I'm fifty-six, with three sons, they're living all around the country, about your age or a bit younger, so that's me.' We mumbled sorry about your hubby. To which she replied, 'That's okay fellas, I don't dwell on it, I just wanted you all to know where I'm from.' With that, she continued, 'Oh, the steward with me is Mike Brown, he's a nice young bloke, only nineteen. I asked him to go down and see if he could get some watercress from the creek, he'll be back before dinner. So you will catch up with him later. I have already met the two young air force blokes, now I do know your names as DOC gave me the heads up, so who is Sam?' Sam lifted his arm. 'It's a pleasure to meet you, Margaret.' 'Maggie,' she answered. 'So Shane must be the other big bloke.' Shane got up and gave her a hug. 'Nice to have you around, Maggie,' he said. 'Nice to have men around too, it feels a bit like home,' she grinned. She turned to me. 'You must be Bob.' I smiled, at least I could look her in the eyes; she was as tall as I was. 'Pleasure, Maggie, we welcome you to our family.' With all the intros done, she went on, 'Well I must get back to making dinner, it will be about six-thirty. When you hear the bell, dinner's ready.' She walked off into the kitchen, which is part of this enormous room. We watched her moving around in her own familiar routine.

We went back to the chopper and started to unload it. It took us about an hour to stack all the food in the cooler. There was even a solar-powered freezer for us to use. It will run on fuel from the generator when the sun goes down and on days when there is no sun. The air force boys will ferry fuel up for it when needed. We picked our rooms. Margaret was close to the toilets. They even had female ones. The young steward was in the dorm, as were the pilots since they were staying only occasionally. I was over the moon; as we three had our own rooms. There was a gun rack in the main room where we left our rifles for easy reach, although we would keep the bolts by our beds. We were sorted and soon settled in nicely. The beds looked comfy. With good food and hot showers, it will be like a home away from home. Tony gave us a yell, 'we are off fellas, catch you tomorrow, I won't forget that stuff you mentioned Bob.' The noise of the chopper silenced the bird life as it lifted up off the ground, with a wag of its tail, a wave from the pilots, and it was as small as a mossie in no time at all.

Sam went outside saying, 'Let's take a look around. How about walking down to the knoll and get a feel for the country we are going to work in.' With the sun in our faces, we took a leisurely walk towards the wee hill. From here, looking back to the hut and beyond, you could see the mist coming off the sulphur pool. Over on the left was a small river or creek, which over the years had formed pools of water as it headed down to Lake Taupo. Sam informed us, 'There are pools of all different temperatures, so if you want to sit in one, put your pinky in first. They range from about twenty-eight to forty-two degrees. Our own hot pools!' We could see the bush line clear and straight. It was as if someone had drawn a straight line across the landscape, through the bush, light scrub, volcanic rock and shingle. 'As far as the eye can see, that's our shooting area,' Sam pointed out. 'I'll go over the maps with you both tomorrow so we can all familiarise ourselves with the area we will be working in. About one kilometre from here, there is a creek, to the right,' he pointed. 'You can just see it if you squint your eyes a bit. We will follow that down to the next block, about three kilometres. It can get a bit foggy down there and sometimes the mist from the lagoon seeps down through the bush, giving you an eerie feeling. The fog can be pretty dense, so it's important to have all our gear with us when we are out, tents, and food: the lot. Once the mist comes in you can lose your sense of direction, even with a compass or GPS; you cannot see your hand in front of you. So we would have to camp up until it blows over. It shouldn't last for more than a day, most likely less. Just a phenomenon in this area. A combination of mist, low pressure, rain, wind and heated steam from the hot pools and lagoon. I was caught in it once, and it can be spooky.'

'Make the most of it while we can,' Shane muttered. 'Everything is a bonus on days like this.' We stood looking around at this picturesque area when I picked up movement about five hundred metres on our right. 'Pig at two o'clock,' I said to the boys. 'Where?' said Shane, then he saw movement. 'Bugger me, Bob, you sure have good eyesight.' 'Shame we didn't bring our rifles with us.' 'We won't let that happen again,' insisted Sam. 'We might make it a rule to have at least one rifle with us when we decide to take in the scenery.' 'We could ping that bloke easy,' grinned Shane. We watched it rooting for tucker. 'There is another one with him,' I remarked. 'I can just make out a shadow, could even be three.' These pigs don't usually travel in groups, especially the males, but now, and again they do. The sows usually form groups with other sows and piglets, so if you latch onto one of these groups you can take out half a dozen altogether. Some of the young bachelor males will form small groups as well. They move around though, up to twelve square kilometres for the males. The females don't travel anywhere near as far. The ones we were watching down there in the bush line might not be here when we start shooting in a few day's time. They will hang around if there is plenty of food, though. Well, we hope so. 'It's a good omen,' Sam said. 'I think this is going to work out fine. To see a big porker like that without trying is neat. I've marked that bugger, white with black spots; he must have been around for a while. Tomorrow, once we have a squizz at all the maps, what say we go down to that point? I'll see how far his tracks go in.' 'I forgot you track, you still do that?' I exclaimed. 'Yeah, I do.' 'Well if you do that, I'll hang around on the wee mound here, and if I see movement, I'll signal. From there I should be able to pick him up if he comes out further down.' 'Bob, you could pick up an ant on a possum's bum,' Sam replied.

The sound of a bell rang out. 'Hell, it's six-thirty already!' Sam blurted out with a grin. 'Din-din time.' You have got to love him; food was his god. 'I'm hungry.' Well, we all were. So walking a bit quicker than the stroll down, we returned to the hut. We went in, cleaned up and ran into Mike, the steward. He was a skinny bloke, about one metre seventy five, maybe a bit taller than I was. He suffered a bit from acne. He came across as a nice kid. 'Go on through, Maggie has all the food in the pots,' he said. 'Just help yourselves, its army style.' He went on in to butter the bread and get our plates for us. 'When this is finished there is apple pie in the oven, fresh cream on the table and fruit for afters. I'll heat the kettle when you are nearly finished.' Maggie was there telling us to tuck in. Oh, this is a favorite of mine. Chicken paprika with rice and peas, freshly baked bread with real crust. Ooh-la-la, I was happy. She must have heard about Sam as she joked, 'There is enough for two helpings, so you eat, I'll cook. You will never eat me out of house and home. I'll win every time.' I think this was a challenge to Sam, as he tucked in and by the end of dinner, he was chocker. 'Hell,' he said. 'That must be the best meal I have ever eaten. I have just enough room for a bit of that apple pie.' We all had a laugh. 'Good to know, Sam, you will be well looked after,' Shane grinned, 'We'll put Maggie on a pedestal.' We had our dessert and a cup of tea or coffee, and then sat back, 'foo the noo'. I think we need to do a lot of tramping; otherwise, we are going to put on weight, with the way Maggie is feeding us. We all offered to help with the dishes, but Mike was taken aback. 'No, that's my job, don't worry about it, but thanks for the offer.'

Maggie was sitting down having a well-earned rest. Shane and Sam went outside for a walk around after the big feed. I wandered over to her and said, 'Maggie, could I ask you a favour? It's Shane's birthday tomorrow, and we have a cake for him in the fridge. Would it be possible to make up some pancakes for him for breakfast? It's his favorite morning meal, with a piece of bacon or two on the side.' 'That's fine Bob,' she replied. 'No trouble what-so-ever. Are you boys out tomorrow?' 'No, we will get ourselves sorted then start on Tuesday. We'll have a couple of beers tomorrow as well. Tony is bringing in a slab for me. We never normally drink on a tramp, but this is special. The flyboys will not be able to have many anyway. There is enough for everyone, including you and Mike.' 'That's good of you Bob, but I don't drink, so young Mike can have mine. I will cook up a nice dinner for Shane as well. So does he like steak?' 'Oh yeah he does, we all do.' 'Well that's settled then, easy as,' Maggie replied 'Thanks Maggie, you are a real pal.'

I strolled out to catch the boys sitting on the outside seats yarning. Sam moved over, and I whispered to him that I would see him after and tell him the arrangements for Shane the next day. The sun was starting to set. The silhouette of the mountain cones was throwing shadows on the hut. You could feel the temperature drop as the final rays slowly slid down the slopes of the mountains, pale light, and then darkness. We sat in the dark for a while, taking in the noises of the night. Then we heard the sound of possums coming out to feed. There was a squawk from the roof as one was chasing the other. 'Oh bugger,' I moaned. 'Hate them on the roof, they shag all night and make a terrible racket.' 'Where's the 22?' Sam asked. 'I'll get rid of those sods.' Shane and I collected the torches, and Sam retrieved the 22 from the rack. Coming out of the hut, he exclaimed, 'the colonel left nearly four hundred rounds, enough to kill all the possums near the hut.' There are about sixty million of these Aussies in New Zealand, and they are a real pest. Sam found a box to stand on, and I hung onto the window frame, a bit ungainly. Shane supported me, so I could get a fix on the sods. I spotted the possums on the roof. Their eyes shone like red diamonds in a sea of black. Sam up and shoots. 'Phiff.' The suppressor quietens the gunshot. He reloaded so fast that I just managed to spot the other one and 'bang!' down it goes. 'Good shooting,' I said. 'I'm afraid you'll have to get them down Bob, as you are the lightest. We will chuck you up onto the roof, and then we'll bury them out there in the bush somewhere.' The noise had brought out Maggie and Mike. 'You got them, that's good,' she beamed. 'They kept me awake all last night.' I climbed over the boys, and they heaved me up onto the roof. I threw the carcasses down, following them, rolling as I hit the deck just as I was taught all those years ago on the parachute course. 'Well, Maggie,' Sam remarked, looking behind him into the dark. 'We will bury them, so they will be out of the road.' 'Let me skin them first, Sam,' she stated. 'I would like to make some possum boots. I made a lovely warm coat a few years ago with some of them.' She went and fetched her knife, skinning them both within a couple of minutes. 'Okay, you can bury the rest. I'll stretch and peg these skins out tomorrow.' Grabbing the shovel, I walked down the hill a wee ways into the scrub, scooped out a hole and buried them. 'Well, that's that,' I yawned. 'I think I might hit the pit, it's been a great day, and I would like to see the sunrise, from the knoll.' 'On your own,' the other blokes declared. 'Since we don't have to shoot, I might have a lie in,' Shane added. I replaced the shovel and turned to Sam as soon as Shane was out of earshot. I explained about the arrangements tomorrow for Shane. Sam smiled, 'Brill, we can always rely on you. Good on ya mate, the big fella will be pleased.'

'Off to bed.' I called out 'Night!' to everyone, had a quick shower and was drifting off to sleep when I heard pitter-patter on the roof – bloody possums! I wasn't quite asleep when I heard the tramping of boots in the hall. 'They're not going to get the better of me, the bloody sods!' I heard Sam saying. He stuck his head around my door.

'You awake mate? There are mobs of the buggers on the roof, and they are really pissing me off. I'm going to knock them off. Want to spotlight for me?' 'Yeah, okay, mate.' Shit, I was nearly asleep. 'I'll just chuck something warm on; see you in a few minutes. Where's Shane? 'Couldn't wake him', he was grinning, 'I really didn't want to, with his birthday and all.' Sam looked up at the ceiling, 'they are getting up my nose, Brill, hope you don't mind.' 'No mate, all part of the fun.' ' I went outside with both torches. We found a ladder at the back of the hut that is used for maintenance. I wish we had looked before. We both very quietly crept up until I was at the top. I slid over onto the roof as Sam came level with the top of the hut. 'Snap and shoot,' he instructed. I listened for the sound of them calling, fighting or whatever, and then I flashed the light in their direction. Once I had a target, Sam will just shoot. With luck, they will not know what hit them, as hardly a sound comes from the gun. 'Okay?' he whispers, I shone the torch into the area where they should be and saw a mob of them. They stopped what they were doing, mesmerised by the light. 'Phiff, phiff.' I switched off the torch, back on again; then more hissing noises from the gun. The possums are just sitting there, looking around: with no noise, they don't know what is happening. Once more I shine the torch and left it on a bit longer, then saw they're all down. Sam had killed about ten of them. 'We'll get them in the morning, Brill; I don't want to walk over the hut's roof at night.' 'Okay mate.' 'You are still as good as ever. That's excellent shooting considering you haven't used that gun before.' 'Oh, I don't know,' he said. 'I was pretty close, and they were milling around like ducks on a pond. I think a blind man could have knocked them off.' We clambered down the ladder and went into the kitchen. 'Do you want a cuppa?' Sam asked. 'I'll make it,' I replied. 'You clean the gun, I'll put the pot on.' Sam came out with the cleaning gear, and we sat and yarned for about half an hour. The roof was quiet. 'There must be a lot of possums around here?' 'Yeah,' Sam replied. 'They need to bring back possum hunting. I don't like the 1080 poisoning. Hunting will also give people jobs. I spoke to some old possum hunters; they made good money, and it's cleaner as well. I have seen our native birds die from that shit, but can you tell the powers that be? No! No one listens.' 'Well, this time I'm off to bed,' I said. 'I'll catch you in the morning. First one up throws the dead possums off the roof.' 'Okay,' says Sam, 'night.' In bed for the second time and no noise. Quiet as a graveyard. It takes a while to come, but eventually, I fall asleep.

CHAPTER SIX

Dawn. I love this time of the day; fresh, clean, and you can touch the sky. The dawn chorus was going strong. All types of birds were out and about, making a racket: tui, bellbirds, tomtits and the last of the morepork as they nestle down for the day. It's only six degrees! Boy, it's cool in the mornings up here, even in summer, but it looks as though it's going to be another cracker day.

The hut was quiet as I threw on some clothes. I could hear Maggie stirring in her room as I quietly padded past her door. I picked up my rifle and went out onto the veranda. First things first, I thought, get those dead possums off the roof. As quietly as possible I climbed up the ladder. There were nine of them; I had counted roughly ten last night so one must be playing possum. Oh, too early in the mornings for puns, I thought. However, I doubt whether the wounded one would have survived. As I was chucking them down off the roof, Maggie came to the door. 'Lovely. I'll skin those to, and dry out the pelts. Thanks, Bob.' Off she went with an arm full of dead possums. I picked up my rifle and slowly, savouring the early morning, started to walk down to the knoll. I had not put my boots on but had slipped on my jandals as I wasn't going to do any major tramping, just a nice quiet walk in the morning. Hope this weather stays with us, I thought as I walked, at least until we get a good routine going. I clambered up to the top of the small hill then sat down to look below me just to relax and enjoy the morning. Out of the corner of my eye, I saw movement at the edge of the bush. Luckily for me, I was upwind; this bloke would have been away in a hurry if he had got a whiff of me. He was a big boar, snuffling the ground and rooting for tucker. I saw another movement in the bush line, but he never came out into the open. This bloke I was looking at had two enormous tusks. Even from where I was sitting you could see he was a big daddy. They were about four hundred meters away. Then I saw more movement in the bush, could be he had a harem. Lucky bugger, I thought as I slid down for a better firing position, hoping that he would just stay still until I was settled. He must have been onto a food source as he rooted around, not moving from his find. I slipped a shell into the breach, safety catch off, stock into the shoulder and was sighting him through the old lens when he turned side-on to me. This made a much bigger target and through the lens, it looked as though I could just about touch him. I took up the slack on the trigger and bang! I ejected and reloaded in a few seconds and did not take my eyes off him. The bullet went through his ear and dropped him instantly. He was dead before he hit the ground. I saw the bush behind him shake as the other pigs took off.

Of course, the noise of the gunfire brought out the other

blokes. I could see Sam and Shane belting out of the hut, guns in hand, making a beeline for me. They slowed as they approached me then crept up quietly, whispering, 'did you get him? Has he moved?' 'No, he's dead,' I said. 'He hasn't stirred. I was just waiting for you two blokes to waddle down to take a look. Come in from the right flank, I'll keep a bead on him so if he does move I'll put another one into him. He might be fibbing; I doubt it though.' 'Good shot,' they said and off they went. I watched them heading down to the pig whilst staying out of my line of fire. It wasn't long before I got a wave and a thumbs up. I waved back. I wasn't going down, not in jandals. The boys can bring the pig up to the DZ for me, and that's just what they did. I watched as Shane tied the legs together, front left to back left and same with the other side. He then slipped his arms into through the legs like a pack and stood up. The pig would have weighed at least one hundred and forty kilograms. Shane always makes it look easy. They headed back to the hut. By the time they climbed up I was there with the net out for the chopper to hook onto, once they arrived later today. Sam was saying it might be the one we saw last night, same colour, but whatever; this is a good omen. The first morning, even with hardly moving we had our first kill. Shane had dropped him into the net. I looked at the tusks; they sure looked enormous. Young Mike came out for a look. He said to me in a low voice, 'I'll take those tusks out and fix them up for Shane's birthday. I work a bit with bone as a hobby thing, and I brought some of my stuff with me. Just get him inside and I'll work on it when he is not around.'

We traipsed inside and Maggie yelled out, 'Happy birthday, Shane. Get washed-up fellas. I have a special breakfast for the big bloke here.' So into the showers, we went and came out squeaky clean. We sat down as Maggie brought over Shane's favorite breakfast: pancakes, maple syrup, bacon, eggs, and toast. Shane was surprised. He looked at the food and said, 'How the hell did you know that I liked this stuff?' 'Oh, you have good mates,' Maggie replied. She handed us our plates. 'Tuck in, you blokes. You don't think I would forget you, do you?' Feeling content after the big breakfast, we were sitting on the bench outside with a cuppa in our hands when young Mike turns up. We hadn't seen him all morning since we went inside; a good hour or so. 'As a birthday present, I want you to have these.' He handed Shane the two tusks from the pig. They were buffed and shone white in the sun. He had drilled a couple of holes through the top and attached a leather thong. 'You can adjust it around your neck to your liking.' Shane just sat there with a stupid look on his face. 'By God Mike, that is bloody good of you mate. This is a really nice present. I don't know what to say.' He got up and shook Mike's hand; hard. The poor bloke's arm was going up and down like a pneumatic drill. 'You are a good bloke,' he kept saying. I nodded to Sam, as he got up and went inside. Coming back parcel in hand, Sam said to Shane, 'Let that poor bloke's arm go, it's about to fall off. This is from me and Brill.' Shane sat down on the bench and ripped off the paper; refined is our Shane. Uncovering the bipod that we had bought him for his rifle, he said, 'Heck fellas.' He looked at us both. 'This is a cracker of a present and one I really wanted.' 'As long as you don't kiss me, you can kiss Sam,' I said. 'Be gentle with my arm. Sam, it doesn't matter, he can take a pounding. Me, I'm too brittle.' He slapped me on the shoulder, grabbed Sam and shook his hand. I hate to be around him when he is really happy. He went and got his gun, turned it over and lined up the slots. Click the bipod slipped in like a bought one. Flicking the legs down, he laid on the floor with the rifle barrel pointing out the door, stock into his shoulder. 'Oh shit, this is so good,' as he played for a while. 'This is the best birthday I have had,' he said, hugging his gun and stroking the tusks.

Sam had arranged with the air force guys by radio to come up about four pm, to pick up the pig and take it to Taupo. I could hear him talking to them. 'A good first run to get ourselves sorted. It's about an hour return for the flight. Plenty of time for you to get up and back before dark.' So the first flight was arranged, and we now had to use radio protocol each day, with the army camp and mountain radio watch. I would use the mountain radio, Sam the army and Shane would tell us if we forgot. Sam turned to Shane and suggested, 'What say we go over the maps this morning? Then after lunch see how that bipod works in the wild.' 'Now that's a good idea,' I chipped in. 'The pigs should be back because I left some offal down there,' said Sam. 'That will bring them in when they smell it. They're like kitchen tidies, just devour anything they can get.' So a plan was formed.

We went over the maps, getting used to the area where we would be shooting. A big area when you are on foot, but we all love the bush so for us it's real fun. Maggie gave us lunch and at about one pm we walked down to where I had shot the pig that morning. The offal had not been touched. Maggie had given us some rotten fruit which Sam dropped further inside the bush area. He tracked their spoor for about ten minutes then came back and reported his findings. 'There were two more with the one you shot, Brill. No females, they took off down towards the creek. The wind was now, blowing lightly from the west. That should take the smell of all this crap down to them. Whatever is out there will get a whiff of it and they will be back.' Sam turned to Shane. 'Grunt, pop up onto that saucer area. With the wind behind you, you will have a clear shot. Brill and I will go farther nor'east in case they come up from that way. Whatever direction, one of us will get the sods.' Shane went up to the natural saucer. Placing the bipod on the lip of it, he tracked the bush line with long slow sweeps. We were up higher to the left of him all waiting quietly, listening to the sounds of the bush. It was about an hour or so later when we heard a rustle, about 350 metres from Shane. Sam whispered to me, 'they're back.' Before Sam could give his bellbird signal, Shane had his thumb up. Sam whispered again, 'that's the one I saw yesterday.' I could see Shane getting himself comfortable. The larger of the two pigs was trying to keep the other away from the food. They were snorting at each other; the big one then turned and charged the smaller one. There was a bit of a tussle until the smaller one retreated to the edge of the bush line, keeping out of the bigger bloke's way. Big guts went back to his feast. I could see Shane line him up, then, 'crack,' seconds later; another 'crack' and both were down. We waited until we were sure they were not faking. Sam and I moved down to look. Two clean kills. 'This is cracker,' said Sam. 'We haven't even got a routine yet, and we have three pigs already.' I brought the rope with me and looped it around the legs on both pigs. Shane came down to help. 'Oh, this bipod is so neat. The rifle was steady as. I'm happy, this is another plus for my birthday mate.' I squatted and picked up the smaller of the two pigs. Sam took the big bugger, and Shane grabbed the rifles. We made a slow procession back up to the hut. Dumping them into the net, then looking at his watch, Sam advised us, 'it's three pm, that's bloody good going. I left some meat back down there and will check that spot again in the morning, might be some mummy ones around.' Maggie yelled out to us. 'Cuppa?' 'Yeah okay,' we said, 'just cleaning our gear, will be with you shortly.' Shane stripped his gun. I hadn't used mine this time, but it was a habit to wipe a spot of oil over her to keep her clean 'I'll do yours as well while you whistle up the flyboys,' I said to Sam. With the tea brewed, we entered the dining area. 'They will be here in about an hour, so we can relax.' Out comes the harmonica and the guitar and, with Sam tapping away on the tin can, we played a few songs that we enjoyed. Then sang at the top of our voices 'You will be my long lost friend, I'll call you Betty and Betty you can call me Al'. Mike came out smiling and hummed along. He was shy and didn't want to make a fool of himself. We don't care when it comes to music, we become lost in the song.

Around three forty five pm we heard the chopper, in the distance, coming in fast. We wandered outside. She hovered above the net, letting down the hook. I coupled it up, and then it took the strain slowly. When everything was checked at our end, thumbs up, it lifted slowly into the air. The pigs were swinging slowly in circles under the kite, as she lifted to about one hundred metres, swung left, and took off for Taupo. 'Well, we should see them back before five,' Sam commented. We all piled inside. I went and had another shower; I could smell pig's blood on my hands. Shane had a lie-down, and Sam went over the maps again. I called the mountain radio at four thirty pm and was told everything was okay, the weather was holding for now although, in the high country of New Zealand, the weather can change in ten minutes, so you have to be prepared for anything.

The noise of the chopper once again had us all outside as she settled onto the DZ. Tony jumped out with a grin. 'The MAF boys and DOC are stoked, fellas. They were not prepared to have any pigs just yet, and they were running around like blue arse flies. They are in the cool store now. The local iwi wants to thank you all when you are down their way. The rangatira was quite vocal. Happy as a pig in shit. Nice bloke, good Māori name, Jim Cochrane.' We had a laugh. That's New Zealand for you. You never know who's Māori or not, by their name sometimes. I sure love this country. Tony came over to me. Quietly, he whispered. 'Beer is in the back. I've wrapped it so Shane won't see it. I'll drop it into the cool store. ' 'Thanks, Tony. You're a real pal.' He continued, 'I got it from Taupo, so there is some change.' 'Keep it mate, shout Don a beer when you are back at base. You did me a favour.' Maggie came out. 'Dinner will be ready in half an hour, so if you want to get sorted you better get a move on.' I helped the air force blokes tie down the chopper for the night, put a cover over the windscreen and fixed the blade to the ground. 'Don't want that rotating on its own,' Don pointed out. Then they went up to the hut, stowed their gear, had a quick shower, and we were ready for dinner just as Maggie's gong was struck, by Mike. 'Pork steaks,' she said. 'I took some off the pigs, didn't think the Taupo lads would mind.' I didn't care if they liked it or not. Pork steaks are the best – wild pork is better. I went out to the cool store and retrieved the beer and the cake. I announced to Shane. 'Here's a beer mate, and a happy birthday.' 'Huh,' he stammered. 'Not like us to have a beer on a tramp, mind you, I'm not complaining.' 'Special mate,' I said. 'Tony got it for us from Taupo.' I placed a beer in front of everyone. We were only going to have a couple each anyway. Young Mike sat down, and I passed him a beer. 'Thanks,' he grinned. Everyone raised their drinks once again and toasted happy birthday to Shane. It sure went down well with pork. After dinner, we insisted that we help with the dishes except for Shane, that is. Then we all had the last of the beer and the biggest piece of cake. Afterwards, we brought out the guitar, Sam's harmonica along with his ukulele. A great night with nice people. The evening was getting on. From now on, it would be an early start for us. We said goodnight to all. As we were heading out to bed, Maggie informed us, 'I'll have a lunch packed for you each morning, but when you go overnight, it might be best to also carry normal dry rations. Though I shouldn't need to teach you blokes how to suck eggs.' I countered, 'Maggie, it's nice to know you have got our backs.'

So we hit the pit, content that we had started on a good note. Shane had a decent birthday, what with the substantial meal and that bloody big chocolate cake. I'm not sure how we managed to crawl into our beds. We could hear Maggie pottering around in her kitchen and Tony, Don and Mike, we're talking quietly. I was pleased that they had made Mike feel at home. It's hard for officers to talk casually to the lower ranks. It's different for Tony and Don, as they were air force pilots with a good education; Mike was an army steward. The armed service was their common ground. I had played rugby with the air force, and we had every rank under the sun in the team. It was the same with the army and navy. All were teammates on the field. Once back into our jobs, ranks reverted to normal, one of the quirks of the armed services. I was drifting off to sleep; feeling satisfied that the stage had been set. We had our routine all organised starting from tomorrow, up at dawn and shooting till lunch. Any pigs we cull will be carted back to the DZ before one pm. Lunch then and back out by three pm. Any pigs shot after that will airlifted at six pm. Then there would be time for the boys to fly up to Taupo and be back for dinner. They would do a couple of trips if it was needed. Flexibility was the word.

So things were falling into place. I was happy as, as I drifted off to sleep.

We arose early, just before dawn, and collected our gear. Maggie was up making our breakfast. She had already put our lunches into our packs. I carried all the dry food we had enough for the week and the boys took the daily rations. The weather was holding, and it was going to be another magic day. The sound of the dawn chorus started to wind up as we headed out. We went down to the bush line, and Sam started to track. There were tracks everywhere, pig rootings and a few mud-wallowing holes. Every twenty steps or so we would stop and listen. Shane had good ears and if there was a noise, he would point in that direction. We were travelling in single file, guns ready to shoot. You just never know if a big porker is going to attack you. The birds were noisy, so it was a bit hard to communicate. Sam came to a fork. We looked left and saw a mummy pig walking casually across the track about 100 metres from us. She didn't even see us, as she had six little weaners chasing after her, kicking up a racket. We slowly followed them until we came to a clearing with a small creek running through it. We dropped our packs quietly. There were three adult females and twelve wieners. We took up our positions. We would fire together. Hit the mothers and the little ones will run around in circles. Sam gave the thumbs up, and we lined them up. We fired three shots together and the bush went mad, birds taking off in all directions. The females went down, and the little ones had no idea what was happening. We quickly lined them up, another crack, twice more, and they were all down. We waited for about ten minutes, no movement, so we slowly went over to the bodies, and they were all dead: fifteen pigs in one hit. 'Oh, DOC will be over the moon,' Sam said. 'Do you reckon the flyboys will be able to drop the hook here Brill, it would save us time if they could?' I looked up. 'Yeah, there is plenty of room for them. Give them a call with the reference number. It will only take them a few minutes to get here.' Sam called on the hand held to Don. 'Yep, that's fine,' Sam was told. 'I'll be there in ten.' We heard a noise at the back of us as we moved the pigs into the middle of the clearing. I looked up to see this big bastard running at me, all tusks and mad as hell. I had no time to aim; I just flicked the safety off, pointed the rifle and fired. I drilled him right through the swede. He nose-dived as his front legs caved in and his snout made a groove in the grass as he came to rest nearly on my leg. 'Shit,' I said. 'He scared the living crap out of me.' 'You and me both,' Shane piped up. 'The good side is, we don't have to lift him, just leave him there,' said Sam. Ten minutes later, we heard the whine of the chopper overhead and then the hook came down with the net. We laid it out and piled all the porkers onto it. Sam was talking to Don on the walkie talkie, 'are you going to take them back to the DZ mate?' 'No,' Don replied. 'We will take them straight through to MAF now. There are thirteen here, which will keep them busy for a while.' 'Okay, that's fine with us, catch you for lunch.' The chopper lifted and turned, with its load swaying in the breeze, and off it went in the direction of Taupo.

So the routine was established; we shot that afternoon, same the next day, morning and afternoon until the first block was cleared. Sam had been taking photos, for the record; we culled fifty-six pigs in that first week. 'That's a lot of pigs for one hangi,' Shane acknowledged. 'They are not going to need all this lot, and this is just the first week. I bet they share it out. Probably most will take a truckload home for the whanau.' We were happy and Sam was over the moon. 'The amount those bloody pigs ruin our bush, and to see that many gone in just one week is a real plus. This area will rejuvenate now, and our ground birds will have less to worry about. Then there's only possums and rats to eliminate, they're destructive bastards as well.' he commented. He had been putting traps out, in an additional effort.

The weather held up until the second week. Then we were hit with a southerly. It went from twenty-five degrees to six degrees in fifteen minutes, rain was just pouring down, and we were out in it. We stopped under shelter and put on our thermals. It hadn't rained for nearly two weeks, which is a drought for this area, but the weather was making up for it now. As it drove in from the south, the rain was dripping off our hats and down our necks, making our lives bloody unpleasant. It didn't deter us though; we just went at it slower. Sam quipped, 'There'll be snow on the tops fellas. When this blows over it will take a few days to warm up again.' We only got six pigs that day, and had to leave them in the nearest clearing – the chopper wouldn't fly in this weather with the cloud so low. We marked the reference point to pick up the mob we left, on the first fine day. Then headed back to base, thinking of a nice hot shower along with a hot meal We looked like drowned rats as we came up to the hut. Mike was there with hot tea as we went inside. 'Get that down you fellas, there is a fire going in the hearth.' The place was warm and cosy. We finished our drinks, removed our wet gear, and climbed into very hot showers. Thank goodness for the thermal activity providing the heated water. I dressed and returned to the common room to catch up with the boys before dinner. All our wet gear was hung up in the drying room; we had never had it so good. Light snowflakes drifted against the window outside, an early night was the story for us. Tony had been checking the chopper. When he came in he said, 'All's good, winds dropping and that snow is only light. It will be gone by morning, you mark my words.' We had dinner, and I was looking forward to bed with the sound of the rain on the roof. 'Well, I'm off to bed, catch you all tomorrow,' I yawned. Sleep came easily. Tony was right, the next day dawned bright but cold.

CHAPTER SEVEN

Another early morning, fine and sunny, a really good sign. While getting our gear together this morning, I thought I would take a bit more ammo this time. I had a feeling that it would come in handy. One hundred rounds seemed a good number. Sam and Shane said the same. Funny how things pan out, we were all thinking alike. Our packs were ready, and we had checked in with the mountain radio. They like to know what we are up to, it is a safety requirement. Their forecast was for fine weather, though there could be a shower in the late afternoon, nothing to write home about.

Firstly, we checked the dead pig we had left out as bait well, bits of it anyway. Then we swung around and headed towards the Waipu Creek. We were getting farther away from the hut now and we were planning to stay out for a few days this time. Well prepared with tents, food for a week and all our warm clothes. You just never know. Phones and GPS were fully charged. Oh, yes, we were real pioneers. So the packs were just that much heavier. In the valley of the dead pigs, about four kilometres from the hut, the bush had thickened up and the going was slow, but it was enjoyable not having to rush. We took our time stepping over roots of trees, sliding under branches and making a detour when the trees blocked the tracks. Because of this, it was sometime later in the morning when we arrived at the dead pigs. We had not heard one snort the whole morning. This was to change. We cautiously approached the spot, when we saw this big daddy of a pig with his head in the guts of a dead one. As Sam dropped to his knee, lined him up and shot him, we heard other pigs escaping through the bush. I went to see if our pig was dead and dragged him out, as Sam followed the track of the runners. Coming back he said, 'Sows and piglets; could have been his girlfriends.' We tracked them for two hours until we saw a piglet that had fallen behind trying to eat a dead possum. Shane just up and shot him, and then we carried on. An hour later we came out onto a nice grassy clearing with a creek running clear over rocks. On the left, we saw four sows and about six little ones wallowing in the stream. We laid our packs down and went into the prone position. 'I'll take the left, Sam you the middle and Brill the right,' Shane said. 'Then lay into them, it should be simple.' We relaxed, and then opened up, the boys were good, and in half a minute they were all on the ground. We could put out a good rate of fire. We waited until we felt it was safe, then moved in slowly. We saw no movement from the pigs and sure enough, they were all dead porkers. 'Good morning's work fellas,' Sam said, 'Eleven to start the day, can't get better than that.'

We dragged them all out into the middle of the clearing in clear view for the chopper. We really didn't notice the change in the weather as we worked to get the pigs out into the open, but it was changing. We could feel the cold as a misty fog came slowly rolling down the valley. I got in touch with the base and was told the weather was getting foggy and they would do the pick up when it clears. So that was that. 'Shit,' Sam said. 'We better get the heck out of here, otherwise, we will be caught in this crap, as I said it can get quite bad in this area. We'll follow this track; it will take us deeper into the bush and it'll give us a bit more protection. If we're lucky, we'll find a dry place to bed down until this blows over.' It was continually getting thicker as we headed off down the track. The mist was starting to wisp around the trees in front of us, but we could still see okay. Looking back though, you could not see from where you had come. Within fifteen minutes, the mist was so thick we could hardly see each other. 'Sam,' I said. 'I think we need to stop and get ourselves settled, this is thick stuff – I have never been in a fog like it.' There was a smell of sulphur in the mist as well. 'I'm sure there is a cave or overhang down here, if we haven't come across it in another 10 minutes then we'll stop,' Sam replied. I have good eyesight, but I could hardly see Sam's pack in front of me. Then out of the gloom, we came across a rock wall with a slight overhang, this would do the job. We climbed up to see inside the rock face. It took us a few minutes until we got to the ledge, where we found a cave about three metres deep, bingo! It was nice and dry with natural freshwater seeping through the rear of the rock wall. 'This is not the one I was thinking of, but it will do the job,' said Sam. We dropped our packs and looked outside. God, it was eerie! The fog had become thicker, the sulphur smell was really quite noticeable and we could not see where we were at all. 'I'm pleased we are here mate, I don't think I would have liked to go any further. I reckon if we had kept going, we would have been in deep shit,' Shane speculated.

Sam rang base, but all he got was static. I pulled out the GPS. 'That's strange,' I said, 'I can't pick up a signal; either it's packed up or we're in a black spot.' I looked at my watch. 'Bugger me, it's 4 pm, what happened to the day?' 'This whole fog thing is weird,' said Shane. 'What do you think, Sam?' 'Well,' he answered, 'I have run into fog like this around here before, but nothing as thick as this. It is serious stuff, to affect the radio and the GPS. There has to be a bloody big storm out there. At least we will be dry here for the night. We should make ourselves comfortable.' We hunted around picking up dead branches to start a fire. The temperature had fallen quite a bit and it felt like it was less than ten degrees. We changed into our cold weather gear and got the billy going. Then we sat down with our backs against the wall of the cave. We were looking out into the mist while eating the sandwiches that Maggie had made for us and enjoying a hot drink when we notice a golden swirl in the fog. 'What the hell's that?' I said. 'God knows,' replied Sam. 'I have never seen golden fog or mist before.' It swirled around the entrance to the cave, making the hairs on our arms stand on end, our skin tingle and we felt a bit dizzy. Then a few minutes later, we felt normal again. 'That sure was strange,' said Sam. 'Did you blokes feel dizzy?' 'Yeah, that felt weird' we answered. 'Well, it must have something to do with the sulphur in the lagoon. As the crow flies it's about four kilometres south of us, with the wind bringing the smell this way.' We sat and debated the ins and outs of the strangeness of our situation to the point of killing the subject. 'That golden stuff was dry though fellas,' I added. 'Mist isn't dry' 'Do you think it was a chemical?' Shane asked. 'I don't think so; well, I hope not. If it was, who would do that sort of thing in NZ?' Sam replied. 'Yeah, sounds a bit dozy when you say it like that,' I said.

It was only just after five pm and the day was getting quite gloomy. It seemed too early to be so dark in February. Then we heard an unusual sound, *coo-ee, coo-ee.* Sam sat up straight, turning his head to the sound. 'Did you blokes hear that?' 'Yeah,' we said, 'sounds like someone calling out.' We walked to the edge of the cave and looked out. That was a waste of effort because we couldn't see a thing. The sound came again on the wind. With the third *coo-ee*, Sam was beside himself. 'I've heard that sound before on a tape in Wellington DOC HQ,' he said. 'It was the sound of the laughing owl.' 'That's great,' Grunt remarked. 'No, you don't understand, it's been extinct for over eighty years.' We looked at him. 'Well, it can't be that,' argued Shane. 'But what if it is?' insisted Sam. 'It would be like finding the Takahe in the forties after everyone thought it was extinct. 'We could be famous,' I laughed, 'in our own lunchtime.' 'Shit fellas, I'm serious, this is big deal. Just make sure that your cameras are at the ready, just in case, okay.' 'Yeah, good as gold, mate,' we echoed. I'm thinking Sam might need to get out of the bush for a while. He now hears stuff that is probably his imagination. I heard the sounds, but it didn't sound like a bird to me. 'It could be a couple of people lost and trying to make contact. Voices will travel in this weather,' I concluded. 'Yeah, you're most likely right,' Sam admitted. 'But keep your cameras ready anyway.' We were all a bit paranoid; things were just not right. 'Let's prepare dinner fellas,' I said. 'It will take our minds off this stuff. Once we have a full gut and our minds are working normally, we will feel better and be able to look at things rationally.' We looked at each other and grinned. 'Yeah,' we all agreed. We needed to make a big effort to stay focused. Food always helps and we had lots to eat.

The stove quickly heated our meal and we sat down to mushroom soup, sausages and eggs along with Maggie's mixed salad, apple pie, fresh fruit bread, tea and coffee. By the time it was over we all felt better. We cleaned our gear and yarned for a while until Shane announced, 'I'm dropping off to sleep, I'm feeling quite buggered. I'll catch you two in the morning.' Within five minutes his breathing was deep and it made us decide to hit the sack as well. I pointed out to Sam. 'It will be good as gold tomorrow mate, the fog will go and we will get more pigs, and everything will be back to normal.' 'Yeah, Brill,' he frowned. 'I hope so. Night mate.'

The bird noise woke us, it had crept into our sleep like a living thing, and it was like being in an aviary with a thousand birds. The noise went on and on. Waking up groggy, I went out for a pee. The fog was still thick but maybe not as bad as last night. I still could not see much. Though I was feeling better and confident this would soon lift. Sam and Shane came out, 'What a bloody racket,' they grumbled. 'I have never heard bird sounds this loud.' Sam commented. We went into our routine: wash, breaky and then clean up. We'll see how the day pans out once we have had a feed. With breakfast over, we sat on the lip of the cave with a tea and coffee in our hands, looking at the fog swirl around but getting lighter and lighter. Slowly the shape of the bush became more distinct, but we were still puzzled about the bird noise. It really hadn't let up. The last of the morepork's cries vibrated off the bush, as the misty morning slowly turned grey, then to white and finally, the sun peeked through the canopy.

Sam was trying to raise base on the radio. 'Not even static and the GPS is still not working,' he grumbled. 'I tried the mountain radio; nothing, not even a peep. Hope we can get hold of them soon, otherwise, they'll be out combing the bush for us. I don't know what to make of all this, I'm stumped.' We went outside; the fog was just about gone. 'That's a plus.' I said. Shane nodded, 'Yeah, fellas have you noticed the size of these trees. I have never seen Matai, Rimu, and Totara for that matter, so tall. Just look at them, and the size of the tree ferns. That's Rata over there,' he pointed. 'Bloody hell, it's a monster, it's a good thirty metres, but it should have some flowers left, as it is only the middle of February. Look at all the wood pigeons in there. I have been watching them, I counted twenty-two. When was the last time you saw twenty-two in a Rata tree?

There's Tuis as well, and I have never seen so many Kaka. This is only one tree fellas, and there must be hundreds, this bush is thick with them.' Just then Sam raised his gun to use the scope and yells. 'This is bull, it cannot be,' he exclaimed. 'What's wrong mate?' we both ask. 'See those birds just about halfway up the Rimu tree?' 'Yep.' Shane was squinting, 'Oh yeah, got it.' 'That's a bloody Huia.' Sam announced. 'And not just one, there are about five of them. They must be a family group. Dad's got the long curved beak and mum has the smaller one. Look, it's turning, orange wattles on its cheek. Oh shit, fellas, they have been extinct since about nineteen hundred and seven.' He looked at us and went on quietly. 'The owl last night, the Huia now and this bush noise; I'm a wee bit worried, I really don't know what to think. Once could be coincidence, but twice? Two extinct birds within twenty-four hours, I just don't know.' Shane theorised. 'You know this bush reminds me of the movie Jurassic Park.' 'I must admit it does look primaeval,' I answered. 'Well,' said Sam, 'I have never seen bush like this. It's like it was before man got here. There has to be an explanation, but I think we should get ourselves sorted and try and pick up the trail.' The day was starting to become fine but not warm. Sun rays were penetrating the canopy, although not with any great effect, so it was cool and damp underneath. I suggested, 'Until we figure out what this is all about, no pissing off by ourselves. Sam, you walk twenty paces in front and check for a path. I'm in the middle, Shane you take the rear guard, we'll keep in contact at all times until we work it all out. Is everyone agreeable?' 'Yeah, you're right Brill, we won't break ranks,' voiced Shane. 'My eyesight is not going to help us here fellas,' I said, 'Though you two have been in situations like this before, so let's play it by your rules.' 'Okay! But safety catches on at all times and no shooting at all, just in case. We don't want to get into trouble,' Sam replied. 'I still cannot figure out what that golden glow was last night, it was dry and gave me queer sensation. Something is different, I just don't know what,' I said. 'Okay,' Sam suggested, 'So let's go and find out.'

We packed up our gear, carrying our rifles we slid out of the cave. 'We will head back the way we came,' Sam remarked, as he took out the compass which fortunately still worked. 'Right, south,' he instructed. I looked at my watch; the time was nine am. The bush just dripped with moisture and big trees closed in as we tried to make a track to the south. 'It's a jungle mate,' I whispered to Shane, 'Look at the vines, they are everywhere. Even the Urewera National Park is nothing like this. I thought that bush was thick but this beats everything I have ever been in. And where the hell's the track we followed yesterday?' We slipped into a routine: every twenty paces we would stop and Sam would scout around looking for signs. The floor of the bush was thick with dead leaves and litter from the trees. Sam had seen plenty of kiwi signs as well. The bird noise was starting to quieten down as I looked at my watch, eleven am. I felt we might have done about one and a half kilometres, which wasn't far, and still, no tracks found. Shane had been marking trees with his Bowie Knife every twenty paces so we could find our way back to the cave, if need be.

We had warmed up but left our thermals on as it only felt about twelve to fifteen degrees. We had no idea what the weather was going to do. We were making slow progress, climbing over dead trees, bending under branches and moving bush and ferns out of the way. Robins were bouncing just behind us, eating the insects that we disturbed. When we stopped they would step over our boots to look between our legs for any morsels they might have missed. It was a joy to watch them. There were ten of them. I have never seen ten robins at one time. I had taken some shots with my camera and so had Shane. I got a good one of Sam when a Kereru flew in and sat on his rifle barrel. We had never seen anything like it. We watched as he took a look around then flew off into the canopy. 'He was a big bugger,' Sam grinned. 'Pretty heavy sitting on the gun. Didn't want to disturb him. He is such a neat bird.' About midday I was going to suggest we stop for a bite to eat when Sam's hand went up. We slipped into the bush just in case and waited till Sam gave us a call. After five minutes we heard Sam's familiar call of the bellbird. Time to find out what he saw. He waved us in and whispered. 'Look, a single track heading from south to north east, or as close as possible. See, there are a couple of footprints in the wet here and here,' he pointed. 'A big toe and heel. He is walking quickly, not running. It's a male about eighty to ninety kilograms, about one point seven five metres.' I looked at him. 'You managed to get all that from those small marks!' I said, 'I'm impressed mate, means not a thing to me. All I can make out was a toe and that was dubious.' 'He's heading north-east, but we are heading south.' Shane observed. 'Yeah,' I said, 'Well, I think we should maybe follow this bloke, he might know something. It's been three hours and this is the closest we have come to seeing a sign of human activity.' 'Grunt, what's your opinion?' Sam asked. 'I think Brill might be right, this is the first bit of evidence we've had all day.' 'Yeah,' Sam replied, 'I think we should pursue him also. He is a few hours ahead. What we've come through has been pretty rough, –well, no track at all, really – but I think it will be okay from here on tracking this bloke. This trail seems to be formed somewhat. The thing is though, he's bare-footed, and being in the bush with no boots on is a thing we never do. Look at this bloke's imprint, he has feet of iron; I have never come across anything like it. This bloke could kick rocks and he would not feel it. Another mystery.'

'Okay, we will stop for a quick drink.' I said. We got off the track, made a clearing and opened our dry rations of scroggin, fruit and finished off with water. Feeling much better we sat there thinking. I was looking at the boys when I mused, 'We need to get our thoughts out in the open. So whatever we think, no one takes the piss okay. I have some ideas, but Sam, you are the most experienced so what's your opinion?' 'Well,' he replied, 'First, and I cannot explain it, is that we are not in the Tongariro area as the land is different.

'Second, I have never in my life seen bush like this. It's untouched like before it was inhabited by humans. Look at the moss on the south side of this tree, it's nearly as thick as my arm.

'Third, there are birds by the hundreds. When have you seen all this activity? Never!

'Fourth, the owl last night and the Huia this morning. I thought they were both extinct.

'Fifth, the fog last night was not damp, it glowed, that is not normal.

'Sixth, it's quite cool; it's February so it should be warmer than this. This is more like autumn.

'Seven, no cell phone coverage. Eight, no GPS, and no radio signal.

'Nine, we all feel a bit uneasy as if we know there is something wrong and cannot put our finger on it,' Sam concluded.

'I have this idea,' I replied, 'Which is blowing my mind, so before I say anything, what's your thinking Shane?'

'Ten,' Shane added, 'I don't recognise this area.

'Eleven, no possum traces. I haven't seen a sign of them anywhere.

Twelve, no pig traces yet. In bush like this, we should have seen something. Thirteen, that footprint, who would run around with no boots on out here?' he wrapped up.

We looked at each other, Sam sort of shuffled his bum, and I said, 'Well, I'm going to make a statement. Jump in if you think I'm mad.' I thought for a moment, and the boys were looking at me. 'Do you think we have come through a time door? We are in New Zealand, I think, but in a different century.' 'Oh bull shit, Brill,' Grunt said, covering his head with his hands. 'Now you're getting out there mate. I think we are just off course and in an area that we have never been before. I think you are way off my friend. What's your opinion, Sam?' Sam looked at us, 'I have an open mind, Shane. Can I leave it like that? I think I would like to make a decision when we can catch this bloke up or see some town or road. Then I'll give you my opinion. I have an idea though not far off Brill's.' We all looked at each other. 'Okay, I think we should still be careful. Sam in the front, I will be in the middle and Shane at the rear. Is that okay with everyone?' 'Fine by me. But if I see a T-Rex, you can have him, Brill,' Shane smirked. 'Shit Shane, I want to be proven wrong because mate, I'm really uneasy.'

We set off again, heading north-east, taking our time. We did not want whoever was in front of us to notice that we were following until we had a chance to look the area over. There might be a town nearby. Slowly we followed the makings of a track, wide enough for only one person, it twisted and turned but gradually kept heading north-east. The bird-life was quiet; being the middle part of the day, we could hear a bit better now. I was enjoying the tramp. I would have enjoyed it better if this nagging thing in my head would stop telling me I'm in the wrong century. The bush never got any thinner. About three hours we came to a fork in the track that went in a westerly and easterly direction. Sam scouted the area while we slipped into the bush. 'He went west,' he said. 'I've also come across some men with boots with an odd pattern, I've never seen that type before. It looks like it could be an army squad of about ten to a dozen men, they're carrying heavy packs. I have a feeling they are tracking our friend.' He pointed. 'Over there one of them dragged the butt of a rifle. Bit of a puzzle, fellas, we need to be bloody careful now. Also, I think we will get that black paint out of my kit. We don't want to be seen. I don't like this at all.'

When Sam gets worried, we all are. So we took his advice, camouflaged our faces hands and any other bits that stood out in the daylight. Well, we didn't need much; our beards were thick and dark. Shane looked like a mountain man, you could hardly see his face for hair. Sam had a red beard, so it took more to darken his face. The red hair on his head was lighter in colour, so he made sure his hat was pulled down hard on his head and any that stuck out was blackened. When he had finished, he was black all over. Me, I was brown as a berry but ended up with black everywhere until Sam was happy. Shane looked at us and sang 'Mammy mammy'. We had to laugh, albeit quietly. 'Okay,' said Sam, 'Brill, because you have bloody good eyesight, I want you up my arse, just in case I miss something. Shane, keep a look out the back, there might be more blokes with guns. You both know the drill, sharp lookout and if we see anything out of the ordinary we hit the deck.' He ordered, 'Okay, let's move out.' We moved off in single file once more, keeping our eyes peeled. Sam had his head down a lot, following the footprints that now I could see clearly. 'I can't pick up the barefooted bloke now,' he whispered, 'The squad have ruined his track. It's completely obliterated.' 'You can get a bit closer, Brill,'

Sam said. But it was a waste of time as the bush never got thinner and the track twisted and turned so much I dropped back, but not as far as before. 'These soldier boys aren't disguising their tracks at all, they are walking through the bush like a herd of elephants,' Sam muttered.

He had just finished talking, when out of the bush came this blood-curdling yell. He came at me with rage on his face and lips. 'Kei te haere ahau ki te patu a koe rewera pango.' 'I'm going to kill you black devil,' he was yelling. The bugger was so close to me the spittle from his mouth was being sprayed in my face. His stone mere was raised above his head. All I had time for was, 'SHIT!' and ducked. It put him off balance for a few seconds as he swiped at my head and missed. When I ducked, I kicked hard at his knee, which dropped him onto his other leg. As he tried to right himself, Shane came tearing in. The big bloke can move when he wants to. He went at him and flattened him with a punch. His fists are like lumps of iron. I heard his jaw crack and I saw the Māori bloke's eyes roll back into his head. He went down and just lay there not moving at all. 'Oh bugger,' said Shane. 'I hope he doesn't cark it.' I got up and stuck my finger on his jugular vein. 'No, you're right mate, he's out cold.' I checked his jaw. 'It's not broken. He'll have a headache, but that's about all.' We're only talking about ten seconds, and the fight was all over with the stone mere laying on the ground. 'This is a serious attack,' barked Sam. 'What got into him?' 'He could be a bit mad,' I answered. I turned to Shane, 'Did you understand what he said?' Shane replied, 'All I got was black devils, what a dumb arse. Well, we will sort this bugger out when he wakes up. If he is aggressive, we will take him to the nearest police station.' Looking at the bloke, I felt really nervous. I don't like this situation one bit.

CHAPTER EIGHT

We were looking at his clothes as he lay on the track. 'Looks as though he has been to a costume party,' Grunt remarked. Sam looked at his feet. 'Bloody hell, they are like concrete! This is the bloke we have been tracking. Are you sure he is okay?' I felt his jugular again for good measure. 'Yep, just out for the count, Grunt sure knows how to hit someone.' 'I didn't hit him that hard,' Grunt said defensively. 'There is a big difference between what you say and what the poor bloke will say. A big difference.' I joked.

He started to stir and moan a few minutes later. I knelt beside him, lifted his head and popped a couple of paracetamol into his mouth. Then I squeezed water in from a water bottle and held his mouth shut until I could see that he had swallowed the pills. He came to, coughing and spluttering, holding his head in his hands. 'Someone ran over me with a horse.' He said in English, with a bit of a Pommie accent. He sat up wide-eyed and looked at us. 'Are you going to eat me?' he blurted out. Grunt burst out laughing. 'You are too stringy mate,' he grinned. 'You are black devils,' he stated with a worried look. We looked at each other, grinned and I reassured him. 'No mate, this is just paint, to keep us hidden in the bush. We didn't want anyone to see us.' You could see the relief on his face. 'Who are you?' he asked. 'Before we answer your question mate, I think you will have to answer ours first,' I replied. 'You speak differently from other Pakeha,' he stammered. ' Are you English?' 'It has to be the ringing in your head,' I answered. 'We will ask the questions okay?' 'What's "okay?"' he returned. Sam grinned, 'Where is this joker from?' He turned to us. 'Let's get off the track, we don't want to be around if the fellas with the guns come back. You okay to walk?' he asked the Māori. 'I'll carry him,' said Shane. He grabbed his arm, threw him over his shoulder and walked into the bush. The Māori was mumbling in Māori and English about being undignified. Sam asked, 'is there a clearing close by?' 'About one hundred yards from the track,' the Māori replied. Sam backtracked to the right spot. It was not a very big clearing, but enough for the four of us to sit. 'It will do fellas,' Sam said as Shane lowered the Māori gently to the ground. 'Okay,' I decided. 'We need to get a coffee on, and maybe have a bite to eat. We have all those rations that Maggie gave us, and if we don't eat them, they'll go off. Now, what's your name?' I asked our newly acquired friend. 'Wiremu,' came the answer. 'Oh, that's Māori for William, so we will call you Bill.' 'Funny,' Bill replied. 'A lot of English people call me that. Why?' We didn't bother to answer him. I got to work getting the food out. We still had bread, cheese, ham, tomatoes, scroggin, apples, plums, peaches and bananas that were starting to go black. Bill was all eyes. When Grunt got the stove going, Bill crawled over and said, 'What's that?' 'It's a stove,' Grunt declared. 'Nothing like I have ever seen before,' frowned Bill. Grunt turned on the gas and lit it with the lighter. 'Oh! Magic fire stick.' 'What the hell are you on about, you stupid bugger,' I fumed. 'Haven't you seen a lighter before?' 'Not until now,' he answered. The man was an idiot. 'When we get to civilization, you are going back to your hospital bed, mate,' said Sam. 'I'll have a coffee, Brill.' 'Okay, mate.' Unusual for Sam to drink coffee. Maybe the situation was catching up on all of us. Well, we would sort it out after we have had a bite to eat and a hot drink.

'Okay fellas, food.' I passed around the sammies and the fruit. We shared everything with Bill, who was stuffing the food down. 'This is good kai,' he grinned. 'Ham is good, but what's that black thing?' 'Are you kidding me, it's an overripe banana,' I grab mine and took a bite, then handed the rest to him. 'Try it,' I offered. 'Oh, that's good, your food is different but good.' I gave him my mug and I had my drink out of my pannikin. We watched him as he was starting to relax. It was getting to the time to ask some questions. 'What made you attack us?' I asked. 'When do you just, out of nowhere, jump out at someone and try to kill them? This is not the wild west.' 'I don't know what you mean,' he said. 'All I saw were black men, black! That's devils' work and you had to die.' 'You stupid prick. What were you thinking? Killing someone is against the law.' I protested. 'Maybe,' he said, 'but not out here.' 'Then why me?' I asked. 'You looked the easiest,' he admitted. 'If I had killed you I would have escaped into the bush. My ancestors would have praised me. Then you swerved and kicked me in the knee. It still hurts a bit, by the way. Then the big man hit me. I did not see that coming, and I woke up with all you staring at me. Who has my patu? I don't want to lose it, it's the only weapon I have. Not a good one, but beggars can't be choosers.' 'Here it is,' said Shane, who had been looking at it with interest. 'Rough but it would do the job. If you raise it above your head, within reach of us,' he continued, looking at Bill and pulling out his bowie knife, 'I might have to use this on you.' 'What a wonderful knife,' Bill blurted out. 'I have never seen a knife that big. That would be worth a lot of women,' he smiled. 'Not for sale,' grinned Shane. 'Just be aware it's here, step out of place and you will find out how sharp it is.'

Bill tried to stand up to get his patu off Shane but was so wobbly he had to sit down again. 'Shane gave you a hay-maker so you are bound to be a bit unwell for a while yet,' Sam laughed. 'So it might pay to sit quietly until you feel better.' Shane leaned over and placed the patu in Bill's hands. 'We are mates now,' he told him. 'Now we want some of our questions answered. Why no shoes?' He looked at Bill's feet. 'I don't like shoes, I cannot understand anyone wearing them, never had any, never will,' answered Bill. 'I can believe that,' said Sam. 'He wouldn't need to wear boots in a rugby game.' 'What's a rugby game?' Bill asked. 'Oh piss off Bill, that's bullshit mate,' Grunt grumbled in frustration. Bill just sat there looking puzzled. 'So what are your names? I have heard five names and there are only three of you. 'Okay,' I said.

'I'm Bob, but my nickname is Brill. The bloke that hit you is Shane, we call him Grunt, and the bloke over there is Sam.' Sam took his hat off and his red hair fell out. 'Oh,' Bill noted. 'Are you a fairy from the bush, with white skin, red hair and blue eyes, supernatural children of the mist?' I had to laugh, Sam as a fairy, made me snigger. 'Well, you got the mist right,' Sam replied. 'I'm a bloke just like you.' 'What about the word "mate," you say it all the time?' he asked. 'You only hear that word on ships or in the navy, never the way I think you mean. Do you mean friend?' 'Yes, friend, but also any man. It's a figure of speech. So we are all mates here.' Sam answered. 'You are not devils then, you are Pakeha?' 'Yeah,' Sam laughed. 'This is camouflage paint as we said before, so we cannot be seen.'Bill looked around. 'Are you all the same?' 'We all are,' I said. 'But Shane has a little bit of Māori in him.' Bill looked at Shane and frowned. 'A bit big for a Māori, both you men are. Bob is about normal for a Pakeha.' He turned to Shane. 'You have Māori blood?' he asked. 'Where are you from?' 'Mate,' Shane replied, 'it's diluted. I know a few words and a bit of protocol, that's all. My family are from Taupo and Tokoroa and the rest from Kaitaia; that was a long time ago.' Shane really didn't really want to get into the details of his whanau, the way things seemed to be shaping up. 'Good mixture,' Bill said. 'Half your family wants to eat the other half.' That brought a smile to our faces. This bloke was no dumb cluck. We looked at him and I asked, 'Your dress, why do you dress like that?' 'Well, you dress funny too,' he replied. 'I have never seen clothes that resemble the bush, and I have never seen cloth like that, or packs like those, or that thing on your wrist. Is that a pocket watch? So I have questions too. To answer your question,' he continued as he leaned against the tree, 'These are my clothes, I bought them, I did not steal them if that's what you are thinking. All Māori are not thieves.' 'No mate,' I said. 'We did not mean that it's just that they look old fashioned.' 'Well, these are the clothes that all Pakeha wear. I just never liked shoes, so I never wear them.' 'Why are there soldiers here, are there maneuvers here or something?' 'Don't you know anything? he answered. 'There is a war coming, the British Army is over there,' he pointed vaguely north, 'they will be here soon. The Māori here will not back down. Rewi said he will fight till he dies.' My head was starting to spin. 'REWI!' I yelled. I swung around to Shane and Sam, then turned back to Bill. 'What the hell is the date?' The boys just looked at me. 'What are you on about, Brill?' they barked. 'The date, Bill, what is it?' 'It's the second of May, 1863. Why don't you know that?' We all looked at him and the boys said 'bullshit' over and over again. It cannot be, it's bloody impossible, I thought. Oh hell, is this real? 'For Christ's sake, Sam punch me, this is a bloody nightmare.' Sam gave me a smack. Shit, that hurt, I am still here, I'm not dreaming. The worried look on our faces got worse, this was just too much to take in.

'Sit down fellas,' I suggested. 'We need to think this through. We must have somehow come through that mist and into the past. I have no idea how it happened, but it looks as though we have. All those pointers we talked about earlier. This place has not been touched, it hasn't been turned into farms, and the birds are still here. No human contact except for hunting parties, oh shit, this is a bloody disaster!' We looked at each other in horror, how did this happen? All this time Wiremu was looking at us. 'Not from here then?' he questioned. 'You could say that,' Sam said turning to me. 'So what do we do, Brill?' 'Buggered if I know,' I replied. 'You blokes know the history; we need some input, I'm completely out of my depth here.' I turned to Bill. 'Where are we mate?' 'Not far from Pukekawa,' he replied. 'It is a small kainga, farming kumara. About six whare, consisting of mainly women and children, though; they have a warrior for protection. I snuck in there a few nights ago and stole some food, another reason to stay out of their way. I have been out here for three days waiting for a chance to get across the Waikato River.' 'Why, aren't you from here?' 'No,' replied Bill. 'I'm from Hokianga, Ngapuhi. This is the Waikato, Tainui country. There is still some animosity between Tainui down here and my tribe, so if I'm caught, they'll most likely kill me, then stuff me with kumara and roast me. I would taste quite good really,' he jested with a grin. 'I cannot get my head around this, fellas,' Shane groaned. 'I think I would really like to go home, but how?' 'Bugger it, Shane, I would too,' I voiced. 'But how the hell do we do that? We are nowhere near Tongariro where the mist was, and it's now 1863. Anyway, how would we get there, there are no tracks? Moreover, you have to remember at this time in history, it's just before the New Zealand Wars when the settlers from Great Britain fought the Māoris over the land. Eventually, the English get the upper hand and the Māori Chief, Rewi Maniapoto, pulls his warriors back to Taumarunui into the King Country. Nobody, especially Pakeha, will be able to get through there for years. I think a post office was set up about 1885, but really not until the rail went through did any Europeans feel very safe in the area. That's about 1907 or 1908, forty-odd years away yet.' 'Oh shit,' cried Sam. 'What about our parents, my wee sister? Shit shit shit, I'll never see her again.' Bill was looking at us as though we came from another planet. 'So what's the problem?' he asked. I just wanted to hit the bugger. It wasn't his fault, of course, but the way I felt and the boys felt, we just wanted to lash out. I ignored him and turned to my mates. 'We would all like to go home, but at the moment it's out of the question until we can get to a safe place and figure all this out.' We were starting to fall apart and I had to do something about it. 'Let's look at what's in front of us first,' I continued, 'one day at a time. The conditions we came through might happen again if we can get back up on the mountain. So let's be positive, or let's just go and get pissed at the nearest village.' That got a smile, as we were all thinking of our families, but what we needed to do is focus on the time right now, and worry about tomorrow, and the future later.

I turned to Bill. 'So Bill, how come you're here?' I hoped that talking to him would stop us from thinking about ourselves. 'Oh, the short or long version?' Bill replied. He had a turn of words for a Māori in 1863, I thought, but I didn't know how they spoke really. You never hear about the average Joe Blog, it's always the chief or someone higher up. 'Just tell us your story mate, we seem to have plenty of time,' I said. 'Well,' he went on, 'I was born in Hokianga on the sixth of February, 1840. I was a treaty baby. I was sent to a native missionary school in Rawene. Then I was sponsored by Mr. White, a lay preacher at the Anglican Church, to learn a printing trade in Auckland. I have been there since 1856. Now I'm a printer in my own right. I work for Mr. Edward Wattle on Queen Street in Auckland. I live on the premises in a room out the back. Well, I did. 'I have strong views about the land,' he continued, 'and did not like the idea of an invasion of the Waikato by the English, so I printed off leaflets and circulated them around the town, much to the disgruntlement of the inhabitants. They kicked me out of town. Instead of shipping me off home up north, they threw me across the Waikato River into Tainui territory with the comment, "All black bastards should be thrown out of the country". I think we all look the same to them. I know there is going to be a war here, the settlers want land, and they will take it. Governor Grey, he talks and smiles about how he will help Māori, but behind their backs, he is building up his forces. We will all be in the middle of a battle soon, and I'm not staying around. This is a Tainui war, not mine. 'Being Ngaphui, our tribes have a few outstanding debts against each other and if I was caught I could be in for the chop. Therefore, I'm trying to stay alive and out of everyone's way. I hope to get to the West Coast, steal a canoe and head back up north to my home in the far north.' He thought for a minute. 'Is the story to your liking so far?' He grinned before continuing,

'I had this feeling of being followed, so I hid off the track until the soldiers walked past. I waited until they were completely gone, giving them a good hour and then I saw you, black devils. All my Christian upbringing went out the door, and I reverted back to being a warrior. I thought black was the devil and had to be killed otherwise there would be death everywhere. So I went for the shortest one, screaming my war chant and other things.' He grinned again. 'Then I woke up with you ugly men staring at me.' 'Ugly? Have you looked in a mirror lately?' I retorted. 'So you are a printer?' 'Yes, my employer tried to help me, he is a good friend. I told him I'll contact him as soon as I can. He's going to open a paper up north; when I get back I'll be in charge. So I'm keen to go home now.' 'So where is the nearest pa?' I asked. 'Oh, that's about five miles east,' he replied. 'Meremere.' 'Oh heck, that pa is one of the biggest in the Waikato. There are trenches, palisades, the works, about thirty-two kilometres from Port Waikato to the Hunuas. How the hell are we going to get across that? So it's May you say?' 'Yes of course.'

I turned to the others. 'We have two months, fellas, to get ourselves organised. Otherwise, we could be caught up in the biggest bun fight in New Zealand's history. I've just had a thought, about getting out of here, it's a small seed of an idea, however, I will need to think about it before I babble forth. How are you blokes holding up now?' They had been looking at me, but whispering to each other. 'Brill,' Sam started, 'Shane and I have been talking. Look, mate, we are not good with this history stuff. We need to do things that we are familiar with and we are just not capable of being at home in another time. We are confused, mate. You seem to be holding yourself together better than we are. We have decided that we want you to lead us. Whatever you say, we will do. But if something happens that requires our expertise, we will take control, okay?' 'It hasn't come to that yet, fellas. We will be okay,' I assured them. 'Yeah, Brill, but you know what to do,' Sam replied. 'This thing with Rewi, who is he? That pa you mentioned, all I know about Meremere is that it used to be a coal power station or something. If you ask me to take you to Tongariro, I'll walk on water to get us there, mate, but the getting there is going to be through your knowledge of history.' 'Shane, what do you think? How do you feel?' 'Yeah, I'm with Sam, Brill,' Shane replied. 'You are the best bloke for the job, piss poor in a fight,' he grinned, 'but you know your history. You can rely on us, it goes without saying. In a scrap, if it comes down to it, we will be there with you, boots and all. Just point us in the right direction. You are the best in this situation. You also have the gift of the gab, mate, it might help us down the line.' I looked at them. 'Okay.' I was humbled. 'I'm not too sure how I feel about being in charge, and it wasn't in my CV either. We will leave it like that for now. But one thing we need to do is make sure that no one reveals our equipment to the locals. We are going to stand out like a sore thumb the way we are and the way we look. We don't need anyone noticing our GPS or phones. We need also to cover our weapons, as they are far too modern. The most important thing is that we must try not to harm or do anything to help the locals as it may change history. I don't know about this, though, it could be all bullshit. Are we part of history now or will we stuff it up?' 'Well, we could have changed the past already with Grunt belting Bill here,' Sam answered. 'Yeah, you could be right; but all I'm saying is we must try, that's all.' I must admit I had no idea and I was just clutching at straws. Old nosy-parker Bill here has already noticed the watch and, like a fool, I had snapped off a couple of photos with my camera. So we weren't helping ourselves at all well, I wasn't.

'I think we should try and skip past this village that Bill mentioned,' I pondered. 'If we can get across the Waikato and into Pakeha territory, we might be able to blend in, though you two blokes stand out you might have to bend over a bit.' 'What about our clothes?' Grunt pointed out. 'They have nothing like this.' 'I'll think about that, mate,' I answered. 'In the meantime, let's try for the Waikato River.' I turned to Bill. 'You okay with that, mate? We could use you as an interpreter if we get into difficulty. We can say that you are our guide, who got us lost while pig shooting. You're a useless bloody guide, though. Are there even pigs here?' 'Oh yes,' Bill replied. 'Plenty. But there is one condition: you help me get home, okay? I like that word,' he smiled. 'I'll help you if you help me.' 'Deal,' I agreed. 'What's your last name, mate?' I asked as the boys were preparing to break camp and clean up. 'Hohepa,' he answered. 'Hohepa!' I gulped, my voice sounding strangled. 'You wouldn't have a sister, Mary, would you?' He looked at me. 'How did you know that?'

The boys gave me a puzzled expression. 'Oh for the love of God, shit, do you know a family by the name of Tilly?' 'Yes, the Tilly's are farming in the Victoria Valley just out of Kaitaia. David Tilly is the son and my sister Mary is the housekeeper for the Tilly family. I think she has an eye on the young man David. They are a nice family. They speak our language, are fair-minded and Mary just loves being there. She is also a good friend of their daughter, Ann. She must be about the same age. She eats at their table.' I could not believe what I was hearing. Bill was my third-great-aunt's brother, therefore he is bloody family! I looked at him, thinking he also knew my third-great-grandmother, Ann Tilly, who would later become the wife of Robert Kydd, my name's sake. I was not listening to him at all. I was staring at him in a daze when he said 'You okay? How do you know Mary?' 'Oh,' I said, snapping out of it. 'It's a long story. I will tell you one day when we have the time.' Grunt came up and whispered, 'you okay?' I whispered back. 'Yes, I just found out he's my third-great-uncle. Things are really getting complicated. Who will we run into next? I don't know much about the family, but his sister married my ancestor, David. I have never been able to find them when tracing my family tree. She would be only fourteen at the moment. I cannot get my head around any of this mate.' 'Well, you better try and clear your head because we are relying on you to be switched on. We will worry about all the other stuff later,' Sam cautioned. Shit! I thought. I laughed to myself: do I call him Uncle Bill? I'm getting overloaded with too much information. Shane laughed nervously. 'Oh God, this whole thing is a bloody great farce. Who would believe all this? I'm here and even I don't believe.' 'Well,' I said, 'as long as we can look on the bright side and be positive. All we need to do now is to get out of the Waikato ASAP.' Bill came over to me. 'If we can get to the Alexander Redoubt, there is a ferry there that will take us over to the Pakeha side.' 'That's a good idea; we can bullshit our way across. Do they have a ferry master?' 'Yes, on the Pakeha side. I think it's under the army control now. The whole area on the border is army. In the past before the war of words, you would just call out for the boat to cross over. So we need to have a good excuse as to why we are here, no Pakeha should be on this side of the river. It's Tainui land and Pakeha are not welcome.' 'Right,' I said. 'I was thinking, fellas, we need to be military. Before we head out we need to sort out our rank, so we can bluff our way through. So I'll be the captain, both you blokes will be lieutenants, and Bill here is our native guide with the rank of staff sergeant. If anyone asks, we are on a secret mission, and if they persist, tell them to piss off. I think, that as long as we act like officers, we will get by. We all have been in the services and officers get away with murder so just act as if you know everything and we'll be right.' Bill, listening to all this, remarked, 'You men are funny, I don't understand a lot of your speech and what you are even talking about. I have no idea what your equipment is for and everything about you is unusual. You don't have an accent that I have heard before, not like the English I know. You must have come a long way.' Sam turned to him. 'You will never guess in a million years, Bill. The distances we have travelled might be insurmountable for our return home. I hope not, but I'm not holding my breath. When we have a quiet time we might give you a hint, but you will not believe it and it will be impossible for you to understand. Just be aware we are friends who are lost and all we want to do is go home to our families.' I looked at my mates. I had never seen them like this and they looked out of their depth. I went over to them and place my hands on their shoulders. 'The one good thing is we are all together.' 'I blame myself for getting us into this, Brill,' Sam replied. 'Oh bullshit, mate. When we get back, what a bloody story this will make. There is a reason in life for everything. So think about why we are here. There must be a reason for it. C'mon, fellas, let's get moving. Sam in front; Bill, you are with me; and Shane in the rear. We don't want to run into those army blokes if we can help it.' We entered the track. The afternoon was slipping by. There was still plenty of light on the tops of the canopy, but the track was dim and it was hard to see as the bush was very thick.

CHAPTER NINE

Silently we crept back onto the track. The bird life was starting to come back to full chorus as the afternoon set in. We had been tramping about thirty minutes when we noticed that the bush seemed to be getting thinner, as more light was shining down onto the track. The path was now well worn; many feet had come this way. Bill whispered in my ear. 'The Kainga is not far in front and if we're going to detour around it, we need to do that at the fork that's about ten minutes away.' 'How far to the village?' I asked. 'Fifteen minutes,' came the reply. Oh bugger, that was getting a bit too close for comfort. I crept up to Sam, who was lead, and said, 'Ten minutes to the fork, we are pretty close to that village, and so we need to be on our toes.' Although my saying this to Sam was like teaching a duck to swim. He's the most competent man I have ever seen in the bush. All he did was give me a thumbs up and I snuck back to inform Grunt in the rear.

We came to the fork earlier than expected, to hear the sound of musket fire from the direction of the village. Sam dropped to the ground and the three of us melted into the bush. 'What the hell?' I whispered. Bill, who was hugging the ground pretty tightly, spoke up. 'I think it must be those army soldiers,' he muttered. Sam slipped back for a yarn. 'They are not far ahead. Sounds as though they might have attacked the village. They have left it until this time of the day, by the looks of it, so the bird noise would disguise their shooting. We are quite close, the sound of the muskets are getting louder.' 'There are only women and children there,' Bill voiced, 'With one able-bodied man and a few older men who do the gardening.' He went on. 'Those army men will take that village easily, though the people will fight, even with sticks, it could be messy. Those English soldiers are porangi.' We huddled in discussion. Looking up the track, Grunt spoke. 'Fellas, we will have to take a look. With only women and kids there, in all good conscience, we cannot just pass by without helping.' Glancing at my mates, I thought about how they always try to do the right thing. I looked at Shane. 'You are right, mate, we cannot just walk on by.' Turning to Bill, I asked him, 'Are you up for this?' 'Oh yes, a bit of utu is good for the soul, especially on the Pakeha that threw me out of Auckland. So I'm right behind you,' he grinned.

'What's the layout, Bill?' Sam asked. He closed his eyes for a tick then replied, 'All the whare are clustered together on the right of the clearing, close to the creek at the back. The creek and the kainga back up to the bush. There are kumara gardens to the right and left of the clearing. Coming out of the track into the village it is completely clear with good vision. There will be a big cooking fire out in front of the largest whare.' 'Thanks, mate,' said Sam. Bill continued, 'it was easy for me to come in from the back of the whare to steal food. They have no guards so I can just came out of the bush grabbed what I could and disappeared. They didn't even know that I was there.' 'Okay,' said Sam. 'Brill, can you and Bill come from around the rear. Grunt and I will go in from the front. We will assess it first to see what the situation is when we get a clear view of the village. If they are only stealing food, maybe we can leave without interfering, but if they are causing any bodily harm, we will have to do something. Is that agreeable with everyone?' I was happy with whatever Grunt and Sam came up with. This was where their judgment came into its own. I agreed and Bill was only too happy to go along with anything, I think he was enjoying himself. 'When we get closer,' Sam said to me, 'You and Bill scoot around the back. I'll give you a bellbird call twice, nice and loud.' 'Okay,' I replied. 'One thing though, unless it is really necessary, no shooting. I would rather lay them out with a whack to the head. We don't know the consequences for the future.' 'We have to be careful,' Shane conceded. 'That's fine, but if someone points a gun at me, I'm not going to sit there and let him shoot me. Same goes for you blokes either. Shoot first, ask questions later.' 'Yeah okay then,' was my reply, 'if in danger we have to protect ourselves.' I thought, shit, I hope that doesn't happen, but it might, and if that's the case then it's in the hands of the gods. I was a bit out of my depth with this time-travel stuff. For all I know we were part of history now, and whatever we do is supposed to happen. Oh shit, I was a very confused chook. I asked Bill, 'How is your knee? We will have to move quickly, will you be okay?' 'I'm fine,' he grinned. 'Don't worry about me. You still look like black devils with the paint on your faces. I think the English will be a bit scared of you.' 'Well, I hope so,' I said. 'I don't really want to kill anyone.' 'They won't be expecting us so that's in our favour,' Sam put in, 'And we do look scary. If I saw Grunt I would shit myself, so that's another advantage to look like we do. We need to be quick and hit them hard before they know we are there.' 'Okay fellas; eyes peeled Brill.' We crept back onto the track. We heard musket fire again. 'Bugger, it is getting serious,' Sam spat. 'They are really dopey buggers doing this with not being at war. Their officers will be pissed, especially the top brass.'

Everything had gone quiet, as the musket fire had silenced the bird noise. We edged up to the clearing and gave the area a once-over. We saw three bodies, two in the garden and one who looked like he had been defending a small whare. Two soldiers were lying not far from the middle of the clear area rolling around in pain. It looked as if the bloke by the hut had got a couple of well-placed shots off before he was shot himself. 'Looks as if the English bastards have killed those blokes,' Shane said. 'No,' I said, 'the one by the hut just moved.' The women and some of the kids were attacking the soldiers with whatever they could get their hands on, led by a woman who had a moko. We counted nine army blokes in the open, seven attacking the women, plus the two who were shot. Also, there was one who was rounding up the kids, but we couldn't see any NCO's. We heard this young bloke yelling at his mates. 'If any of you bastards hurt these children, I'll ram my bayonet up your arse, you hear me, you English shits.' He had a broad Scottish accent. We watched him gather up the kids taking them right away from the fighting, and depositing them in the small whare.

'While the women are keeping the soldiers occupied,' Sam whispered, 'I think we should have a go at them since these buggers are distracted. We don't need to go around the back after all, as they are all clustered together. We will go in like a forward rumble, over the top and ruck the buggers out. Bill, you come in behind and tap them with your mere. Quietly as possible; we don't want any others who may be around to come out firing.' The soldiers nearly had the woman under control when a couple of young boys of about eight or nine got amongst them with small stone mere and started to hit the blokes on their knees. You could see that this pissed off the soldiers in a big way, as they swung their rifles, hitting the kids on their backs and flinging them onto the ground. I felt Grunt tense. 'Bugger that, they're just kids.' Knowing our mate, we knew what he was going to do when he took off, so we went with him. Going like the clappers, three blokes in a row, with Bill at our rear, we drove into the English soldiers. They didn't even see us coming. Fists and rifle butts were tossed around willy-nilly as they popped out to our rear, with Bill whacking them on the side of the head. It didn't even last thirty seconds and we weren't even breathing hard. When the fighting stopped, the women immediately were all over the English. I yelled, 'Don't kill them, I need to ask them questions!' The woman with the moko said, 'we will tie them up.' This is when we heard a scream coming from the small hut that the Māori man had been protecting. A high pitched scream, like someone, was being hurt. We took off in that direction. Shane didn't even stop, he just plowed into the hut with murder on his mind. Shit, he's scary when he gets like this, which is hardly ever. A young boy called out that his whaea was in there. 'Don't worry, we'll help her,' I yelled as we ran past him, following Shane into the hut. We were just in time to see him slug this sergeant in the side of the head so hard that he fell through the wall. The sergeant's pants were down around his ankles with his legs in the air. You would have laughed if it were not so serious. There was a woman on the ground with her face covered in blood, and there was another younger woman about eighteen or nineteen, standing over her. She had been using the knife to defend the older woman who was on the ground. I think she must have poked the sergeant, hence the yelling. The two soldiers against the wall had a surprised look on their faces. They had been expecting to be included in a nice bit of gang rape, but it had all gone tits up. Now all they had for their effort was their sergeant out cold outside and three angry looking black fellas who turned on them and smacked them with the butts of their rifles.

We watched as they fell to the ground, and then we turned to the women. Shane went over to see if they were all right. The younger woman had had her shirt ripped off by the sergeant and her exposed breasts had us all thinking god, she is a good-looking woman. She was about one point seventy-five metres or five foot six inches, had black hair down to her waist and brown eyes that flashed in anger. She looked a fiery wee thing. Shane nearly got the knife in his guts as she said, 'Stay away you black devil, you are not getting near me or my mistress. You are the devil's spawn.' We had forgotten about the face paint and Shane was a bit shocked. He turned to me. 'Brill, get that jacket off that bloke on the floor and let's give her some modesty.' The woman kept flicking her knife at him. 'You are not lying with me. Keep away or I'll chop off your manhood.' I took the jacket off the soldier and handed it to Shane. He threw it at the young woman, not wanting to get too close to her. 'We aren't black, this is just paint to disguise ourselves in the bush.' He wiped his cheek, and the light brown of his face become clear for her to see. The look on her face was one of surprise, as she looked at the three of us. 'You are not black?' Her mouth sort of twitched, then a lopsided smile spread across her face. Her expression changed just like that. She was all sweet and lovely, and thanked us for the jacket, as she put it on. She then knelt down and helped the woman on the floor to get up. 'I have to check the bloke out the front,' I said. 'Shane will you see if this woman is okay, then tie up these three and put them with the others outside. Sam, will you check the kids, and the other women, to see if they're alright? Leave that young Scottish bloke with the kids. He did a good job keeping them out of harm's way.'

Only minutes had passed since we ran into the camp. I rushed outside and went straight for the Māori bloke near the whare who had been shot. I could see he was moving, but he'd lost a lot of blood. Oh shit! I thought it looked like a femoral wound. I threw my pack down, opened the first aid kit and jammed a clotting pad into the wound. The elder woman with the moko came over. I asked, 'can you organise guards on those soldiers? Use their rifles. I need to get this man inside, otherwise, he will die.' She yelled out an order, as the women came up and took the guns. They sat down in a circle facing the men. 'Shane,' I shouted. 'I need your help. As he came towards me I asked, is the woman okay?' 'Yep,' he said. 'Just a smack on the nose, she will be good as gold. I just finished tying up the NCO's. What do you need?' 'We need a bed or table and hot water for this bloke.' I turned around and saw the elder woman next to me. Can you supply them?' I inquired. 'Yes,' she replied. 'Can you bring them to the big whare?' I asked. 'I'll organise it for you now.''Do you need a hand to pick up the Māori bloke, Grunt?' 'She'll be right, mate, no worries.' Shane bent down and lifted him in his arms. Didn't even break a sweat. I held his legs up high above his heart, trying not to think what was going to happen when we got him onto the table.

As we were walking into the whare, we saw the young bloke who had helped the Māori children assist the two wounded men back to the group of soldiers. He then settled all his charges together and afterward headed over to see the woman with the moko. I got the impression the women felt okay with him, as he didn't take part in the attack and protected their children from the line of fire. He was about one metre eight or five foot nine inches, with a strong build and young looking, about nineteen. He had light reddish hair and pale skin. He looked like he hadn't been in the sun at all and his eyes were blue like Sam's. He had the youngest children with him and I heard him say he would prepare some food for them. Before long, off he went with ten kids following him like the pied piper. The Māori woman laughed and then turned back to the prisoners with scowling faces of very pissed-off people.

Sam had checked the two old men who had been working in the garden, but they had died instantly. He also checked the kids and fixed up their bumps and bruises. As I settled the wounded bloke inside, I thought about what was going to happen to the soldiers. Shit, these days they hung you for stealing bread. Nevertheless, I couldn't worry about that yet; I needed to concentrate on the task at hand. First, I need to wash myself and also clean this bloke up with the hot water. The pressure pad I had put on the wound was holding, but as soon as I released it, I was sure it would start gushing again. 'Keep his legs elevated,' I said to Shane. Then the water arrived. I stripped off and got rid of the gunk from the day. Then I relieved Shane as he washed up. Once cleaned, we gathered our packs together and went through them to see what we might need. 'Clamps Shane, I've only got the clamp on my Swiss army knife.' I exclaimed. After I explained to the elder woman what I wanted, she said she had some sort of food tongs. 'They will have to do. In addition, we need more hot water and a fire going in here to keep it hot, so we can sterilise our instruments,' I said. She had no idea what I was on about, but after I explained she sent the girl out to do our bidding. This was the same girl that Shane had given the jacket too. She came back with what was needed, and I talked them both through how I wanted them to cleanse themselves for the operation. They looked at us with frowns on their faces but did as we asked. Now Shane and I sterilised the equipment then scrubbed our hands thoroughly with the soap and hot water and we were ready. I took my Swiss army knife from the pile and began.

'Okay,' I said to Shane, 'He is still out, but I think he needs a bit of morphine to keep him that way, and also for the pain.' I took out the needle and jabbed him with enough to help. What I needed was to get both ends of the femoral artery and join them if they were ripped. I was pretty sure what I was going to do was right, but had my fingers crossed that it wasn't too bad and that I could do it before he bleeds out. If it was completely severed, he would lose his leg. I would have to cauterise it and take it off and that made me feel a bit sick. While I was getting everything in order, Shane had exposed the leg. I had the needle threaded for speed and said to him, 'I need to clamp the artery at the top to stop the flow and pull up the bottom piece so I can attach it to the top, then sew.' Shit, it sounded easy. This was a major operation and we were in a whare, in the middle of nowhere in 1863. I was really out of my depth, but I had to try. I picked up a clamp while Shane removed the pad from the wound and it started to bleed. I widened the wound, then put my hand inside his leg and grabbed the femoral artery. I had to be quick but thank God it had not been severed. I clamped the artery above the cut. I then asked the young woman to hold on to it as I held the bottom portion of the artery, pulling it up to join with the top. I then, without much delicacy, stitched it together. I was quite surprised at the strength of the tissue. My handiwork took quite a while and the sweat just poured off me. Thankfully, the Māori man's wife occasionally wiped my forehead during the procedure. It seemed like ages, but finally, that was done, and I asked the girl to release the clamp slowly as I watched for further bleeding, but it seemed to hold up. 'Yay!' I yelled. 'Shane, we need our torches, it's getting dark in here.' He took them out of the packs and with some tape, he attached it to my head. He held the other and gave the third one to the elder Māori woman. Their eyes were wide with fright. 'They're all right,' I said. 'They won't hurt you.' 'It's light without fire,' she said. 'God's light,' added the young woman. I didn't have time to explain. I started to sew up his inner thigh, and once completed we turned, him over very slowly, so I could check the musket wound in his back.' The ball was through the meaty part of the shoulder and neck. It had missed the artery but was still under the surface of his skin. I took my knife, cut along the bulge and out popped the ball. Washing the wound out I thought it was clean enough, but I got a second opinion from Shane. 'Looks good,' he said. Then I stitched up the hole. I turned him onto his back, keeping his legs raised so as not to put too much pressure on the leg artery while I checked the entrance wound of the ball. It was dirtier here, with cloth stuck in the wound. I widened it slightly and cleaned it out until the blood was a deep red. I then stretched the skin and stitched it together. I used a soft clotting pad on his neck, then strapped his arm to his chest. With bandages on his leg and upper body, he was starting to look like a mummy. I looked at Shane. 'I think we have done it.' The sweat was still pouring off me and once I stopped, my hands started to shake. 'I need a coffee,' I said to no one in particular. The young girl went to get one for me. I turned to the wife and said, 'He will need to be laid in a comfortable bed and make sure you keep his leg raised for the next twenty-four hours. No walking for at least three days, and even then only for short times on his feet. This could take a few months to heal properly.' I was not sure, but my advice sounded okay to me. The women were looking at both Shane and me with open mouths. Well, to them we must have looked like magicians. Here we were in white masks and surgical gloves. I had jabbed needles into their tribesman and had been inside his leg stitching. Then there were the lights that needed no fire. How's that for not interfering in the past? The elder woman said, 'I have never seen anything like this; it's magic.' 'No, not magic,' I said 'Just my very limited knowledge of medicine. This is what we do in our place, but with qualified doctors.' Shane spoke up. 'Will he be okay?' 'I'm not sure, mate. I'll give him a penicillin jab, and a few more painkillers which he can take when he wakes up. He needs complete rest.' I turned to his wife. 'What's his name?' 'Watene,' was the reply. Shane just looked at her. 'Do you have a last name?' 'Yes,' she said, 'Te Nana.' I felt the hairs on my arms stand up and I started to cough uncontrollably. 'What is yours?' I choked out. 'Aroha,' she replied. That wasn't the name I had heard in Shane's family story, but that is his family name. This bloke is most likely a relation of his or even his third-great-grandfather. Shane then asked, 'Do you sing, Aroha?' She smiled. 'Oh yes, I love singing in the chapel. They say I have the voice of a Tui; some of our people even call me that.' We just stood there like big dummies staring at her. Shane was looking in her eyes for a spark of recognition. He then looked at Watene on the table. I cannot imagine what was going on in his mind. Aroha broke the silence, saying, 'You remind me of my father. He was not as big. I have never seen such a big man as you; but the way you walk, your eyes, the way you hold yourself, I feel family with you.' Shane looked at her and you could see he felt like weeping. 'I feel the same,' he smiled. 'From now on we are whanau.' I looked at Watene. 'Shane,' I said. 'He has lost a lot of blood. I think he needs a top up; he's looking a bit pale. I think you are a descendant of this bloke, so will you give him a transfusion? I hope it will be compatible. It's a longshot, but I think we have to risk it.' Good old Shane never hesitated. 'Good-oh, Brill, we'll need another table to get me level.' I turned to the elder woman. 'Do you have another table like this?' 'Yes I'll get it for you,' she replied. ' While you are about it, can you sort out a bed for Watene in his hut? He needs to be as comfortable as possible, and I want his leg raised up a tad.'

Aroha left with the girl. A table arrived and we set it up next to Watene's. I took the intravenous needles from the pack and swabbed the areas on both Watene and Shane's arms. I then inserted them, taped them and watched the blood flow. 'I think I'll give it about ten minutes mate.' Fingers crossed, I hope this is correct. I could see wide eyes poking around the doors, looking at the lines of blood flowing between the men. The elder woman ordered, 'Leave these men to get on with their work. We need food for tonight, and all the English will need to be fed.' One old girl grinned, 'Shame they are not for the hangi.' I smiled at her, but I think she meant it. I turned to the elder woman. ' I don't know your name.' ' You can call me Rita.' 'Nice name,' I said. 'Have you a last name?' 'Yes, Maniapoto after our tribe.' I looked at her. 'Are you related to Rewi?' 'He's my brother.' 'Bugger me, not *the* Rewi?' I stammered. 'I don't know what you mean,' she replied. 'There is only one, he is a paramount chief.' 'He is a great general and will be remembered forever in the history of our country.' I spoke without thinking. Then I thought, shut up you dumb bastard. 'What do you mean by that?' she asked. 'Oh,' I said, 'He is a very famous chief even amongst the Pakeha.'

The ten minutes were up and I took the needles out of Shane and Watene's arms, hoping that the break in conversation would get me out of hot water with Rita. I turned to the young woman. 'Shane will need something like a big cup of sweet tea. Do you have sugar?' 'Yes,' she said. 'I also have some sweet potato and Māori bread, will that do as well?' 'Thanks, could you do that for him please.' She was off like a rabbit down a burrow. 'Just take it easy, mate.' I said. 'We will get Watene fixed up in his whare and I will need to go and check out those pommie soldiers that were shot. You okay here for a while?' 'Yep, fine mate, you do that, I have a young woman running around after me.' Shane smiled from his table. 'Yeah,' I laughed, 'she has you in her sights.' 'Nah mate, she's too young,' he replied. 'Not this day and age kiddo, she didn't look too young to me without her shirt on. She is at a child-bearing and marriageable age and her sights are set on you.' 'Bullshit mate,' he grinned. 'Relax mate,' I replied. 'Catch you later.'

As I came out of the whare, I counted ten women surrounding the soldiers, who were all nicely tied up and not going anywhere. A group of children we're talking and playing around the Scottish soldier, while he continued cleaning up after their meal. They sure are resilient kids. I called Sam over. 'I need to check those two soldiers that were wounded, can you give me a hand to take them over to that tree stump.' 'Yeah, okay mate.' Sam had cleaned himself up. Now with a brown face, red beard, and his enormous size, he was intimidating to those who didn't know him. He stepped over the prone bodies and helped the two blokes get up. He supported them over to where I was setting up my gear. 'Thanks, Sam. While I'm doing this, we need to separate the NCO's from the pack. Find a place in the open. They don't deserve it, but put up a shelter for them if you have time. Make sure you tie them together. I don't want them running off and get a couple of the nastiest women you can find to guard them. Maybe one of the family members those poor buggers that were killed. That should keep them quiet. Ask Bill to give you a hand.' I watched as Sam went back amongst the prisoners and picked up both NCO's, one under each arm, making it look easy. You could see the redcoats were impressed with his strength. The sergeant and corporal were yelling all sorts of curses, but old Sam just ignored them. He took them to an ancient manuka tree and chucked them down. Bill tied them to the tree, warning them any more noise and they would get a whack on the head. That shut them up. We heard rustling from the bush and Sam went to investigate.

I turned back to the wounded soldiers. Shit, they were shorter than me and not as bulked up either. They had bushy beards, white faces, and skinny frames. They seemed okay, and not in too much pain. 'I need to check your wounds fellas. So I'll need those coats and shirts off. I'll untie your hands, but any funny business and I will beat the shit out of you and tie you up again, okay?' They looked at me and then looked over in the direction of where Sam vanished. 'Okay means alright,' I added. 'Oh, we won't give you any trouble.' they answered. A Māori boy had come over to watch what I was doing so I asked him, 'Can you speak English?' 'Yes,' he replied. 'Good, do you want to help?' He nodded. 'Okay, go and get me a big pot of really hot water.' As he was turning, I said 'What's your name?' 'Henare,' came the answer. 'You just helped my papa.' Now that is interesting, I thought, he must be Shane's second-great-grandfather, as a boy. My head was in a spin; all these relations kept turning up. Bugger it, I thought. Get this job done first, then worry about the relations later. The soldiers had stripped off their jackets and shirts. Rita came over. 'Would you like me to help you clean their wounds?' I was a bit surprised. 'After what they did to your village?' 'I'm a Christian,' she answered. 'You help where you can.' The army boys looked sufficiently embarrassed. I took out a pair of surgical gloves as Henare came back with the water. I inspected the men's wounds. 'You boys are lucky: the wounds are through the top of the meaty part of your arm. You will be sore for a while, but okay.' I passed a pair of gloves to Rita. She looked at me. 'These will keep germs out of their wounds when you are cleaning them,' I told her. 'What are germs? Funny word,' she remarked. 'Oh, they cause infection and are everywhere. That's why you need to wash your hands with plenty of soap. Cleanliness is a protection from germs and these gloves are better still.' 'You people are porangi,' she said, but obliged me. We cleaned the wounds and I gave them a penicillin jab. That took them by surprise. 'Why are you poking needles into us?' they asked. 'This will help the wound from becoming infected,' I replied. I gave them a couple of painkillers, which they took easily enough, and then I bandaged them up. 'When you get back to your camp, if you get back, this will need to be changed. Make sure you, or whoever looks after you, has clean washed hands and uses clean cloth bandages on the wounds.' 'We have never met a surgeon like you,' they mumbled. 'They are usually covered in blood with rusty instruments.' 'Not this bloke,' I answered. We gave them water and I said, 'I won't tie your hands, but I will your feet. Keep a short distance from the others. Any funny moves and those ladies will kill you.' 'Thank you sir,' they said. 'We won't make trouble.' That done, I sat down for a minute. What the hell's next, I thought; what will tomorrow bring? I anticipated the warriors would be here in numbers. I just didn't want to think about it.

CHAPTER TEN

During the time it had taken to work on the two English soldiers, the others had moved Watene into his hut. I popped in to see him. He was out like a light, but he looked peaceful and his breathing was normal. I said to his wife, 'Keep an eye on his temperature, do you understand?' 'Of course,' she said, 'we are not savages.' I grinned. 'You're surely not. Make sure you have his leg elevated tonight, and I'll pop in order to see him through the evening.' 'I'll be with him all night with my tamariki. You do not have to worry. We have been fighting for generations; he will be well looked after, and thank you for your help,' she answered. I left the hut to see the women cleaning the bodies of the two old blokes that had been shot. They were singing quietly as they prepared the bodies for burial. I gathered they would be taken to the main pa at Meremere.

I caught up with Sam, who told me he saw two young boys dash off into the bush heading east. Shit, I thought that meant we are going to have some angry, bloody warriors here in the morning with utu on their minds. 'We should be okay,' I said to Sam. 'We have helped these people, but I'm going to have to negotiate with them for the redcoats.

We cannot let them be killed; it's up to their own people to decide what to do with them. That young fella who has been helping with the kids; what's his story?' 'I don't know, Brill,' Sam replied. 'He has hit it off with the kids, a good bloke by the looks of it; Scottish and a redhead like me, so he must be okay,' he grinned. 'Well,' I replied, 'we need him out of uniform and into something rough. We will keep him out of the way of the warriors, and away from his mates. I'll get Shane to have a yarn with him when he gets up.' 'That young sheila still running around after him?' Sam asked with a smirk. 'Good looking kid, she could run around me and I don't think I'd complain.' 'Yeah, she is,' I grinned, 'Taking a real fancy to him.' There might be trouble down the line, I speculated; I hope not, for everyone's sake. I just wished it was me though; there was something about her that touched my heart. 'Oh, by the way,' Sam said, 'There's a pig hanging around, I'll clear him out, so if I'm not here, then that's what I'm doing. There is a rubbish pit out back and it's into the muck.'

I looked up to see Shane coming out of the hut, with the Māori girl walking beside him quite animated. He wandered over to us. 'How are you feeling mate?' I asked. 'Good Brill,' he said. 'That kumara and bread with the sweet tea did the job. A good meal tonight and I will be back to normal.' 'Grunt,' I said. 'Will you have a yarn with that Scots bloke and find out his story? We need to keep him out of harm's way, so ditch his uniform and find some clothes for him. You okay with that?' 'Yeah, easy as mate. You don't have to mollycoddle me, fellas,' he said,

'I'm fine. I only gave a small amount of blood. I'll have a yarn with the wee Scottish bloke now.' He left with the Māori girl trailing behind him. As she passed me, I asked her, 'What's your name?' She stopped. 'Wahine.' 'Yeah. I know you are a woman, but that's not your name is it?' 'That's what I'm called,' she said, and took off after Shane. I thought that was strange; however, many children had unusual names, maybe the family just ran out of one, who knows. I went back over to the wounded soldiers. 'How are you blokes holding up?' They just looked at me. I rephrased the question. 'Are you alright, no pain?' 'We are fine,' one answered. 'Are you up to talking?' I asked. They were sitting away from the rest of the men, with a couple of scowling women with rifles guarding them. 'Will they shoot us?' one inquired with a worried look. 'Only if you move or do anything stupid,' I replied. They looked at Bill. 'What about the Māori with the stone weapon?' 'He'll only hit you if you piss him off,' I said. 'So what was this debacle all about?' Rita came over. 'I would like that question answered as well.' The skinny one started to talk. 'The sergeant said that this was a rebel hideout. We were to get in here and clean them out.' Rita interrupted. 'We are not at war with you, why would he think that?' 'We are sorry, missus,' he said. 'We were only following orders. If we didn't, the sergeant would have hit us with the barrel of his rifle, he's a bully. Afterwards he would have put the blame on the Māori for hurting us. We were forced to come, we had no choice.' He stopped for a minute subsequently went on. 'When we came out of the bush into the clearing, the sergeant fired his gun at one of the Māori in the field. Then the Māori near the small hut shot me, after that my friend.' I wondered if this is where Grunt got his shooting expertise from. He continued, 'Before he could get a third shot off, the sergeant ran up and shot him twice. The corporal shot the other old man in the field, and the rest of the boys charged the huts. They didn't expect the women to fight back. I have never seen a woman fight; they were just like men, even the young boys. Then I saw a church-type building out the back. I thought we were supposed to fight savages, not people who are of the Christian faith like us. My father will be disappointed with me.' The troops fired at the women. 'Hold on,' I said. 'I didn't find any women with musket wounds.' 'No, we are not good shots,' He gave a weak grin. 'Most of the lads have been here in New Zealand less than two weeks. First time I have held a gun; I know nothing about the army; we arrived from Sydney Town, straight off the boat. We were recruited over there with the promise of land.' I could feel the hackles of Rita go up a notch. 'A few days of marching, fire the gun twice, and we found ourselves here on the border. We were supposed to just stay on our side of the river, but the sergeant bribed the ferryman who brought us across at night; so even the officers have no idea where we are. They will be worried about what has happened to us, and might send out someone to find us.' 'Not on this side of the river,' I stated. 'You are in a right old pickle. So where are you from?' 'London. The land offered was too good to turn down; we have never owned land in our lives.' Rita was pissed, she couldn't hold herself back. 'Our land,' she yelled. 'There will be blood spilled, I can tell you that,' she spat. They shrunk down; she was very frightening with the whites of her eye's showing. 'We will see,' she growled. I turned back to the soldier. 'Go on,' I encouraged. 'When I saw the men start hitting the children with their rifles, I was angry. I'm married with two children, and I found it a bit much, seeing them harmed like that. Then that Scottish lad rushed in; I heard him yell that he would shove his bayonet up someone's arse if they touched those children, oops, sorry missus for the bad language.' Rita just waved her hand. 'We saw him gather the children up and take them to the hut over there, whilst he kept a watch from the door. I had never met him until the other day. He comes from down south somewhere I think. Arriving from London to Auckland was like walking back in time, it's so primitive.' I had to laugh. 'Yeah, I would agree with that,' I grinned. 'I'll try to get you back across the border, but no guarantees. The Māori are very good with revenge, that's 'utu,' they will want someone's balls for this attack. Two old men were killed, and the kainga was violated.' I turned to Rita. 'Can we talk?' I left the soldiers, and she followed me out of hearing range of the prisoners. 'I want to get all these men over the river and take them to Drury,' I whispered. 'You know, and I know that's General Cameron's headquarters. I'll make sure that their leaders over there,' I pointed to the sergeant and corporal, 'will be punished.' I was thinking on my feet, and I did not know how she would react: these were her people who were killed. 'Would your leaders accept that?' She looked at me. 'Someone has to pay,' she hissed. 'This is a violation of the treaty. But I can also see that if we extract utu at this moment, it brings the hostilities earlier, and we are not quite ready, you understand?' 'Yeah, I do,' I said. 'Maybe more than you think.' 'You are a good man, so are the other two with you, and that pale young fellow. He looked after our children, and I would not like to see him suffer for the stupidity of his sergeant.' 'Nor would we,' I smiled. 'He's a brave lad, going against his own troops,' I added. 'That Māori warrior with you is Ngapuhi,' she said. 'How do you know that?' I asked. 'Oh, I know. He will be welcome to stay, but most likely won't, as there is a feeling of distrust between our tribes.' She went on. 'You and your friends are wanderers; that large man Shane, he is part Tainui and Pakeha. That other big man you call Sam, red hair, brown face; he is a man of the bush. He is at home here. You are the thinker; you will be tied to Tainui and Ngapuhi when you get home.' I just looked at her. 'Can you see the future?' I asked. 'No. I'm a woman, who can see the future?' she beamed with a glint in her eye. I didn't know whether to believe her or not, but it dawned on me, she said 'When' I get home. Oh hell, I hope she's right.

'You are amazing,' I remarked. 'I better introduce myself, I'm Bob.' We performed a hongi. 'You do know who I am?' she asked. 'Yes,' I replied. 'I hope you have some influence with the tribe, so we can get these blokes out of here.' 'Why are you here?' she inquired. Oh bugger, I wondered when that would come up. 'We come up from the south over the fire mountain of Ruapehu, passing Taupo. We got lost and after a long time floundering all over the place, we ended up here just before this attack.' 'Hmm,' she whispered. I don't think she believed me. 'Even we don't go there, it is tapu.' 'If we had known, we would not have gone,' I replied. 'What about the Ngapuhi?' she asked. 'He was thrown out of Auckland,' I answered, 'for delivering pamphlets around, denouncing the government's land-grab of your land if your tribe doesn't heed the government decree. Instead of chucking him out into the Kaipara, they chucked him onto your side of the river.' 'Oh,' she said. 'I heard about those letters; it was him?' 'Yeah, it was Wiremu.' 'A point in his favour,' she admitted. 'Look, Rita,' I said with a bit of desperation. 'If I promised you to make sure that those two NCO's are at the front of any attack on your pa, would that go down okay?' She stared at me. 'You speak so differently to the other English I know,' she replied. 'What I meant,' I corrected, 'Would this be favourable to you and your tribe?' I was hoping that she was influential; she was after all the sister of the chief, Rewi. 'I will have to think about it,' she replied. I went on. 'You have a large pa at Rangiriri if that is attacked, they will be in the front of the attack. Would this be utu enough for your tribe? Or maybe even guard duty in Camerontown, which I know Rewi will attack?' 'What makes you say that?' she demanded. 'No, I'm saying if they do. They will be in the lead or on guard duty,' I insisted. 'I promise.' How the hell I was going to sort this out, it was bloody near impossible, but I needed to save the rest of the poor buggers, who had to follow a bastard of an NCO blindly. 'I will think about this also,' she muttered, then added, 'I sent two boys back to the pa at Meremere. The hapu will be here tomorrow, so all you have said will be taken into account.' 'That's fine, thank you, Rita,' I answered. Well, I've done as much as I could do. 'I saw what you have done for Watene,' she stated. 'A good warrior. He did his best, his mana is admirable. He was outnumbered, but he stood his ground and tried to protect this kainga, as did his sons. Big boys for their age; they reminded me of your friend Shane.' Bloody woman's perception again, I thought. 'Does he know he is of their family?' she added. I thought for a minute. 'Yes, he does; they don't. It has to stay that way. We are from a different place; it would be too confusing.' 'Hmm,' she hummed thoughtfully. 'Wahine is becoming a true friend to him.' 'Yes,' I remarked, 'About that, why the name Wahine funny name for a woman?' 'Not really,' she answered. 'She is a slave.' 'What?!' I spluttered. 'A slave?' 'Yes, why not. She is a slave to Watene and Aroha and our iwi. Watene's father, years ago, was with a raiding party on a pa in the Hokianga. They took many woman slaves. Her mother was one, pregnant at the time, so the daughter was a slave too. She was treated like all our children, went to the missionary school, learned to read English and do arithmetic. She can be released from this condition on the say so of the iwi, or a chief that sees that she did extraordinary feats. I think she did that today, don't you think?' I was blown away. Shane's family having slaves, bugger me, that wasn't passed down in the stories of his family. She went on. 'She fought off the sergeant and protected her mistress; do you think that this qualifies?' 'I reckon,' I grinned. 'Funny word, but I think I know what you mean,' she replied. 'The chief can release her or give her away to a young man. I will have to think about that also.' 'How can you have slaves now you are a Christian?' 'I do not see it as a problem,' she answered. 'In biblical times people had slaves; nothing has changed, has it?' 'Okay,' I mumbled. Shit, this was getting above my pay grade. 'Yes, I will think on all the things we have spoken about tonight,' she said. She started to turn away but then stopped, adding, 'Don't you think that they would make strong children?' She looked in Shane's direction as he came out of the hut with Wahine in tow. I had to smile. 'I don't think he's at the right time in his life,' I joked. 'Oh, that is where you are wrong, it is the very right time for them both,' Rita answered before walking off.

Oh hell, I thought. This is not getting us home. My head was whirling, I just didn't want to think about it. I walked over to Shane, who was sitting on the ground being fed by Wahine. She was putting bits of pork onto his plate. He didn't even notice, bloody hell, Darby and Joan. This was getting to me. Only yesterday we were in a chopper shooting pig, now we are in 1863 shooting people. I just hope I could sort out something to get us all home in one piece. Small steps, my mind was screaming, small steps. 'Shane mate,' I started. 'It looks like a hapu will be here in the morning. We need to get all those men into the hut and out of sight tonight. They need to be told the truth; to be quiet, not a peek out of them, or they might be tomorrow night's hangi.' 'Yeah, good as gold mate. I will sort it out now,' he said. 'You still feeling okay?' I inquired. 'Much better, thanks. I don't feel dizzy now, the rest and food have been the right medicine,' he answered.

We both ambled across to the prisoners, and I ordered, 'fellas, listen up.' They looked at us the best way they could. 'We are going to cut your leg ropes, and once this is done, you will quietly walk to that hut over there,' I pointed to the huts by the kumara fields. 'You will be fed and watered, then you will be retied. The wounded men will only be tied at the feet. Any noise at all and you will have this Māori bloke ' I indicated Bill, 'give you a whack, alright?' There were nods of affirmation. Shane pulled out his Bowie Knife. 'If I hear a bloody word out of anyone, I will cut off the left nut of each man, and the man on his right will be forced to eat it. Do we make ourselves completely clear?' That got their attention. 'Yes sir!' they shouted together. 'The warriors from Meremere will be here in the morning. I want you as quiet as mice. We have to convince them not to kill and eat you. So once again it's in your hands.' 'Yes sir,' came the reply. Shane went to each one and slowly cut the ropes. Letting them look at the knife, there was a look of horror on their faces. The sergeant yelled out, 'What about us?' Sam hppened to be walking past them with a pig on his back. I had wondered where he had got to, I had forgotten he had told me about the pig; he had been gone a wee while. I hadn't heard a rifle shot, Sam must have stuck the pig. I have seen him do it in the past, just go out with a knife, you have to have nerves of steel to do that. He passed the sergeant and shouted at him. 'You, you prick. If anyone deserves to be roasted with this pig, it is you two, so shut the hell up.' Shit, he looked angry. This thing about being eaten was all bullshit, but those boys did not know that, and it was good to keep them on their toes.

So we marched them over to the hut and got them to settle in. Rita looked in to see how things were going. 'Can we feed them?' I asked. 'Yes,' she replied. 'The women have the food prepared, and we must thank Sam for replacing the kai we've used. That pig had been making a nuisance of itself for a while around the scrap pit, so we are pleased, he killed it. He is a good provider.' 'Don't you go marrying Sam off as well,' I remarked. She just grinned. 'Would that be so bad?' I hoped she was just pulling my tit.

We went into the hut and all the men were sitting with their legs tied, but their hands were loose so they could eat. 'Right, you bastards,' I boomed as I walked around the hut. 'I want to go over a few points with you. My name is Captain Kidder.' I heard Sam cough as he tried to smother his laugh. 'You are the biggest pack of shits I have ever come across. What was done here today is inexcusable? You will be taken back to Drury for punishment. That's if the locals let you go. So we need you all to be quiet and to behave if you want to live to see your families again. This red-headed gentleman next to me is Lieutenant Mack. If anyone of you try to escape, well, this man can track a snail for fifty kilometres.' Oops! Wrong word, I thought, I corrected myself, 'Miles; you will not get far.' Then the big bloke came in. Shane seemed to fill the room, and together Sam and Shane blocked the light of the door. 'This is Lieutenant Lang.' I did not want to use our real names so shortening them would disguise who we were I hoped. 'He's a mean bugger: big, strong, and loves nothing better than punching some witless private to a pulp. So it does not pay to get offside with these two officers. 'This man here,' I pointed to Bill, 'Is Staff Sergeant Hohepa.' Good old Bill had the biggest smile ever. 'He is our ticket out of here; he's our guide and interpreter.' We had to give them all something to think about, and hope is a excellent thing. I went on, 'there will be guards on you all night and also on the shit heads of NCO's out there tied to the manuka tree. Okay, so settle down. I want quietness, not a peep out of you. I need an answer!' I demanded. 'Yes sir!' they yelled their reply. 'Good, we will be in and out throughout the night.' We turned and went out. 'Bill,' I asked, 'could you do a watch for the moment. I'll get a roster sorted out so we can all have equal time keeping an eye on these men. I'll jack up some food for you also.' 'Who's Jack?' he inquired. 'Sorry, I'll arrange food for you,' I amended. 'Yes, that will be, okay,' he grinned. I laughed with the boys. 'You are catching on with how we say things, Billy.' Shane smirked. Rita caught up with us. 'The women will take the food to the men now,' she informed us. 'I would like them to stand guard throughout the night, especially with the sergeant and corporal.' I was pleased with that. 'That's excellent,' I remarked. 'If you can arrange for them to be looked after, I'll organise the guard on the hut. How is the young Scottish fella getting on?' 'Oh,' she grinned. 'You wouldn't recognise him. I'll send him over to you when you have your kai.'

We sat down with our backs to a hut. 'Right,' I started. 'What say we do two hours on, two hours off?' 'That's fine by us,' they replied. A couple of women came over and sat down facing us. 'We will guard the Pakeha redcoats.' 'Fine, that's good of you. Would you like to do the three am to five am?' 'We will be there,' they answered, 'when the old ruru starts to hoot.' 'The owl?' I asked. 'Yes, every morning at that time, he hoots; and wakes us, so we will be there.' 'Fine, thank you,' I grinned. They got up and walked away. I turned to my friends. 'Toss to see who gets the first duty.' Sam ended first up. 'I think we should start at about nine pm; we'll leave Bill there with a couple of other women till then.' I got the eleven to one, Shane the one to three, with the two Māori women already in the three to five slot. 'Then Bill again from five am, he can wake us all up. We also need to check the NCOs, and I will pop in to check Watene and the wounded soldiers.' 'Good-oh,' said Sam. 'We have a plan.' Sam and I went over to check the NCO's. They looked like tied-up chooks and pretty uncomfortable to boot. The women guards still looking as mean as hell. Shane went over, picked the NCO's up and propped them against the tree. They looked at him with wild eyes. 'Do you know who we are?' I insisted. 'Yes, we heard you talking,' the sergeant replied. 'You are Captain Kidder, and the big officer is Lieutenant Lang.' I squatted in front of them. 'Why?' 'Why did you do this stupid and illegal attack? You have not only put yourselves at risk but all your men as well. You are a bloody disgrace, both of you. Why?' 'What's your name?' I demanded. 'Router,' was the sergeant's reply. 'And you, corporal?' 'Smith, sir.' 'Well, Sergeant, Corporal; you are both in big trouble. These people will demand utu, that's revenge. We are going to try to talk them out of it. You had better pray that we win the argument. How did you think you would get away with it, Router?' 'I thought this village was only small. Give the black bastards a lesson. I didn't think that the women would fight back.' 'You didn't do your homework then, they are not easy beats. They all fight: men, women and at times, children. The way I feel at the moment, I should just hand you over to them. You are a bloody waste of time.' 'You won't, will you sir?' the Corporal piped in. 'They will eat us, I have heard all the stories.' I turned to the women. 'Would you want to eat these two?' 'Not fat enough,' the old woman replied. 'Shrink his head maybe.' They all laughed. I grinned and Shane said, 'Tawara kino, bad taste.' 'Pakeha kawa,' the women giggled, 'Sour white man.' I watch the two men; the poor buggers looked beaten and scared. It was not going to be a nice night for them. I asked the old woman, 'Has the guard duty been arranged?' 'Yes,' she replied. 'We will be here all night until the hapu arrives. These men are not going anywhere. Not even to relieve themselves.' She looked at us and said with a smile, 'We want to thank you for your help,' then turned back to the NCO's with a familiar scowl on her face. We left them in capable hands.

We headed back to the hut and sat down. 'Okay,' I asked, 'What about that young Scots bloke, what's his story?' 'I had a yarn with him,' Shane replied, as he looked a bit uncomfortable.'What!' I exclaimed. Shane looked at Sam. 'Okay,' he continued. 'He came up from Dunedin on a cutter to buy grain for his dad's General Store. Something to do with the gold rush in central. He had no sooner got off the boat than he was swooped on by the army. They told him Auckland was a garrison town, and every able-bodied man had to be ready to fight; they stood over him while he signed up. He's only 19, what a pack of shits. He was saying he managed to get a letter off to his father. He has only been in the army a couple of days. What the hell are they thinking of he is as raw as hell and should not even be with this mob?" 'Yeah,' I stated, 'But you have to remember what he said, Auckland is a garrison town, so all able-bodied men from sixteen to fifty-five are roped into the conflict.' 'What's his name?' I asked. Shane just looked at us then. 'What's wrong mate?' Sam inquired. 'Oh shit Sam,' Grunt replied. 'His name is Stewart McInnes.' 'So what, same name as me, lots of Scots in Dunedin,' Sam replied. 'Yeah, that's right,' Grunt stated. 'But his younger brother name is Angus, isn't he on your family tree you mentioned it to me ages ago? Sam looked at me then Shane. He groaned. 'Bullshit, oh no, not again.' I asked, 'Did your family have a store?' 'Yeah,' Sam replied. 'Princess Street in Dunedin. Oh shit, shit, what does that make him to me, Brill?' 'Um, he would be your second-great-grandfather's brother that makes him your second great uncle.' 'For the love of god,' moaned Sam. 'In one day each of us have met long dead relations, what are the odds of that happening?' 'Well,' I reasoned, 'New Zealand had a small population at this time, so it's only natural that we might run into a few. However, this is bloody weird eh.' 'I cannot get my head around any of it,' Shane remarked. 'I wish there was a way to head home.' 'Me too, Grunt,' I admitted. 'We need to pace ourselves fellas, one day at a time. We will get home, I'm sure of it.' I wasn't confident though. I was as uncertain as my mates, but I just could not allow them to see it. 'Quite honestly, Brill,' Shane stuttered, 'I'm really confused. Okay on the outside but terrified inside. How are we going to cope? We haven't come across any run-of-the-mill people, and we talk and act differently. I'm getting a bit paranoid.' 'It's only natural, mate,' I comforted, 'But as long as we stick together. Look, we just keep saying we are not from here, and this is how we speak where we come from. There are a lot of different accents at this time in New Zealand. You have heard how the Pommies here have spoken; we are just another voice in hundreds that are around. We can bluff our way through. If in doubt, leave it to me. I can talk shit till the cows come home.' They both grinned. 'Well, you have a point there,' affirmed Sam. 'I feel a bit better talking about it, getting it out. I'm pleased you have taken the lead; I don't think I could do that. What's your opinion Grunt?' 'Yep, I'm with you on this, Sam. Brill can make the decisions on the important stuff, and we will advise on tactical stuff, just as we have been doing. All we have done today is go from one stressful situation to another.' 'I'm pleased that the day is coming to an end. It's hard to believe we were pig shooting yesterday,' Sam added. 'Right, a feed and a hot drink, and then we can relax for a while,' I said. So off we went looking for Rita and the food. Three bewildered men out of their depth, maybe, but with a determination to go home.

CHAPTER ELEVEN

The women did not have the time to put down a hangi, so the meat had been cooked over the open fire. The meal was well in hand as we walked over to check out what's for dinner. Wahine, seeing Shane, gave him a radiant smile then quickly filled a flax plate with food for him. Her hand held his plate a little longer than normal to get his attention, and he looked puzzled, then seemed to notice her for the first time. I was envious. She turned and passed us all full plates as well. 'Thank you Wahine,' we said. She smiled in return, but her eyes slipped back to Shane. I looked at Sam; he grinned and rolled his eyes. Poor old Grunt was being chased, and I think he was only just starting to notice. Oh, I hope this doesn't get serious, it would put the cat amongst the pigeons for sure.

We took our food and sat down with our backs to the wall. Stu came over and sat quietly, not saying too much, he looked a bit out of sorts. We introduced ourselves. He had been over with the army blokes but was trying to distance himself from their stupidity. Wiremu wandered by to pick up his meal and also came to sit with us, saying 'Two ladies are looking after the soldiers while I have my dinner.' We tried to be inconspicuous, but now there are five of us and even more noticeable. How the hell did that happen? We needed to downsize to be more low key. I think a bit more thought will have to go into it. In the future, that thought would come back to bite me on the bum. We sat and ate our meal, thinking about the day. Then Wahine came over with more food for Grunt, she sat down in front of him and started to refill his plate. Bugger me, he was in a trance now, watching her every move. In twenty-four hours, he went from being a gorilla to a teddy bear. What the hell we were going to do about it, I didn't have a clue. Cups of tea were passed around, and we sat and listened to the bird sounds slowly quietening down as the village slipped into darkness. The moreporks started their first calls of the evening. 'We have worked out the roster to guard these soldier boys,' I said to Bill. 'Will you do now until nine pm, then come on again at five till six am, wake us at six, so we will be ready when the hapu arrives?' 'Yes, that will be fine. I can do that,' he replied. I continued, 'Sam is nine to eleven, Shane has the eleven till one, I'm one to three am, the women will make up the three to five am. Then back to you, Bill again. Rita came over, and I gave her the women's roster. 'They will be happy with that and don't worry about the women, they will be there. They'll take care of the NCO's as well,' she said. So that's the sergeant and corporal all sorted; it's nice not to have to think of them tonight. I thanked her for their help. She's a nice woman for a Tainui,' Bill confided, as she walked away. I would not like to make her angry, there are hidden depths with that woman, I wouldn't be surprised if she is the Tohonga.' I turned to Stu. 'Mate, you need to get your head down.' I didn't want him to be around and pick up anything unusual in our conversation. The Māori women had changed him from a soldier to a civilian. Black woollen longs, with a Māori skirt around his waist to his knees. Dark-blue shirt and jacket and a woollen navy hat pulled down over his ears. They also rubbed some wild blackberry stain onto his skin, taking away the whiteness of his face and arms. He wasn't the same bloke. .'Tomorrow, I want you out of the way, 'I insisted.' There will be some warriors, at least a hapu coming in here first thing. That's about twenty-five men. So you stay out of sight and out of mind. If we get away from here, we will try to get you back to Auckland, then onto a ship home to Dunedin. It's not a promise, but we will do our best. I will also try to get an army discharge for you. How, at the moment, I don't know; I'll need to think more on that.' He turned to us. 'Thank you for all you have done. I don't know where I would have been without you. If I get out of here, and you ever come to Dunedin, my place is your place as long as you want. We Scots are loyal. I'll take my leave and see you in the morning.'

Wahine had gone back to the cooking fire to clean up. Shane was looking at her move around the fire, with a thoughtful grin on his face. After a while, I asked, 'How is everyone coping at the moment?' The floodgates opened once again as my mates start talking both together. The gist of it was the same for all of us. How the hell did this happen, will we get home? We were all worried about our families; would we ever see them again? 'Fellas, I have a gem of an idea, but a lot of it relies on Bill here to help.' I looked at Bill. 'You're a printer, right?' 'Yes,' he replied. 'Qualified, and work for Mr. E Wattle in Queen Street, Auckland.' 'Good,' I said. 'Who does the government printing in Auckland?' 'That's us,' he grinned, my eyes shot up to look him in the face. It was a bit hard to see, as it was getting dark now, but my mind was ticking over until he asked. 'Why?' 'Who does the governor's printing?' I asked. 'Oh,' Bill replied. 'We do that as well. You see, if the governor wants to make a proclamation or some official document, he writes out what he wants to be printed. He sends his secretary down to see us, and we print it for him. I usually take it up to Government House when it is finished. We have all the necessary papers in the office. Mr. Wattle has them in his desk; they are already signed, just in case something is needed to be printed in a hurry, even if the governor isn't there.' I sat there looking at him, taking that all in and said, 'Shit, this is the best news I have heard all day mate,' slapping him on his shoulder. 'What are you talking about, Brill,' Sam whispered. 'How is that going to help us?' 'Well,' I continued, 'I have been thinking along the lines of getting documentation to legitimise us, and I think I can do it now with Bill's help.' 'How do you mean?' asked Grunt. 'This is the gist of my thoughts at the moment,' I said. 'If you think, I have gone off half-cocked, let me know. Even so, it might work, as long as the governor is not around. Now if I remember rightly, at this time he was tearing around the country doing his thing with the settlers, meeting up with Māori chiefs from tribes all around New Zealand, and trying to get the Kingites to buckle under. So we might be in luck that he is not in Auckland.' As I was explaining to them my ideas, the boys remained quiet, they knew me well enough to know not to interrupt my thought pattern. 'Okay,' I stated. 'This is how I think we can do it. We get ourselves to Auckland after dropping off these army blokes in Drury or whatever. With the help of Bill, we'll write out an order from the governor to Captain Kidder, who is on a secret mission with you two blokes. The letter will state that we will have the authority to use whatever means to achieve our goals which only we know about. Everyone who comes into contact, especially officers, will be shown this order to shut them up if they get a bit antsy. It will have our rank, names and be signed by the governor. That official paper we need is in the desk where Bill was working, and that's where we need to go.' Before the boys jumped in with questions, I carried on. We will create another document, which we can show to the paymaster in either Fort Britomart or Albert Barracks. We will date it a couple of months ago, that way we can get a bit of back pay. We need money here for board and lodging in Auckland, and also clothes. If we wander about the place like we are at the moment, we will stand out like a pimple on a bum, so we'll dress like the population, and blend in. Each of us will have the same document, if we get separated, we have evidence of who we are. The big question is, can you help us, Bill?' I asked, turning to him. He looked at me, and I thought shit, I hoped so. He grinned. 'You three men are the most unusual men I have ever come across. I cannot work out your reason for all of this, but I do know in my mind you are all good men. I will certainly help. If you can write what you need for the documents, I will print them.' 'Oh, one other thing,' I said. 'I need one more document with the governor's name on it for Stu, to discharge him from all army duties with a discharge payment of 20 pounds and a free ticket to Dunedin, as his effort to supply the army will be paramount in the future.' Bill, thought for a minute. 'Four documents with an order from the governor, and four for the paymaster. Is that all?' 'What about you?' I asked. 'No,' he replied. 'I have a feeling you won't be around to be found out, but I might be. I would rather go north with a clear conscious, and I will start the print shop up there without having to look over my shoulder.' 'You are a good bloke, Watene Hohepa,' I smiled. 'So are you all, you are like my whanau.' We all laughed, it was as close to the truth as he would ever get; I mean, he was my third-great-uncle. I was still trying to get my head around that, and the boys were all feeling the same way. 'One thing,' he pointed out, 'Mr. Wattle lives on the premises; he will need to be out of the way while I do the layout and print for at least two hours. There is also another small problem: remember I was thrown out of Auckland. I don't want to be seen there if possible.' 'We will work on that, Bill,' I assured him. 'You are a little cracker mate.' 'I don't know what you mean, but it sounded okay,' he grinned. 'Don't forget you have been promoted to Staff Sergeant; if there are any problems with that, I'll send Grunt and Sam around to sort it out. I don't think there will be any trouble you're in the army now. Don't forget Bill, there are plenty of Māori in British uniform. You will blend right in, mate, a lot of them are from your iwi, as you know.

'So fellas,' I continued, 'What do you think?' 'What does a Lieutenant get?' Sam asked. 'I'm not too sure about that,' I answered, 'It might be twelve shillings a day. We should get a bit more, as we are "on a secret mission," so I'll up it to seventeen shillings or a pound a day each.' 'Well, fine, but what is a shilling?' asked Sam. 'Ah, about 10 cents, so we would be on a dollar seventy to two dollars a day.' 'You must be joking?!' 'No, that should be ample for us while we are here. We are going to get back pay for two months, that could be around sixty pounds each. Some clothes could set us back three to four pounds each; food and lodging for a few days, even a week, will come to say two pounds at the most; we will have plenty. Anything over, when we leave we can donate to someone who needs it, and a lot of people at this time were on the bones of their bums. 'Shane, who was sitting quietly, then questioned, 'Do you think it will work, Brill?' 'Yeah, I do mate,' I replied. 'The doco will get us through the lines if we have to come back this way or on a boat to New Plymouth.' A boat, I thought, not on your bloody life. 'When we get back into bush gear, if any nosy officer tries to ask questions, we just show him the document. The same with our rifles; we cannot let the buggers get their hands on them, so the order will tell them, in no uncertain terms, to piss off.' 'Well, if you're happy, I'm happy. I would have never thought this through in a million years,' Shane remarked. Sam was nodding his head in agreement.

'Bullshit, fellas,' I voiced. 'You would have worked it out sooner or later. And besides, we short blokes can multitask and be good looking at the same time,' I joked. That got a grin from the big oafs. Turning around, I added, 'Thanks Bill.' 'If you cannot help your friends …' is all, he said. He looked over to the others. 'I'll go back to guarding the English soldiers.' 'Okay mate, till about nine, then again, in the morning. Remember to wake us at six, so we have our wits about us when the boys from Meremere turn up.' Bill smiled. 'I hope I don't have to crack some Tainui heads. It would be a shame, as I'm getting quite fond of a few of the wahine guards.' He was still smiling to himself as he turned and walked away.

Once he had gone, Shane said, 'I do feel better listening to and discussing our plans. I know we have talked about it before, but I'm not at all comfortable with the way things are at the moment. I keep thinking of my family, and I'm worried that we might not get back. I'm really out of my comfort zone. Anyway, you've made me feel a bit more optimistic Brill.' 'Yeah,' Sam remarked. 'I'm with Grunt on this, I feel the same way. I'm okay to a point; it's the uncertainty of the situation that is my biggest worry. Just the other day we were all pig shooting, flying in helicopters, with all the mod cons, and now it's back to wiping your bum with a bit of grass.' You had to smile. 'Well,' I explained. 'We might be able to contact the family. I know it doesn't sound plausible, but if we all write letters to our families when we get to Auckland, and put our home addresses on them. We can deposit them into the ANZ bank vault, with "Not to be opened until March 2014," written on them. We wil leave some of our normal money in the vault, and that would pay the postage when the vault is opened. The bank can then post it on to our folks. I know it sounds dumb, but it might work. The ANZ opened for business in 1863 and is still going strong.' 'Would it cost us anything to put it in the vault mate?' Sam asked. 'I don't know, but we can find out when we are there.' 'I have 50 dollars on me,' said Sam. 'That should be tons to courier them to all our parents. That's a good plan Brill, even if we don't get home in our time they will get this letter a few weeks down the line explaining what happened. At least then they will know what happened to us. I could not bear to have them worried for the rest of their lives.' 'Thanks Brill,' Shane added, 'That's another load off my mind.' 'Look fellas, I'm the same as you blokes, I'm worried stiff. I don't know whether what I have been suggesting will work. We just need to try to do something. If nothing else, this will give us focus,' I sympathised.

We yarned until Sam spoke up. 'I think it's about time to raise our spirits.' He went to his pack and took out his harmonica. 'A bit of music is the best cure.' 'We can all sing, let's see if the crowd, here is receptive to our music.' 'Okay,' he beamed. 'I like this one.' He started to play an 80's number, by Simon and Garfunkel. 'You can call me Betty, and I'll call you Al.' So he played, and we sang and pretty soon there was a group of ladies, sitting in a half-circle in front of Sam, clapping lightly to the music. 1980's music with an 1863 backing, I thought to myself. It made me laugh, and I snapped off some photos secretly. I didn't know how they would turn out without the flash, but the flash would have scared the living hell out of everyone. Wahine came over and sat down next to Shane. Then he did what was natural for any man and woman, he put his arm around her as she leant against him. She was humming to the music. Sam went straight on to another song, then another until he announced. 'Here's one you might like. It's an oldie but a goody.' He started playing an Abba number, 'Fernando'. We jumped in singing, and by the end of the song Wahine had the chorus down nearly to pat. So Sam played it again. The second time she only stumbled over a few words, and then he laughed. 'Okay girl, you sing it all the way through, and we will help out if you get stuck.' He started it again. This time she had it completely right. My god, what a voice. Dressed in modern clothes and with all the gear, she would have been at home on any stage in New Zealand in our time. She was so good-looking and with a voice to match; as we sang I watched Shane looking at her, just mesmerised. We were all taken up with her voice and when she had finished everyone clapped. Shane was sitting there with a big grin all over his face. 'What a voice, my god she would be right at home on any stage,' he said. I laughed. 'Two minds think alike!' Rita, who was sitting with the women, came over and remarked, 'I did not realise you had such a beautiful voice, Wahine. What a talent! I do believe that your name from this day forward will be Tui, as you sing like one. Is this agreeable to you, Aroha?' Aroha came out from the whare to listen to the music with her kids. 'I agree,' she replied. 'That was so uplifting.' I thought back to the story that Mona, Shane's mother, had told me it had a bit of truth in it after all. 'Also, while everyone is here,' Aroha went on, 'I would like to relinquish our family hold on this woman. If this is agreeable with you Rita?' My ears picked up at that she must have a bit of say in the proceedings and with the rest of the iwi. Calling her by her new name, Aroha announced, 'Tui, you are free, not only have you brought mana to yourself but also to our iwi. You stood up to the English soldiers today and when I was punched to the ground, you stood over me and took on that foul-mouthed English soldier, allowing time for this man Shane to burst in and strike him to the ground. You are free now to become a member of our iwi and to marry whoever you wish. It is our right to allow this to happen, and it is now done.' Rita nodded in agreement and all the ladies applauded. At the conclusion of this pronouncement Tui turned to Shane and stated, 'If I can marry anyone I want, then I want you.' I dropped my cup of tea all over my lap. 'Shit, that's hot,' I yelped. Sam almost swallowed his harmonica. Shane just sat there. 'I can't,' he sputtered, 'I hardly know you girl.' She threw herself at him like a rugby forward. Then, kneeling in front of him and grabbing both sides of his beard, she pulled his face to hers. 'Look at me,' she said. 'Look at me. You can feel it, can't you? Look into my eyes you can see what's there, it's the same as I see in yours. Feel my body against you; you feel the same as I do. When I'm near you, I go all dizzy with happiness; we are meant for each other. The first time

I saw you when you wiped that black off your face, I knew then it was you who I had been waiting for. You feel the same about me, I know. I watched your eyes change, from hard to soft. Look at me,' she said again, 'Don't tell me this is not right, even now this energy is running through us, it's like a fire, you can feel it.' She knelt there looking into his eyes; not blinking, not doing anything, just staring at him, as though she was touching his soul. You could see Shane was the same: he did not move, but I could see he was swallowing hard. I thought, oh shit. He's not coming home with us, she's got him. It was the only thing that would have stopped Shane going home: a woman. I knew it. I could feel the electricity in the air between them and I just about cried. Not for him, but for me and Sam. I don't know if Sam felt it, but he was sitting watching the proceedings not breathing, just staring. I saw Shane swallow hard, and his features went from an expression of tenseness to becoming relaxed as he made a decision within. He took her hands, looking at this beautiful young lady, who was twelve years his junior and smiled. 'Yes, I can feel what you feel. It has never happened to me before, but I know exactly what you mean. I cannot keep my eyes off you, I want you close all the time, all day I have been either looking at you, or for you. I will be your husband.' I heard a whoosh of breath as Sam inhaled sharply. I just looked at them; my mouth had dropped open and my tongue was dry, until a couple of sand flies buzzed in, and I closed it quickly. Shane and Tui were still looking at each other. Then she kissed him. All the ladies clapped, and suddenly Rita was holding the hands of the couple. 'On this day at this hour,' she declared, 'at the kainga Pukekawa, Tui is married to Shane Lang. This will go on the records of our tribe through the chief Rewi Maniapoto's people. Even though the woman Tui is of Ngapuhi, she is also Tainui; wherever she goes, she can claim the iwi of both tribes. Shane turned to us. 'mum was right,' he said. 'She said one day whenever I fall for a woman, and it would be love at first sight.' He grinned. 'Wait here,' insisted Aroha. She was gone for a few minutes and came back with a greenstone mere, which would probably be worth thousands of dollars in our time. She handed it to Shane. 'Usually, it is the man who gives a wedding gift to the woman's family; but today this woman, who was a slave, was freed by saving my life. It will be my family who will give the bride gift to you, with thanks to all your men for saving my husband Watene. I would like you both to use the whare next to mine for your first night together with no distractions.' Tui smiled. 'I have never slept alone in all my life.' 'What does she mean?' Sam asked me under his breath. 'Oh, communal sleeping,' I whispered back. We looked at our mate as he walked up to us, the bride in tow, and put an arm around each of us with an apologetic look. 'Sorry fellas, this is going to hit you as hard as it will hit me.' 'Mate,' I stated. 'We are thrilled for you whatever happens. You are our mate, and Tui will always be our friend: it is your decision. You're old enough to make your own decisions, your happiness is the most important thing. We are happy for you both.' Sam gave Shane a cheeky grin. 'I agree mate, she's better looking than Brill and I; you have never looked into my eyes the way you did with Tui's.' He laughed. 'I hope someday I can find a woman just like her. We really are chuffed mate.' They both looked at us and smiled. 'Thank you Sam, Bob,' Tui said. 'I hoped your friendship would not alter because Shane has taken a wife, and that is the way it should be.' She turned to him. 'Where you go, I go and what you decide I will agree, but if you are wrong, I will tell you.' 'Your mum would like this woman, mate; strong-willed, strong opinions and smart,' I said. Rita came walking down to the fire. 'A wonderful end to the day,' she said. 'From anger and hate to bliss. Your whare awaits you, Tui, Shane.' 'Don't worry about your shift on duty,' I told Shane. 'We will sort it out.' 'No, I'll do my bit,' he threw back. 'Not on your nelly mate,' Sam chipped in. 'This is your wedding night: you stay with your bride, we'll sort out the guard duty.' Together the new couple walked off into the dark. All the women walked beside them, singing softly until they disappeared into the whare.

I turned to Sam, 'Well, mate, this is one for the books.' 'Yeah it is,' he replied. 'Not sure what's going to happen, but I have this feeling he might stay.' 'I think the same, mate,' I answered. 'His mum and dad will be devastated, but it is Shane's life, and he must do what is right for himself, and now Tui. We need to get some photos for his mum and dad, Sam. If you are out near the bush line and no one's around except Shane and Tui, get a few shots in as close as you can. At least, we will be able to take a few photos of him and their daughter-in-law. Take my camera as well just in case, just snap them off.' 'Good idea,' he agreed. 'You okay to do an extra hour at the end of your shift mate, and I'll do the same?' 'Yeah, good-oh mate, that's fine.' 'Okay then, you are from nine till twelve, I'll go on till three the woman till five, then Bill from five till he gets us all up at six am.' 'Yep, good as gold,' Sam replied. 'You haven't lost your touch with the music,' I grinned. 'You can make that harmonica sing.' 'Yeah, I enjoyed it, but I would love to play the piano again.' 'You never know,' I remarked. 'Things are all tits-up at the moment, you could even end up in a band.' 'Yeah right,' he laughed. 'Anyway, you get your head down till nine pm; you've only got an hour.' 'Nah mate, I think we should check on the prisoners just to make sure they know we are on the ball.' We both got up and went into the hut where all the prisoners were tied up. Bill and some lady guards were whispering together, the cunning bugger, he was doing a bloody line. But he was not inattentive as he looked up as he said, 'Is that you, Bob?' 'Yeah, just doing a quick inspection, mate. Shane won't be doing a shift tonight.' 'Yes, I heard. He is a lucky man. A good Ngapuhi girl, he might have his hands full, but she will be loyal; all our women are.' I had to grin. 'Mate, on your marae they cannot speak,' I replied. 'I think they just might have a job trying to keep Tui quiet. She has been brought up Tainui, and can have as much say as the men.' 'Yes,' he grinned. 'Silly people.' 'Sam and I will do the extra time for him, you still okay with the five till six shift?' 'Yes, that's still alright with me.' 'Good-oh,' I said, 'I'll just check the injured blokes to make sure they are okay.' I went inside the hut with a lamp, stepping over bodies. I found the wounded blokes against the back wall.

'You boys okay?' I asked. 'A bit sore,' one whispered. 'Hang on to the lamp, I'll give you a pain-relief pill.' I fished into my pocket and got a couple of pills out. 'Swallow these, use your water bottle.' 'Thank you, sir,' he mumbled. 'You okay?' I asked the second one. 'Yes sir, I'm fine. I don't need a pill.' 'Okay then, I'll look in throughout the night. Keep quiet and behave.' I boomed a bit louder, so they could all hear. I went outside; Sam had been over to check on Watene. 'He is still sleeping,' he reported. 'No temperature. Bloody hell mate, he must be the luckiest bloke around. He could have died if the quacks had got him; they would have at least taken his leg off. You and Shane did good work mate.' We took a walk over to the NCO's. They were tied up like chooks. 'Are you happy?' I asked the guards. 'Yes,' one of them said. 'It's a shame they don't move, I would love to shove this bayonet into them. However, Rita said I can only do that if they move, and they won't move, it is so disappointing.' The soldiers' eyes were opened wide; you could see they were scared stiff. 'Okay,' I said to the girls. 'We will call in throughout the night. See you later.' 'Haere rā,' they replied. The night passed quickly. It was quiet, as we did our rounds of duty. When I did get to sleep, I dreamt about Shane, Tui, and children, with a mixture of all our families. It was all very confusing.

CHAPTER TWELVE

A shake in the morning from Bill brought me out of my sleep. It was still dark and cold. 'There is a fire going outside,' he said quietly, 'And a hot drink.' Sam sat up, rubbing his eyes. 'I wonder how Grunt got on last night.' 'Well,' I said, 'He would have at least been warm.' 'It's a bit bloody cool this morning,' Sam agreed, scratching his head. 'I feel peeved that we've missed summer.'

We went out and walked over to the fire. A woman handed us a cup of hot tea. 'Ka pai,' Sam thanked her. He turned to me. 'Do we wake the hubby?' 'Give him a few more minutes. We should check the Pommie boys to see how they are, and the shit-heads by the manuka tree.' We wandered over to the sergeant and corporal. 'You blokes okay?' I asked. 'No,' the sergeant complained. 'We need to relieve ourselves, the binds are too tight, and we can't feel our hands or legs.' I looked at them; it was so dark it was hard to pick up any features. 'What do you reckon Sam, walk them into the bush one at a time and let them pee?' 'Yeah, probably mate. You take a look at the others, and I'll look after these two.' I watched for a minute or two while Sam explained to the lady guards what he was going to do. They insisted they would watch just to make sure the men didn't run away. I had to laugh; this might take a while. They dragged the sergeant up onto his feet, cut the cords around his legs and frog-marched him into their toilet area. Sam followed, smiling like a Cheshire cat. I imagined the woman watching them pee, which I'm sure will stop their desire to go purely through sheer embarrassment. I laughed to myself.

I went over to the whare to check with the guards and to see how they were faring. I offered to get them a hot drink, but they declined: they already had one. I asked how the night went. 'Very quiet, not a noise out of them. Well, maybe light grumbles but that was all.' I thanked them. Then I went inside to see how the wounded boys were. I took a lamp with me, and I could see the fellas sitting up against the wall. 'You blokes okay?' I said. 'Yes, we are fine if that's what you mean.' 'Good. We will get some hot food and drink into you. Remember fellas,' I spoke to all those awake, 'We are going to have a hapu come running at dawn. A hapu, all looking for blood, so for the love of god keep your mouths shut.' I went back to the fire, to see Sam helping the corporal up and taking him for a pee as well, the same procedure as with the sergeant. I was still smiling as I reach the fire and asked the Māori women if it was possible to get the prisoners some hot food and drink. 'It has been arranged,' she replied. 'Rita organised it last night. You have no need to worry, it will be done.' I should remember this was a working village; everyone had a job to do, and it was normal for everyone to help.

It's a shame we didn't have communities like this in our time. Oh, we have a few; however, here, this was normal for these people.

Eventually, Sam came back. 'That was the best laugh I have had for a long time,' he said. 'See the old lady over there, she undid his fly buttons, dragged out his dick and held it the whole time. I could not help but laugh, you should have seen their expressions. Even in the dark, you could see the redness from their neck and their faces, they were so embarrassed. Oh shit, it was funny. I don't know what the girls were talking about, but it had to be size, I nearly choked with laughter. I bet they won't want a pee in daylight. They would rather pee their pants I reckon than go through all that again. Great stuff.' He was still giggling as we headed for Shane and Tui's hut. Pretty hard to knock when there's no door so Sam called out. 'Coo-ee, are you awake in there?' We could hear shuffling in the darkness of the hut, then this big shadow wandered out through the door. We looked at him; he had this silly look on his face. Sam said quietly under his breath, 'that's a satisfied-look.' I don't know whether Grunt heard or just ignored it. 'Everything okay, mate?' I enquired. 'Yep, fine,' he replied. 'All okay out there? No trouble through the night?' 'Yeah everything's good, a quiet night. We need to be organised by daybreak. I'm sure the hapu from Meremere will arrive about then, so we need to be out the front and just as mean-looking as they are going to be. We will need our rifles, and our army faces on.' 'Will do, Brill,' Shane said. 'Tui okay?' Sam asked innocently. Shane turned to his mate. 'Yeah she is, thanks for asking and thanks also for giving us the night off, fellas. I know it was inconvenient, but this was out of the blue.' 'Are you still happy with last night's decision?' Sam asked. 'Yeah, I am, even more so. I don't expect you to understand, but I have never been so happy. I never really thought it would happen to me. I would die for that woman.' Sam embraced his mate. 'We are happy for you Grunt, we really are. We know things will be different now. But we will always be here for you both. No questions asked. What you are to us, she is to us also.' 'I concur,' I mumbled. I straightened up. 'Now all we need to do is get our shit together and get out of here in one piece.' 'You blokes are something else,' Shane said. 'Okay, so we have sorted out daybreak, anything else?' Sam asked. 'Well I think we will leave the two NCO's where they are, a nice distraction, and the Māori can vent their anger in the appropriate place. As I said before, we will be out front. Guns, packs and looking mean. I hope to have Rita with us on our side.' 'What about Tui?' Sam asked, looking at Shane. 'Well she won't be in the background,' he replied. 'I can tell you that she will guard my back. That greenstone mere sits nicely in her hand.' 'Well, that's something,' I said. 'We have seen her fight to protect whanau. I think, mate, that she will fight even harder for you.'

I went looking for Rita and asked what she planned to do. 'I'm still thinking about it all,' she replied. That was not what I wanted to hear. 'You and your friends will be fine,' she said. 'Not sure yet about the English. Whatever happens, it is out of your hands.'

Dawn was approaching. It was just after seven am, by my watch. A little Māori girl came over and grabbed my wrist, asking, 'What is that?' Shit, I thought. If a kid can see what we have, the locals will have a field day. 'It's a piece of jewellery,' I said. 'Where we come from everyone has one.' She accepted that with a smile. 'If I come to your marae would I get one too?' she asked. 'Of course,' I said, 'they have nice ones for the pretty young girls.' She went away happy. I'll have to watch myself. Take the bloody thing off your wrist, my mind said. I stuck the watch into my top pocket; I hope I don't lose it. My sister Sasha gave that to me for my twenty first, and it reminded me of her. Whenever I wanted to think of home, I could always touch the watch.

I caught up with the boys and Bill. 'You game for this Bill?' I asked. 'Yes,' he replied. 'If I want to go home, I will have to be with you. I have an English gun and my mere; I will be there with you.' We picked up our rifles and gear and did a quick check. 'Right, I'm sure when dawn breaks they will come tearing out of that path over there,' I said. 'So we will stand just in front of the fire, nice and handy to the NCO's just in case. Shane whispered, 'One up the spout for good luck.' Our rifles were loaded; all we had to do was wait. I saw Tui coming over towards us. She looked different somehow, satisfied looking. I don't know, but she's so good-looking and proud with it. My heart did a flip. Heck, I thought, catching myself. Don't be stupid, she's Shane's wife. Hell, I envied him. I'm sure I'm in love with her, but I couldn't let that show. She came up to Shane and kissed him on his forehead, with him bending over double for her to reach. She squeezed his hand and stood beside him with this bloody big greenstone mere in her belt. I looked around and saw Stu looking out of a hut further along. I yelled for him to keep out of sight, and he quickly pulled his head back inside.

Then a call went out, and an answer call came from the village. No mucking about, no protocol, the hapu came running into the kainga. They all looked to be fit, tough men. Only two had the facial moko of chiefdom: the leader and the bloke by his side. As for the rest, some were wearing traditional Māori gear; they had tattoos from their knees to their bums. Others were dressed in European clothes: jackets, woollen trousers, waistcoats, and derby hats. They looked funny, but these blokes were serious. They had an assortment of weapons as well. The traditional mere, taiaha, a fighting staff, a few of them had European axes in their belts and a tao, a short spear; and of course a putu, which is a mere made of stone. On the rifle front, they had English Lee-Enfield muskets, some had the tupara. This is a double barrel percussion shotgun, a good weapon in the bush. Not everyone had a gun, which gave me the impression that this was their Achilles heel. But they still looked formidable. The leader did not speak a word. He sent a few men around all the whare to check them out, and a couple went over to the NCO's to take a look at them. The warriors reported back before the young chief spoke up. 'You,' he said in English to Shane, 'Are not from here, I have never seen rifles like that. They would buy a few good women, I would think.' It was hard for

Shane to keep a straight face. 'Yes they would,' he said, 'but I only want one woman, and she is standing here beside me.' 'Wahine,' the chief said, looking at her. 'Not anymore,' Shane replied. 'Her name is now Tui, and she's my wife.' The warrior looked at him. 'I'm pleased you are a big man: it will take all your strength and effort to keep her under control,' he said with a slight grin. Then he went straight back to being serious. He directed his gaze at Sam. 'We were told stories of big redheaded men in our past. I wouldn't believe it, and then I heard that you play a flute as well. Are you a supernatural fairy?' They were looking quite apprehensively at Sam. 'I'm a man like you,' Sam replied. 'I come from the bottom of Ngai Tahu Country, where the snow falls and there's ice on the ground and where a brave Tainui warrior would cry with the cold.' Oh shit Sam, I thought, don't start throwing out challenges. The chief looked at Sam then laughed. 'I think you are no fairy,' he said. 'I have heard of your exploits with this kainga; fairies do not do that.' He turned to me. 'How come the shortest is in the chief?' 'I can negotiate,' I explained. 'My friends are warriors and to a point, I am too, but in all tribes, there are people who organise, and who would like to think of different outcomes: that is me. Don't get me wrong, I'll fight with my friends because we are as one. Our tribe from the south are strong as well.' You all speak different than the English here,' he replied. 'We are not English,' I said. I could see he was a bit confused. He kept looking at our weapons with a bit of envy. I was thinking how he would love them. Though, thinking about it, all the soldiers rifles had disappeared among the tribe and would be of use to them in the coming war. He turned to Bill. 'You,' he pointed, 'Are Ngapuhi?' 'Yes,' Bill said proudly. 'I am and it was a Ngapuhi that helped save your kainga with the help of these Southern men.' 'Would you stay to fight the Pakeha?' 'No, this is not my fight. I have a fight of my own. I need to be revenged for the indiscretions that were done to me by the Pakeha in Auckland. I need to extract utu; after that I will decide whether I will come to help you. 'This young chief was no dill: he was ascertaining what he would do. He looked a capable, good-looking young bloke; all the warriors were looking at him. One word and they would be onto us, then while we were getting a thumping, they would certainly slaughter all the soldiers. 'Why do you want to protect these men?' he asked, pointing to the NCO's. I spoke up. 'I don't want to protect them, but to kill them now will bring a war to your tribe. You are not ready; a few more months and you will be. Killing them will give you a bloody great headache, and I don't think your chief would somehow want that.' 'How do you know how we think?' he questioned. I walked a bit closer to him, and he placed his hand on his mere. I stared directly at him. 'I know all about the trenches from the sea to the pa and up nearly to the Hunuas. I know of the big pa at Rangiriri, of the other fighting pa as far south as Te Awamutu. I know of the new tactics that your chief Rewi wants to try out. Hit and run.' His eyes widened. 'This is all secret, only known to a few men.' ' Well,' I said, 'I told you I know about words, and I can see into the future. I'm a Pakeha tohunga.' He stepped back and took his hand off his mere. 'Will you tell the

English?' he asked. 'No,' I replied. 'What happens in the future is for the future. The information I know will never come out otherwise down the line things might change, and maybe God would be angry with me. I don't want that. However, these men here, I want their own people to punish them. The men in the hut were only following orders from their chief over there.' He knew about them, as he had sent his warriors to look around.' I pointed at the sergeant, 'he is to blame for everything that has gone on here. So I say to you, there should be utu on these two men, but not now, in a few months.' Once again I walked closer and whispered, 'I will guarantee that these men will be in the front of any attack on your people. They will be there for you to extract utu. I know there will be an attack in a few months at the supply depot at Camerontown.' His eyes just about popped out of his head. 'You know this?' 'Yes,' I said. 'I can have these two men there on guard duty. This will be the time to extract your revenge.' 'How come a Pakeha does not mind us attacking a white village?' 'We are not from here; it is not our fight. I do not want to change the future – it would be wrong to do this, but I can help you in your quest for utu, and if you let me take these men out of here today, then I promise, one warrior to another, this will be done.'

This was when Rita came up to the young chief. 'Mother,' he said to her in Māori, 'you were not hurt?' Oh heck. Rewi's nephew. No wonder he was in the know. 'No,' Rita replied, also in Māori, 'These men here have been good to us. This man you are talking to has performed a miracle on Watene. I have seen nothing like it, he is a powerful tohunga. This man here,' she pointed to Shane, 'has Tainui in his blood, even though he does not show it, and he is tied to our tribe through his marriage to Tui last night. The red-headed man is a warrior also, and can sing the birds out of the trees. Strong and fair, with his friends together, they are one. Tui now is married to Shane and will bear his children well. Even now she carries his child. Wiremu is a warrior. He did his best for our tribe even considering there is ill feeling between us; he did not hesitate. What we could do if all the people of this land were united?' She continued, 'There is a Pakeha man, Scottish, from the deep south like these men, who helped our children when the English attacked. He threatened the English soldiers with a bayonet if they did not leave our children alone. So my son, all these men here are honourable. They helped our people, our children, in time of need. I believe this is not the right moment to do your duty with those two men tied to the manuka tree, or the soldiers in the whare. I believe we need to trust this man Bob with his word.' She gestured to the whare where Watene lay. 'The wounded warrior in the whare has mana. He stood up to the attack and shot two English before he was shot himself. His boys also fought the English; they are only aged eight and nine and accounted for themselves well. Bob here worked for hours to save Watene's life. He would like to ask you a favour. Is it possible for Watene's family to go south to Te Awamutu or Taumarunui to recuperate? He is no good as a warrior at the moment. I thought that wouldn't be a problem. Wouldn't you agree?' The chief looked at his mother and smiled. 'You have thought this through, Mother,' he said. 'You and this Pakeha are good with words. You could be related.' She laughed. 'I think not, but I like him. In fact, all of them they are honest men.' 'I'll leave that for you to sort out,' he replied. 'I cannot leave you any warriors, but there are a few back at the Pa, who are weakening with age. It might be best if I send them to you to help move his family south.' 'Thank you, my son,' she said.

He turned to me, switching back to English. 'I have listened and thought about what my mother has said. I will go with my inner spirit, which tells me you are a good man. I'll give you an escort to the English fort. But any trouble with these men and I will kill them. Is this fair to you?' Shit, I was relieved. I don't know how she did it, as it was all said in Māori, but I could have kissed her. 'I think you might have underestimated yourself,' he continued. 'Your argument was well done, and I commend you on it. My mother put, how do you say, put the icing on the cake?' It's funny listening to Māori speak like this, I thought to myself. In our time, we are so used to language more like, 'hey bro.' The chief turned to his warriors. 'I want those two men standing up against the tree.' They went over to them and yanked them up. Both men went white, and the sergeant looked quite ill. The chief then got all his men individually to go over to them and look at their faces. 'Mark them well,' he said in Māori. 'When we go into battle, these two men will be there, and we will extract utu on that day.' Twenty-five warriors slowly walked up to the two men, and unblinking stared at them, marking every part of their features. Down the road when the fighting starts, they would be remembered. The chief came over to us. 'I'll send six men with you; that should be plenty to take care of them on the trail. I would suggest you tie their hands in front of their bodies. It will give them more balance. My men will stand no nonsense from them if they even look defiant, I have told my warriors to kill them.' 'I will relay that to the men,' I said. 'Good.' He came up to me and pressed his nose to mine in a hongi, then he went down the line until he got to Bill. He looked him in the eye, but Bill came forward and instigated the hongi and everyone went away happy. He hongied then kissed his mum on the cheek. I wasn't sure if they did that, but why not it's his mum. He took a last look around, turned with his remaining nineteen warriors, and disappeared into the bush. I sighed with relief; quite honestly I was scared as hell, thank goodness for Rita.

I asked if any of the warriors could speak English. One spoke up. 'Yes, old chap, I learnt it with the missionary teachers.' Bugger me, he spoke with a plum in his mouth. 'Good,' I said, 'that will help. I'll communicate through you.' 'Fine old man,' he replied. 'Most of these chaps speak a bit of the mother tongue.' I nearly laughed. I saw Sam catch himself and Shane just stared at him. 'What's wrong?' the warrior asked. 'Is it something I have said?' 'No, not at all, it's just your English accent is a bit funny to us.' 'Yes, I can understand old boy, this is the way I learnt to speak. You men speak funny not the Queen's

English. However, that is by and by, we need to get these nasty men over to their side of the border.' I needed a photo or video of this bloke. He was talking like this with a Māori skirt, a woollen shirt, and tattoos from his knees to his bum; god it was precious. He didn't look like how he spoke though: a big barrel of a chest, big legs, a scar on his face and half an ear. 'What is your name?' I asked. 'You can call me Peri,' he informed me. 'If I had been with my teacher, it would not have been good form to let anyone use my first name. But out here it is not as important. Can I ask you your name, my good fellow?' This was bizarre. 'My name is Bob, the red-head is Sam, the big fellow is Shane, his wife Tui, and Wiremu.' 'Pleased to make your acquaintances, gentle people,' he greeted. Shane just about swallowed his tongue with choking noises. 'Are you well, Shane?' Peri asked. Shane pretended to get a coughing fit. 'Yes, I'm fine, just something caught in my throat.' 'How come you don't talk like this bloke, Bill?' I queried. 'Different teachers, mine came from London.' I meant it as a joke, but it went over Bill's head.

'Okay,' I said 'let's get this party on the road.' Bill and a couple of the Tainui warriors collected the men from the hut, cutting their leg ropes and retied each one with their hands to the front. Stu came out looking relieved. 'I was a bit scared when they came into the hut,' he said to me. 'You would have been okay,' I said, 'Rita was on your side. Don't forget you are at the back with Shane and Tui.' Hell, he was only Tui's age. Speaking of Tui: she had gone into the whare and brought out her worldly belongings in a small flax kete. She went up to Shane, put her hand in his, pulled him down and kissed his cheek. 'I'm ready,' I heard her say. 'Wherever you go, I go to.' Well, that was sorted. Shane waved Stu over. 'Keep in between Tui and me,' he ordered. 'I want your army mates to see as little of you as possible, so there's more of a chance they will forget you. They don't know you very well, so that's in your favour.' I arranged the men and lined them up in the direction of the track to the river. 'Okay, listen up,' I said. Whether they understood this expression or not, I couldn't care less. 'We are going to the Alexander Redoubt. We have a guard of Tainui Warriors. They have been told by their chief that if any one of you looks defiant or causes trouble, they will kill you. Is this understood, Sergeant?' 'Yes sir,' came the reply. 'Okay, we will move out.' All the men were tied to each other so if one tried to break away, he wasn't going to get far with twelve others dragging behind. Sam and a Tainui warrior went point, the rest of us slowly followed them out of the village.

The women had given us food for the trip when we had said our goodbyes, which we would share with everyone. I guessed a normal tramp to the river would be two hours, so I allowed four as it would be much slower with the men tied. I took a peek at my watch: just after ten am; we will stop for thirty minutes at twelve. The bush closed in on us as we left the village, and it started to rain, cold driving rain the soldiers looked miserable as they walked slowly in single file interspersed with the warriors. The Māori boys were happy: they were smiling and walking up and down the line, making faces, sticking out their tongues, and scaring the shit out of the English, while saving their most ferocious looks for the two NCO's. We made good progress by midday and I called a halt. The English drank from their water bottles which they carried with them. Tui came down the line handing out food to the soldiers until she got to the sergeant, where she spat into his food and threw it at him. 'Quite lady like,' I said to Sam. He grinned. 'I would not like to be on the end of an argument with her.' The rain had stopped and the sun was trying to come out, but it was still quite cool. Sam wondered aloud, 'Why in hell would the English attack at this time of the year?' 'I don't know mate,' I answered. 'Once they start they get bogged down for weeks. Dumb really, should have left it until spring or summer. These people aren't going anywhere.' I checked my watch. 'Okay you blokes, on your feet. Another couple of hours and you will be home in a nice warm cell.' Some of the men were talking to each other. I let them, as it took their minds off the tramp and their immediate future. They continually glanced at the warriors when they walked passed. We had no problems on the hike to the river; I was thankful for that. Once again, I felt sorry for them. Most of them hadn't been in New Zealand more than a week, and this was so not London or Sydney. This was going to be a shooting war, against men who knew how to kill. They had been doing it for centuries so this group of soldiers were a little bit out of their league. As we got closer to our destination, you could smell the water and the sound of the river got louder until we burst out of the bush. In front of us across the river, there it was: Alexander Redoubt.

CHAPTER THIRTEEN

The redoubt looked pretty impressive. Four metres high, with a two-metre ditch around the perimeter. An army behind the walls would have the upper hand. Oh, it wasn't impregnable, but it depended upon how many lives you wanted to waste taking it. Personally, I would cut their supply line and starve them out. All the same it was good, solid and well fortified, with clear views up and down the Waikato River.

We had come out opposite Namuheiriri Island. Well, it's not really an island as such, only when the river is in flood. That's when the water swirls around the right bank, turning it into an island. But at the moment it was still attached to the mainland. I asked Peri, 'What does the name mean?' He mumbled something about 'Bloody sandflies', and he wished the beggars would go away. So maybe the name meant sandflies be gone, or whatever – the bitey little buggers were having a go at us now. The Māori boys had collected some kawakawa leaves and were rubbing them onto their exposed skin; we did the same. It gave some relief, to a point. There was a small ferry on the other side of the river with a flat bottom. To get it you just undid the rope and pulled it across, then used the second rope to pull yourself back. If the river was in flood I don't think it would be used – a bit too dangerous I'd say. At the moment, mainly because of the animosity between the Māori and the English and this being the border, and the boat was just lying idle. I wondered why the ferry was still here, but was pleased it was. The only problem I could see was that we needed someone over in the redoubt to untie their end. I was surprised that no one had stuck their head up over there to take a look at what was happening. I mean, they had lost a patrol of twelve men, I would have thought they would have been more vigilant. Shane and Sam were thinking along the same line as me and shaking their heads.'

I ordered the prisoners to sit down. I had a funny suspicion that they were grateful for that order. The Māori boys were looking at the redoubt with interest. Peri commented, 'I would not bother about attacking from the river, but from the rear at night it would be splendid. We blend in lovely at night,' he grinned. 'Then we would have a wonderful time attacking their relief columns when they resupply and such like. It would tie up so many of their troops protecting their back. Wonderful stuff.' I still could not get over a Māori with an upper-class English accent. It threw me off, him talking like he did with his tattoos, dress and rugged battle marked face but no one took a blind bit of notice to the way he spoke; I suppose if we were around him for any length of time we would get used to it as well. I turned to the boys. 'Here goes fellas, bullshit from now on. Let's hope I can pass muster.' I walked to the edge of the r iver, and with the most impressive yell, I called out. 'Hello, the fort. You there in the redoubt are you listening.' A face peeked over the edge of the palisades, looking down on us. I yelled again. 'I want your officer now, there's a good chap.' A few minutes went by and another head popped up. 'Who are you?' I asked. 'Ensign Smyth,' came the answer. 'Where is your captain and colour sergeant?' I yelled back. 'Drury, for the conference,' was the reply. Oh shit, that was good; I should be able to bullshit this young bloke without too much difficulty. 'My name,' I boomed out, 'is Captain Kidder. I need an armed escort here now. I have your lost patrol under arrest. I want you and your men down here and I want the ferry over my side sooner than later. Have you got all that, ensign?' 'Yes, sir,' he yelled. 'Right away.' His face disappeared from the ramparts. It was not long until we saw a line of men running down the track, with the young ensign in behind. 'Get that boat untied, corporal,' he ordered. 'I want you and six men to come with me. Lance Corporal Brown, stay over here to guard the men who come across.' There was a lot of 'yes sirs' as the ferry was untied. His men jumped aboard and pulled themselves over to our side. The ensign came up to me and saluted. 'How can I help, sir?' he asked. He was looking at the prisoners, then turned and looked at Peri's warriors with a worried frown. 'Well, I need these men locked up tonight,' I said, 'And accommodation for myself and my party. I will need to write a report about these idiots here who broke every rule in the book. I'll explain it all when we get them across and into a holding cell or barracks.' 'We only have one small cell, sir,' he replied. 'That's all right, you can put these two men together,' I ordered, pointing at the NCOs, 'the rest, I think, will not cause trouble. They can bunk down in the barracks or the stable – just keep them away from those two.

Let's get them tucked away, then we will talk.' 'What about these Māori warriors?' 'Oh, they helped me bring the patrol back to the Redoubt; you don't have to worry about them.'

In groups of six at a time, the soldiers walked to the ferry and boarded with their six guards. The ensign went over with the first lot as the NCOs were in that group. I asked that he put them under lock and key as his first duty. I watched as they slowly walked up the track to the redoubt. Then the boat returned for the next group. We waited until that group had gone and I turned to Peri. 'My thanks to you, and also give our thanks to your chief. It was a real pleasure to meet you and your warriors.' He smiled. 'If you attack our pa in the future, just yell your names. We will fire over your heads. You men are too good to kill in battle.' I had to admit, Māori warfare is a bit different than elsewhere. We all hongied and as they turned back into the bush, Peri called out, 'Wonderful to meet you, next time we will have tea,' then disappeared from sight. We had a giggle. 'Can you imagine the Māori boys talking like that in our time?' I smiled. Oops, Tui and Stu were listening; I keep forgetting. I told the others to watch themselves, but I always get caught out.

There was a yell from the bank. 'Coming across now, sir, when you're ready.' The ferry touched our side. We all jumped on, grabbing the rope and dragging ourselves to the left bank. A private tied up the boat. 'Follow me sir. The officer has a hot drink ready for you all.' He was looking at Tui and Bill. 'Oh, this is Lieutenant Lang's wife –' I informed him, gesturing to Tui, '– Mrs Lang, and this

Māori gentleman is Staff Sergeant Hohepa.'

Thank you, sir. Please follow me, sirs and madam.' We traipsed up the path to the double doors at the top with sentries on both sides. As we went through, they presented arms and Shane ordered, 'At ease.' The private escorted us into the officers' mess. 'Would you prefer the sergeants' mess?' he asked Bill. 'Not at the moment, private,' I jumped in. 'I want him with us – we need to talk to your officer.' I could see he was not happy with a sergeant in the officers' mess, but he was not going to argue with a captain. We entered the mess. Tea and cakes were on the table and the ensign was there with another younger officer, who only looked about 16. 'Please take a seat, sirs and madam. This is Ensign Robb.' Ensign Smyth looked at Bill and Stu. 'I want them here for the moment,' I growled, and then enquired, 'Do you have a writer?' 'Yes sir, do you want him now?' 'No, I'll have tea first, then I'll give you our story that I want put down in writing. When will your CO arrive back?' I asked. 'About three day's sir, after the conference,' he replied. 'They left me and Ensign Robb here to look after the redoubt.' 'When the patrol went missing, we searched straight away, up and down our side of the bank. We went further than Camerontown, which is just over four miles west of here. We did not expect them to be on the other side of the river. What possessed them?'

'Yes, well it wasn't really the rank and file, Ensign, it was that bloody sergeant and corporal. They coerced their men to do something stupid by threatening them. So really, the other ranks are not the problem. It was that sergeant, and by a lesser degree the corporal. They need to be in irons. I would like to take them to General Cameron's HQ. They could have caused the war to be brought forward by months, and our chaps are not ready. The Governor would have been very unhappy.'

The mess steward came in and served us cups of tea, with milk poured from small a silver jug and cakes on a fancy plate. 'Oh, so refined.' I heard Sam say. 'How long did you search?' I asked. 'All day and night until I sent an orderly off in the dray to Drury to inform the CO and the general. I sent out patrols again today; one is still out there. I would have still kept sending them both up and down the river, with the hope they got just got lost and, continued until the captain returned. We went about 3 miles past Camerontown today, and the same the other way.''These men went over on the ferry,' I divulged. 'You need to give the ferry man a boot up the bum.' He went red. 'There is a lady present, sir.' Oh bugger, I thought, Victorian niceties. 'I do apologise, Tui, I will wash out my mouth with soap.' 'It's quite alright, Bob,' she smiled. 'I understand this is a man's mess. It's not usual to have a lady around; a slip of the tongue.' She went right up a notch in my estimation.

I sat down and told the two ensigns the story. 'My god, sir.' They were horrified by the time I had finished. 'We are so lucky you were over there. I cannot understand why the sergeant did this; he's been in the service for twenty years.' 'A little bit of rape and pillage was on his mind, Ensign.' 'Err, how come you were over there in the first place, sir?' he asked. 'That is a question I cannot answer. All I can say is that we have been over there for quite a few months with the authority of the governor. We report back to him and only him, and the information is then related to General Cameron. No one must know about our assignment, and these bloody idiots nearly put the whole exercise in jeopardy. We had to show ourselves, just because some of your men with amorous thoughts wanted some easy pickings. Unfortunately for them, it bit them on their bums– oops, sorry, Tui.' She smiled sweetly.

'So young fella, what do we do? We need transport to Drury, have you got anything at all?'

'No, sir, we only had one horse and dray. Supplies come in once a week and the last was only two days ago.' 'Looks like shanks pony,' I said as I turned to the boys. 'How far is it, Ensign, to walk to Drury?' Oh, about six hours, sir.' I thought for a moment, 'Okay, this is my plan. We will all write a report; you too, Ensign. I will leave the main body of the squad here. I was going to take the sergeant and corporal to Drury, but I think in hindsight, they should be left here for your commanding officer to deal with. I might catch up with your CO or colour sergeant on the road. When they are punished, if possible, I would like them to be put on permanent guard duty in Camerontown for at least six months after a bloody good flogging.' I felt myself cringe, but this would be normal punishment, or even a firing squad for them. After all, they did shoot two men. 'I'll have a yarn, ah, a talk with the general and see if we can come up with a consensus. I will put my recommendations in my report.' 'That is fine, sir,' he replied. 'Oh, and I need a jacket for my sergeant. Where we have been it hasn't mattered, but back in civilization I don't want the local population to think he is a rebel.'

'I'll fix that right away, sir. What about yourselves? Very unusual clothes.' He was looking intently at our camouflage gear. 'Well, our uniforms are all made down south; we did not think we would have to use them, but this wee incident has changed things considerably. Buying another uniform at this time is not an option. I think we should get by until we get to Auckland.' 'I have a tailor here, sir, I'm sure we could fix you up something before you leave.' 'Thank you, Ensign, that won't be necessary, but I would appreciate you fixing up my sergeant. I can see why the captain felt the redoubt in such good hands, when he left it with you.' You could see the young bloke's shoulders come up; I'm sure his head got bigger. 'Oh, one other thing. We have been away so long, and until we get ourselves sorted, we will need a chit for vittles and accommodation. Once in Auckland we will be fine. I will just go to the bank. But I cannot, in all fairness to the other officers and Mrs Lang, live on nothing until we see the paymaster.' 'That will be no problem, sir, Ensign Robb is the paymaster here. He will give you more than one chit, enough to pay your bills till you sort out your finances; it will see you through to Auckland. You will want to be incognito up there, sir, so can I suggest the Union Hotel on Queen Street. Much more elegant than a few of the others around. I'll have the chits made out for the six of you for a week, and any money can be paid back once you have settled with the paymaster up there: either through him, or drop it here yourself when you pass. We must keep our records up to date. Also, as you head up to Auckland on the Great South Road you will pass a few more redoubts. I'll give you a chit for your vittles for these redoubts, you can use them for food and accommodation.

'I'll fix up a tent for Mr and Mrs Lang, sir, the others can use the NCO bunks – they won't be using them, as they're in the cells. Sir, you two gentlemen can use the officers' quarters at the end of the hall; there are two bedrooms, so you get one each.' 'Would it be possible to allow Mrs and Lieutenant Lang to have my room? It would be more comfortable for her, and I will have the tent. Mrs Lang might be in a delicate condition.' Tui gave me a funny look.

'Oh certainly, if that's fine by you, Lieutenant Lang.' 'Yes, thank you, Ensign,' Shane said. 'That would be wonderful, she has had a bad time of it lately.' Tui gave him a frosty look as well. 'I'll go and get the writer and get all this down, sir. Dinner will be at six pm, sherry at five; Mrs Lang will be our honoured guest. Sergeant, you can dine in the sergeants' mess.' He paused for a minute then went on. 'Would you like an escort to Auckland, sir?' 'No, we should be fine. I think with the unsettled environment here it would be wise not to downsize your garrison. You can use the rest of the prisoners for normal duties, but the two NCOs stay locked up. The two who have been shot – we attended to their wounds and they need to only be on light duties until their wounds heal.' 'How about you, sir?

You look familiar.' He turned to Stu, who went red. 'Oh,' I rushed in, 'he is under the sergeant's care; he will stay with him. He is undercover with us and quite honestly, what he has to say is the utmost importance to the governor. So I would appreciate it if he is fed in his room. We do not want anyone to know he is here.' 'Fine, sir. You know best. That will be arranged. I'll get things sorted now, sir, and we will see you at dinner.' He got up and both ensigns went out.

There was a collective sigh. 'They didn't recognize Stu, thank god. I think I got in first – well, I hope so.' I remarked.'My God, Brill,' Sam began, 'I did not know that you could bullshit your way out of a paper bag. Even I was starting to believe all the crap you were talking.'

'I told you fellas, I can talk rubbish.' I was grinning. 'Yeah mate, that was great. I'm pleased the rest of the squad might be handled differently than the NCOs,' Sam replied. 'When you look at it, a few of them did get a bit carried away with whacking the woman and the kids, but a good "twelve of the best" might bring them back to earth,' I replied.'You mean a flogging?' 'Yeah, I do, mate. As much as we had no trouble with them, they did lay into the woman and kids. There were only the three that didn't: Stu and the two wounded. So they should take a bit of responsibility for their actions.' 'Yeah,' agreed Shane, 'but I don't want to be around when it happens.' 'Nor do I,' Sam admitted. 'Well, that makes three of us,' I answered. I turned to Tui. 'Tui, would you help when the writer comes back. Your version will help the officer in charge?' 'Yes that will be fine. I'll paint the picture so black the Sergeant will never command men again; if this is all the utu I get, I will be happy.' 'Well, Bill, Stu, you both get to sleep in a warm bed tonight. I think having a jacket with stripes on Bill will stop a lot of wagging tongues. And you Stu, being in your room will keep you incognito until we get to Auckland.' 'I don't know what you meant in half that conversation, but I will keep my head down,' he replied. 'Good man.' I grinned. At this point, the sergeant came in. 'Sergeant Hohepa and the young sir, if you will follow me and I will show you to your quarters.' 'Bill,' I cut in, 'We will be off at daybreak about seven-ish.' He looked at me. 'Fine, we will be up and ready.' As he was leaving, the sergeant focused on him. 'The officer called you by your first name, and don't you call your officers "sir"?' 'Yes,' I heard him reply as the door slowly closed behind him, 'At least once a day.' I could hear him sniggering down the hall.

Later there was a knock on the door, and a little old bloke puts his head through. 'I'm Mr Frost, are you ready for a writer now?' 'Come in,' I beamed. 'You're a bit old for the army,' Shane observed. 'Oh,' he smiled. 'No, I'm not in the army; I'm just here to keep the books straight and to shuffle paperwork around. Not enough men can read or write, so they asked me to come down from Auckland for a few months to get the paperwork up to date. So how can I help you?' 'How many quills have you got?' I asked. 'I have three here and a bottle of ink, blotting paper and the official seal.' 'Okay, if you can write down what Mrs

Lang dictates to you, we will write down our reports on the other pages.' He set up the tables, putting the ink in the middle and started talking to Tui. When he had the gist of her story, he started to write. Now and again he would stop and ask a question. We got stuck into ours and within the hour they were done. It was hard going. None of us had written with a quill, so there were a few ink blots to try and clean up. At the bottom of my report I suggested that the men responsible for the attack be sent to Camerontown for six months permanent guard duty, and be reverted to the ranks, and with the compensation of half their wages to go to the families of the dead warriors. I didn't know if this was usual, but I'm sure the army didn't want a war right at this minute. Mr Frost looked up with his glasses on the end of his nose. He read what he had written and handed it to Tui. 'You can read, Mrs Lang?' he asked.

'Yes, thank you, Mr Frost.' The mess went quiet as she reviewed her report. 'Thank you, Mr Frost, you have written that down splendidly.' He smiled. 'It was my pleasure, madam, you are a very brave woman. I congratulate you on your fortitude. You must be very proud of her, Lieutenant,' he added, looking at Shane. He turned to me, 'Would you like me to check that everything is in order with your reports, Captain?' 'Thank you, Mr Frost, that is most kind.' Bugger me, I was falling into their way of talking. He took our reports settled down to read. We left him to it as we wandered out of earshot to yarn about tomorrow.

'That was good thinking, Brill, about the chits.' My mates grinned. 'We never would have thought of that.' 'I didn't think of it till the last minute,' I replied. 'We need to eat and have accommodation so this works out well for us. I'm hoping the Union Hotel is only a short distance from the printers; that would be an added bonus. It's a bit of a hike from here to Auckland though, about 60 kilometres: a good couple of days' walk, without hold ups. If it gets too late, we will doss down overnight somewhere and carry on the next day. As we get closer to Drury we may get lucky, there might even be a cart heading north. It's the main supply route to Auckland so I'm hoping there is a bit of traffic heading into the city.' A slight cough got our attention. 'Remarkable story, sirs,' Mr Frost mused, 'You have it down on paper eloquently. The commanding officer will not be able to complain about the evidence; it's all here. Thank you for being so precise. A couple of words I'm not sure of, but overall a wonderful piece of writing from you all. Now I will fold them and put on the regiment wax seal. This will go to the ensign who will hold it till the CO gets back from Drury. A capital day.' He was smiling as he waxed each report then gathered up his gear. 'Will we see you for dinner?' I asked. 'Oh no, that would not be proper, me in the officers' mess. No no, I will have my dinner with Mrs Frost. Thank you all the same.' And off he went. 'I cannot get my head around how formal everyone is,' Sam confessed. 'Tui, you are a natural, where did you learn to act like a lady?' She smiled. 'All the children went to the mission school. If we did not speak or act properly they would cane us, so you quickly learnt to adapt to what they wanted. We got our own back, a little bit of utu, when we left school for the last time. The teachers loved their gardens and one evening we released a small flock of sheep into it. The next morning, everything had been eaten and all the ground was trampled. All our whanau knew it was us, but the teachers thought is an accident. It was a victory of sorts.'

Five o'clock came around and we all met in the mess for drinks. I don't like sherry and the boys didn't either, but we endured. At six there was a sound of a bell and the ensign announced, 'Dinner, gentlemen and madam. Would it be proper for me to escort Mrs Lang into the mess?' 'Why thank you Ensign,' Tui responded, 'You will be a fine catch for a young lady from Auckland. Impeccable manners and good looking to boot.' Shane was just about having to step over his bottom lip as we smiled, walking into the mess Dinner was quite amazing. I wasn't expecting much, but we had pigeon pie, kumara, fresh peas and gravy. I heard Sam say, 'I hope this is not kereru.' For dessert they gave us apple pie; the crust was so thick. I hadn't eaten anything like this ever. To top it off, there was fresh cream from the house cow, so the steward informed us, as he poured generous quantities of the stuff all over our pie. Sitting back with a full belly, Sam spoke. 'Ensign, that was one of the better meals I have had. Would the cook still be around?' 'He would, sir.' 'Point me to the kitchen, I want to thank him for his effort.' 'Well sir, it is not normal for an officer to go into the kitchen unless it's for an inspection.' Sam replied, 'Well, it's time for an inspection then.' He jumped up. 'I'm going to inspect the kitchen, is that okay by you?' 'Um what do you mean?'

'Do you object?' 'No, sir.' 'Good-oh,' said Sam, and was gone. 'Let's have a glass of port, Ensign.' I suggested. I thought it would take his mind off Sam belting around the kitchen, frightening all the men.

We all had a glass in our hands when Sam came in with another plate of apple pie. 'Bloody hell Ensign, that man needs promoting. Bang him up to sergeant, he deserves it for the meal he cooked.' 'Ladies present, sir,' the ensign reminded us with a frown on his face. 'Oh, sorry Tui, keep forgetting, I'm your humble servant.' Shane just laughed. 'Humble would not be the right word, mate.' 'I say, you fellows speak so differently,' Ensign Robb jeered. He had been very quiet all night. 'Don't you think you sound a bit common?' I looked at Sam. He turned and gave the young bloke a fiery look and we watched the Ensign visibly shrink away. 'No, young fella, we don't sound common; not to us anyway,' he snapped. 'If you judged everyone by the way that person spoke, or how they act, just because it's different than what you are used to – when you don't know a thing about them – then that would make you the common one. You are an officer, so who comes first in this man's army: you or the men you command? You should, by all rights, not have to even think about it. The men come first, second and third. If the men are happy, you are happy. If they bitch and moan then there is something wrong with your commanding abilities. So to be a good officer, you put the men first. I believe by that statement you just uttered, you have had a sheltered life, and this is your chance to grab this experience and become a great officer – one that the troops like and want to be led by. Don't miss the opportunity. Now this "common" bugger is going to bed.'

With that Sam rose, turned to the rest of us and muttered, 'I bid you gentlemen, and Tui, a good night. I'm looking forward to a normal bed.' And off he went. There was a hush. The young ensign was red from his throat to his brow. 'Don't take it hard, son,' Shane offered. 'That advice will be with you forever, you just have to take heed of it. Start tomorrow and see what reaction you get when you treat everyone with respect. Just don't judge people by the way they speak. It is amazing what you can learn from the lowest on the pole to the highest. Sam did not want to belittle you. Just a gentle reminder that the army is run by good men, whatever way they speak, and with positive thinking you can be one of them. It's what's in here,' he touched his heart, 'that's important. Here ends the lesson. Brill, Ensign, I will see you tomorrow.' 'Goodnight, gentlemen.' Tui walked across to Ensign Robb, and kissed him on his cheek. 'Cheer up,' she whispered. 'He is on your side.' Then, arm and arm with her husband, she walked out the door. That left me and the two ensigns. 'Are you all right, Mr Robb?' I asked. 'Yes, thank you sir,' he mumbled. 'No one has ever spoken to me like that before. I'm embarrassed.' He was obviously humbled. 'The information that the Lieutenant spoke of was well worth listening to.' Acknowledged Ensign Smyth. Robb turned to me. 'I'd would like to think on this advice, and before the Lieutenant leaves, I will apologise to him.'

'I think you will be a good officer young Robb. If you learn from your mistakes and the mistakes of others, you will do fine,' I replied. 'Thank you, sir. I will have all the chits ready for you before you go, at seven am.' 'Yes, well, thank you, Robb,' I replied. 'Everyone's turned in early so now I will too. I will catch up with you both tomorrow. Goodnight, gentlemen.' I walked out the door to my tent thinking, bloody hell, what have we got ourselves into.

CHAPTER FOURTEEN

It seemed as though my head just touched the pillow when an insistent voice entered my head. 'Sir! Sir, time to get up.' The steward was lightly shaking my shoulder. I stirred, not too happy to be woken; it was still bloody dark. I sat up, staring into the candle lamp, rubbing my eyes. 'Crikey mate, it's cold,' I moaned. I think he might have been taken aback a little, on the familiarity of my speech. So he ignored me and went on. 'I have set up a wash stand for you: there is hot water, soap and a towel. Would you be so kind, sir, as to leave it on the bunk when you take your leave? I have arranged the same service for your other officers. I'll leave the lamp with you as well, sir, breakfast is in fifteen minutes. Is there anything else I can help you with?' 'No, thank you, steward,' I responded, peering at him through gummy eyes, 'You're a pal.' His eyes shot open. An officer calling him a pal that would be all around the baggie's mess like a bush fire. I wasn't thinking; too bloody early in the morning to think straight. He had this look on his face as he turned and walked out. I jumped out of bed, stripped and did the old basin bath trick; quickest wash I had for a while. I vigorously rubbed myself all over and felt a bit of warmth creeping into the joints.

I grabbed my pack and headed out to the privy. What an awful stink. Bugger me, the hygiene was not all that good, and no place to wash your hands after as well. No wonder more men went down with an illness than killed in action; I was surprised that more didn't get sick. I eventually found a bucket of water and washed my hands, then headed for the mess. As I passed the sergeants' mess, I called out to the bloke near the door. 'Is Sergeant Hohepa up?' 'Yes sir,' he answered. 'He went in about ten minutes ago.' 'Thank you. I'll catch up with him later.' I was first into the mess, and I wandered down through to Shane's room. Knocking lightly on the door, a big head came out from behind it. 'Oh, g'day Brill, everything okay?' 'Yeah, just checking to see if you are up. This is for Tui,' I said, passing him an extra toothbrush. 'It's new, she might enjoy using it instead of stringy flax.' 'Good-oh, ta,' he said. 'We'll be at breakfast in a jiffy.' As I was turning to go back to the mess, Sam and Stu came out of their room. 'G'day, Brill,' Sam smiled. Stu just nodded. 'I slept well, went out like a light. How about you?' he added. 'Yeah mate, I did too,' I answered. 'I think,' he continued, 'That I might have pissed that kid-of-an-ensign off last night.' 'Nah, mate,' I replied. 'No, he was alright, he really needed to be told. The problem with the army at this time is that the kids have had their commissions bought by the parents to get them out of their hair, and then they've been shipped out to the colonies. They really have no idea about men at all. I feel a bit sorry for him. The older one is handling it okay, but the younger kid … I would not like him to lead me out of a paper bag, let alone a shooting war. You cannot blame the men for not having any faith in their officers with blokes like that around. It's not their fault: it's the system. 'I have to tell you though, he was affected by what you said to him, I don't think he realised what he said was offensive, but now he knows better. You have to remember he's only about sixteen. You did a good job mate; I hope he does take it on board, he will be a better officer for it.' We left Stu to his ablutions. He was having breakfast in his room and keeping out of everyone's way; we didn't want him to be recognised.

We strode into the mess, both ensigns were standing at the table each holding a cup of tea. The lamps were lit: it was not as bright as we were used to, but enough to see who was around the table. 'Oh, good morning, sirs,' Ensign Smyth called out. 'Good morning,' we replied. I informed them that the Lieutenant, and his wife will be along presently. Ensign Robb placed his cup down on the table, walked over to Sam and looked up at him. I had to grin: the little bugger was shorter than me. Sam must have seemed like a giant to Robb, and he bent a little forward to make it easier to look the ensign in the eye. 'Lieutenant Mack,' he began, 'I most sincerely apologise to you, and all the officers for being such a cad last night. I didn't realise that I had offended you all with what I said. I would not have done that intentionally if I had known better. You were right when you said I have had a sheltered life: I have not mixed with men, or even young men of my own age, so I'm not too sure how I'm supposed to act. I think what you all said to me is the best advice anyone has given me. I have this opportunity to do well and sir, and I would like to think at the end of the day you will be proud of me. Please accept my apologies.' Sam grinned. 'Of course I do. Both of you blokes will make good officers, but if you don't try to understand the men you command, you will be a useless as a pimple on a bum.' They both looked a bit shocked at the language but returned the smile he gave them. 'Now,' Sam announced, 'I think we are all mates, so let's have breakfast.' He put out his hand, and the young bloke shook it. I could see the relief on his face. He thought he had really put himself in hot water, but now he was relieved it was behind him. 'I have never met officers like you,' he stated. 'You don't act like Officers yet you are all close. We are the opposite. All the senior men are quite remote, you can never relax around them like we can with you.' 'I do sympathise,' Sam responded. 'Just try your best, that's all anyone can do.' At this point, Shane came in with Tui. 'Morning all,' he said. 'We could both eat a horse.' 'Mate!' Sam exclaimed. 'That's my line.'

Tui was wearing a European top and skirt. She looked really good, with her black hair past her shoulders and her arms bare. The young blokes kept looking at her. She had a cape to put on once we left the building. I don't know where those clothes come from; It must have been in her kete. Funny though, you could see her toes sticking out every now and again from under the skirt. I don't think she likes shoes either. 'Good morning Lieutenant, Mrs. Lang. Please be seated, breakfast will be served in five minutes,' Robb advised. He came over to me and gave me an envelope. 'These are the chits, sirs, for accommodation and food on the road to Auckland, and in Auckland itself. There is also money there for you to get by on, until you see the paymaster at Albert Barracks. I think I have given you enough, sir. If you would be so kind, once you have sorted out your arrangements, to return the money to me. That will put our books back in order. I don't have to tell you what a stickler the army can be with records.' 'I cannot thank you enough, Ensign,' I replied. 'I will put in my report that both you men are a real asset to the army. You will have this money back on your books as soon as possible. You have made our time here very enjoyable.' 'Thank you, sir,' he answered. 'On the contrary, you have done more for me than I have done for you. You have opened my eyes.' He turned back to the table. 'Let's have breakfast.' Breakfast arrived on large platters, and small talk went on around the table as the sun slowly came shining into the room. It was time to leave. I got up from the table. 'Once again, Ensigns, our thanks for your hospitality; we hope that we have not caused you any inconvenience. That problem with your men, I'm sure will be dealt with in the proper manner.' 'I'll try to get the results of the outcome to you, sir,' he offered. 'Leave a message for me at the ANZ bank in Auckland or the post office – we don't know where we will be, we are at the governor's convenience.'

We walked outside, heaved our packs onto our backs, picked up our rifles and took a last look around before heading out the gate to where Bill and Stu were waiting.

We then took the road to Drury. For the first mile or so the bush had been cleared. The further we travelled north, the more thicker the Kanuka and Manuka trees grew. Along the road, the number of Totara, Rimu and Matai trees increased as we progressed. Eventually, they closed together over the track with just enough room for a wagon to travel through. The ensign told us to keep our eyes open as lately they had had a bit of trouble with marauding Māori. They were not affiliated with any tribe, just taking the opportunity of robbing and making a bloody nuisance of themselves, which wasn't helping the situation here at all. This was another excuse for the governor to invade the Waikato, though the English didn't need an excuse. With the bush closing in we become more vigilant. I turned to Sam, 'It's hard to believe that all this will be gone in thirty years or so. A real shame.' He frowned. 'If this was my time, I think I would have fought with the Māori: to lose this is a bloody crime.' Sam was a greenie, and this was his environment. We didn't see eye to eye on everything but to lose all this in thirty to fifty years is really sad. The bush in New Zealand was stripped out, we will never get it back to the way it was, but at least we have some really large national parks in our time. In fact, ten percent of our land is national park now. However, unless we can clear out the introduced species, which would allow us to rejuvenate our bird life and native bush, we are pushing shit uphill. Looking around, I thought the only natural bush to survive in this area is the Hunua Ranges. Back in our time, it is a Forest Park and a water reservoir for Auckland City.

A lot of wagons use this road so the track was quite firm. It's only a wagon-width wide, but it's good enough for us to walk in pairs. Sam didn't though, as he was up ahead on point, making sure there were no evil buggers out there who were preparing to jump out and give us a scare. I walked with Stu, then Bill, and at the rear came Shane and Tui. I took a squizz at them every now and again, but he was always looking at her and wasn't really concentrating on the job in hand. I was looking so what the hell; he was as happy as a bee in a clover patch. Tui was the same. She had pinned her skirt up to stop it dragging in the dirt and was hanging onto his arm, looking up at him with adoring eyes chatting away, completely unaware of her surroundings. Showing her legs was highly inappropriate in Victorian New Zealand, but at the moment she couldn't care less. So we walked with our own thoughts, and the bush got thicker. Stu was talking. 'I will be pleased to get home to my parents. I hope they recieved my letter, I sent before I was bundled off to fight for Queen and Country,' he said with a laugh. 'Next time Stu,' I answered. 'Get your grain from Wellington or Sydney, until all this blows over.'

At last, the bush thinned, and we saw Drury in the distance. We stopped for a conference and decided to skirt around the redoubt; we didn't need the hassle of questions at this time and honestly, I was getting a bit peeved with all the bullshit that went with it as well. We had spent five hours on the road, and we had not run into a living soul. 'Must be to do with the conference for the officers at Drury HQ,' Shane commented. 'Let's hope it stays like that.' I had a letter to give to HQ, but I did not want to be hassled again. So when push came to shove, I'd give it to the paymaster in Auckland and let him sort it out. Drury, looked very busy, lots of comings and goings; in fact, it was the most activity we'd seen all day, and I wanted no part of it. As we looked for a bypass track, a voice from our rear yelled out, 'Captain, Captain, hold on a minute, sir.' Oh shit! What now, I thought. He was from the redoubt we'd left this morning. Sweaty and dirty, he had been chasing us for over five hours. He must be a fit bloke. 'What's wrong?' I asked. 'Lieutenant Lang left his wallet in his room; we found it under the bed when the steward went to strip it. Ensign Robb asked me to catch you and hand it back.' Grunt came up and he thanked the private. 'Shit. That would have been interesting, my driver's licence, credit cards and all the stuff we have today is in there. They would have wondered what it was all about,' he whispered to me. 'Did anyone open it?' I asked. 'Oh no, sir, we would not do that, it's private. One more thing, sir, the ensign also gave me this envelope to give to you.' He handed it to me. 'You will understand when you opened it.' 'Thank you,' I replied putting it into my pocket. 'May I ask you a favour, private? We would like to make Auckland tonight but have got behind a bit. Would you deliver a letter to HQ for me? It would save us a lot of time.' 'Of course, sir,' he promised. 'Find your CO and give it to him. It's a report on what happened yesterday. It will keep him up to date.' 'That will be fine, sir, it will be an excuse to have some vittles before heading back. Though, I'd rather not be out at night on my lonesome.' 'Well, stay the night then private. Just mention it to your CO and say I suggested it. I'm sure he's a thoughtful man.' 'Thank you, sir, I'll do that.' I handed him my letter. He saluted then turned and walked off smartly in the direction of Drury, to mix with the thousands of men just waiting for something to happen, which would throw the country into bloodshed.

Sam wandered back to us. He informed us that he found a track that kept close to the inlet, and followed the shoreline, to cut back onto the main road some way ahead. From there, fingers crossed we might get a wagon ride north. The track brought us out a couple of kilometres west of Papakura; there was a lot more farmland here. The bush had been cleared to make room for the new farms. Black, burnt stumps of trees covered the paddocks, where a few years ago primeval forest once stood. The Papakura redoubt was in front of us, and the road swung left to pass it as it headed north. The northern and east-facing sides of the redoubt were heavily fortified, and earthworks had been thrown up to four metres with a ditch about two metres deep dug around the outside. They must be expecting an attack from the Hunua Ranges, because the rear of the redoubt was not as well fortified. Strange, I thought. Māori would probably attack from the least protected side. Maybe the army thought that with the bush being well cleared, they would have a better field of fire, as there was no cover but if the Māori ever attacked after dark, I reckon they might just stroll right in. In the distance, you could see the church with its steeple; it was fortified as well. The church was not taking any chances.

It was getting near to two pm and we had not stopped at all. I was getting hungry and surprisingly, Sam had not said a thing about food, though for all, I know he could be eating his shoe leather. 'We need to stop for lunch,' I said. Looking north, I could see the road curve and Sam had disappeared around it. He came back and waved, and as we walked up to meet him. He reported, 'There is a house up ahead. I think it might be a hotel, good place to stop for a bite.' 'Great minds think alike,' I agreed. As we got closer, we could make out a single-story long-house, with a half-veranda out the front. No gate or fence, just walk up and knock on the door. A shingle out the front said Manurewa Hotel. A large woman opened the door with a big smile with her sleeves rolled up. She had a dirty apron around her ample body and flour on her face. She stared at our camouflage gear. 'You're different,' she commented. 'What sort of clothes are those?' 'Oh, special gear for the bush, we are not really allowed to talk about it,' Sam warned. 'Army secrets,' she clucked. 'Oh spiff,' waving her arms in the air. 'Come in, come in, you all look hungry.' The room was large, but as usual, Sam, and Shane filled it. She looked up at them. 'I have never seen men the size of you, where are you from?' She had a soft Irish accent. 'We are from the deep south of New Zealand,' Shane replied. 'The colder it gets, the bigger we grow,' Sam laughed. She smiled. 'Well, young gentlemen and madam, we have beef stew cooked in brown ale, fresh-baked bread with new butter and a tankard of ale. Please take a seat; I will only be a few minutes.' As she started to walk out I quietly asked her if there was a privy. 'Yes, out the back with the canvas sides,' she replied. I wandered outside. You could smell it before you got within five metres of the place: it stank. I held my breath, had a pee and got out of there quickly. I found a barrel of water and washed my hands. While I was still alone, I took the envelope delivered by the private out of my pocket. I opened it and inside was another twenty-five pounds in coins and notes, along with a note.

My Dear Captain Kidder,

I've thought about it, and felt you could have delays en-route, and I don't think the ten pounds would be sufficient for six people. So with this extra, it should last you at least a month or longer. It would not be good form to have officers left in an embarrassing situation. Once you have arranged your own money, you could deliver it back personally or through the paymaster in Auckland.

Your obedient servant, E Robb Ensign 48th Foot.

Bugger me, he was a good lad. This would help us no end. I pocketed the money and went back inside in time to see the cook bringing out a very large cauldron of steaming beef stew. She ladled it into each person's bowl, generous to a fault. 'There is more where that come from,' she quipped. She was busy cutting bread and buttering the massive slices with thick creamy butter. The bread itself was a meal on its own. We filled our faces to bursting, and with the ale, I didn't want to move. However, move we had to, so reluctantly we lifted ourselves off the chairs with a bit of a groan. 'Right. How much do we own you? I asked. 'Let me think,' she said. 'Tuppence each for the stew, six ales at tuppence each, and a penny for the bread each: say, a half-crown.' I looked at the coins in my hand. I had three shillings in coin: that was three bob. My grandparents use to talk about the old coins, and 'bob' stuck in my head. I gave her the lot. 'Sir, you have given me too much.' 'No, you take it,' I offered. 'You fed us all well, we are content, and a bit more profit will do you no harm.' She smiled, 'Thank you sir. A lot of army fellows would try to beat the price down.' 'Thank you again,' we all chorused as we walked outside to restart our journey north.

It was now after three. 'I don't think we will make Auckland tonight,' I declared. 'We should make a beeline for Papatoetoe. I think it will be a couple more hours so with luck we'll be off the road before dark.' There was more activity heading north on this part of the Great South Road. We had started to stand out a bit, as our clothes were not in line with the rest of the population. We'll just have to bullshit our way through again; we were getting good at it. If I continued like this I would start to believe the crap was true myself. About an hour after leaving the hotel, we heard the plodding of a horse and cart coming from behind us. We stopped to let it catch us up, and as it came abreast the driver pulled up. He looked at us then Bill Hohepa with his sergeant's stripes. He was an army bloke, with a mate who had a rifle perched on his lap. 'Can we give you a lift, Sergeant?' he volunteered. 'We are going as far as Papatoetoe redoubt.' 'Ka pai,' Bill replied. Pointing at us, Bill did the introductions. 'This is Captain Kidder, Lieutenants Lang and Mack, Mr. McInnes, and Mrs. Lang.' 'Oh!' the driver mumbled. 'Sorry, sirs, I didn't recognise your uniforms. They are uniforms?' 'Yes,' I replied. 'Special ones for a special duty. Thank you private, we will certainly take up your offer. Jump aboard fellas; Tui, rest your weary bones.' We slowly got back to a plodding pace, which was quite enjoyable watching the road slip by a little bit quicker than if we had walked. 'Do you get much trouble here private?' I asked. 'A little bit, sir,' he agreed. 'We have had a few Māori shoot at us from the bush. The way things are going, I think there will be a lot more of that in the future. I was farming over the other side of the river, south of Tuakau. I had no problems at all with the tribe over there. I didn't own the land, but leased it off them; it worked out fine for everyone. I think that if we all did that, sir, we would not have to fight: no war and that will also be good for everyone.' He went on, 'My children did their schooling with the tribe at Pukekawa, and they are good friends with the Māori children. But, we had to move out … so I moved the family to Auckland. Then I got called up. We are just making ends meet: the pay in this man's army is not good, and prices in Auckland have risen to the point of stupidity. I hope it will all be over soon; I want to go back to my farm.' Well, that was an earful, I thought. If I had been a normal officer, I think he might have got an earful back for his outlandish views. 'Excuse me, Mrs. Lang, you look familiar. Did you live in Pukekawa?' He paused a minute, thinking, 'Hmm, family name Te Nana?' 'Yes,' she replied. 'I remember you now, your children went with our children to the mission school. I'm married to the Lieutenant here.' She smiled. 'I remember your name: Luke Robinson, you have lovely children and so is your wife Lily.' 'The Chief Piripi came and saw me, he told me to move out as there was going to be a shooting war, they did not want us to come to harm. When it's over, we will be welcomed back. So we took his advice and moved out for the duration. Your people are good people; I hope nothing happens to them.'

He went quiet, and the steady plodding of the horse lulled us into a trance, we were deep in our own thoughts until Luke announced, 'We are nearly there sirs.' The redoubt was a wee way up ahead; it looked like a large fortress. 'Private Robinson, are you going on up to Auckland tomorrow?' I inquired. 'Yes sir,' he answered. 'I might get to see my family. We will be leaving at day break, sir.' 'Will you be okay, err, happy with us hitching a ride with you?' 'Of course, sir. Sydney here,' he pointed to his offsider, 'is not good with that gun. If he had to fire it, there will be all noise and little else. With you with us, it'll give us much more firepower. We have had a few incidents between here and Otahuhu, so I would be pleased to have you with us, sir.' He was looking at our camouflaged guns. 'They seem smaller than ours,' he remarked. 'Yeah, very secret specials, private, so not a word about them,' was my answer. 'Well, sir, I cannot even make them out, so I can't say anything about them if I can't see them.' I thought to myself, why is this bloke only a private?

Oh, that's right, the class system. If he had joined a colonial militia, he might have been better offand he would have had more in common with the men, though he might not have had the option.

Slowly, the walls of the fortress became clearer. St Johns Redoubt was one of the largest forts with nearly two hundred men, including a small cavalry attachment. Arriving there as the sun went down was a blessing, I hoped; we won't be scrutinised as much, fingers crossed. The trouble was that every time we go somewhere, Sam and Shane are so bloody big they just stand out. Oh, there were large men around, but these two still dwarfed them. What we took for granted in our time, was different here: anyone over six feet was big. My blokes were six feet five or six inches and wide as well. Very hard to disguise. We could not change it, we'd just have to live with it. Having a Māori wife in New Zealand was common, so that was not an issue, although even if it was, I'm sure Shane would sort that out. Coming up closer, we got a better view as the bush had been cleared for over two kilometres for a clear field of fire. Like all earth redoubts it was formidable, but this was one of the biggest. It was the barrier to stop the tribes invading Auckland. They were pretty serious about no one getting through to the capital of the country. Looking at the place as we drove up towards the gates, I was thinking I would really have to hone my bullshitting technique. There could be a colonel at least in command of this establishment. I turned to the boys as we pulled up at the gate. 'Here we go again.'

CHAPTER FIFTEEN

The dray slowly pulled up to the main gate. The sentry came over smiling, and walked around to the driver. 'Hello, Robinson. I see you have picked up a few stragglers.' Luke grinned. 'Yes, Corporal, just an hour out of Manurewa. This is Captain Kidder,' he gestured to me. The smile wiped off the sentry's face as he turned to me. 'Sorry, sir,' he spluttered. 'I did not recognise your rank in those clothes.' He turned, yelling to his men, 'Officer at the front.' They all seem to jump up at once and presented arms. I heard Shane say. 'Impressive.' I jumped off the wagon and inspected the guard. Out of the corner of my eye, I saw Sam smirking. I kept telling myself play the part, or we could be in hot water. 'Very good, Corporal, duty well done, at ease.' He relaxed. 'Is the CO expecting you, sir?' he asked. 'If so, you will have a long wait: he has gone to the conference at General Cameron's HQ in Drury with all the senior officers.' My ears picked up, oh, that is so good, I thought. 'No he wasn't, but it is not that important. We're on our way to report to the Governor, and unfortunately we've missed the General as well. This is just a courtesy stop.' 'We,' I continued, waving my arm toward the others in the wagon, 'Are on special assignment. So, Corporal, I have to tell you and the men, you have not seen us. I will talk to your acting CO and explain the situation to him but please inform the guard, no loose wagging tongues.' 'You are not here, sir,' he said with a grin. 'I'll take you to the acting CO.' 'Who is the commanding officer, while your CO is away?' 'Lieutenant Frost, sir. I'll take you myself.' Turning to the driver, he directed, 'Drive through to HQ Robinson, I'll meet you there.' He turned to me 'I'll just have a talk with my men, sir, to explain what you said. You will have no loose tongues from my troops; you can count on that.'

We drove through the gates and slowly headed for the building to the left of the flag pole. The redoubt was quite sizable, about an acre, that's about half a hectare. It was formed as a large square, with thick earth walls surrounding the stables, along with tents. Getting towards the middle of winter these boys were going to be cold and wet. I was trying to remember if there was ever an attack on this redoubt … I didn't think so, but it was a bit hazy in my memory; I might be wrong. I did know that between here and Otahuhu, there were some problems, but I was not sure what. I didn't think it was anything too serious. We plodded on into the base and came to a halt outside the flap of a large tent which must be the base HQ. The corporal came running up as we jumped down from the dray. 'This way, sir.' There was nowhere to knock, so he yelled out, 'Knock, knock!' Sam muttered, 'I bet the next words are "come.' Sure enough, 'Come!' was barked from inside the tent. We all crammed in with a bit of an effort. The lieutenant looked up, saw us and jumped to his feet, buttoning his jacket up over a very ample stomach. He was about forty-ish. I thought that promotion must have passed him by, or he didn't have enough cash to buy the captaincy. He looked a real prick; I would hate to be under his command. 'Who are these people, Black?' he spat. 'Why are these people in my office?' His face was like thunder. Before Corporal, Black could say anything, I spoke up. 'Ah, Lieutenant Frost, good evening. I'm Captain Kidder; these men are Lieutenants Mack and Lang, Mrs. Lang, Mr. McInnes and Staff Sergeant Hohepa. We do apologise for disturbing your early evening, and arriving unannounced, but the matter is all out of our hands due to the circumstances.' I didn't let him get a word in. 'We are on special assignment for the governor. We need accommodation and vittles tonight and tomorrow morning, then Private Robinson will convey us on to Auckland where we will wait the governor's pleasure.' 'The governor, you say,' he muttered. 'My god this must be important.' 'Yes it is Lieutenant, but not a word. Though I need not give you that advice, a well-trained officer like yourself.' Shit, I saw his stomach go in a few inches as he pushed his shoulders back. I had a feeling that this was the highlight of his career, or as close as he would get to be in the limelight. 'Of course, sir,' he answered. 'What you are wearing is unusual attire, is it not; I don't recognise any regiment at all, and no rank insignia.' I leant forward and whispered close to his ear, 'Yes, well, it's all part of our little secret; we are trying them out in the bush, for the governor. The cloth comes from a very special Chinese formula which we are not allowed to talk about.' Shane got a coughing fit as he tried to suppress a laugh. 'So, not a word once again: all you see is top secret.' 'Thank you, sir, for keeping me informed. Now, accommodation; don't you worry about chits, this is too important to worry about that, and we don't want any record of you, so we will do things incognito? I'll make sure that we feed you together, away from prying eyes. We have a few tents right out the back away from everyone that should do nicely. You might have to sleep with the sergeant. I don't agree with being too familiar with the lower ranks, but needs must, isn't that right, sir?' 'You are right, of course,' I answered, we will get by. I cannot thank you enough Lieutenant, and when we see the governor, I will personally bring to his attention your wonderful help.' He actually smiled. 'That is very kind of you, sir. I will get this sorted right away.' He turned and yelled to the Corporal, 'Black, get me the quartermaster, then go back to your duties.' No please, thank you, kiss my bum, and this was him in a good mood. I would hate to be around him when he was in a shit.

Another corporal showed us our tents. We were given bedding, and supplied buckets for ablutions, which included a night bucket. They fed us and with, 'I'll wake you all an hour before dawn,' and left us to our own devices. I was pleased that we were out of the way; it was getting a bit hairy, bullshitting to all in sundry every minute of the day. It was tiring me out. Sleep came quickly.

It seemed that I just put my head down, and some bloody idiot started to trumpet. "Reveille." Bleary eyed, I staggered out and used the bucket. I wondered what the noise was, then I realised it was pouring with rain, my brain doesn't work that fast in the morning. The water was coming down in sheets. Good old North Island weather. Oh wonderful, I thought; we had about twenty kilometres to go and with the rain, you could bet your bottom dollar that the road would be a quagmire. In my head I was trying to work out how long it would normally take a walker to travel the twenty kilometres: I thought about five kilometres an hour, so say about four hours. We would be travelling by horse and cart, which just plods along, but the road was uphill, and it will be boggy, so that means a lot of pushing and shoving. It could take up to six hours; we were in for a really miserable day.

The steward delivered us breakfast, and we sat on our cots and ate. Sam was chewing his bread, saying, 'Let's see if we can con a tarp out of them for the back of the wagon. It will keep the worst of the rain off us.' 'Good idea,' I said. 'When the steward gets back I'll ask him. I'll have to see if he'll scrounge up a coat for Stu and Tui as well; all they have is what they stood up in.' When the steward returned I made my enquiries. 'Do you think you could get Lieutenant Frost to organise a canopy for the dray, and capes for Mr. McInnes and Mrs. Lang?' 'I'll drop these dishes off first, sir,' he replied, 'Then go over and talk to the quartermaster. I know him well; we should be able to accommodate you.' Off he went. True to form, when we left the tent, standing by the dray was Luke Robinson and his mate Sydney putting a cover over the wagon. Tui was given two coats, one which she passed to Stu. 'It was nice of the corporal to do this,' she commented. 'I'll drop them back when we return this way.'

Bugger that, I thought. I hope I never see the place again. Lieutenant Frost came out to say goodbye. 'Everything to your liking, sir?' He quivered, rain running down his face. He was looking quite uncomfortable in the wet weather and by the look on his face, he wished we would just bugger off so he could get back to his warm tent or office. 'Thank you, Lieutenant,' I replied. 'Your name will be mentioned to the right people. We cannot thank you enough for your kind hospitality.' Looking at the sky, I grunted, 'I think we need to be on the road, it looks as though it's going to be a tiresome day.' 'Be careful,' he yelled at me. The rain was getting heavier, and you had to yell over it to be heard. 'We've had a couple of incidents, nothing too major, just a few hotheads. The cavalry will be out today, even in this weather, patrolling the road north as far as Otahuhu, so you might come across them. They are all colonials,' he snorted with distaste on his face. 'Why they promote these people I will never know; they don't even think like us.' He gulped when he suddenly remembered that we were colonials as well. He steps back, saluted, then turned and walked away. 'What a miserable little sod,' Sam whispered. 'Let's get the hell out of here.' We all piled into the wagon underneath the tarp, and settled down for the first part of our trip.

Surprisingly, even with the miserable weather, we weren't too bad off under the tarp. The boys up front though – driving this cart, they would be getting a soaking. The rain was beating down like a drum on our heads, and we sang along with Sam on his harmonica. This might not be too bad a trip after all I thought

I don't know what happened next: it happened in a blur. We were plodding along at a good rate when the sound of musket fire brought us to our senses. We heard then felt the horse go down with a thump; a musket ball had hit him in the head, and he died in the traps. Soon we were tumbling over ourselves and there were sounds of shot's slapping into the wooden sides of the wagon. Sam flung himself out. 'Get under the wagon!' he yelled. 'Brill, we need your eyes.' I slipped out over the tailgate. There was a lull in the firing, which gave us time to get organised. Luke, who had been driving, had fallen off the wagon when the horse went down and was lying beside it. Dazed but okay, he had his rifle at the ready. His mate Sydney was spread-eagled in the mud on the road. Tui dashed over to check him. I heard her say sorry to Luke: Sydney was dead. She hurried back and slipped under the wagon with Shane. He took his bowie knife out and gave it to her. With her greenstone mere, I would not like to get close to her if I were the enemy; she looked formidable. Bill was all teeth: the warrior was coming out in him. 'What can you see, Brill?' Sam whispered. 'Nothing yet.' I was trying to focus through the deluge. The rain was concealing the country around us. I could make out a few tree stumps, which would be ideal for the attackers to hide behind, so clearly I would have to have my wits about me. Nothing happened for several minutes, just the sound of the rain all around us. I was crouching at the rear of the wagon, taking quick peaks when I saw some movement on the left. I yelled, 'Eleven o'clock, twenty metres.' The boys swung their rifles to that position and waited. Through their scopes, a blurred form appeared. Sam didn't waste any time as he shot at the blur. We heard the whack as the bullet hit a body and a grunt as it fell down. Another salvo of firing; it was like mozzies all around us, buzzing over our heads. I heard a 'shit', and I thought someone was hit so I yelled, 'Everyone okay?' 'Yeah fine,' Sam yelled back, 'Don't worry about us. Keep your eyes peeled, good work for the last one mate.' The rain eased and for a minute I had a clearer view. There must have been about a dozen tree stumps out there, enough protection for that many men. I saw movement again and yelled, 'five o'clock.' This was Shane's side. He had his rifle ready on his bipod and took aim through the sights. 'Got it,' he growled, and fired. Another sickening whack and then a whimper. Two down. I crouched low. 'I think they are going to do a rush, fellas.' 'Look to your front, Luke,' I yelled. 'Be ready mate.' The rain was back, and it was starting to get hazy again. Mud from the road was clinging to our clothes, the wheel ruts were full of water and we were standing and lying in the stuff. 'From one to five o'clock,' I roared out they were coming in with a rush. We slammed them with a volley of fire. I supported my rifle on the backboard of the wagon to give myself stability; the boys had the ground for that. I was watching man after man drop, until the last couple just turned and hobbled away. I counted six down, two that were shot before the rush, and it looked like two wounded. Ten men wasted for what? One Māori bloke had got quite close to the wagon, but Tui had lashed out with the bowie knife and cut his Achilles, and he took a bullet in his head as he fell. He was the closest; none of the others were anywhere near us. We waited a minute or two and Sam called out, 'Are you okay Luke, Bill?' 'Yes,' came the replies. All we could hear was the rain, then, in the distance, what sounded like horses. As they got closer, we could hear them properly: the cavalry had arrived. I came out from behind the wagon and pointed into the gloom. 'They went that way,' and off they went. Shane and Tui came out from under the wagon, then Sam followed by Wiremu; all covered in mud, wet, cold and a bit pissed off.

Sam stood guard, whilst we went and took a look at Sydney, poor bugger. He would not have known what hit him, clean through the head. We picked him up and place him gently in the rear of the wagon. Then Shane stood guard as I went with Sam to check out the Māori who had fallen. All were dead; their dress was an assortment of European clothes. Why had they attacked? Easy pickings, a lone wagon; who knows? I went out further until I got to the tree stumps with Sam following behind me. Suddenly, this big bloke came up with his patu and tried to hit me. He had been wounded, so the force was not in his arm, but he glanced my shoulder and it hurt like hell. I swung around, hit him with the butt of my gun, and he collapsed like a bag of old rags. 'Are you okay Brill?' Sam said in a worried voice, running up to me. 'Yeah, I'm fine, arm is a bit tingly; It must have hit a nerve. I think I'm going to have a bloody big bruise. Let's get this bastard to the wagon and find out what all this is all about.' Sam threw the bloke over his shoulder, and we both walked back to the wagon. Tui looked up as we arrived. 'Oh, you have one, is he alive?' 'Yep, he tried to take Brill's head off,' Sam grinned. 'Nearly did as well, but he lost out, Brill whacked him one. When he comes to, we can find out what this debacle is all about. We aren't going anywhere, we have no horse … it's going to be a long wet walk into Auckland.'

'Once we get to Otahuhu,' I suggested, 'We will freshen up and dry out, then I suppose we will have to make a report. Blast, if it's not one thing, it's another. Trying to be invisible is bloody hard to do.' 'We do our best mate. As you said, play what's in front of you,' Shane grinned. 'Your words not mine.' Tui was looking at the warrior I had smacked. 'He's from the Urewera area,' she said. 'See his warrior makings on his face, from either side of his nose down to his chin. They have aligned themselves with Rewi, but I don't think he would be stupid enough to let this happen. They have done this on their own initiative.' 'Oh great,' I exclaimed, 'Like the English boys at Pukekawa. Shit a brick, why don't they just talk before going out and killing people?' I checked the warrior out; the wound wasn't too bad, a nasty groove across his shoulder and one on his arm, and of course a lump on his head where I had slugged him. I got my stuff out and cleaned him up; he was still out like a light. 'Any of us hurt?' I asked, to which the others shook their heads. 'No one? Well, we were lucky.' I felt sorry for Sydney though. A bloody waste.

We heard the cavalry before we saw them. They came straight in, with white lather on the horses' flanks: they had been ridden hard. The officer climbed down. 'I'm Lieutenant Metcalfe,' he announced. 'Who is in command here?' 'I am,' I replied. 'Captain Kidder.' 'I wouldn't have recognised you, sir. No insignia, I have never seen uniforms like that; you must like mud.' He grinned. 'Did you find anything out there?' I asked. 'No, not a thing, we saw drag marks. It looked as though someone was helping a mate.' My ears pricked up at the word. 'Mate?' I said. 'Oh, sorry sir, we throw that word about.' 'I know what you mean. We do too,' I replied. 'Ah,' he replied, 'you are not English born either?' 'No, we are all Kiwis,' I grinned. 'I like that,' he commented. '"Kiwis," that rolls off the tongue.' He went on, 'Yes, well, we were all born here, we're a small group. I got the commission. We raced for it, I won, and the second rider ended up sergeant.' 'Most likely better than paying for a commission,' I laughed. 'Well, they do have a lot of officers whom I'd not like to go into battle with. We try to stick to ourselves, but we know that what we do is completely useless in the bush. It's alright here on the open fields and roads, but take a horse into the bush or even, god forbid, attack a pa, and we might as well throw rocks for all the good we would do.' 'How many men have you got?' I asked. 'Twelve, a real large fighting force, only half a dozen of us today.' he laughed. 'The worst thing about all this is that we know a lot of the Māori personally. We've worked with them, as we are from around here. They would not accept the governor's ultimatum and crossed the border, but they are our friends. It's alright for the army, after this is over, they all go back to England, but we live here, and will have to mend fences. We don't want to be in the firing line when the shooting starts. Hell, we don't want to kill friends. That is why we suggested a "colonial cavalry" not much use in bush warfare.' I noticed his uniform once he had taken off his cape and handed it to Tui. It wasn't the normal run-of-the-mill uniform I was used to seeing: it was all brown and blue, well, nearly black, even the webbing was brown not white. It exhibited a muted effect. This mob was a little bit ahead of their time. 'Good uniform,' I remarked. 'It blends in.' 'Just like yours,' he replied. 'What do you call yourselves?' I asked. 'Oh, the colonel got a bit unhappy when I gave him the name Auckland Rough Riders that's when he saw our uniforms I thought he was going to die, he was spluttering and swearing. I told him to take it or leave it as we paid for everything ourselves. They could use us or not, we'd be happy to go back to our own work. So here we are, not beholding to anyone. They cannot understand us at all, we are now under General Cameron's command to keep the Great South Road clear. This is really the first time we have struck an all-out attack, and we weren't here to help, sorry about that.' 'You did pretty well in the circumstances,' I offered. He noticed the wounded Māori in the back of the wagon. 'Oh he's from the Ureweras, I heard they had jumped in with old Rewi.' He looked at Tui. 'Do you recognise him at all?' 'No, never saw him before, he must be new here,' she responded. 'Though I have heard there are as many as five hundred coming up to help Rewi.' 'What did you do before the call up?' I asked. 'I farmed with my parents up north in Whangarei, and a small holding here in Mangere. Oh, by the way, my name is Abraham. Most call me Abe.' 'I'm Bob,' I said, then pointing at everyone, introduced, 'Shane, Sam; Tui there is Shane's wife; Wiremu, we call him Bill; Stu, and Luke here is the driver.' Poor old Stu and Luke had never been introduced by first name to officers before, so were a wee bit perplexed. 'Hello, fellows,' Abe greeted them. My sergeant is William, we call him Billy.' 'Someone in common, Bill,' I said to our Bill. 'Richard, Isaac, John and lastly there is Henry. Technically, Henry was not born here, but he's one of us. He's also a Wesley preacher, so he gets to be called padre.' Henry smiled. 'I'm the oldest so all my infinite knowledge is always in demand.' I thought it was strange to have a minister in the cavalry. He continued, 'Anyway, I'm more of a help here, saving souls at the hub of this conflict which we all know is coming. So, good friends, let us bury our enemies with dignity.' 'What about Sydney?' Luke asked. 'We will take him onto Otahuhu and bury him there with military honours,' the padre commented. 'He's left two boys, and his wife died last year. He has no family here in New Zealand, what's going to happen to his children? They are only three and five years old.' 'Don't worry Luke,' the padre sympathised, 'we will work something out. Where are his children now?' 'They have been living with an old couple in Auckland, in Grey Street. Sydney passed all his wages on to them. Now he's dead, I'm not sure what they will do with the children. I would take them, but I haven't got hardly enough money for my own family. I will, though, if that's the only way.' No social welfare here, I thought. 'We'll put our collective heads together and work on it,' I added.

We dug a communal grave for the Māori men who lost their lives. Gently we placed them into the ground, and the padre did his stuff. Then we filled in the grave and marked it, so we could pass the site on to Rewi's people if we got the chance. 'John, your horse was at the plough wasn't he?' Abe asked. 'Yep,' came the reply, 'He's pulled a wagon before.' 'Right, we will cut this dead one out and hook yours to the wagon. You can drive into Otahuhu in complete splendour.' Abe turned to me. 'I'll send a rider on now to explain what has happened. I'll ask that the CO to have a place for you all to dry out in and a hot bath ready. You don't want to be in those clothes all day, especially Tui. He smiled at her. 'Love your knife, by the way, though I don't want to get too close as it might be fatal.' She replied with a smile, 'You are too nice to stick like a pig. I only do it to horrible men.' He laughed. 'Thank goodness.'

While all this was going on, Billy had ridden off in the direction of Otahuhu to give them a heads-up on what had happened here. The dead horse was pulled away from the shaft; then John's horse was backed up, harnessed, and within thirty minutes, we were on our way. The road was just a sea of water with the wheel ruts waist deep. The wagon wheels slithered through the mud and many a time we needed the other horses to give us a pull when we got stuck. I turned to Sam. 'Hard to imagine this is the main road.' 'I cannot get over any of this, I'm still in a daze,' Sam stated. As we got closer to the Otahuhu redoubt, I got to thinking about the attack. I started to shake and vomited a few times over the side of the wagon. Shane slipped in beside me. 'A natural reaction mate,' he empathised, 'First time is always the hardest.' He handed me a canteen of water. 'Sip that until the shakes stop,' he suggested. 'You did well, Brill, for a flyboy.' It was nice of him to say so, but I felt like shit.

Passing the time, the padre rode up beside the wagon. 'How long have you been married, Shane?' he queried. 'Oh, quite a while,' Shane answered with a grin. 'A couple of days.'

'Oh well done,' the padre said, 'A nice church wedding?' Shane looked at him. 'Nah. A Māori wedding.' 'That's nice, but would you like me to make it official this side of the river?' he asked with a smile. 'I don't know,' Shane replied. 'I feel married, and so does Tui.' Turning to her, he asked, 'How do you feel about a church wedding?' She smiled. 'Oh, that would be nice, but I don't have anything to wear. It's same with you Shane, and your friends.' 'Oh, we can organise anything, if you would like to be married in the house of God. Think about it, and I'll see what I can do.' He pulled back on his reins and slid behind the wagon. As I listened to Shane and Tui debate over the situation, I got the feeling that this would be another hold up.

Slowly, the redoubt came into view. This was the main HQ for the southern route. There would likely be someone in command here higher than a lieutenant, which was a bit of a worry. I was pleased to have Abe with us as he would help give us credibility. They were used to him, with his speech being a bit different than the English. I had been listening to him, and his accent was not English as such a bit between ours and theirs, which showed me how our language started to evolve. We came up to the redoubt just as the rain stopped. It took nearly six hours to travel the five-to-six kilometres. We were wet, muddy and tired. I still felt queasy. An officer and a woman were waiting for us as we drove up to the gate. The officer stepped forward as we stopped. 'Good afternoon, I'm Lieutenant Bates, and this is my wife Elizabeth,' he said. 'I'm Captain Kidder,' I called in response. 'I have everything arranged for you to clean yourselves up. You have a married woman with you, I hear.' He turned to Tui. 'Madam, we have a bath ready for you; if you would like to follow my wife, she will attend to you. You have all had a time of it. We will get everyone cleaned up and fed, then we will talk.' 'Are you the commanding officer?' I asked. 'Yes,' was the reply, 'The colonel, with his senior officers, are in Drury.' Thank you Lord, I thought, this bloke seemed much more sensible than the idiot at Papatoetoe. 'Driver, will you take the wagon around to the doctor please; he will make the arrangements for the private who was killed in action. We will give him a military funeral tomorrow, if that suits you gentlemen?' Well, how the heck could we refuse? 'You all look a mess; come on, follow me. We have scrounged around the place and managed to find some baths. If you give the steward your clothes, he will wash them and dry them in the kitchen. Uniforms to fit you are going to be hard – you are big men, and I think we will have a problem, but if we can find something for you to get about in without being too undignified, we will do our best. I have arranged a hut for the married couple, and the rest can share the biggest one. No problems all sleeping all together?' he asked me. 'Not at all. What we have been through together, rank does not come into it.' 'Yes, I thought not. It's hard for us from England to get that in our minds, but we are learning,' he said with a smile. 'I'll ask Lieutenant Metcalfe to stay as well until we put it all down on paper. Now come along with me.' 'Another uneventful day,' Sam laughed, as we followed the officer to the bathroom and the bath, we were all looking forward to.

CHAPTER SIXTEEN

Washed, cleaned, and fed, we sat on our cots waiting for our clothes to arrive. Sam was talking. 'It's getting me down, all this, Brill. I wish I was heading home.' 'You and me both.' I confessed. We were talking quietly since Bill, and Stu were in the same room with us.

Bill turned to us. 'Stu and I were talking,' he remarked. 'We have come to the conclusion that wherever you fellows are from, it's not from here. We have listened to the unusual way you talk to each other, so unlike us, and the casualness of your comradeship is very different to what is typical here. Not only that, it's your equipment and everything about you. I know you've tried to hide this from us but most of your gear, neither of us has ever seen. The guns are peculiar, and the fire power was amazing. There is nothing like that here. Your medical skills we don't comprehend. The list goes on and on. I have seen you pointing a square shiny thing at people then you look at it and put it in your pocket. I saw Shane with a thing I cannot even describe, but it lit up when he pushed a button. I don't understand; it is so confusing. We know you have nothing to do with the army, yet you have been military I'm sure. Please don't get us wrong, we are with you all; it's just that things don't seem right about you, and it makes us hesitant.' Sam moaned, 'Oh shit.' Not another problem, I thought – we were doing so well but obviously not. We just come through a fire fight, so naturally they would have seen the rifles. What the hell are we going to say to them? I got up, 'Be back in a minute.' I went over to Shane's room. 'Can we talk mate?' I asked. I explained to him what Bill and Stu had said to us. 'Oh,' he said. 'I have been trying to answer those same questions to Tui. When you are living with someone, you cannot keep secrets, anyway, it's not a good way to start a marriage.' I looked at him, 'How the hell did she react, did she take any of it in?' He grinned. 'She thought I was porangi. She accepts we are from some distant place where things are different, as we dress and talk differently. She is curious about the stuff she has seen and in the end, I showed her the phone, but she has no understanding of it. She did like the light on it though, and wondered how the words got behind the glass. When I showed her a photo, she just could not believe it until I took her photo then showed it to her. She was like a kid in a lolly shop. Sorry mate, but I could not live a lie with her – it's not fair. So we are all sorted. She accepts that we are a bit different, and she can live with that. The boys might be another matter though. Do you want backing?' 'Nah mate, I'll be right. You go back to Tui; Sam and I will sort it. I'm pleased you've straightened it out with her. It's hard going every day, one lie after another. I'll catch you later.' I turned back to my room.

Back in the room, it was quiet. Sam looked up and said, 'What!' 'I spoke with Shane; Tui is okay about things.' Then I turned to Bill and Stu. 'Look fellas, yes it's true, we aren't from around here, and yes our gear is different,' I explained. 'We were not even supposed to be here, but this is where we turned up. It's hard to explain, but our people are more advanced in technology than you and there is a consensus that if we introduce things gradually, it will benefit everyone. We're not ready to show to the world yet, but we will in time; you just have to believe that we are all good people who are not doing anything wrong, we just want to go home. I hope that you can both accept this. Everything else you might have heard us talk about is the means to get us home. Like you, we have been diverted into things that we have no control over.' I went silent. 'I don't know about Bill, but I'm happy to call you my friends,' Stu confided. 'All you've done, or tried to do, since we met at the village has been praiseworthy. Moreover, you have been helping me, and are still trying to help me get home. You have made my life interesting, and I accept you all at your word.' He continued, this time looking at Sam. 'I have this empathy with you, which I don't understand,' he said with a weird look on his face. 'I feel you're family, but that's impossible. So rest assured I will stand by you all. You don't really have to explain if you don't want to, I will accept your privacy.' He thought for a moment; now with his attention on me. 'But I do have a real interest in the box thing though, in your pocket.' I nearly choked; they had even seen my camera as well. We were a bit too obvious, it's hard to keep things hidden when you are living close to someone. Bill jumped in. 'I'm interested in getting home as well, but I have to admit my interest is in your weapons – they are unbelievable. I accept that you are honourable men. You could have killed me back when I jumped out at you near Pukekawa, but you didn't, and since I have gotten to know you all, I have found you admirable. Even so, some of the things I have seen are so weird, I don't think there's a word for them. For instance, I saw a flat black thing like a mat, with a string attached to a box, which Sam left in the sun. I had a good look at it, but could not understand its purpose. One of many things I cannot make sense of. I respect you all, even though you are different. I like the way you talk and act, and your casualness. It feels like whanau and for me that is all that matters, though I still love your guns,' he said with a grin. Sam turned to me. 'I think we need to tell them something, mate, to put them out of their misery.' 'That's it,' said Stu, 'the way you just spoke to Bob no one talks like that to a superior officer or an employee. Even at home when I work for my father, around customers, I have to say Mr. McInnes.' 'Yeah, we are casual in our speech,' replied Sam, 'it's where we come from. All of our people talk a bit like this, and I must admit we do stand out. We try not to, but you can't change thirty-one years of the way we speak in a few days, and I don't want to anyway. Tell them something Brill; no one will believe them at all.'

'Okay, Stu, Bill; I'll show you this because you must have seen it anyway. Have you seen anyone take a photograph?' 'Yes,' they both nodded. Bill added, 'It's very expensive, and it takes a long time to set up. It's called holography. It's starting to become very popular. A few studios have opened in Auckland, they advertised with us. You have to stand still for quite a while, and then there's a flash of manganese. A few days later, your image is on a glass plate.' 'Well, this is the more modern version.' I took my camera out of my pocket and gave it to Bill. 'What's this?' he frowned. 'A camera, like the one you saw, but more compact.' 'I think you might be having a joke at my expense,' he blurted out. 'And mine,' said Stu. 'Right mate. Stu, sit next to Bill, now look at me.' I turned it on and the lens pushed out. Bill was startled, but Sam remarked, 'it's nothing to worry about fellas.' 'Smile,' I said. They did their best to grin, but both were very nervous. The flash went off, and Stu jumped off the bed as if he had a candle up his bum, in fright. 'That's usual, it's to give more light,' I explained. 'Remember the other camera you saw, Stu, it's a larger version of this, but this is much more compact.' I turned the camera around, found the picture then handed the camera to them. Both blokes stared in awe. 'That's me,' Stu stammered. 'And me,' whispered Bill, 'that's the cot we are sitting on, the nail on the wall for a cape. It's all here and in colour.' 'This,' I declared, 'is an ultra-modern camera which will be used by everyone in the future.' They both took turns looking at the picture, and eventually they handed it back. 'How?' they asked. I wasn't going to go into that. 'Just accept it, okay,' I replied. 'What a wonderful piece of machinery,' Stu commented. 'You could make big money with that.' 'A bit more complicated to print it off,' I told him, 'and all that machinery is back at our place.' 'Are you blokes all right with this?' I inquired. I took a couple more photos, and they soon started to relax to the point of pulling faces and laughing fit to burst when they saw the pictures. When I showed them how to use it, they were over the moon. 'It's so easy, and what about the eye glass?' Bill said. 'It's like a telescope.' 'My father,' Stu laughed, 'called it a bring-it-in-close apparatus, but this is so much better.' We played around for a while, it didn't take them long to get the hang of it, until there was a knock on the door.

I hid the camera away out of sight when a steward came in with our clothes. 'All done, sir,' he declared. 'We have ironed them as well of course. Unusual material, but they came up well. Yours took a bit longer, Mr. McInnes, Sergeant Hohepa; however, we got them all spic and span. The CO would like to see you in his office in an hour.' He turned and walked away, not waiting for a reply. We dressed, tidied ourselves up and an hour later we were in the CO's office, with the writer present to take down our statements. 'How is the Māori warrior?' I asked. 'He's fine,' the lieutenant answered. 'He came to, and the doctor reckoned you did a good job with him. There was nothing more he could do. We asked him why they attacked your wagon, and he mumbled something about it was utu for Pukekawa. Do you know what happened there?' Bugger, I thought. It had come back to bite us on our bums. So we went into the lengthy explanation. 'How bloody ironic,' the lieutenant exclaimed. 'You rescued them, and you were attacked for your troubles.' 'I don't think they knew it was us, most likely any wagon on the road would have been attacked, but I bet it was not sanctioned by Rewi; he will be livid,' I replied. 'What will happen to the Māori?' Shane inquired. 'We have a prison hulk off Rangitoto Island; we will send him there. Officially, he will be a prisoner of war, even though we aren't at war yet. Nevertheless, that's a technicality as we soon will be.' We gave our reports one by one, and the writer kept telling us to slow down. A couple of hours later, he finished. He read it back, and most of the facts were there; we signed it, and away he went, a happy wee chappie.

The CO announced the funeral for private Sydney Walters would be at the new Anglican Church, at ten am. 'We expect you to be there of course. A full military funeral. I have arranged for all messes to take a bucket around for donations for his children. We hope this will help.' He looked up at Shane. 'Also, it's been arranged, all right, Mr. Lang?' Shane nodded; I wondered what this was about. 'A wedding will take place for Shane and Tui, in the same church tomorrow at four pm. The bride has been given my wife's wedding frock, and Mrs. Bell, with the aid of my wife and a couple of Māori women, will decorate the church. Not the time of the year for flowers but they said they will get by. We couldn't find uniforms for you all, only you Captain Kidder; it will be up to you if you want to use it. Tomorrow will start in sorrow and finish in happiness. And that's it gentlemen, will see you all for dinner at six pm. I'll leave you now as you will have things to discuss.' We walked out of the office, and Shane said,

'Sorry to throw it at you fellas. By the time it was arranged I didn't have time to tell you both.' What could we say, it was Shane's decision and whatever he decided we were along for the ride. Shane turned to Sam. 'Would you be my best man? Don't be hurt Brill; Tui would like you to give her away.'

It was all getting a bit much for me. 'Give me a minute,' I stammered, as I walked behind a hut, placing my head on the wall, I felt like crying. Shane was real serious now. A church wedding, we seemed to be running around in circles. We should have been in Auckland by now with the paperwork to get us out of here. At this point in time, I would have taken a ship to go anywhere, but here, and for me, that was saying something. Are we going to get home? I was starting doubt it. Nevertheless, I had to be strong for my mates and support them whatever they decided to do. I felt a bit better as I returned to them. 'You okay, mate?' Shane asked, sounding worried. 'Yeah mate, I'm fine. It's just everything is piling up; I'm fine now. Of course, I will give Tui away, it will be an honour. I'll arrange it with her.' I took off the signet ring that my mum had given me; I always wore it. I handed it to Shane. 'You will need a wedding ring mate, use this,' I suggested. He took the ring and studied it; he knew how much it meant to me. Then he grabbed me and gave me a manly hug. 'I'll never forget you mate, ever.' At this moment, his words went over my head, figuratively and quite literally. Sam reached over. 'I'll look after that,' he quipped, taking the ring from Shane, 'as it is my job now. And no sleeping with the bride before your wedding night; all the fun is after, remember.' Shane grinned, 'I'm at your mercy.' 'Well, I'm off to see the bride,' I informed them, 'but Shane, you are banned from her room, you sleep with us tonight. If you are feeling randy, you can have anyone except me.' I turned away with a 'bugger off' in my ear.

Tui was in her room working on the wedding dress. 'Hi,' I called out, after I knocked and poked my head around the door. 'I'm your dad.' 'Come in, Bob.' She jumped up and hugged me. 'I wasn't sure if you would agree,' she whispered quietly. 'Of course, I would do anything for you both. It's a no brainer. You are both my favourite people. So we need to be at the church at five past four; a bride must always be a bit late. I'll arrange for a wagon to take us there. Can I help with anything else?' 'Well, sit down Bob, and you tell me the little things about Shane,' she smiled. Oh, I thought, this might take a bit of time. 'Okay Tui, I'll try to give you an insight into him as much as I can, this could take a while.' I told her about Shane, just changing the circumstances. His parents and sisters. His idiosyncrasies and in general what a great bloke she had. His love of children, and the medals he won from saving them. His love of music and how he was a clever engineer. 'You've got a good bloke, Tui. Sam and I hope you are going to be very happy.' She hugged me again. I could get used to this, but it was a sister hug, and I had to look at her now as my mate's wife. 'Thank you Bob, I don't have any family that I know of, so it's a blessing that you and Sam will be part of my family.' 'Okay,' I said, 'I think that is sorted. Does your wedding dress fit you all right?' 'Oh yes,' she said, her eyes bright with happiness. 'Mrs. Bates has some lovely small flowers for my hair. I will even wear shoes for him tomorrow. 'Okay, I'll catch up with you at dinner tonight, and I'll pick you up at three thirty tomorrow afternoon.' 'No,' she replied, 'I'll have dinner with Mr. and Mrs. Bates. I can't see Shane until I'm married.' 'But what about the funeral?' I burst out. 'I went and saw Luke and explained it to him. He is quite happy that I cared sufficiently to see him, and that was good enough for him. So I will see you tomorrow afternoon.' She kissed me on the cheek. 'Good evening Bob, I'll see you then.'

I left her room and wandered over to the mess since it was close enough to six pm. The Reverend Henry Talbert, aka Padre, was there talking to Shane. The Padre turned as I approached them. 'Ah, you might be wondering what a private is doing in the officers' mess. My profession seems to change things for me and confuses all in sundry. I was just telling Shane that the Reverend Gould, who is the minister at the new Anglican Church, has granted me permission to marry Shane and Tui. He is a splendid fellow; he will play the organ. So all is well. I will see all parties at four pm with the Lord's blessing. I expect you will all be at Sydney's funeral? The Reverend Gould is the officiating minister. I'll head back to my mess for dinner now, and I will see you all tomorrow. Good evening, gentlemen.'

We had dinner at six pm, then the officers of the mess had a few drinks to celebrate Shane's forthcoming wedding. It went on a tad longer than expected. Good old Shane had a couple too many, and we carried him back to our room. I had managed to find an extra mattress for me to sleep on the floor as the groom had my bed. He was pissed, telling everyone how bloody good both Sam, and I were, best mates in the world, and he would fly anywhere to be with us. Fly, I heard one bloke say, he must be drunk. The night passed with Shane snoring and making slobbering noises. I didn't get that much sleep, with everything happening to us. It was par for the course. We woke to the six am reveille. Shane was looking like a bag of shit so we left him to sleep off the wonderful night he had. The rest of us went to the mess for breakfast. Afterwards, I wandered down to the stables. The farrier sergeant was there so I spoke to him about a wagon which I could use to take the future Mrs. Lang to the church at three thirty. He thought for a minute. 'Well, I have the Colonels plus-four trap,' he suggested. 'I'm sure he would let me use that for a wedding.' 'I'm the father of the bride,' I grinned. 'Is it big enough for both of us?' 'Plenty of room, sir, it's just the ticket. You and the bride can sit in the back; there's ample space for you both. Have you anyone who will drive you?' I didn't think of that. 'I'll get back to you. I can rely on this plus-four, will it be ready?' 'Don't worry about a thing, sir; I'll get a few of the lads to give it a good clean, and we have a lovely horse for you. So everything will be arranged.' 'Thanks Sarge,' I said. He looked at me with a sloppy grin. I don't think anyone had called him Sarge in his life before. I caught up with Stu. 'Mate, what's your driving like?' 'Oh, fine why?' he queried. 'Would you be the driver for the bride's party this afternoon?' 'Of course, it would be a privilege,' he said. So that was sorted. 'Please be at Mrs. Bates house at three thirty; I'll meet you there. If you go and see the farrier sergeant, he will give you all the information. Thanks Stu, you are a pal.' 'No Bob, thank you for asking,' he replied.

Shane eventually rose with a head full of crabs and a mouth like an Arab's armpit. Red-eyed and dozy, we went to work to make him presentable for the funeral and his wedding. It took effort, but
he slowly started to become a real person. With umpteen cups of coffee later, and some food in him, he was presentable before the funeral started. As we walked down to the church, the men marched beside the coffin on the wagon with the Union Jack draped over it. Sydney was to be the first person to be buried at the new church. I bet though, he would not have wished for that honour. Everyone was in their best uniforms with lots of braid, swords, rifles; the whole nine yards. We were in our camouflage uniforms, looking smart. Since we had no hats, the lieutenant had supplied us with forage caps from the quartermaster. Each hat had '58th of Foot' on the badge. As our hair was so thick, they sat perilously on our heads with the band under our chins to hold them on. The funeral guard walked the coffin into the church and placed it near the altar, and Reverend Gould began. 'If man believeth in me he will not die.' The service went

on for an hour until finally the pallbearers came forward, lifted the coffin onto their shoulders and walked outside to the rear of the church. A guard of honour was there to farewell Sydney as they gently lowered him into the ground. The Reverend Gould finished off, 'ashes to ashes, dust to dust,' and the guards fired three rounds into the air, ordered arms, then turned away to walk at a faster beat than whence they came. So it was over; another mound of earth which could have been avoided.

We walked back to the redoubt in silence. When we reached the barracks, Shane remarked, 'It brings it home fellas, to make as much of your life as possible. Don't let an opportunity go by. Sydney was our age, the poor bugger, and now there are two kids without a dad and no one to look after them. We will have to do something about that.' Stu was thoughtful. 'I have been thinking,' he said slowly, 'I have an elder sister Mary.' Sam looked at him; I could see his mind working furiously. 'She was married at eighteen, and now she's twenty-one and still without children. She wants them so much. I caught her crying over it we are very close, and she confides in me. Her husband Thomas is a real nice man, but sometimes these things happen. I hope I'm not embarrassing you.' 'No, not at all, carry on,' Shane urged. 'Well, if these two boys haven't got a family, I'm positive my sister would take them with open arms. She'd be only too happy to. I know her; if she ever found out I knew of these children, she would be so mad at me if I didn't do something about it. What say I suggest it to Luke and see what he says, it would be a load off his mind?' Sam turned to him. 'Stu, you are a real good bloke mate. It is an honour to know that the gene pool is so good.' Stu was a little taken aback. 'What do you mean, Sam?' 'Oh, just nice to know there are people like you who care.' 'I think,' Stu replied, looking at us all, 'it's only a small thing, compared to what you all have done for me.' 'Nah, not really' I replied, 'children are for life.'

Stu went off to find Luke while we had lunch and then started to prepare for the second part of the day. The weather was fine and about sixteen degrees; it was a good day for a wedding. I left the boys to sort out their part of the proceedings and went over to see Tui. Mrs. Bates came to the door, and I asked if there was anything I could do. 'Yes, I have these primroses for your buttonholes. Would you deliver them for me please? I still have so much to do. Will we see you back here at three thirty?' 'Of course,' I affirmed. 'I'll see you all this afternoon. If there's anything I can do or any problems I'll be in the mess,' I added. Stu was checking out the plus-four and the horse. He saw me and gave a wave, yelling, 'Everything is good.' I took the primroses to Sam. 'Thanks, Brill. I'll fix lover-boy up with one and keep one each aside for Stu and Bill.' Bill was pleased, he would be in the front pew on the bride's side of the family. Well, they were both from the same tribe after all. The afternoon dragged on until three fifteen, when I went to find Stu. 'Ready mate?' I asked. He was sitting with his flower in his buttonhole. The jacket had been given to him by someone in the mess, his shoes were cleaned and there was a crease in his pants: he was ready.

'Stu, would you be able to use my camera?' I inquired as I handed it to him. 'I want to get photos of this day.' 'Do you mean it?' he asked breathlessly. 'Yeah, mate. But don't look too obvious; people will start asking questions. We didn't do too well hiding it from you, did we?' 'Yes, I understand.' 'Do you remember how to use it?' I checked. 'Oh yes, I do,' he exclaimed. 'Okay mate, do your best. Any problems, come and find me.'I looked presentable as I could be with what I had to work with. I had my primrose pinned to my shirt, but I didn't wear the hat; it looked bloody silly. My beard was long, as was my hair, but that was normal for this time period. We drove over to the Bates residence. I went inside and there she was, looking a picture. White frock, pulled tight into her waist, showing her ample bust; soft veil, pink primroses in a bouquet and petals in her hair; she looked really beautiful. I hope Stu gets some good photos for Shane and also for his parents. 'You look stunning,' I blurted out. 'My God! Tui, you really are beautiful.' She gave me a big smile. 'Thank you father,' she giggled. 'Okay, daughter,' I said. 'Let's get you to the altar.' Mrs. Bates helped her into the trap through the rear door; I went in beside her. 'Are you coming with us, Elizabeth?' I asked. 'No, but just go slow and let me get in front.' So we gave her five minutes, and then slowly moved forward. There was quite a guard of honour for her, as all the men waved when we passed, grinning and saying good luck as we plodded towards the church.

Five past four, good, we made the sod wait. 'Are you ready to be married again Tui?' I asked. She looked at me with a tear in her eye. 'He has my soul.' 'Then let's put him out of his misery.' We came to the door, and the wedding march started to play. The church was full with officers, men of all ranks and a sprinkling of women filling the pews. The Kiwi cavalry boys with Lieutenant Metcalfe were all there also. Everyone stood as we walked down the aisle. The Reverend Henry Talbert was there in all his regalia; it was quite an experience. Shane stood tall with Sam beside him, both big men, looking at Tui. I saw Shane's eyes light up: he was so much in love with this woman. She smiled as he took her hand and turned to face the padre. And so it started. 'We are gathered here today in this house of God, to bring together this man and this woman ....' Within half an hour they were married. As they walked out of the church the men threw rice at them, then they climbed onto the trap and slowly headed back to base for a wedding breakfast that the Bates had organised. We slogged up the low hill behind them. 'Well,' exclaimed Sam, 'it's done, this time properly. I feel as though I have lost an arm.' 'Same here,' I muttered. It didn't seem like a celebration to Sam and I, more like a wake. That was unfair I thought; Shane was happy, what right have we got to interfere with that? We went into the mess. Stu was off to the left, taking photos as much as he could without being noticed. I arranged all of us together so Stu could get us all in the photo. I was hoping he was doing it okay. I'd check later. The CO claimed the meal was ready, so we moved into the dining room. All the senior officers were there, including the padre. I had to smile, a private eating in the officers' mess. The Reverend Gould and his wife

Fanny were also included. We sat at the top table when the best man started his speech. I watched Sam, hoping he wouldn't sail too close to the wind. Thankfully, and of course, he didn't. He kept it to the now, how we all were thrilled Shane found the right woman, and so on and so forth. Through all this, I ate, drank and got pissed, until I was in no state to walk back to our room. Stu, with the help of Sam, guided me to my vacant cot at the same time that Shane was back in the marriage bed. 'Oh shit, Sam,' I blubbered. 'He's not going to come home.' In my drunken stupor, I remembered the words, 'I'll never forget you, mate.' I put my head on the pillow and swallowed: shit, shit, shit! The bastard was going to stay, he knew, she knew, and now I knew. I was completely devastated, and Sam would be too.

CHAPTER SEVENTEEN

I opened my eyes to another morning but this time, I woke with a feeling of loss. I felt like giving it all away, to hide under the blankets, so everything would pass me by. Sam was lying in the cot next to me; he was awake and looking at me. 'You look lost, mate,' he said. He could be perceptive when he wanted to be. 'Yeah, I feel completely out of my depth. I think I'm going to pieces. It's just getting too much for me Mac,' I said. I hardly ever shortened his last name, so he knew when I used it, I was not one hundred percent. 'I know what you mean. He's not coming home with us, is he?' Sam groaned. 'No mate, I don't think so. I don't even know if he knows. I don't blame him – we both know that he will be hurting, thinking of his family, but he has a new life, a new purpose. Tui is great for him; it's just that we will not be part of it, and I think that's why I feel this way.' 'Well,' Sam replied, 'we need to make the best of the time we have with him.' Bloody hell. He had thought it through, and I was acting like a baby. 'You are mostly right, mate,' I sighed, 'but it's everything. mum, dad and my sister; Grunt's parents and the girls; your folks and your sister; how will we explain it?' 'Well, Brill, we just need to concentrate on getting home. I would rather worry about all that when we're home, don't you think? Why don't you get up and head down to the church and have a think about it in I'll go organise the wagon for today's wee trip north.'

I got up, washed, dressed and wandered down to the church. Fresh-cut timber permeated throughout the place as I went inside and sat down on the back pew. The smell of primroses lingered from the wedding. I was still feeling lost, and even though Sam had done his best, I was depressed. I was just staring into space, hoping for divine intervention when I heard footsteps coming from the vestry, and the Reverend Gould walked in. 'I'm so sorry to disturb you,' he said. 'Please stay, I will only be a minute.' Then he noticed my face. 'Is everything all right, Captain Kidder?' 'I'm a wee bit mixed up, Padre,' I said. 'I seem to have this wall around me that I can't climb over. I'll be fine, you carry on.' He came over and sat down. 'Losing a friend sometimes does that to us, even though they're not lost as such it just feels that way. You and the lieutenant are close, it's a natural reaction. We need to be happy for others as well as ourselves and live our lives to the best of our abilities. Each day is special, God has made it that way. These obstacles are like hurdles: once we realise we can go around them, we know we have learnt that lesson and can move on. This is your hurdle. Wish him all the very best and let him go, you will find it's simple when you do that. You haven't lost him; he's in your mind and your heart forever. When you have accepted that, concentrate on your next hurdle. That's life, we can't change it, we just have to try to make the best of it and all you can do, is your best. Make peace with yourself, and this is the best place to do that. Remember, we are here only for a short while so make every day count. Once the warmth of Christ has penetrated your soul, your life, that you love, will return. I must go; here endeth the lesson.' He smiled. 'I'll leave you to your thoughts.' I sat there thinking about what he said, and what Sam said, and came to realise that we had done the best that we could. If Shane wasn't coming home, Sam and I would still do our damnedest to get back to our time. We would let his family know that he was happy. If I can't get home, then I would make a life here, I will just have to accept that. I was aware of a weight coming off my shoulders and felt a bit better. I would always have memories of Shane; bugger me, he's not dead, he's still my mate. I'm being selfish of them both by only thinking of myself. I got up, said a thank you to the ceiling and walked out the door. My steps were lighter as I headed back to the redoubt.

The wagon was in the yard, and they were all waiting for me, including the Kiwi cavalry, who I was told would escort us as far as Newmarket before returning and heading south again. 'You okay, mate?' Sam asked. 'Yeah, I am now, thanks Sam, you're a good mate.' Lieutenant Bates arrived as I climb up into the wagon. 'Safe travels, Captain,' he said as he handed me a purse. 'This is the money we raised for Private Walters children. Twenty-two pounds.' I was astonished, that was a year's wage for a servant. 'Use it how you see fit for the children. God speed, I hope to see you all again,' he added. 'Thanks for the hospitality, and everything else,' I replied. It appeared that everyone had said their thanks to the Bates family for the wedding. 'Off you go, Private,' he ordered Luke. We plodded out of the gates heading towards the metropolis of Auckland.

We settled down for the trip. It was about fifteen kilometres that would usually be around three hours, but the road was just mud so it could take double that time. We should be there around two pm at the latest if all went well. It's hard to believe in a car in our century, on a normal day with the traffic flowing, the trip would only take fifteen minutes. We yarned amongst ourselves and the cavalry boys as we travelled. The road was so bad, in a few places, we had to use the cavalry horses to get us out of the bog. Even though it was only a gradual climb to Newmarket, it was slow going. Finally, Lieutenant Metcalfe pulled in. 'This is where we leave you. Safe travels to you all, I hope to see you all again. Good luck, Shane and Tui, on your new life together.' They waved goodbye then swung around and headed south back to Papatoetoe. We passed Mangere Mount, One Tree Hill, and both Mounts Eden and Hobson. There were more houses popping up all over the place now, as we slowly plodded into Newmarket. This area was feeding Auckland City, which had a population of 14,000 army personnel and 12,000 civilians. Auckland was a garrison town, and food was a priority, hence the market gardens in Newmarket. We turned onto Khyber Pass Road, which climbed up to meet Symonds Street. It was a real slog getting to the top, so we all jumped off to allow the horse to pull the wagon without the weight of us on board. At the top of the hill was Grafton Heights, a well-off suburb of Auckland, with large houses that dotted the hillside. Partington's Windmill stood out above all the houses dominating the area. We followed Karangahape Road on the ridge, heading towards upper Queen Street. From here, we could see all the area out west to Dedwood that was starting to be developed. Traps and wagons of all descriptions filled the roads. Looking out towards the harbour, ships of all shapes and sizes were anchored. Behind them Rangitoto Island, a familiar landmark in our time, was protecting the Waitamata harbour. There were fifty-two islands out in the Gulf; it would become a boaties paradise in the future. The settlers already celebrated Auckland Anniversary Day every year on the 29th of January with a sailing regatta. Boating is the lifeblood of the young colonial city.

We turned into Queen Street, Auckland's main street, which was all mud and grit. From here we could see right down to Queens Wharf, one and a half kilometres away, at the far end of the road. 'There must be ships heading down to Dunedin from Auckland all the time,' I said, looking at one large four-master in the roads. 'You'll be home soon Stu.' We gazed at the buildings as we slid and sloshed our way down the street, passing Grey Street on our left. There were some clapboard shop fronts with only a few well-serviced shops, and I noticed wooden footpaths in front of some of them further down the street. 'Here's the Union Hotel,' announced Bill, hoping his army uniform was concealing his identity from the population in general. Anyway, if anyone recognised him, in his uniform, he should be accepted. 'It's not far from our printing shop; see, over there.' He was pointing to a store on the other side of the road, about six doors down with 'Wattle Printers Books and Musical Instruments, painted on the front. He continued, 'If you look further down, on the right you will also see a men's clothing shop, Woodward's. For you, Tui, also on the right is a draper and millinery shop run by a Miss Milne, and woman's clothes can be bought a little further on at Mary Jane's Emporium.'

The hotel was a two-story brick affair, with a balcony on the second floor overlooking the street. Its entrance was grand as it had double doors made of copper, with a lion's coat of arms in the middle which split when the doors were opened. It was modern for its day. We all traipsed inside after thanking Luke for all his help. He was to meet up with Stu later to organise what to do with the children, and to book their passage after I got the discharge papers for him. I walked up to where there was an arrogant-looking bloke standing behind the counter pretending to be doing something important. I stood there for a few minutes, but he didn't look up. I then leant across the counter and roared, 'Are you the manager?' He looked up and leered at me. 'No, I'm not,' he stated. 'Well,' I fumed, 'get him now. I don't want to be pissed around with a prick like you. We are on the governor's business. I don't think he would be too happy when I report to him that I was shagged about by a little upstart.' Shane grinned. 'Do you reckon he got any of that?' he muttered. I turned back to the desk clerk and added, 'Did I make myself clear?' 'The governor, sorry sir, how can I help?' he bleated. It's amazing, name dropping in whatever century, and they are all over you like a rash. 'We want three rooms to sleep six people, for at least a week; It could be more, depending on how long the governor will be away. Can you do that?' 'Will those two Māori with you be staying as well?' he blurted out. I sensed Shane next to me as he leant across the counter and hoisted the clerk out over the top. He was squawking like a stuck pig. 'Put me down, put me down,' he cried. Lucky for us, the place was quiet with no one around. Shane stuck his face right up to the clerk's and asserted, 'This woman is my wife, you piece of shit. If you don't apologise, I will hit you until you're a blob of meat.' The clerk's face went purple. 'So sorry, so sorry,' he panted. 'I do apologise madam, I really do.' Shane lifted him up and placed him back on the other side of the counter. 'Apology accepted,' he growled. Sam was trying to keep a straight face and Stu conveniently walked outside to get some air. Bill was so happy. 'I love it when you get porangi, Shane,' he grinned. 'Three rooms, yes, yes, all on the top floor,' the clerk spluttered, his cheek twitching nervously. 'They even have their own privy,' he whispers to me, going red in the face. 'Is there a bathroom?' I asked. 'Yes, we will give you a key to the room at the end of the hall. We need about an hour to get the water to you so it has to be booked. That can be done by ringing the bell in your room, and a porter will come up and take the details down. Dinner is at six thirty in the main dining room. The smoking room is on the left, there is a lady's lounge on the right and a pool room at the back.' 'Do you accept army chits?' 'Oh yes sir, that will be fine,' he answered. I wondered how much extra he would put on the bill, but I didn't really care. We still had our money in our pocket. 'All the shops now accept army chits,' he said 'even the millinery.' 'Are we too late for lunch?' I asked. 'Yes, it has finished, but I'll see the kitchen and get something up to your rooms in half an hour.' He was falling all over himself to set things right. I handed him a chit. 'All the expenses will go onto this chit for our time here, including our beverages; we will need to open a tab in the bar as well.' 'Who shall I put it under?' he asked. 'Captain Kidder,' I replied. He rang a bell, and a young boy of about thirteen came running up to us. 'Take these people up to rooms five, six and seven,' he ordered. 'We will carry our own gear, you show us the way,' Sam smiled at the boy. We followed him up the stairs to the second floor. He opened doors as we went, waving everyone inside their rooms and explaining the amenities. We thanked him when we arrived, and I gave him a shilling. 'Oh, sir, that's too much; the desk clerk will take most of that.' 'Oh will he? Well, you can tell him you got this,' I handed him a penny, 'he can have that, and you keep your shilling.' 'What do you get a week?' I added. 'Three and six pence plus food and lodging, sir. One day off a week, from six in the morning till six at night.' I had just given him a third of his weekly wages. 'Don't tell him, okay,' ah, I forgot myself again, 'all right, I mean.' 'Thank you, sir. That's most kind. I'll be back with your food, and I will set this table up for tiffin in here, that is, if it is agreeable with you?' 'That will be appreciated, thank you,' I answered, as he closed the door behind him.

I looked around the room. There were two single beds, a wardrobe, a wash basin with a pitcher of water, a table and some lounge chairs which looked like camel hair and hard as hell. However, there were gas lights on the walls, adding a modern touch. Doors opened out onto the balcony, and you could see down Queen Street to the wharf. Sam jumped on the bed. 'Hard right enough, but we have slept on harder,' he said. The privy was in a closet. It had a wooden seat with a bucket underneath so it was, for all intents and purposes, an inside dunny. We had a laugh, then Shane & Tui came in. 'Very fancy,' she said with admiration as she looked around, 'I have never been in such a fine establishment.' 'This will have cost the army a dollar or two,' Shane chimed in. 'Seven pounds a week for us all, including meals.' 'Is that expensive?' Sam asked. 'A bit, but we have over thirty-five pounds to see us through, and this is on a chit, so no cost to us at all. We need to get ourselves organised after lunch. We can't rest on our laurels; we have to have a plan. Bill and Stu wandered in. 'Ready for something to eat, fellas?' I asked. 'Yes,' they replied. 'It should be here soon. In the meantime, Bill, how should we go about getting this printing done?' 'Well, I thought I would discreetly go around to the back of my old firm and inform my boss, I'm here with the army; that will put him at ease. I will mention I need to do some printing, and if it's alright with him, I'll do it when he is not in production. We need to get him out of the building. I'm just not sure how yet,' he added with a frown. 'Hmm, I suggest we take a wander down to get the lay of the land.' I responded. 'But clothes are also a priority, we need to blend in. So what say after lunch Shane and Tui head down to the women's wear shop and get some stuff that Tui needs? After looking around at the printers, Sam and I will meet you in the menswear shop. You stay in your uniform, Bill, that's your cover; but anything you need, just ask. Stu, you can sort out yourself and the kids' clothes.' 'Kids?' he inquired. 'Sorry, children, we call them kids.' 'Don't worry about my clothes,' he offered, 'my bag is at the shipping office. Mr. James, who we buy our grain from, is looking after it for me, so I'm fine.' I handed the money for the children to Stu and said, 'You better look after this. You might need it to help the old folks out.' 'Well that's not a bad plan on such short notice.'

There was a knock at the door, and the young bell boy arrived with the food and a couple of maids who followed him into the room. He put everything on the table, including a big pot of hot tea; there were ham sandwiches, cakes, and fruit, enough for everyone. 'Thank you, what's your name?' asked Shane. 'Albert, sir,' the boy replied. 'Okay Al, thanks mate, we will catch up later.' The poor kid had never had his name shortened or had anyone being so familiar. He was taken aback but he smiled saying, 'Just ring the bell when you've finished, and one of the maids will be up to clear it away.' We all sat down in the chairs and on the beds to eat, and enjoyed our lunch together. It had been a while since it was only the six of us. 'Bill,' I started, 'I'll need to write out something for you to print. When you see your old boss, could you ask for some writing paper for me?' 'Yes, I know where we store it; I'll pick up a few sheets for you.' So we ate and yarned until the plates were empty. 'Tui, I bet you will love shopping, have you done much before?' I chatted. 'No, I've never been shopping in my life, so it's going to be quite thrilling for me. I do need a few things though, and Shane will need a jacket, shirt and trousers.' I handed Shane a chit. 'Fill your boots, mate.' 'Thanks,' he replied, 'I'll open an account at the men's shop too, but if you beat us to it, you open it. I'll take another chit just in case.' So I handed him an extra one; I could see that Tui was really excited. I continued, 'Sam and I will take a look at the print shop and meet you at the store.' Stu cut in, 'I'm off to see Luke, to arrange the children's board for the rest of our time here, and to see what else I can do.' 'Okay, we'll meet back here at six pm for a debrief,' I replied.

Bill opened the door to leave after Stu, then turned and said with a grin, 'fingers crossed that my boss will be okay with me.' He continued out the door. He was starting to pick up the way we speak. Shane and Tui strolled off to the women's clothes shop, and Sam and I took a slow walk over to Wattle's front entrance to have a good look around. It was quite a large shop, with large front windows full of musical instruments. Books lined one side of the shop, with a counter down the other. There was a door at the back which led, I thought, to the printing press. Sam and I took a quick look around. 'Oh shit Brill, look, a piano.' He was in like Flynn. He plonked himself down and stroked the ivory keyboard. 'These are real,' he said, 'not imitation. That should make me angry about it, but this is so beautiful.' He started to play some music from Beethoven, and then went on to Bach and Mozart; he was in a world of his own. People going past stopped, coming in to listen. He was good, very good, in fact. It was then that I had this gem of an idea about getting Mr. Wattle away from this place through the day. I thought, what say we give a concert for the troops and civilians alike. I had noticed a hall on the corner of Grey and Queen Street. We could just ask for a coin donation, and at the same time promote Mr. Wattle's shop. My thoughts were interrupted when Sam stopped playing. By this time, there were about twenty folks in the shop and everyone was clapping. 'Well done old fellow, well done,' a man from the crowd said. Sam looked up and smiled at his audience. He whispered to me, 'as long as they don't throw their underwear at me, I'll be happy.' Mr. Wattle came out from behind the counter. 'That was absolutely splendid, my dear chap,' he said. 'My name is Edward Wattle. I'm the proprietor of this establishment.' 'Hi Eddy, my name is Sam; this is Bob.' He was taken aback. 'I'm not sure if it's proper to call me by that name.' 'Well Eddy,' Sam grinned, 'my full name is Samuel, I prefer to be called just Sam. This is the way we speak where we come from; there is no disrespect intended, it's the complete opposite. Anyone who has instruments like this is a gentleman. This shop is amazing.' He was walking around looking at what they had. 'Woo, Brill, he has a guitar.' 'Yes,' Edward boasted, 'it's a bit different than the mandolin. It's just in from the Americas.' 'Can I have a play?' Sam asked. 'You can play it?' Edward sounded shocked. 'Yes, I can, and so can my mate.' He picked it up. 'It's a bit heavier than the modern ones.' He listened as he strummed. 'Yep, she's pretty close to being in tune,' he asserted and started to play some classical tunes. The crowd were spellbound. Sam was good at the guitar too; he was wasting his time in the bush. He handed the instrument to me to have a go. One of my favourites for the guitar was 'White Rabbit', so I played that. Oh, it felt good to lose yourself in the music; I had forgotten what it was like. The people clapped after I had finished. 'Never, never have I heard music being played like that on a string instrument. Wonderful, wonderful,' a man from the audience said with enthusiasm. A few other people came up to us both and thanked us. 'Do you sell sheet music?' I asked Edward. 'Yes, they're in the draw.' 'How much?' 'Threepence.' 'Hang on, folks,' I called out to the people in the shop. 'You can buy this music, and practice at home.' I sold six copies. Old Eddy was so pleased. I was hoping to make a good impression, as I was about to make a suggestion to him. I turned to him and said 'Edward, I have an idea. What would your thoughts be on us putting on a concert, on Saturday afternoon, to promote you and your music shop? Sam, he will play the piano, and also the harmonica. I will play the guitar, our friend Shane can play the mandolin and guitar, and his wife can sing. You could ask for a donation, so the people who can never afford to hear this type of music would come. We'll fill that hall, up the road; we'll do it for nothing, and you'll get all the credit. We could play for a couple of hours, say from two until four pm. If you print off a leaflet to tell everyone about the concert, you could add an advertisement for special deals for your shop at the same time. Then, the only cost will be the hall.' He was listening intently. 'I could get that hall for a pound.' He was thinking out loud. 'Donations? We would get the riff-raff.' 'You might, but they will be riff-raff that will enjoy music and later, when they have money for a few special things in life, your place will be the place to come. I'm sure the Auckland Carol Society would back you and give you a hand to set up. Though we could do that for you as well. We'll come up with a programme and will introduce some different types of music and songs. It will be an enlightening experience for the mums, dads and the kids.' He looked at me. 'What?' 'Oh. The mothers, fathers and children,' I corrected. 'They could bring their whole family for a special afternoon out.' 'There is merit in what you say. I heard your friend, he would be welcome on any stage in the world; he plays exquisitely, and yourself. I have never heard a string instrument being played like that, it was wonderful,' he enthused. 'Well, you should hear my other mate's wife sing, and he's also a wonderful musician and singer,' I claimed. 'What's today, Wednesday, can I get it organised by Saturday? There's a bit to do, but this town needs a bit of music – it's all, war, war, war, and I would like to lose myself for a few hours. I'll do it. Mr., err!' 'Just call me Bob,' I said. 'Alright, everything is topsy-turvy today, but Bob it is. I'll get onto it right away. Will you need to practice?' 'Yes, maybe tonight and tomorrow, would that be alright? If we can get the piano up to the hall on Friday we could practice up there in the afternoon,'

I said. 'Splendid, splendid, I'm looking forward to it. A shame the governor is not here, but donations, I don't think he would come, mingling with the great unwashed,' he laughed. 'We will make it an afternoon to remember.' Sam and I shook Edward's hand. 'We will be here tonight about eight, is that alright? We won't keep the children up will we?' 'It will be educational if you did, and no, the children are right down at the back of the house. I'm sure my wife would love to watch though; would that be acceptable with you all?' he added. 'Of course, there is no need to ask.' My mind drifted elsewhere, thinking we needed to get a programme sorted for Tui so she could learn a few songs before Saturday afternoon.

Sam and I left feeling quite good about how it all went. 'That will give Bill a free reign on Saturday to do the printing,' I chatted to Sam as we walked down the street. 'That was good thinking Brill, now we just have to work out what we should sing. Even if we do some 70s and 80s music, I don't think people will remember, over the years. A two-hour show, it will just be a myth in 150 years.' 'Even if it's not,' I replied, 'what does it matter? Who the hell cares; I certainly don't. We should enjoy ourselves as tomorrow we might not be here. That's how I'm starting to feel,' I added, sounding disheartened. 'Bugger me, Brill. You have changed your tune, mate,' Sam burst out. 'Yeah, I'm fed up having to second guess every move we make, worrying about how our actions might affect the future. We can't go on like this forever. I'm going to live my life Sam if this is it, then we should enjoy it. Let's pop in and see what's on offer at the menswear shop, and we better tell Shane and Tui what they are in for. That should be interesting.' I was feeling better now, that I'd gotten that off my chest.

We ran into Shane and Tui as we were about to step into Woodward's. She had a few parcels in her hands and looked as happy as a sand boy. We told them about our suggestion for a concert and asked them what they thought. Tui was all excited. 'What a treat to sing for an audience, I haven't sung in front of anyone before. The last time I sang was in the congregation in the chapel.' 'So I will take that as a yes, you don't mind singing then,' I laughed. Shane and Sam had to bend slightly to get through the door of the shop. Tui and I slipped in just fine. I said to Sam, 'Bet they don't have anything to fit you.' A young man came out from behind the counter and stood and stared at us. 'Oh my, you are going to be hard to fit,' he stated. 'We would like shirts, trousers and jackets for all of us,' I declared. 'Are you all army? I don't recognise that material at all,' he said, having a closer look. 'Yes, we are and yes, its army issue. A special product for bush warfare.' 'Yes, I can see how that would blend in,' he commented. 'We might have something for you, sir,' he said, looking at me, 'but your friends are big men; we will not have anything for them.' 'Well, what can we do?' I asked. 'I'll ask my father, be back in a minute.' He went out the back, and we stood looking at material. It looked as though there was nothing 'off the peg'; everything was handmade. Meanwhile, senior Mr. Woodward arrived. He took one look at us, picked up his tape measure and started to take measurements. He tut-tutted as he worked and ended up measuring us all. 'How many do you want?' he asked. 'One of each,' I said. I turned to the others, 'Is that okay, fellas?' Tui piped up. 'You will each need an extra shirt.' 'Hmm! I can do three trousers and jackets with three shirts, and I'll throw in another shirt each for six pounds, or with an extra pair of trousers for seven pounds, and I will still give you each an extra shirt. All up, with a small discount, say eighteen pounds for everything.' We looked at each other, and I replied, 'Okay, we will go with the seven pound order, that's twenty-one pounds, and we are grateful for the discount.' 'Cash or chit?' he asked. 'Oh, chit, the army took our clothes months ago. They could be back in England by now.' He smiled. 'That is fine, good sirs. I'll have them all ready for you tomorrow at this time.' My mouth opened like a goldfish. 'Are you sure?' 'Of course, we will work all night on them; we have done it before and no doubt, we will do it again. Good service always comes at a cost to oneself.' I handed him the chit. 'Thank you, sir, we will see you tomorrow.' A thought occurred to me. 'Oh,' I said, before turning to leave, 'do you like music sir?' 'I have not the time,' he conceded, 'but my son here is quite keen.' 'Well, give him two hours off on Saturday, between two and four. We are putting on a concert at the cost of a donation. Mr Wattle is organising it. Your son would enjoy it. Well, all your family would, if you let the boy go.' I did my best to entice him, but I could see the miserable shit was going to say no. 'Add another pound to the bill, our treat,' I pushed. 'Well, in that case, of course. It might make him appreciate the finer things of life; I might even let my daughters go as well.' With that, he turned and walked to the back of the shop, yelling, 'Wife, we need all the girls here now.' The young bloke murmured, 'Thank you, my sisters and I will look forward to the concert.'

CHAPTER EIGHTEEN

Back in our hotel room we all relaxed. It was a relief that we had our accommodation arranged, our clothes sorted and Mr. Wattle organised to be out of the way for Saturday afternoon. 'I need to write the Official Letters for Bill to print, is there anything else?' I questioned. 'Yeah, the letters for the bank to send to our parents,' replied Shane. 'Oh, thanks mate, I forgot about them. We also need to sit down and work on some songs for the concert and to teach Tui the words.' It was three-thirty pm, with only three hours or so until dinner. 'I'll need to get the letters written. If we organise most things today that would give us the rest of the week to practice, and it will also keep us away from prying eyes.' Sam was humming away to a song in his head. 'I have a few things in mind for Tui to sing, leave all that to Shane and me. You concentrate on the other stuff.'

At that point, Bill rushed in. 'Mr. Wattle accepted that I was in the army only temporarily and was really pleased to see me. We even talked about the press shop up north. He only left me when Sam – I think it was Sam, started to play. I was out the back and heard everything. Now, I have the paper you wanted. I checked to see if the official forms are there, and they are, so I moved a dozen, to be on the safe side, into the printing area where only I will find them. I think I got enough: one each for you three, one each for the paymaster, one for Stu for a discharge and five spare just in case." 'I think,' I said, 'we will use an extra one for Stu. He deserves his pay for the inconvenience the army put him through. Let the army pay. Once he has that, he can then book his passage and be on his way home.' 'Okay,' agreed Bill, 'eight pages. That will take about an hour-thirty to two hours to print. We have a bit of leeway, and Mr. Wattle won't come home straight after the concert; he will stay for a natter if you could hold him up for a bit, say an extra half an hour or so. Yes, that should be enough,' he said, running through all the logistics in his head. 'Good, that should be fine,' I agreed. So the plan was set. Now to write out the fake orders.

We separated; Shane and Tui used their bedroom with Sam, to work on the music for the Concert, and Bill and I continued on in my room. I took the blank paper from him and said, 'How do we go about it? If it doesn't sound right, you'll let me know I hope, as you have done this before.' 'Like all important documents, they are all flowery, so we'll start with that.' Bill replied. I thought for a moment and then started to write. *'I, Lieutenant Governor Sir George Grey, representative of our Majesty Queen Victoria, defender of the faith and Supreme Commander of all Armed Services in the Colony of New Zealand ....'* I read it out to him and asked, 'How does this sound?' 'Well done Bob. This is looking good,' he said leaning over my shoulder. I continued to write, *'By the grace of God, I entrust my authority to the holder of this document, the said Captain Kidder. Under this order, he has the full cooperation of all commanders of both army and navy to travel throughout this colony without hindrance in the service of the said Supreme Commander. This mission is of the utmost secrecy. This order is in place until I, the Supreme Commander, rescind this document. Dated by my hand, in Auckland, New Zealand, on the 9th day of May in the year of our Lord 1863.'* 'Will that pass inspection?' I asked as I put down the pen and blotted the ink. Bill looked it over. 'Yes, that's good. I have a few squiggles to add to make it pretty, but what you have written down is just fine, Bob.' 'Thanks, Bill,' I said, 'so all you have to do is change the names on the other documents to Shane and Sam.' 'That is easy,' he asserted. 'Now, you want a document for the paymaster. It doesn't have to be as flowery this time.' He carried on, 'Something like, *'I, Governor Sir George Grey, authorise moneys to the said Officer, Captain Kidder, at one pound per day, back dated from the 12th day of March 1863. To be paid through any paymaster in the colony, or a draft from the ANZ bank wherever they are situated.'* Then I'll date it the same date, and I have his signature to should finish it off.' 'Great, that will be the same for the other blokes as well,' I stated. 'Now Stewart's document will be similar, with the normal introduction,' he continued. "I Sir George Grey,' then, 'I authorise the said Private Stewart McInnes to be discharged from today's date.' Once again, I have his signature. That will do it nicely. You don't need anything else; as long as the governor's name is on the order they will all fall over themselves doing his bidding. It won't take long to print it out. I'll set up one press for the main order, and then all I have to do is change the names. Same with the pay order. Lastly, we have a small press on which I can run the discharge papers for Stu. All in all, a good afternoon's work.' Writing with a quill is hard work so it took time, but I eventually finished. With the pages blotted I gave them all to Bill to scrutinise. He sat down and went over them carefully. When he looked up, he grinned. 'They will do Bob, a grand piece of writing. I will take these down to the shop and put them in my hidey hole. We don't want them to be found.' I was buggered; it took a lot out of me, shit I'm getting soft.

Bill went out, closing the door quietly. I thought I should really start this letter to mum and dad, something I wasn't looking forward to. It was like a final goodbye, and I wasn't in the mood. However, I needed to do it, I had suggested it, and I wanted to be the first to have it down on paper so my mates would follow. Once again, I picked up the pen and started writing our long, drawn-out story to date. Adding at the end, *If you are reading this, then I never made it home; I tried, and failed.* I then told them I loved them all, and that I'm giving my house and everything I own to Sasha to either sell or keep, whatever she wanted. I also wrote a will to make it all official. I would get the boys to put their signatures on it later. That, I think, was all that needed to be done. Well, I thought that's all I had to do, I had no idea really. I sat back on the chair and reread what I wrote. If I got this in the mail, I'd think the sender was bonkers, but I had to try. There was a knock on the door. 'You in, mate?' called Shane. They didn't wait for the affirmative; Shane, Tui and Sam just bowled in with grins on their faces. 'I think,' Sam divulged, 'we have the music sussed for Saturday, so we wanted to keep you up with the play.' Thank god, I thought, I needed something else to think about, besides the letter I had just written to the folks. 'Okay, what are we going to do?' I asked. 'Well, we thought maestro, here could play about fifteen minutes of his favourite classics,' Shane said. 'We have four songs that Tui can sing with us in the background. Remember, there is no sound system, so we will have to sing louder than normal; we think Tui has the voice range.' She smiled up at him as he continued, 'That will take, say, thirty minutes. Sam can do another fifteen minutes from the stage shows, like Hello Dolly and My Fair Lady; he has a repertoire as long as your arm and most likely can carry on for hours if we let him. You can do a few of your favourites with the guitar, then I can do mine. We can break for five minutes to wet the whistle. Then repeat it again, for another forty minutes or so to keep it going for over two hours. Tui has never done this before, so we will keep an eye on her until she feels comfortable. If she falters, we'll be there to jump in.' 'That's carefully thought out,' I responded. 'Okay, what sort of music have you decided on?' 'Middle of the road,' replied Sam, 'we can't have our modern stuff mate, it might not go down well, but classics are always good.' I rolled my eyes; he grinned. 'For me, anyway. Some country stuff like John Denver, where they can get their feet tapping, and a bit of, say, Roger Whitaker, for some of those dreamy songs of England and Karen Carpenter. Tui has the voice. A few of the other classics like songs from Mary Poppins and the Lion King. Shane and I will get Tui ready, you just have to practice on your guitar, though you haven't lost your touch, mate.' 'Yeah, well, I have a few tunes in mind so if that's okay; Shane can jump in with me.' We threw the ideas around, until we had a semblance of a concert. Now all we had to do was get Tui up to scratch. Thinking about it, even if she made a complete balls of it, the audience would be none the wiser since the music we were playing for them was a hundred or so years in the future. As long as it kept Edward Wattle out of the printing shop, I would have done handstands on the stage.

'First practice after dinner,' Shane announced. Sam went over to the table with Tui to write down a list of the songs we intended to play and to write out the music with the lyrics for her. Hell, he had a good memory for this sort of thing: he would play it once and remember it forever. Tui picked up his first sheet of music and started to memorise the words. While they were doing this I talked in general about the letter I had written to my folks and also the will. Shane picked it up and took a look. 'That's good mate, I better get it done also.' He didn't give me any inclination that he was going to stay, maybe he still hadn't thought about it, but Tui must be wondering about us all now as we were talking freely in front of her, as though she had come through the mist with us. 'Would you mind if I copy what you wrote mate?' he said. 'I also need to tell my folks, I'm married and that's going to be very hard to put in writing. mum and dad are going to be so disappointed for not being at the wedding.' 'When we get back mate, you can have another one,' I replied. 'Yeah,' was all he said, but he never looked me in the eye. He just got stuck into writing his letter. Then Sam took an interest and said, 'I'd better do it also mate.' They sat side by side writing their story, occasionally looking at my letter. It took an hour or so before they sat back. 'Heck, it looks awful,' Shane sighed, 'ink blots everywhere.' 'It's down Grunt, that's the main thing,' I said as I leant over to look at his letter. They folded their letters and asked 'What now?' 'Oh, will you blokes witness my will?' I replied. 'And I'll witness yours.' 'Do you think we should do the same, Brill?' Sam asked. 'Yeah I do mate. If we don't get back, it's best to have everything sorted for the families.' So they sat down and made out their wills, with all of us witnessing each other's. 'Tomorrow we will take them to the bank and put them into a deposit box. Let's hope they turn up in 2014. It's a long shot, but it's worth a go.' 'There's another way also,' I proposed. 'If none of us get home, the least we can do is leave a paper trail. Make sure that throughout our lives, we vote, get an occasional mention in a paper, register any marriages,' I looked at Shane, 'but it needs to be done under our own names, not the ones we have now. That way, maybe someone in our family might, just might, find us and realise we were happy with a good life, that we had children, a house, and good jobs.' 'That's a bloody great idea,' Sam observed, 'good thinking, mate.' 'I agree with

Sam, mate,' Shane nodded. ' I turned to Tui. You've been very quiet; 'Do you understand what we are talking about? I hope you don't think you have married a fruit cake.' 'I don't understand what you mean about a fruit cake, but Shane has explained in his own way what has happened. I know you are all quite different from the people around here, I accept that, and if Shane wants to go home, I will be with him. I can fit into wherever he goes and I think that goes for him also.' 'Good,' I said, 'I don't want you to think we are nuts.' 'No, I don't think that, different is the word I would use. However, from the future, I can't believe that, it's inconceivable to me, but I trust Shane explicitly.'

There was a knock, and Stu stuck his head around the door. 'Hello gentleman, Tui, sorry to be away so long, I had a lot to organise,' he apologised as he came into the room. 'They are really nice children, and to tell them their father was not coming home was tragic. I don't think the youngest got any of it, but the eldest boy understood. At five, going on six, he remembered his mother dying last year, so he has taken it hard. I sat them down and explained what we will do for them. I told them about the wonderful lady in Dunedin who has no children of her own, that would be excited for them to live with her and her husband. I mentioned that she was my sister, and if they would like to go to school to learn how to read and write, my sister would arrange all that for them too. At least, I left them with some hope for the future.' 'The older couple they are staying with at the moment are very good, not like the impression I got from Luke. They have been looking after the children to the best of their abilities. When Luke had explained what happened to Sydney, they were genuinely upset. They are not well off, so I gave them five pounds towards food, clothes and shoes for the children and a couple of suitcases. I said any leftover was theirs. They were very thankful. I'll leave another couple of quid when we leave as well.' 'Then I walked down to the grain merchant; he had my bag. All my family's grain is to be loaded on the Te Awa tonight and will sail with the tide on Friday morning. I have decided to take the children and go home with it. The merchant has already booked a cabin for me and the children. Now, I know I haven't got my discharge papers, but would it be in your power to post them to me or hand them to our agent at the grain depot, and he will send them down? I know it's inconvenient, but I don't want to stay a moment longer than necessary. I'm not interested in the money from the army. If I'm due any monetary allowance, please give it to the older couple who have been looking after the children; they deserve it.' Well, you could have knocked me over with a feather, quiet waters run deep. Sam was the same; it had to run in his family. 'Stu,' Sam stated, 'that's great, you have done so much with taking responsibility for the kids. We will make sure that the papers will be passed on to the grain merchant for you.' 'Thank you all,' Stu replied. 'You have been like family to me, even though we have only known each other a short time, it seems like we have known each other forever.' He looked at us. 'If you ever get down my way, I will expect you to look my family up. You are all very welcome, anytime, and if you need anything, anything at all, look for our name, McInnes. We are going to be the biggest store on the gold fields. I didn't tell you before, but that's where I'm heading. My father thinks, and rightly so, there is money to be made there, not digging, mind you, but providing a store. That is where we will make our name. So if ever you are down our way, head out to the diggings in central, you will find me. My house is your house.' Bugger me, this kid had his head screwed on. Shane momentarily had this look on his face, which I couldn't fathom, but it was gone in a blink.

There was another knock at the door. 'Good evening whanau,' Bill acknowledged as he came into the room. 'I was asked to let you all know that it's twenty past six o'clock, and dinner is in ten minutes. Shall we meet for a quick drink and upset the natives?' He laughed. I love this bloke. 'Yeah, let's do that,' agreed Sam. 'Can a woman go into the bar?' I thought about it. 'Well, if she is not allowed, we will take our drinks into the woman's lounge.' True enough, that's what happened. 'What's that woman doing trying to come into our bar,' some bugger yelled. 'Out, out, this is a man's place.' 'This is bullshit,' Shane growled as he went up and scowled at the loudmouthed bloke. Everyone went quiet, and it stayed that way until Sam ordered our drinks, and we waltzed into the ladies' lounge. The bar returned to its noisy self as we shut the door behind us. The ladies' lounge was empty; it was better for us as we wouldn't draw attention to ourselves, and we could have a drink in peace. Dumb really, to think like that in a way, since come Saturday afternoon every bloody man, woman and dog will see us singing for our supper on stage in the hall. The bell rang but we took our time finishing our drinks, and then went through into the dining room. It was nearly full. We got some wonderful stares with people whispering as Tui and Shane walked past to sit at our table, which was stuck right in the far corner away from everyone. We did appreciate the kind gesture. The waitress came through with the menu, curtsied and delivered it into the hands of Shane. In her eyes, he looked most likely to be the boss, as he was the biggest of us, all and the most impressive; with his marvellous beard, he was too good looking for words. He smiled at her, saying thank you and passed the menu around. We all took our turn deciding what to have. The choice wasn't too bad, so we ordered roast duck with veg, rhubarb pie and a cheese board. If you had money in early New Zealand, you could live quite well. Even so, like today, there were more haves -nots than haves. We enjoyed our dinner, good company with good friends. Looking at the time on the grandfather clock in the dining hall, we saw it was coming up to quarter to eight. Shane announced, 'Time for the first rehearsal; on a full stomach, I think it might be a flop.'

We waddled out of the hotel and down the street to the Wattle's shop. Edward was there waiting with his wife. 'Oh,' she gushed to Tui, 'I'm really quite excited, this will be so much fun. I'm thrilled that Mr. Wattle agreed to this venture, and I'm sure it will be positive for the business.' 'I'm excited as well,' replied Tui, 'I have never done anything like this. Sam has been organising the songs for me to sing; I haven't got that much time to learn them, but I will do my best, and the men are so supportive.' Sam got us all together with a few of the songs on his list, and with a lot of work we had made a wee bit of progress after a couple of hours. 'A lot more work is needed,' he suggested, 'but we should be right on the day.' Mrs. Wattle brought out tea and cake for us at the end of the practice. Babbling how wonderful it was, and how much she loved the way we played and that the music was so invigorating. 'Tui has a wonderful voice,' she enthused, going on to say that she was so looking forward to seeing us on stage on Saturday, as were the children. Edward was as happy as a sand boy. He told us that the piano would be shifted to the hall tomorrow, and that we had full use of the place till we had finished. This was good news; we still had a few things to do, and then we could hide away until the show. By Sunday, or most likely Monday, we would be able to get out of town, on a fast camel, anything really that walked quicker than us. I was ready to go home. We thanked them for their courtesy and headed back to the hotel. Bill was waiting for us in our room. 'Did it go okay?' he asked. 'Yep, it did,' replied Sam. 'We need a lot more practice for Tui to get the words down pat, and then she'll be right.' Bill looked at him, scratching his head. 'I didn't understand a lot of that, but I gather it will be okay.' 'Yep,' Sam grinned.

'I won't be with you all, from Sunday,' Bill told us. 'There was a scow in today from Houhora. I spoke to its captain, a Captain Subritzky, and I have a ride back home with him. He leaves Sunday morning. I'll be working my passage, but I have done that before. I've seen Mr. Wattle and told him I'll be going home; he was pleased to have me go north. He was worried that with me being in the army, his newspaper up north would never get off the ground. Now I will be able to open the press office in Russell and start up their brand-new evening newspaper, The Far North Evening News. Sunday is the tenth of May, and all the press machinery should arrive up there by the end of the month. We have the building, and we hope to have it up and running within a month of setting up. So that's the end of June; I'm looking forward to it.' 'Heck Bill. We are sure going to miss you, what with Stu heading home on Friday and now you; it's going to be a bit quiet without you all. However, mate, we have really appreciated what you have done and what you are going to do on Saturday. Let's hope there's no hiccups,' I offered. 'If that means problems, then don't you worry about a thing, Bob. Everything will run like clockwork. I have printed for years; there won't be a problem.' His confidence was reassuring. 'Well, I'm off to bed,' Bill informed us. 'Oh, by the way,' he said, handing me a slip of paper, 'you better give this to Stu. I printed it out tonight when you were all practicing. It's a letter of introduction from the general to anyone who tries to enlist him again, saying that he's under the general's command and to be left alone … or words to that effect. He's been walking around forgetting that he was dragged into enlistment a few weeks ago, and I'm afraid that some over-zealous officer will grab him again and put him back into uniform.' 'Hell,' I burst out, 'I didn't even think of that, thanks Bill.' I had just finished talking, and Stu walked in. He had popped around to see the kids and the old folks before retiring. He wanted the kids to get to know him before they left on Friday, as he didn't want them worried about leaving with a stranger. I handed him the letter. 'What's this?' he inquired as he took a squizz. 'Oh, that's very good, is this your doing, Bob?' 'No, mate, it's all Bill's. He will explain it all to you; we are off to bed. Practice tomorrow and I want to be bright and cheerful.' I could hear Bill and Stu talking as they went down to their room; they had got quite close in the time they had been together.

With everyone gone, the place was quiet. Sam turned to me and said, 'Well, that was a good day Brill, we are a bit closer to getting home than yesterday.' 'Yeah mate, it can't come quick enough for me,' I answered. 'Yep, I know what you mean,' Sam replied. 'Sam, have you thought about how we will get back to our time? I mean, do we try and head back to the point up on Ruapehu, or do we try for the cave out at Pukekawa? I'm at a bit of a loss. We entered the mist below the mount, but came out of it in the Waikato. What are your thoughts?' He looked at me. 'Shit mate, I haven't the foggiest.' He scratched his head. 'It's got me beat.' 'I'm a bit like that also,' I replied, 'well, we have those two options. I'm more convinced that the cave might be best, because I think we went back to the past while we were walking to that cave, that's when the mist hit us. So if the conditions came back again, we could leave the cave and back track into the mist. With a bit of luck, we might come out in our own time on the mount once more." 'It's a bitch, Bob,' Sam sighed, 'it doesn't make sense at all to me, but it's a plan. If it doesn't work we can go back up to Mount Ruapehu and start from there again. Whatever you decide, I'll get us there you can count on that.' 'Yeah, we could go in again from our old start point on Ruapehu, but, well, it might send us back further. I don't want to end up living with the Moa, mate,' I replied. 'Do you think?' Sam said, looking shocked. 'I don't know, Sam, I really don't. I just think we should find the cave, hope like hell we get the same weather pattern, and see if it takes us home.' 'Okay,' Sam pondered, 'you're the boss, I'm just not able to really comprehend it all. I'll follow your lead; you have been pretty good up till now.' He grinned. 'And at least we have each other. If we end up going back further into the past, there's plenty of meat on a Moa, we won't starve,' he laughed. 'Okay mate,' I scratched my head, 'I'm going to sleep on it. I haven't mentioned any of this to Grunt. I've noticed he's not talking about home as much to us. I think his mind is made up, he is just waiting for a chance to spring it on us.' 'Where do you think, he'll go?' he asked. 'God knows, mate,' I answered. 'But I'm sure he'll be thinking on the subject. He's a clever bugger; he will go somewhere where they'll need his skills. He's a bloody good mechanic, so engineering would be up his street. Also with the stuff he learnt from his old man, he's a bloody good chippy as well. He will have no problems. You wouldn't either Sam, you're good with your hands and with stock, you would be okay. Me, I'd come up short, a driver, with half a degree in history,' I grumbled. 'Well, I don't know anything about a horse's arse to its elbow.

A labourer? Bugger that. It's hard work labouring in this century before automation. Also there's no railways yet to work on, and by the time they get them in New Zealand, I'd be too old.'

'Oh, bullshit, mate,' Sam broke in, 'you could get a job in business, or anything with words, you would be okay. I would employ you.' I had to laugh, 'Yeah, I could be your silent partner.' 'Well,' he said, 'what about the gold fields? With your knowledge of history, you should know when and where the next strike is. You could make a killing.' 'I didn't think of that, mate,' I replied. 'Keep it in mind, if we don't get back that's a good possibility,' he added. 'Would you be interested?' I asked 'Too right, something different. I'll be in like Flynn.' As I lay in bed thinking of the conversion that we had, I felt a bit better about it all. It's not all doom and gloom; we could make a life here, I just needed to be positive. I thought of the places where gold had been taken. Gabriels Gully was still going and would be for another year. I was racking my brain to remember; there's a claim just out of the gully that made a killing about six months from now. Greymouth Beach in 1864; then there was Wakamarina River, which went through to 1866; Kapinga, Thames in 1867; Reefton in 1870, and a few more. So yes, I could make a killing if I couldn't get home. Would it change history if Sam and I snuck in under the radar before the actual dates? I'm buggered if I knew, but it was a good thought to sleep on.

CHAPTER NINETEEN

Another dawn and I woke to rain pelting on the window. We didn't need to get up too early as it was still dark. I lay back on the bed and thought about the day. How do I get through another day of lies? Well, I was getting really good at it, I would make a good politician; maybe I might do that when I get home. Sometime today, we would go to the bank and deposit the letters; I bet that might cause some toing and froing for the clerks. What the hell, something for them to talk about with their children, some strange men putting something in a deposit box that wasn't to be opened for one hundred and fifty years. We have to be at the Wattle's store, to help move the piano and all the instruments up to the hall, then get the practice under way. Mrs. Wattle informed us, she and her lady friends would decorate the hall to make it nice. So it's practice for most of the day. I needed to organise the hotel to supply us with lunch at the hall; I didn't want to be seen around town. Then in the late afternoon, it would be back to Woodward's shop to pick up our clothes, dinner and an early night. Well, it was best that way; it gets dark so bloody early and with candlelight or even gaslight in the room you can hardly see what you are doing anyway. No wonder a lot of people these days ended up with glasses, having to squint all the time. Well, that was the day organised, that's if the boys agreed. There was no need to get up just yet, so I snuggled down and drifted back off to sleep with the sound of the rain on the windows.

At about the same time that I was dropping back off to sleep, seventy kilometres away at the top of the Firth of Thames and nestled under the Hunua Ranges, was a place called Orere. There, Rewi Maniapoto had called a gathering of warriors to a secret meeting. The call had been sent out as far as Wellington, six hundred kilometres to the south. The purpose was to get help on a project which he was keeping very close to his chest. On this wet Thursday morning, warriors from Ngati Toa, Ngai Tai, Ngati Rauru, Tainui, Nga Tuhoe and many more from around the country arrived in twos and threes at the place of the gathering. Hidden in the bush were five thirty-man Waka, all waiting for strong crews to propel them to wherever Rewi was to send them. Of course, it needed the agreement of the warriors of each hapu in question. As they arrived, they were greeted quietly; not with the normal flamboyant welcome haka, but with a quiet hongi, some hot food and a place to sit, away from prying eyes at the bottom of a valley in the Hunuas. Once they all were gathered, fed and watered, the tribes involved sat with their chiefs and sub chiefs in front, and listened to what Rewi had to say. He announced, 'No one would be able to leave this place until Sunday morning, even if you don't want to continue with this plan. There will be no animosity, we are friends. If you don't agree with what I'm about to say, that's your prerogative.' He continued, 'This is no disrespect to my friends present, but there may be spies working for the English, our own people who will fight against us for the English Queen. So I need to have your word that you won't leave this place until Sunday.' After receiving affirmations from the gathering, he went on to tell the tribes of the attack on the kainga at Pukekawa; of the killing of two warriors and the wounding of another; the attempted rape of a woman; and how some Pakeha men helped his people. Not every Pakeha is against us, he suggested. He then explained to them that the perpetrators of the attack were flogged in Drury and were now on a permanent guard duty at Camerontown.

His plan, if they agreed, was to extract utu on the Pakeha. He looked at the congregated warriors. 'I want you to attack Auckland. Not as a fight-to-the-death attack, but a hit and run, burn and slash, to make the Pakeha understand that we can attack anywhere we want. I will talk about the details later,' he assured them. 'While you are attacking Auckland, I will attack Camerontown. This is the general's largest supply town; my men and I will raze it to the ground. At the same time, we will extract utu on the two men who caused this grievance.' There were nods all around. Utu was an important part of life, it was even in the bible. 'Now,' he continued, 'most of the warriors here today are Christians, and we will be breaking the Sabbath as the attack will be in the early hours of Sunday morning. It has worried me that we have to do this on a Sunday, but it must be done. So I have prayed that God will forgive us; that is all a man can do,' he confessed. 'There will be no moon from now till the first crescent on Tuesday. The dark will keep us safe and in the early hours of Sunday morning, when the soldiers and civilians are tucked up in their beds, we will attack from the beaches right under their noses.' He waited until the murmuring stopped. 'We have five war Waka. Tonight, each canoe will take thirty warriors. You will leave here late and paddle around to the far side of Waiheke Island to Onetangi. I have men with supplies of food and water waiting there for you. You will need to pull the Waka up into the bush line and obliterate the drag marks from the beach. This is to be a resting place until the next evening, that's Friday night or early Saturday morning, when it's at its darkest. You will then continue around the far side of Motutapu to Rangitoto Island, to a place called McKenzie Bay. Here, you will once again pull the canoes up into the bush line. This is where you will be supplied with weapons. Oh, you can take your own personal, mere and such like, but on Rangitoto, we will give each one of you, a tupara or a rifle. You will be given enough ammunition for the job you will do. Fire-sticks of very dry ti kouka leaves to throw at the buildings as you run up the streets will also be supplied.' 'Leaving the supply of weapons until the last evening is a precaution in case you are picked up before your destination. With no weapons, you can say you are fishing or travelling to a tribal gathering and they, the English, will not be able to hold you.' 'You will all be supplied with a kete, one for each warrior. In each, there will be an English Army jacket and waistcoat. There are a lot of pockets in a waist coat as you all know, ideal for carrying extra ammunition. This jacket will enable you to confuse the Pakeha once you are clear of Auckland, and if you are questioned by the English troops, you can say you are kupapa and are searching for rebels. There are four thousand kupapa fighting for the English, so you will blend in. So make sure you put them on after the attack. There you will abandon the Waka and make your way back to the Hunuas. The route will be told to you after all of you have agreed to this venture. When you are safe, you can go back to your tribes or join with us at Meremere for the fight to come. This plan will give General Cameron a fright, and it will cause him to take men from Drury, of which he has 14, 000; he will have to make Auckland secure in case it happens again. The population will demand it. This is my outline of the task in hand. Please talk to your hapu; we will talk again after we have had a midday meal. Remember, talk quietly, the bush has ears.' With heads together in hushed voices they argued the pros and cons of the venture. Most were in agreement: the New Zealand government and the governor were only after Maori land, and it would break the treaty if they took it by force. It was looking like this was going to happen, and we as a people needed to go on the offensive. Rewi said, 'In the past we have had siege mentality, but this has to change and an attack like this would make them take notice. It might, with luck, even postpone the inevitable war and give everyone time to rethink another outcome.'

Long into the morning and early afternoon with the rain falling heavily the men talked on and on, until the women turned up with food and drink. Some of the children had brought tree fern fronds and started to build shelters for the men. While the men ate, the women helped the children until there was enough cover for everyone, then departed to prepare the evening's meal. Rewi gathered them all again after they had their meal and a pipe. 'Have you decided?' he asked every hapu individually. They all agreed that this was right and not one man declined. 'Now I want to go over the details,' Rewi said, and then introduced his sister's son, Te Ruru. 'My nephew has this name as he has the sight of the owl; he knows the old paths of our ancestors and will guide you out of Auckland in the dark, back to this place. Each canoe will have guides,' he continued as all the guides stood up, 'so if a guide is lost to the Pakeha, another will be there to take his place.' He took out a map. 'I have made a copy of this map for each Waka. It is marked in red; it's the path you will take once you have beached. Study this, it shows the streets you need to know and which way to go. Concentrate fully on this task in hand, learn your route. Don't forget it will be dark, very dark, but with the fire from the buildings that you burn, it will help light up your way. Study the map well so in your mind's eye, you will know where you are at any given time. If you are separated from your hapu you will have the map in your head. Follow the lead of your guides; they also know the streets of Auckland well.' 'My men who will supply you with food and firepower on the last night, will follow you into the bay in the Waka iti;

they will attack and release the prisoners from the prison hulk. This will also cause a distraction. The hulk has no sails, but they will cut the anchors and on the ebb tide, it should run aground on Browns Island. More confusion and cost to the Pakeha.' His oratory continued, 'We will attack on three fronts. The first Waka will beach at Official Bay. The warriors will head up Short Street. Burn as much as you can but don't linger – we want noise, fire and shooting to scare and polarise the population. Cross over Eden Crescent and into Waterloo Quadrant. Then, most importantly, head up to the Parliament Building, and burn it. There will be guards there; once again, if you feel you might get bogged down, leave it and carry on, but do as much damage as possible.

Parliament is right next to Albert Barracks, right under their noses. Don't take on the barracks; they have a thousand men stationed there. The confusion and the fires will hold them back a while, so keep that in mind as you head down Victoria Street to meet up with the crews of Waka two and three in Queen Street.' 'Waka two and three will beach at Commercial Bay, right under the nose of Fort Britomart. These two canoes will burn the commercial area of Queen Street and Customhouse Street. One canoe crew will head up Queen Street; the other will go into Fort Street, then on into Shortland Street and will rejoin the other Waka crew in Queen Street. There you will meet up with the crew coming down from Victoria Street.' 'The last two Waka will beach at Freemans Bay. They will fire everything they can, from Drake Street up onto Wellesley Street, and join up with the crews of the other three Waka in Queen Street. When you all come together, this is where you will divide in half. Half will go up Wakefield Street, led by the guides into Grafton Gully, which is thick with bush; the other half will go by Queen Street to Karangahape Road, and then cut left into the gully. This is where you will slip into your English Army jackets. From here you will then proceed through the bush to the Orakei Basin, following the tidal paths to the Tamaki inlet. You will follow this inlet to the Otara stream. Once here, in the swamp of the Otara, you will hide out until the next evening. The main south road by this time will be crawling with troops, but Te Ruru and his guides know the secret paths. You will not need to cross over the road as you will be to the east of it. From the swamps, your guides will take you into the bush of the Wairoa; once there you are nearly home, as the Hunuas are just a hop, skip and jump away.'

That is my plan, I would be interested in your response. The sub-chief of the Ngati Toa stood and responded. 'What a plan. We will tell our children and our children's children how we took on the English in their own backyard. This is a wonderful undertaking.' The leader of each hapu quietly stood and spoke. Each one of the chiefs found favour with Rewi's plan. They all knew the risks, they were warriors, and in any engagement there will always be casualties; they understood that not all would get home. However, to die as a warrior was what they all strive for; to die with no land, bowing to the English was a slow death. They all agreed this was the best way, a payback on grievances of the past.

The plan was discussed late into the day. Maps were pored over until everyone knew what their task was and could visualise where they were on the map. As they all settled down for the evening, there was a peace that came over the men. They had accepted their destiny, and now was the time to act. A lot of water had to be paddled from here to get to the jump-off point of the attack, but they were all confident that everything was covered. Rewi's instructions were explicit: the churches were to be left alone and, if possible, the ministers as well. Rewi had added, 'Though in the heat of battle, if they are silly enough to get in your way, then you have to go over them. War is war. I'm sure God would understand; we are just men.'

That evening at the darkest time of the night, five Waka slipped into the water and quietly paddled to their first destination, unbeknown to the population of Auckland who slept the sleep of the righteous.

All day Thursday, the rain poured down. The streets were just running-rivers of mud; it would be years before anything resembling tar seal would be laid. We ventured out to move the piano to the hall, collected all the instruments we would need, and set up our wee concert on the small stage at the back of the hall. Hell, it was dark. Mrs. Wattle had supplied four dozen candles that made the hall a bit friendlier. Her friends helped with the decorations and the place slowly became a hall of colour. We practiced our program and with the music floating out the door, it caught people's interest as they walked passed.

Though, I thought to myself, only the silly buggers were out in this weather. We stopped at midday and had a bite to eat. Then, leaving Tui to practice her songs alone for a while, we strolled down to the bank in lower Queen Street. Strolled might not be the right word, sloshed would be more like it. We really needed gumboots since the mud came up past our ankles. Shoes wet, socks wet and the bottom of your pants wet, how the hell these people lived like this; buggered if I know. We cruised into the bank. It was a new building with tellers along the back wall, and everything was hushed. It was more like a morgue than a bank. There were three tellers behind a massive counter; they each sat on high stools in open cubicles. We went over to the youngest-looking one who asked us how he could help. We looked at each other. 'Away you go, Bob,' Shane said. 'I'm looking forward to his reaction.' I looked at the teller. 'Ah, do you have safety deposit boxes?' I asked. 'Yes, sir. We do,' he replied. 'How much would it cost for a year?' 'That will be ten shillings,' he answered. 'Oops, too dear,' I complained. It looked as though my idea was going to fall to pieces even before it got off the ground. 'Well, sir, how long do you want it for?' I looked him in the eye. 'one hundred and fifty years,' I answered. He chuckled, 'Sir, I think you are telling me a little white lie.' 'No,' I replied, 'we have some important items to be saved for later generations. It is important that our ancestors open them in the future, like a time capsule.' 'Oh, I understand, sir, just wait a moment.' He disappeared out the rear door and a few minutes later an old bloke popped out. 'Young Mr. Reid has asked me to talk to you gentlemen,' he uttered. 'It just so happens that this company is going to put a time capsule in the vault not to be open for one hundred years. This being our first venture in the colony, it was deemed appropriate. Would that be of interest to you?' 'That is very good of you,' I said, 'but would it be possible if a note was put on our parcel, with instructions not to be opened for another fifty years?' He thought for a moment. 'This item, is it very big?' 'No, not at all, just letters,' I smiled as I pulled them out and showed him the three letters tied together. 'Oh, they are not big at all. I'll tell you what, if you pay for a small steel box to hold them in, I'll attach a note to rebury them until, ah, one hundred and fifty years have gone.' 'That's 2014,' I piped up. 'Yes, that's the year; it's a long time off, this must be important for you all.' 'Well,' I replied, 'we would like to give our ancestors a general idea how we lived, and this piece of history will help them do that.' 'Yes,' he nodded, 'I think it's a splendid idea. Come around the back with me and we will sort it out.' We followed him around the back to where the open vault was. Inside the vault on a table, there were a few small steel deposit boxes and next to that on the floor was square hole; he informed us it was to be bricked in and mortared with a plaque: *Time Capsule, not to be opened until 1964.* 'These boxes come from our parent company in Australia,' he informed us. 'This is marvellous,' I acknowledged, 'so what is the price of a box?' 'I think ten pounds would be a fair price,' the manager replied. 'These boxes are sealed and are completely weather proof.' 'That's good enough for me,' Sam enthused. We all agreed. 'I'm pleased to be of service,' he replied. We paid out our ten pounds and as an extra measure, we wrapped the letters in a waterproof canvas bag before placing them in the box. The box was then sealed, and he asked one of us to place it into the cavity in the floor of the vault. I gave it to Shane. 'You do the honours, mate.' He knelt down and with a bit of ceremony deposited it into the hole. 'Later today,' the manager confirmed, 'we will place our contribution in it as well. We have a bricklayer coming to brick it up nice and tight, and there it will lie for the next 100 years. I wonder what it will be like then?' he added to himself with a thoughtful smile. 'Oh, I reckon very different to what we have here today, mark my words,' Sam responded with a grin. We all thanked him and walked back to the hall. 'Well, that's another job out of the way,' Shane drawled. 'After another few hours practice, we'll be able to pick up our clothes from Woodward's. We should be able to blend in a bit better then.'

Tui had made progress; she called out to us as we came into the hall. 'I think I have got it.' She was very excited and started singing 'Wind beneath my Wings'. She had four songs nearly down pat, and we had a day up our sleeves. Things were at last starting to pan out. Well, we thought they were. Stu called in with the kids at about three pm, just checking on how things are going. 'It's an early night for these young men; we've an early start tomorrow. We sail on the full tide at nine am, so we have to be on board by eight.' A young lady came forward, who had come in behind him. 'Oh,' announced Stu, 'I would like to introduce you to Sofia McFarland, from Glasgow.

Sofia was working in the kitchen at the Union Hotel. We got talking when I had breakfast, and I explained to her, I really needed a woman's touch to help me with the boys on the trip to Dunedin. I asked her if she would like to be a nanny for a few weeks, and if so, I'd find her employment with our family. She's agreed. So I have given up my room on the scow. I'll bunk down with the men, and Sofia can have my bed.' Sam just looked at him with an open mouth, then broke in with, 'Excuse me,' he said looking around at everyone. 'I'll be back in a minute. Bob, I need to speak to you.' I wondered what this was about. When we went outside he whispered, 'Mate, that is my second-great-grandmother. She married Angus, Stu's elder brother, my second-great-grandfather.' 'Oh shit on a stick, Sam, not again. My god, it seems every time we turn a corner, we find relations,' I moaned. We went back inside. 'Sorry,' Sam explained, 'just something that needed to be sorted out. Lovely to meet you, Sofia.' She curtsied. 'I have been told so much about the three of you and Tui, I feel as though I know you all.' 'Do you have family nearby?' I asked. 'No,' she murmured with a big sigh, 'my parents died on the way out to New Zealand, and my wee brother as well. Typhoid, when we called into the Cape. We lost thirty-six passengers; I was lucky. It was so hard, burying my family in the southern ocean. I have to make a life for myself. It might seem a bit forward in your way of thinking, but a woman on her own needs to be strong.' 'Well, Sofia, I have a real feeling you won't be on your own ever again. I'll tell you what, here is a shilling,' I gave it to Stu. 'If you find happiness, it's yours, if not, get Stu to send it back to me. I'm sure it will be yours to keep.' She smiled, heck, for a minute I saw Sam in that smile. 'Thank you Mr. Kidder.' 'No, call me Bob,' I insisted. She looked at me, 'Bob, I'll hold you to it.' 'Well, we must be off,' Stu was looking at his fob watch, 'I'll see you all tonight.' With that, Sofia, the boys and Stu took their leave.

We practised a bit more and then left in the late afternoon to head down to Woodward's menswear. When we arrived, the clothes were already on the pegs for us to try on. It seemed strange to put them on, I was not used to the heavy cloth, but as it was starting to cool down, no doubt it would be a godsend. They fitted perfectly. 'Mr. Woodward,' I said. 'You have done a wonderful job, the workmanship is perfection.' He beamed and replied, 'It's a pleasure.' 'How do I look?' asked Sam. He was dressed in longs, a waistcoat, a shirt with a tie placed outside the collar and a v-shaped jacket. 'Cool mate,' I grinned. We all looked smart, if you could call clothes from 1863 smart. Bill stuck his head in the door. 'I just thought I would see if the clothes came up to your expectations.' He had a grin from ear to ear. 'Oh, yes you look like toffs. I've been in the printing office all day working on strategies with Mr. Wattle for the start-up of our newspaper. Everything we've talked over is going well and Saturday,' he winked at us, 'will be a walk in the park. He's so looking forward to the concert. I printed off one hundred pamphlets and the boys are delivering them around the town as we speak.' 'In this weather?' I questioned. 'Oh, they have coats. What's a bit of rain? Well, I'll get back, see you later for kai,' he finished, and off he went. Mr. Woodward gave us a bag for our camouflage gear, and we left his shop dressed like everyone else around town. It was the first time we felt comfortable in public.

Back at the hall, Tui was delighted at our swanky clothes. 'It's nice to see you all well dressed,' she gushed, 'and Shane, you look so dapper.' I was thinking of another word, and laughed out loud, and got a lopsided grin from Shane. We went on with the practice until it was dark outside. 'Let's call it quits,' Sam suggested, 'we've all done great today, even now I think we could pull it off. Tui, you could be on stage anywhere, you have quite the makings of a really good entertainer.' As we walked back to the hotel, we saw posters in the windows of some of the shops advertising a musical afternoon from two pm till four pm in the hall on Queen Street. *Five artists of renown, to perform music you have never heard before, though immensely entertaining, two hours of capitulating enjoyment. The cost is a coin donation, all welcome, including children. Not to be missed.* 'I think that's us,' Shane joked. 'I reckon, do you think we will get many, Sam?' I asked. 'I think we will, mate,' he said, 'they're screaming out for something. There's no entertainment available for the kids, not like in our day.' 'Well,' I replied, 'let's make it an afternoon to remember.'

Back in the hotel, we washed and got the muck off the bottom of our clothes. Bill came in to tell us it was nearly dinner time, and as it was Stu's last night, so we should get together with a couple of drinks before dinner. This time, we went straight to the women's lounge, and who should be there but Sofia. Stu came in with the drinks, 'My turn to buy,' he insisted. We sat down and yarned. 'It's going to be funny without you, mate,' Sam declared. We all agreed. It seemed a while ago since we met. I was trying to think how long; it seemed like ages. However, it was only four days, although so much has happened in that time. We finished our drinks and I said, 'One more before dinner. Our shout, Stu.' 'I'll get them,' Sam offered. He grinned. 'It's the least I can do for my relations.' 'Will you join us for dinner, Sofia?' I asked. 'Thank you, but no. I have a few more things to pack, but I hope to say goodbye in the morning.' She stood up. 'I'll walk you home,' Stu volunteered. 'Don't be silly Stewart, I am home. Remember I worked here until today, and they let me keep my room until the morning. I'll see you, Stewart, at seven o'clock; that'll give us time enough to uplift the children,' she said.' 'I forgot this is where she was living,' he grinned sheepishly at us. We had a laugh as we walked into the dining lounge. There was nowhere near the crowd as the day before. We were given the same seating at the back of the room, and we ordered our meal, talking until it came. After the meal, we had a port, and with, 'See you tomorrow, Stu,' we left the lounge and wandered up to our rooms.

CHAPTER TWENTY

We had an early call setup for six thirty am. There was a discreet knock on the door. 'Sir, your wake up call.' 'Thanks,' I called back. Sam sat up in his bed rubbing his eyes. There wasn't any rain on the window. 'It might be okay for Stu today,' he said. 'I hope so, he told me he organised a dog cart to pick up the kids,' I replied. 'What the hell is a dog cart?' asked Sam. 'Oh, ah, it's a two-wheeler, where you can put the kids in the back seat, and the cases underneath the seats. Though it'll have to be a big one, since Sofia will have some stuff to take as well.' We shuffled around each other to wash and use the privy, there wasn't all that much room really, and then headed down for an early breakfast. Stu was shovelling food down his gullet. 'I have to be up the top of Cook Street in thirty minutes, so excuse my rudeness,' he gulped, as he slopped his tea down his throat. Sofia came in with a cup in her hand. 'The four-wheeler is here, Stewart,' she announced. 'Not the dog cart?' I asked. 'No,' she said, 'much too small for all of us. It's not raining either, so that is a blessing. I took the driver a cup of tea; he said for you to take your time,' she laughed. 'He is getting paid by the hour.' 'You paying him by the hour, mate?' Sam asked. 'Och aye,' Stu affirmed, 'it will be a bit cheaper that way.' I had to laugh; it was the first time his Scottish nature was out in the open. Sam was never like that, but Stu was closer to his roots. It was funny to hear him come out with it and not blink.

With a roaring fire in the hearth, we sat down to a big breakfast in the empty dining room. Stu and Sofia had left to pick up the kids, telling us that they would call in on the way back and have a cup of tea with us all before heading down to the ship. I thought I ordered some cake for the kids; the waiter should be able to find some. Bill came rushing in. 'Have I missed him?' he asked. 'He was so quiet leaving our room, he didn't wake me.' 'No, he'll be back soon with the kids.' I was asked the same question again when Tui and Shane arrived. They ordered their breakfasts, and they ate in silence. We were content to let the heat from the fire sweep over us. Everyone seemed to be a bit down this morning. I suppose it was saying goodbye to a friend, knowing we'll never see them again. In Sam's case, this is his relation, he only found less than a week ago. Stu and Sofia were only anonymous names on a dusty genealogy file, but now they were flesh and blood and he was about to see them for the last time. The waiter came in with a big fruit cake, which I cut up. 'Do you reckon the kids will like this?' 'Well,' Sam grinned, 'I don't know about them, but I will.' Great, I thought, he's getting back to his usual self.

I left the lounge and wandered outside. It was just starting to get lighter in the east. The grey clouds were moving quickly across the sky as the easterly pushed them out of the way, promising a better day than yesterday. The road was still muddy though; bugger, I thought, I don't want to get all muddy walking down to the wharf, I'll just get a cab or something to take us down to say our last goodbyes. I saw a trap for hire just up the road, and since there was a wooden walkway I strolled up to the driver. 'Are you for hire?' I asked. 'Yes governor,' he answered. 'Have you room for five adults to the wharf, at about seven forty-five, to see the boat off to Dunedin?' 'Yes sir, are you at the Union?' 'Yes,' I replied. 'I'll be there. It's a shilling though, for five passengers.' 'Okay, can you bring us back as well, about nine-ish? We would like to wait and see the boat depart. So how much from seven forty-five, till say ten am?' He smiled. 'Well, governor, for you a special deal, half a crown. If it's raining on the wharf, you can sit in the cab and not get wet, then I'll bring you right back here.' 'Done, mate,' I said as I handed him three shillings. 'If you don't get mud all over us, the extra sixpence is yours.' 'Thanks gov, you're a prince. I will see you at seven o'clock and forty-five,' he answered with approval. I returned to hotel. 'I've ordered a cab to take us all to the wharf to see Stu and the family off, we'll be picked up at quarter to eight. I don't know about you, but I'm personally fed up to the teeth with walking in mud all day.' 'Good thinking, Brill,' Shane nodded. 'It's hard for us but worse for Tui, as she has a hell of a job trying to keep her skirts from dragging in the mire.' 'It'll be a bit more comfortable for us all,' assured Tui, 'well done, Bobby.' Heck, she was starting to sound like Shane's mum.

At around seven thirty am, there was a clumping of feet as Stu, Sofia and the boys tried to remove some of the mud from their feet before coming into the lounge. Everyone was talking at once, and the poor wee kids were hiding behind Sofia's skirt. Tui bent to speak to them. 'It's alright, boys, we're just happy to see you all.' From her pocket she removed a toy canoe, which she gave to the eldest boy. 'What's your name?' she inquired. He was a bit overwhelmed with the toy and mumbled, 'Adam Walters.' 'And what's your brother's name?' she asked. 'Noah,' he replied. He hadn't taken his eyes off the boat. He looked up eventually, and with impeccable manners said, 'Thank you, madam, it is a very good present, I'll share it with my brother.' 'No need for that,' countered Tui. She brought out another toy boat and handed it to Noah, but he didn't come out from behind Sofia's skirt. 'Oh, I see you are a bit shy.' Tui smiled. Sam was looking at the kids. He turned to me and whispered, 'Adam and Noah ... do those names ring a bell for you, Bob? Something to do with Dunedin.' 'Yeah,' I agreed, 'I recall an Adam and Noah Fenton. Didn't they start the refrigeration shipping line from Dunedin to England in the late 1880s? And went on to make a million.' 'My god, Brill,' he stammered, 'is this them?' He was frowning as he looked at the boys, 'Hang on a minute, the name was hyphenated. Oh, I've got it, McInnes-Fenton, that's it. It's them, and they took our last name as well. Mum did say we had a connection to the Fenton's, but we never took much notice. Bloody hell, not again. We keep running into family everywhere, this is amazing. They must have dropped the Walters name, a bit of a shame, but Stu's sister must have made a good job of bringing them up,' he whispered in my ear. We turned back to the boys. Both were now too interested in the canoes to talk to us old people. Sam gave them a big piece of cake, and their eyes opened wide. 'Is this all for us?' Adam asked. 'Yep, young fellow, it's all yours.' 'Thank you, sir,' Adam beamed and broke off a piece for his brother. There was nothing wrong with these boys' manners. Stu put down his cup and announced, 'We must get going fellows, are you coming down to the ship?' 'Too right mate,' said Sam. 'Wouldn't miss it for the world.' We strolled out to the front and Sam lifted the boys into the four-wheeler, also helping Sofia up. Stu jumped up beside the driver and said, 'See you all at the wharf.' The driver flicked the reins, and the horse sloshed off through the mud, heading down to the port. Our cab turned up within a minute of Stu leaving. 'Right on time,' the cabbie informed me. He jumped down and opened the door for Tui, leaving us to struggle aboard ourselves. Soon we moved off after them, sloshing and rattling through the quagmire as we made our way down Queen Street to Queens Wharf. At least on the timber wharf, we didn't have to stand in the mud.

Stu had arrived five minutes before us, and already the crew were taking their gear on board. His agent was there, and Stu introduced us. He told his agent he might receive a letter from Captain Kidder to be sent on to him on the first available boat. The agent said that would be no problem. We stood around talking, then Sofia decided she would go aboard and get the children organised as they were chomping at the bit to look around the boat. We said our goodbyes and good luck, when she smiled and said, 'It was lovely to meet you all.' She looked long and hard at Sam. 'I feel as I have known you for years; it's uncanny.' 'It was really nice to meet you too, Sofia, you will do well,' Sam replied. She took the boys' hands and walked up the gangway onto the ship where an officer was there to greet her, and then took them to their cabin. Stu turned to us all, 'I don't know what to say, you are my friends for life. Please, once again, if you make it to Dunedin, my place is there for you. Even if I'm not there you are welcome, all of you.' He stuck out his hand, and we took turns shaking it. 'Sam,' he affirmed, 'like Sofia, I have this uncanny feeling about you, you remind me of my brother. Please take care and get home safely.' He turned and walked onto the ship. It wasn't long before we heard, 'Cast off forward,' and then, 'cast off stern.' We waved madly to Stu's family as the scow moved away from the wharf. The mainsail went up to give them leeway, and she drifted on the tide out into the channel. We watched as she turned her stern towards us and eventually disappeared around Devonport heads. We were all quiet; it was like a death in the family.

Sam broke the mood. 'I'm pleased he has gone, he needed to go back to where he belonged. When you think about it, his sister will change the lives of those kids. Sofia will be introduced to Angus, my direct descendant. The boys will go on to make a name for themselves, and in the process, show what a small country at the end of the world can achieve in the early days of refrigeration. So we must have been here for this purpose, maybe saving Stu from the army, with him meeting Sofia and taking the children home to Dunedin. It might never have happened if we hadn't come through the mist. So if nothing else comes out of this, I think we've all done pretty well, fellas. We haven't lost a mate, and we've kept history in the balance. I think that might deserve a beer for lunch. After that, we'll have a bloody good music practice.' We all looked at Sam. 'You know, Sam,' I said, 'you're a pretty perceptive bloke. I think you are right: we were meant to be here. Let's get back and make some music; I recon things are going to be okay from now on.'

As we clambered aboard the cab, I heard Tui say to Shane, 'What was it that Sam was saying; I don't understand, about coming through the mist, direct descendents?' He whispered to her, 'I'll explain it all later, I promise, once we get out of Auckland and settle. We'll decide what we're going to do about getting home.' 'I'll keep you to your word, Mr. Langford,' she claimed. Well, she now had his rightful name, but I wonder how much he's divulged. She will eventually have to be told the full story; however, that was up to Shane to tell her. Though, to think of it, he had already told her some of our secrets. We sloshed through the muck on our way back up the road, and I asked the cabbie to drop us at the hall. He left us there, and we went inside. Mrs. Wattle was still working on the decorations with her friends. 'We won't get in your way,' she smiled. 'We're getting a lot of interest with many saying they're coming, and I'm starting to think that the hall will not be big enough, but we will do our best to make it nice for everyone.'

We settled down to another day of practice. After about three hours, the hotel delivered our lunch to us with hot tea and coffee, we stopped for a break. Mrs. Wattle left with her friends, saying the music was so different and very enjoyable. She was sure all the children would appreciate it. All afternoon we banged out our music and poor old Tui had to stop for a while as she was getting a sore throat. We didn't want anything to happen to her voice between now and the concert. We closed up the hall in good spirits at about five pm and went back to the hotel to freshen up, have a drink, and wait around until dinner time.

Bill had been with Edward Wattle all day, working on their new newspaper layout. On the quiet, he had already set up one of the printers with the first page to be printed of the order we had written out. He sat down with a drink and informed us, 'It's all ready to go tomorrow, as soon as the family have left I'll start printing right away. With setting it up today, it won't take so long to finish.' 'That's so good, mate,' I replied. 'Well, I hope it all goes to plan,' he answered, 'as of Sunday I'm off up north, and I don't want to let you all down. I'm sure everything will go the way we want.' We finished dinner and took some beers up to our rooms for a drink and a yarn. Shane and Tui excused themselves an hour later. Bill, Sam and I continued talking. It wasn't long before Bill left us, muttering, 'Busy day tomorrow, I'll see you all in the morning.' So Sam and I decided to hit the pit early as well. It was quiet as a grave outside, no movement anywhere. I shut the balcony doors and piled into bed. 'Night Sam.' He mumbled something, and I went out like a light.

The morning broke with a promise of sun; hell, take a picture, I haven't seen it for a few days, and it sure makes all the difference. First breakfast, then down to the hall to check out if everything was ready. 'How's your voice Tui?' I asked. 'I'm fine, thank you Bob, I can still hit the high notes,' she affirmed. 'Good. Shane, you ready for this?' 'Yep,' he answered. As for Sam, you don't have to ask: he's always ready to play music. So for now all we had to do was wait until 2 pm. We later lunched at the hotel. The waiting staff will be given some time off to go to the concert, so there was a feeling of high anticipation around the hotel and to a degree, around town. We even heard some hotel guests talking about going.

We left the hotel at one pm and strolled up to the hall. Bill was waiting for us. 'Mr. Wattle is already here, and I'm about to go down and get things started with the printing. I'll wait until Mrs. Wattle leaves; I think he said she was only about ten minutes behind him, looking for the children's hats or something.' We watched him head slowly down to the store and around the back. Fingers crossed everything goes to plan. We went inside the hall, finding there were a few people already there. Mr. Wattle's oldest son was at the door with a box for the donations and even now I could see a few coins in there. 'Well, my friends,' said Edward greeting us, 'are you ready?' Sam replied, 'Yep, all set to go.' We went out the back to warm up. The place looked quite nice with winter flowers, ferns and bunting. At a push, I think they would be able to squeeze in about three hundred people; that would be a good size crowd. However, it was better than we expected, and the audience jammed into hall to the point where they stood three deep at the door, and I worried the walls might collapse. 'Two o'clock,' Sam announced. 'Let's get this gig underway.' We moved onto the stage, and I went forward. Of course, there was no microphone, so I had to raise my voice. I introduced myself, then introduced the rest of the group and explained that a lot of the music would be new to them, just sit back and enjoy the show. We began with Sam playing his classics. Next, Tui sang a few songs; then it was my turn on the guitar; and before long Shane came on with his deep voice and sang a Roger Whittaker number. This continued on until the break just over an hour later, when we stopped for ten minutes to wet our whistles. Then off we went again. At the end, the room just erupted; the noise was amazing, everyone was smiling, it could not have gone better. Tui was beaming from ear to ear as she came off the stage. Over and over they were saying, what wonderful music, they'd never heard anything like it in their lives before. It took an hour to clear the hall, and the Wattle's were there the whole time. That went off extremely well, Eddy,' I beamed. 'Oh, it was wonderful and we took nearly forty pounds, forty pounds! That is amazing, I'm thrilled.' 'That's good then, and you'll get some more sales in the future too, from your advertisement,' I remarked. 'Plus lessons.' 'That's right; I have had at least fifteen parents asking about lessons for their children. My friends, you have been so good to give up your time, I need to do something for you all.' I thought, don't you worry mate, Bill has been printing illegal documents, and that's payment enough. Out loud I said, 'Not at all, it's our contribution to the growing city of Auckland. It's taken the thoughts of war away from these folk for a few hours, we don't want anything, we have enjoyed performing for you.' 'Well, please come and dine with my wife and myself tonight. Wiremu is going back up to Russell in the morning, so we could have a farewell dinner for him and yourselves, as I gather you will be away quite quickly as well.' 'That is very generous of you, Edward, our thanks for the kind offer,' I replied, 'we will be there. What time would suit you?' 'Ah …' he turned to his wife. She spoke up, 'seven thirty pm would be fine. I will head home now to prepare.' It was just after five. I watched her, and the children walk down to the store; I hoped that Bill had finished the printing. 'I'll lock up the hall and come back tomorrow to move everything to the shop,' Edward purred; he was in a really good mood. 'You all might want to freshen up. I'll see you all at seven thirty.' He turned and walked back into the hall.

Strolling back to the hotel, nobody said a word. We were all feeling worried after the excitement of the show. We hadn't seen or heard from Bill at all, and we were apprehensive. Climbing the stairs, Sam confided, 'I hope to hell everything went okay. Not knowing is a bugger.' But on opening the door to our room, there Bill was, sitting on the bed with a big grin all over his face. 'All done, my friends. Every last one signed and ready for you all.' I rushed over and shook his hand, pleased it went okay. I then turned to look over the papers he had finished for us. They were spread out on the bed; I picked one up and it was just what we'd asked for, looking all official. I couldn't believe, it was finished, a done deal. I turned to the boys with a big grin on my face. 'Just take a look at these, they will get us everywhere we want to go, no questions asked.' The documents for the paymaster were the same, as was the discharge paper for Stu with his pay document. We were set. I rang the bell for the porter, and when he came up I asked for a bottle of wine. It was duly sent up and we celebrated a day well done. Bill told us everything was finished and cleaned up by four pm, just as the concert was finishing. He had been back at the hotel for nearly forty-five minutes. So he wrote an article on the concert for the paper. He didn't mention our names, but wrote how wonderful it went with thanks to his boss, all flowery and no substance. He hadn't even been there, but a lot of writing was like that in the 1860s. It would be in the Monday paper; I hoped we'd be gone by then. I explained to Bill that we were going to Edward's place for dinner, and he was the guest of honour. He was thrilled.

We all turned up just before seven thirty pm. The door was opened by his eldest son who ushered us into the reading room. 'My parents will be with you in a few minutes,' he told us, 'I did so much enjoy your music. To play the guitar like you did, I would love to be able to perform like that.' 'Well,' I advised, 'it's just practice. If you put the time in anyone can do it.' He then turned to Bill, 'How about you, Wiremu, did you enjoy it?' 'Oh yes, though I have heard them play before. I did enjoy the music, but I think I like newspapers better,' he grinned. The young fellow replied 'Yes, I expect I'm destined for that as well.' Mr. and Mrs. Wattle came in and announced that dinner would be served in ten minutes, so we all stood around making small talk before heading into the dining room. In the middle of the room was a big kauri table with seating for eight; the oldest son would be joining us. We started with toheroa soup, mutton pie and veggies. With glasses of wine, then topped with a treacle roly-poly as a dessert, it was, all in all, a pretty good meal. How the heck Mrs. Wattle produced something like this in just a few hours, for eight people and on a wood fire oven, I had no idea. When we offered to help with the dishes, she was horrified. 'Oh no,' she said, 'that's woman's work.' I grinned in response. 'That would go down well with your sisters, Shane,' I laughed. 'Yeah, we'd have a real verbal encounter if I said that, things have sure changed.' 'Don't your sisters do the dishes?' Mrs. Wattle asked. 'Yes, they do, but the difference is that they like us men to help as well.' 'That is quite strange,' she replied. 'My sisters are different,' he laughed. 'Bob's sister goes one better: she is a captain on a fishing boat.' Oops, he forgot where we were. Mrs. Wattle looked at me. 'A captain?' 'Yeah, I reckon she's a bit different.' Before she could grill me, Edward interrupted with, 'Let us retire to the sitting room.' It was like a lounge in our day. Sam took out his harmonica and played a few songs for everyone. We all sang quietly together, and the

Wattles were thrilled. It was time to leave, they thanked us again for a day to remember and hoped in the future that if we were ever back in Auckland, would we do it all again. We said of course we would, knowing full well that it was the last thing we wanted to do. We had our ticket out of here, and we're going to bugger off. Come Monday, we'll be gone. We said our goodbyes and headed back to the hotel. It was dark as hell: no moon, pitch black, you had to watch your step walking a few hundred metres up the road, but we got there without falling into a mud bath. Heading off to bed, Bill announced, 'I leave on the turn of the tide so I need to be down at the wharf at nine am; it's full tide at about ten thirty am. So I'll see you all in the morning.' We all said our good nights and went off to our respective bedrooms. Dropping off to sleep thinking, two more sleeps and the journey home begins; I hope it was going to go okay. I really wasn't too hopeful. I just had this deep feeling that things were going to turn turtle, and I couldn't shake it off.

Friday night in the harbour was black as the ace of spades. Five canoes had slowly and quietly left Onetangi to paddle around Motutapu Island and then follow the coast of Rangitoto Island to McKenzie Bay. Very early in the wee hours of Saturday morning, they'd pulled the canoes up into the bush line out of sight, and they waited for the next part of the plan. The advance party had killed the fire beacon which was really only a small pinpoint of light, and then helped them with the Waka. The warriors were each given food, water, firearms and the kete with the

English uniforms. The chiefs of each canoe discussed the plans again, for early Sunday morning, they were going to make history. Then they all settled down to sleep. Out in the harbour, a few lights could be seen on the mainland around Devonport and Takapuna. However, it was very sparsely populated, and another dark night was expected for early Sunday morning. This was the view of the tohunga, who said everything was looking favourable for their cause. They slept right through to the sunrise. They were quiet and watchful on waking, then whispering amongst themselves, and preparing for the attack which was to come.

Saturday night, and early Sunday morning, Auckland slept on. The guards at Britomart weren't as vigilant as they should have been; neither were the guards at the Albert Barracks. The war hadn't started yet, there was no need to be too worried. Anyway, when it did start, the English with their enormous firepower will probably overrun the nasty rebels in a week; then, everyone would leave, and the Europeans who stayed behind would have some nice bits of confiscated land to call home. But of course, this was all in the future. And that future was about to change the lives of me and my mates.

CHAPTER TWENTY-ONE

The night was black and heavy clouds scurried across the sky, promising rain in the foreseeable future. The canoes silently swept into the main channel of the harbour with muffled paddles, slipping past ship after ship that were floating, unsuspecting, at their moorings. Under the noses of the ships' crews, who no doubt were not that vigilant, they manoeuvred their Waka towards their destination. This was the most dangerous time of the campaign. Each Waka had to arrive at the beachhead at the same time, or as close to it as possible. The tohunga looked at the stars for guidance, but they were gone, hidden by the clouds, so it was all in the lap of the gods now.

At the very bottom of Queen Street, in the heart of Auckland's trading centre, the first two Waka silently beached at Commercial Bay. The rain started to fall as the last man came ashore, and nothing could be seen moving around town. They quietly gathered and readied themselves for the main attack. The ti kouka leaves that had been wound around manuka poles were lit. The assault began as they stormed onto Custom House Street, breaking windows and throwing the burning leaves into the buildings.

As the first window was broken, about half a mile to the northeast, the second hapu, a single Waka this time, beached at Official Bay. It slid up onto the sand and the warriors jumped out noiselessly, then prepared for their mad dash up to the Parliament Buildings. The rain was now starting to get heavy, but the ti kouka leaves were brittle and caught fire as soon as they were lit. Keeping to the shadows, they ran up Short Street, kicking over the buckets of water that most houses had by their homes as a fire-fighting precaution. One booted the buckets over, while the other threw his burning fire stick into the house or businesses as they passed. They continued into Eden Crescent, creating the same destruction as before. The sound of a bell rang out. A fire watchman doing his rounds saw the flicker of a flame at the bottom of Queen Street. He swung the bell he carried, letting it ring loudly and yelled at the top of his voice, 'Fire, fire.' A Māori who had just turned into the street killed him with a rifle shot, and the noise vibrated around the bottom end of town, but still no lights were lit and hardly anyone stuck their heads out to find out what the racket was. This was soon to change though, since the warriors were burning everything in their path. As they dashed across the quad and onto Parliament grounds, there by the door, under a gas lamp, were two soldiers from Albert Barracks. They looked puzzled; they could see flames and had heard rifle fire but were not too sure what was happening. Then the warriors came into sight firing at the guards. Both soldiers returned fire but soon were overcome and went down as the shotgun pellets blasted into their chests with a sickening whack. The way was now clear for the Māori to break into parliament. Out of the rain, the leaves they left burnt more ferociously, setting fire to the main office inside the door. The two-story building was made of kauri and dry as a bone; it flared up like a roman candle. The warriors took a quick look around and continued on as they headed out of the building, through the grounds and onto Victoria Street, right underneath the noses of more guards from Albert Barracks. Up to this point, very few shots had been fired, and the barracks were just starting to stir. Fort Britomart woke up to the noise of an explosion of glass breaking in the nearby commercial district; they were looking right down onto the fires from their hill. Bugles started to sound as men and horses woke to the crackling of fire all around them. They could also see now that Parliament was ablaze, and the general public were just starting to appear out of their homes, groggy and confused about what was happening.

A detachment of the armed constabulary force rushed into Queen Street from Wyndham Street to be confronted by sixty warriors, intent on burning everything in their path. For the Māori, it was a pleasure to see some men to fight; it was alright to burn your enemy, but to fight men fair and square carried a lot more honour. They turned towards the police who were sent scurrying undercover as the Māori brought up their rifles and laid into them, leaving a couple of men lying in the road, severely injured. The police returned fire, knocking at least one warrior over, but true to their instructions the Māori bypassed them and continued on the rampage. They weren't going to get into a fire fight if they could avoid it. Some of the younger warriors took a bit of persuading that the object of this fight was to keep moving. Soon the police were left behind as the fight and flames moved further up the street.

By now, just to the west of the assault, the third hapu had beached two Waka in Freemans Bay and started their run later than the others. So consequently, as they ran, there were a few more people around who had come out of their homes to see what all the commotion was about. These people were confronted with sixty fierce Māori brandishing fire sticks, and tossing the flames into their houses, shooting all in sundry as they ran past. Three civilians died as they stepped onto their porches and army personnel living outside the barracks with their families took a few hits. Nevertheless, most ducked inside to collect their rifles and began to return fire at the assailants as they ran past. The destruction on this side of the city wasn't as bad, but the number of civilians who had been aroused meant more people were shot and injured. Around the town things were starting to warm up. Fire had engulfed most of, but not the entire commercial district at the bottom of the city as far as the waterfront. Parliament was now an inferno, and the army were still not organised. The Māori who had burnt the building had gone on to run down Victoria Street and torched their way through to the bottom end of the city where they joined the first hapu in Queen Street. Now they numbered less than ninety; they had left a few of their crew members face down on the road. They had already surpassed the outcome that Rewi wanted, and they were still a complete fighting force. They still hadn't caught up with the sixty from the third hapu, coming down Wellesley Street.

Things were going to change a bit now though as the army got itself together. The Auckland Rough Riders were billeted at the Albert Barracks that evening. Lieutenant Metcalfe had woken to the sounds of firing and immediately had his troops up and ready to go as the first and second hapu had merged at Queen and Victoria Streets. The twelve men tore out of the barracks like a bat out of hell. They shot down Princess Street, turned into Shortland, not looking at the fires or the destruction that the raiding parties had accomplished, they concentrated on what needed to be done. They then wheeled left into Queen Street, now only a block behind the Māori who were regrouping for their final run to meet up with their colleagues of the third hapu coming from Freemans Bay. Lieutenant Metcalfe gave the order to draw swords, and with, 'Let's get the bastards,' they flew up the road in line. The Māori didn't hear them coming and turned too late as the horses ran straight into them. Their swords swung, and bodies were slashed; the Rough Riders went through them like a knife through butter. The bodies of the dead mixed with the wounded were littered all over the road. The riders swung around the corner into Wellesley Street to see another group racing toward them down the hill, and they charged. This hapu didn't expect them either, and the surprise was total as the men on horseback went at them with blades and pistols. It was now starting to look like an all-out war. The Māori scattered, using buildings as protection and fired back, taking a few of the riders in a volley. The lieutenant was hit in the leg and arm, but still he turned his horse and stormed back into the Māori who had retreated down the road to meet up with the rest of their mates.

I had woken to the sound of gunfire and was on my feet immediately, but Sam beat me to the balcony door. We crept outside; the rain was coming down in sheets. Bloody Auckland, I thought, it was always raining. We saw the fires straight away and could see that Parliament was ablaze. Sam frowned, and with a worried, voice said, 'I think we're under attack, wake everyone up mate; this is serious.' I shot out of the room and banged on all the doors on the top floor, yelling my head off for everyone to get up. Bill came out wide eyed. 'What's wrong?' he asked. 'It looks as though Māori are attacking Auckland. Fires are everywhere, you can hear gunshots, and they're getting nearer,' I answered. 'Oh no, the Wattles, I need to get over to them,' Bill insisted as he raced back into his room to grab his rifle and took off. 'Sam,' I hollered, 'Bill has just run down to the Wattles to give them protection.' Oh shit, Brill, you stay here with Shane, I'll go with Bill; keep your head down and fire when you think it is right.' He took off, yelling to Shane, 'Stay with Brill.' I grabbed my rifle as Shane came in with Tui; he took a look outside and weighed up our options. He turned to Tui. 'Go downstairs and get everyone away from the windows. We'll need buckets of water, in case they try to burn us out. Get everything sorted then come back up here. If any of the men have guns leave a couple of them down there. Tell the rest to bring the guns up to the second-floor we have a better view of the street up here.' She ran downstairs then started banging on doors, getting everyone up, repeating Shane's instructions. They barricaded the front doors, pulled all the curtains down on the windows that faced the street and then collected buckets of water just in case. Three men stayed there to protect the ground floor and six came upstairs with Tui. Shane directed them all to the balcony looking up and down the street. It was then that we saw a group of Māori heading up the street toward us, trying to burn some of the shops, although the weather was making it difficult now that it was really pouring down. They reached the Wattles' and smashed the window. 'Bugger this mate,' I said as I took a look at the blurred image and shot at one of the group. I saw him throw his arms in the air and drop to the road. His mates pushed inside the building, and I could hear gunfire coming from deep inside the shop. Only one Māori came running out, and then all was silent. The Māori swept past us, smashing glass and doing their damnedest to burn as much as they could. We kept firing at any target we could see, until the Rough Riders came tearing up and through the group below us. I watched them turn back, but then instead they shot up Wellesley Street. The Māori below us dispersed, hiding inside doorways and making themselves as inconspicuous as possible before regrouping further up the road. We continued firing at any movement that presented itself.

The army was now, after thirty minutes, starting to get their act together as they came out of the barracks in good order to the corner of Wakefield and Queen Streets, then set up a defensive line. They started firing as the third hapu came into sight, chased by the Auckland Rough Riders, who were now down to six men. They pulled up and retreated back up the street, not wanting to get caught in the crossfire. The army opened fire at the attackers, but the Māori avoided them and broke through into the business premises, to pass into the next street at the rear, before heading up the hill, bypassing the barricade completely. The army were left shooting at shadows.

That's when the warriors seem to vanish. They scooted up into Symonds Street, then down into Grafton gully away from the town centre. They changed into their English Army jackets and with guides showing them the way, headed southeast; they were not seen again. The authorities were pissed to say the least, how could so many men just disappear without sight or sound? But, disappear, they did. The longer they took to look for the attackers, the more damage that was being done. You could hear the flames of the buildings burning; it was like a living thing. Now that the fighting had finished, the twelve-man volunteer fire brigade came out of their building carrying pumps and hoses and tried at least to rescue some buildings that were saveable. They had only manpower, as the horses had bolted in fright and were wandering well away from the fires. We were lucky it was pouring with rain; it was the weather that helped to stop the complete destruction of the commercial business district.

At last, the army took control. Men from Britomart began to organise the fire fighters and helped control the fires, while other sections went out in squads checking on the community to assist with the injured and move the dead aside for a later count and identification. Meanwhile, soldiers were still running around, trying to find the enemy to no avail. Shane and I stood up. 'I'm worried mate,' he declared, 'Sam and Bill haven't come out of the building, and they should have by now. We need to get down there and check them out.' He shouted to the men on the balcony to stay put just in case. I grabbed my first-aid kit then followed him out of the room and downstairs. Tui had popped downstairs earlier to check on the defences; she had done well with her handiwork, as the front of the building was all boarded up. Shane spoke to her, 'we need to get over to the Wattle's shop to check on Sam and Bill, they haven't come out. We're really are worried.' We pulled back some bracing from the door and stepped out into the street. The fires gave us a clear view as we moved down to the shop. We approached cautiously and called, 'Sam, Bill, are you there, is everything okay? It's alright to come out now, it's all over.' No answer came back. We looked through the broken window and saw there were three Māori bodies lying sprawled on the floor. I found some candles and lit them, and saw both Bill and Sam lying in the corner. Sam's head was covered in blood. It looked as though Bill and Sam had barricaded the door to the house and both of them had been shot. We ran over to them and I gingerly felt for Sam's pulse; it was there but weak. I sighed with relief. 'He's alive.' I then moved over to Bill, but he had gone. Oh shit! All his aspirations were wasted through a kind deed to protect his employer, and he'd given up his life for it. He was my family; I was choked. I turned back to Sam with watery eyes. Shane lifted him up and laid him on the large counter in the shop. He banged on the inner door crying out 'Edward, are you there, it's okay to come out.' The door opened, and a frightened face poked his head around the door. 'Oh my, is it over?' Edward whispered. 'Yes,' replied Shane, 'but Bill is dead, mate, I'm so sorry, and Sam is seriously wounded. We need some water and light, can you arrange that please?' 'Oh, certainly, oh, poor Wiremu, my friend.' They had known Bill for a long time, and his family were going to feel the loss. I was numb; Bill was my family by marriage, and Sam was my best mate, one was dead and the other with blood all over his face. I had to pull myself together for Sam's sake. I pulled the curtains off the back wall and wrapped it around Sam for warmth. Then I took out my kit, found some clean pads and began to wipe away the blood. While I was doing this, Shane checked out the rest of Sam's body to see if there were more injuries. 'I can't feel anything else, Brill,' he said. 'The damage is only around his head.' I was hoping it wasn't too bad, as head wounds always look worse; usually wipe away the blood, and they're just a scratch. Well, I hope so, in this case. Mrs. Wattle came out with a bowl of hot water and some clean cloth. I thanked her as she went away, saying she would boil some more water and make a pot of tea. Tui had arrived, worried about our delay, and offered to help, heading after Mrs. Wattle. Shane lit a few more candles, so we could now see what we were doing. I wiped away all the blood and found three wounds: two welts on the top of his head and one just above his ear in the hairline. I cut away his hair and said to Shane, 'I can see the bone, mate, but it is not cracked as far as I can see. I'll have to give him an anaesthetic, clean it up and stitch it. It's much deeper than anything I have witnessed, so I don't really know the outcome. He might be out for a while.' Mrs. Wattle and Tui came in with another bowl of hot water and more candles; they stood close while I sewed up all the cuts on Sam's head. Then I bandaged it up and turned to Mrs. Wattle. 'We need to get him to a bed.' 'I have one here you can use for him,' she answered. 'It's Wiremu's bed, I'm sure he wouldn't mind if Sam rested there.' Shane picked Sam up like a baby; I really admired this bloke's strength, considering Sam is a big man also. He took him into Bill's room and laid him on the bed. We covered him, and then sat down on the bed looking at him as if he was dead. Shane put his face in his hands. I think he was crying, I didn't say a thing, I felt like crying also, what a bloody mess. I thought about Bill. 'Shane, would you and Tui sit here and look after Sam? I'll go and sort out Bill.' It turned out I didn't have to worry though, as Edward had already with the help of his wife, taken Bill into his lounge and placed him on the couch. I followed and cast my eyes over him; he took a full blast of shotgun fire to the chest. I assumed Sam and Bill had shot three blokes before the blast had pelted Bill's chest. Luckily for Sam, I think Bill's body had protected him as he was riddled with shot and Sam only got a few around the head. If it hadn't been for Bill, Sam would be dead as well.

Meanwhile, a hapu of warriors from Meremere had left Pukekawa in the late evening and jogged the track to pass Alexander Redoubt, then crossed the Waikato one kilometre downstream from Camerontown. In the early hours of Sunday morning, at about the same time as the first attack happened in Auckland, twenty-five Tainui attacked the town. They had circled the supply town and came in from all points. The guards that night were ex-Sergeant Router and ex-Corporal Smith. They had, for their part of the attack at Pukekawa, been flogged, twenty each, and been demoted to the ranks. Their punishment also included six months' night duty at the supply town. If they were to try and run, they would be caught and shot. Afterwards, they would be discharged and sent back to England, with both losing their pensions. Rewi knew this, but as far as he was concerned this was for him, and his tribe, was the ultimate revenge. They came in quietly and at the last minute, Router saw movement right in front of him; he tried to shout a warning, but he was clubbed down with the traditional mere and dropped dead to the ground. Smith didn't even hear the Māori, they were on him in an instant and with a whack, he was also dispatched. Rewi's men methodically went around burning the town. Eight kupapa Māori, who were also guards that night, put up a much better fight but surprise was on Rewi's side. When the place was burning to Rewi's satisfaction, the warriors turned and walked away. The men from the redoubt four kilometres away had seen the flames and turned up just as Rewi was leaving. This ensured a run, hide and shoot tactic, until they slipped across the river and away with only a few men lost. The supply town was a right off; six guards dead, two wounded and the town razed to the ground, all in all, a good night's work. General Cameron was furious. The only bright side was the colour sergeant from Alexander Redoubt received a VC for bravery chasing the rebels through the bush.

To top off a good nights work, the prison hulk had been cut loose in the Waitamata Harbour and had drifted all night on the outgoing tide to run aground on Browns Island. Rewi's men, who were responsible for this, had boarded and killed the guards and then released all the prisoners, Māori and Pakeha alike. When the hulk ran aground, they set it alight and then abandoned ship; most using planks which were thrown into the water and proceeded to float themselves onto various beaches. Some of the Māori prisoners joined Rewi's men in the small canoes and travelled back the same route the warriors had come. Other Māori travelling only at night, found their way through the bush until they arrived back in the Hunuas a few days later. It took the army weeks to capture most of the European prisoners, but not all, and no Māori were recaptured. So, all in all, definitely a job well done.

'The cost to the city is thousands of pounds. The cost to the army is disastrous; they lost face on all fronts, with the public, with themselves, high command, Parliament and last but not least the governor. Auckland is in ruins. Thirty civilians have been killed, including a couple of children. There were one hundred wounded, and forty-five Māori rebels were found dead or wounded on the streets. Three of the rebels died in one building, where an officer and his Māori sergeant had fought off the attack; the sergeant was shot and died immediately, and the officer was shot in the head and still hasn't regained consciousness. These two men saved the life of the publishing family Mr. and Mrs. E Wattle. The only really good thing to come out of this is that the Colonial Rough Riders went on and did what the regulars should have done. If it had not been for Lieutenant Metcalfe and his men, a lot more buildings would have been razed to the ground. Wounded twice, Lieutenant Metcalfe drove into the Māori with no regard for himself; because of this, he was awarded the Victoria Cross, as was private the Reverend Henry Talbert, who with his lieutenant harassed the enemy until they broke off contact. The other four men will receive the New Zealand Cross for bravery. Six of these brave men died defending their city, and will be buried with full military honours.'

The above article was to be placed in the Southern Cross Newspaper but never made print as a block was put on it by the governor. This copy though, came from sources unknown and did the rounds of the town.

Shane and I hung around the hotel area, travelling back and forth to the Wattles, but Sam was not recovering. We were sitting him up and dribbling food into his mouth, until one wet afternoon a week later, there was a knock at the door. A young lady came in and introduced herself as Bella Wrightson. She said that she had heard there was an officer, with a head wound, who had not recovered consciousness. She believed that some fresh air out on the newly-arrived navy boat, HMS Esk, would be just the thing he needed. It was being set up as a hospital for wounded officers. She went on to say that she had done her training as a nurse with Florence Nightingale at St Thomas Hospital London. Hygiene, fresh clean bandages, food and fresh air would help him. She asked if she could see the patient. She took a look at Sam and commented on the cleanliness of his being, and thought she could help. Shane and I were at our wits end; the local quack had no idea, and we didn't know how long a person could stay unconscious before they died. We had no medical equipment to feed him like in our day, and we were worried sick. So we agreed. She took all of his particulars and arranged to set him up on the ship that very day. A few hours later, four matelots arrived with a cart and gently transferred Sam onto it. Miss Wrightson fussed around like a mother hen. They slowly drove the cart down to the wharf through the burnt-out streets of Auckland, which were now in the process of the big clean up. This reminded me of Christchurch after the earthquakes, I hope they work faster than in Christchurch. Transferring him onto a cutter, they whisked Sam away to the large ship in the channel. We had to wait until the next day before we were able to visit.

The next day, Shane, Tui and I took the cutter out to the boat, which was a three-masted single screw steam-powered ship of the line. We were welcomed aboard by the captain, a big Scottish bloke; it was strange but most of the crew were Scots as well. Bella came up and said, 'He finally woke through the night, I sat with him talking. He would wake for ten minutes, then he would drop off; he did that most of the night. I knew he liked music from what you told me, so I sang to him quietly till dawn. I did manage to feed him some broth this morning, I think it is a breakthrough.' We all piled into his spotlessly clean cabin. Sam, lying still on the cot, seemed to have a bit more colour than he had the day before. but, man, he had lost weight over the last week. I was looking at his face and noticed the dark patches around his eyes, then his eyes twitched. I said to Shane, 'I think he's coming to.' Sam opened his eyes, though they didn't focus that well. 'Who are all you people?' he said. 'Bugger, amnesia, this could take a while,' Shane whispered. 'We're your mates, Sam,' he said with a smile, 'you were in a fire fight over a week ago when the Māori attacked Auckland.' 'Sorry, I can't remember, who are you again,'? he stuttered, 'I'm feeling peckish.' 'That's the best news yet,' I marvelled, 'you eat and get your strength back we will be in everyday to check you out.' He drifted off to sleep again. We went back up on deck, it dawned on me, I was on a boat, and I really needed to get off it as soon as possible. It was moving up and down in a way that made me feel real sick. 'Thank you, Captain,' I heard Shane comment. 'We will call again, is that okay by you?' 'Och man, of course, where is the young laddie from?' he asked. 'Dunedin,' I voiced. 'Well, that's good, so am I,' he said, 'he must have the Gallic then.' I had no idea what he was on about; all I wanted to do was to get the hell off this tub. We clambered aboard the cutter, and they rowed us back to the wharf. Tui looked at me and commented, 'You're a bit pale Bob, are you alright?' 'Oh,' Shane replies, 'he suffers from sea sickness.' 'Oh, you poor man,' she sympathised. Once back on terra firma I was okay. I turned to Shane and Tui, 'it's good he's getting his appetite back, I think he is on the mend. I'm not sure how long his amnesia will last though, that's a big worry, but let's get him healthy again and go from there. We'll have lunch, and we'll see what we can do about our pay.' I had to keep busy.

The governor had returned and was renting a house in Symonds Street. Parliament had moved into one of the better pubs, and heads were rolling. We did our best to stay out of the way of all in sundry. The ANZ bank had been burnt to the ground, and a shed was set up as a temporary replacement. We needed the money so that's what we were going to do, get our back-pay and hideout until our mate was okay. Unfortunately, I couldn't get to the paymaster until tomorrow, I had to be content to sit in my room brooding about Sam.

I thought back on the past week. Bill's body was taken up north to his family by Captain Subritzky; he knew the family well, and he said it was an honour to do so. The

Auckland streets were slowly coming back, but it was going to take a while. Meanwhile, there were patrols everywhere: squads of men twenty-four hours a day, seven days a week, travelling from Dedwood to Karangahape Road, down into Newmarket and around Orakei in both directions. New redoubts were popping up at Mission Bay, Freemans Bay, Dedwood, Newmarket, and anywhere they could think that the Māori might attack again. It tied up thousands of men. Letters were sent to the paper condemning the army, but it was a circus, as nothing was ever printed. When evening arrived, Shane, Tui and I sat in the dining hall; it was just a quiet threesome. I wasn't much company, so I mumbled, 'I'll see you both tomorrow before we head over to see Sam.' I plodded off to bed. I was depressed again, it wasn't the same, and things weren't getting any better. Maybe with luck, it will change and be better tomorrow.

I woke early, washed, and then went outside for a walk down to the wharf. Looking out onto the Waitamata on a nice fine day makes you feel alive, and today was no exception. I stood there looking out at the ships and suddenly I did a double-take: the Esk wasn't there. I rushed to the end of the wharf, staring out into the roads; she had gone. What the hell. I started to panic, where had it gone? Shit a brick she had gone, our mate had gone, where had it gone? All the 'gone' words were tumbling around in my head. I took off like a bat out of hell to see Shane, feeling sick to my stomach. Oh God, what now.

CHAPTER TWENTY-TWO

I pounded my way back to the hotel and all I could think of was that Sam had gone. I tore through the doors and took the steps three at a time until I arrived at Grunt's room. I banged on his door then burst in; shit, they weren't here. Dining room. Racing down the stairs again, I shot into the room to see Shane and Tui over the other side by the window. I pushed past people without a sorry or a pardon; there were lots of angry looks directed at me. Finally, I skidded to a halt at their table. Shane looked up startled. 'What's wrong, Brill?' he asked. I blurted out, 'He's gone, mate, bloody Sam has gone.' Shane panicked, jumped to his feet and shrilled, 'He can't be dead, he can't.' 'No, not dead,' I said, shocked at the thought, 'the boat has gone.' 'What do you mean? "Gone"?' 'It's not there mate, vanished, disappeared, the bloody boat has left,' I exclaimed. 'Come on, let's sort this out.' He rose to his feet. 'We'll go down to the harbour master and see what the story is.' At least Shane was thinking with his head, all I could do was panic. 'Finish your breakfast, Tui,' Shane suggested. 'Oh no, I'm coming with you, he's my friend as well,' she insisted. We stormed out of the hotel, leaving a wake of chattering folks behind, and headed back down to the harbour. 'Where the hell would they have disappeared to?' Shane wondered aloud. 'The captain of the ship didn't mention a thing about leaving, I was under the impression that he would be here for weeks.' We both tried to get our heads around it. 'The only thing I can think of,' I answered, 'is orders must have come through last night, and they had no time to let anyone know.' 'Well either way,' Shane replied, 'we'll find out soon enough. It might be the time to use those orders that Bill printed to cut through red tape. We need answers now, not tomorrow.' We walked into what was left of the harbour master's office to see the bloke at his desk. He looked up as we arrived. 'How can I help you gentlemen?' he asked. I bellowed, 'What the hell's happened to HMS Esk?' 'Calm down, Brill, that's not going to help,' Shane warned and turned to the man. 'I apologise for my mate, but we're a bit worried about our friend.' The harbour master didn't like being shouted at so he scowled, 'It left at eleven pm last night. No reason was given to me. Unusual though.' He tapped his quill on the desk. 'The navy are usually quite courteous, but this time they just up and left.' 'Do you know where it went?' Shane asked. 'No idea at all, you will have to see the military commander at Fort Britomart.' 'I'm sorry I yelled at you,' I apologised, 'our wounded mate is on the boat, we have to find him.' 'Apology accepted, I can understand; sorry I can't be much help. The military is the place to get your answers.'

So off we traipsed. 'I hope we don't get the bums rush, mate,' I muttered to Shane, 'I will be mightily pissed off if they do that.' Once we left the office and climbed the hill up to the barracks, you could see the destruction of the lower city all around, though some places survived. Things appeared to be getting done; buildings were cleared, and rebuilding had started. A bit quicker than Christchurch thank goodness,. I could smell the new timber in the air, so things were definitely progressing. I was really upset about Sam, even though he had come to, he had no idea who he was or where he was from. His memories, if and when he did remember, will be of 2014, not 1863; it could cause a few ripples, or they might think he's round the bend and put him away for his 'so called' own good. It was imperative that we got a handle on where he went. On arrival at the gate, the guard wanted to check our papers, so without fanfare Shane produced the papers that Bill had printed for us and gave them to the guard. I watched his face as he read them; he paled a bit, handed them back and said, 'Sorry, sir, please follow me.' He called to the corporal to take his place as we followed him into the barracks proper. We went straight to the colonel's office, the name on the door said 'Jackson'. The sergeant knocked, and went straight in. 'Two officers to see you, sir,' he announced. We thanked him as he turned and left. The colonel stood up and asked what he could do for us. We showed him our papers, and he raised his eyebrows. 'These are hush-hush orders; how can I help?' I went on to explain about Sam being put on the Esk to recuperate, that he had amnesia, and we were quite concerned that he might say something he shouldn't without realising, because of his dilemma. That what he knew was secret, not for everyone except for the governor and the general. We needed to know where the ship went to last night. It was not meant to go for a few weeks, we had thought, otherwise we would not have put the lieutenant on it. He rummaged through his top draw and come up with a document which he read and handed it over to us to look at. It was an order for the HMS Esk to proceed with Governor Grey to Sydney then to continue on to Dunedin, taking all the wounded Scottish officers to their home port. 'Bloody Dunedin,' Shane blurted, 'it's not cool mate, it makes things more difficult.' 'Yeah,' I replied, 'one of us needs to follow him and you know I can't. If he's going via Sydney, say five days each way as she's under steam. Allow a day or so in Sydney and you and Tui could be down in Dunedin waiting for the ship to arrive.' I turned to the colonel. 'Do you know if there is another ship heading down there in the next few days?' 'Sergeant,' the colonel bellowed through the door. 'Have we got a ship heading down to Dunedin in the near future?' 'One moment, sir.' You could hear a shuffling of paper, then, 'The Sea Witch, sir, leaves today about six pm.' 'Good man,' he praised, 'book a cabin for the lieutenant.' 'And my wife also,' Shane added. 'And his wife. Get a chit from the paymaster, do it right away, and bring it straight back here when you've booked.' The sergeant took off like a scalded cat. 'Thank you, sir,' I acknowledged. 'That's a load off our minds.' Shane spoke to Tui. 'Will you head back to the hotel and start packing? I'll catch up with you as soon as we have confirmation of the booking.' She squeezed his hand and went out with a corporal who escorted her from the barracks. We hung around for about an hour until the sergeant came back with Shane's booking; he said it was all organised, and will the officer and his wife be down at the boat by four pm. We thanked the colonel and left the barracks. 'At least the printed orders worked out okay for us,' I remarked. I thought for a moment. 'We need some sort of communication setup,' I suggested. 'If I need to contact you, I think the Thistle Pub in the Dunedin Octagon opened in 1862 or 63, so make that your base, and if you need to contact me, post it care of the post office on Queen Street.' 'Yeah, that seems a good idea,' he agreed.

'The way things are going Shane, we might not get together for a while. Even when Sam arrives down there, he still might not be up to another trip for a few weeks or so. If this is the case, send me a letter; either way we could be apart for a couple of months.' Two months, what the hell was I going to do with myself? I didn't want to get tied up with the army. 'I'll have to go bush, mate,' I proposed. 'I can't hang around here waiting. I'll stand out, as if we haven't already.' I was getting a bit nervous thinking about spending two months on my own. This wasn't supposed to happen. Could I bluff my way around for another month or two? I might be fine with my mates, but by myself, I wasn't confident. No, go bush might be the best course. Shane suggested, 'We need to organise our money today, let's see the paymaster together and get it sorted.' 'Right,' I agreed, 'that will take my mind off things for a while; I hope this goes through without a hitch.' We headed up to Albert Barracks. Soldiers were everywhere and at the gate, we ran into Lieutenant Metcalfe coming out of the barracks in a gig with a driver. 'Hello fellows,' he greeted us, 'nice to catch up with you.' 'How are you, mate?' I asked. 'I'm fine, a couple of pellets through the meaty bits of my legs and arms, but I'm fine. They are sending me home on the Dart today to recuperate back in Whangarei. My father, I think, wants to take me around all the pubs. They are calling our men the saviours of Auckland.' He grinned. 'It's like we can't do a thing wrong, they have stuck us all on a pedestal, so I'm off home. Funny though, I've just been told by the colonel not to mention the attack at all here in Auckland. I'm not sure what that's all about, but the way it came across, I think it would be best to heed it. If asked, I got my wounds on the border. It's a bit strange though. If you make it up north just call in, you are only too welcome. Bye for now, my friends, sorry to rush, but I have a few things to do before I leave.' We waved as he moved off; heck, even he was going. I was starting to feel lonely already. It was weird about him not being allowed to mention about the attack though. We were shown into the paymaster's office and handed over our paperwork. He didn't even blink; he just sat down and worked it all out. Then he said, 'That's a tidy sum, 228 pounds for you all, including the wounded lieutenant. I'll give you his share to pass on when you see him. There's three pounds also for Private McInnes.' I jumped in, 'Can you send that over to Mr. and Mrs. Wilson of Cook Street? That's a payment for looking after the children, and I almost forgot, thirty-five pounds has to be sent back to Ensign Robb at Alexander Redoubt for the money lent to us when we came out of the bush.' 'Yes,' he declared, 'that will be fine.' He made a note in his ledger. 'I'll get you to sign for it, though,' he emphasised. 'The army owes you sixty-four pounds, six shillings and nine pence each, but I'll round it up to seven shillings.' He went out the back and returned with three envelopes which he asked us to sign, plus Stewart's three pounds as well. We were out the door, all in fifteen minutes, hearing the paymaster call out, 'I'll send that money down to Ensign Robb.'

Most of the money was in one-pound notes, but there were a few gold sovereigns and half sovereigns as well. 'That sure is a load off my mind,' I said and added, 'I see he has included the amounts on our orders, paid up to today's date; methodical, that's for sure. You better take Sam's pay, Shane, he will need it.' I handed him Sam's envelope. 'Yeah good thinking, Brill, we will look after it,' he concluded. Back at the hotel, Tui had packed all their gear, including Shane's rifle. We sat around yarning, just small talk; we were all worried about Sam and trying not to look it. I was also really concerned about being by myself, though I tried not to let it show. I looked around their room; it was like a clearing out of the old, the slate wiped clean. A thought hit me: once they were gone, would I ever see them again? I was starting to have doubts if I would see *any* of them again. bugger, I was getting myself down. Come three pm, we started to make tracks down to the wharf. We stood and talked by the gang plank, delaying the inevitable. Tui murmured that she would go aboard and came over and gave me a hug. 'You will always be in our hearts and minds, Bobby,' she smiled, kissing me on both sides of the cheek, then squeezed my arm and walked on board. That left me and Shane to look at each other as if it was a funeral. 'Look mate,' he said, 'I'll do my best. If you haven't heard from me in three months, try and get home, let the family know what

happened.' He took the one-gigabyte camera memory card out of his pocket and handed it to me. 'I have another which I will get back to you somehow, mate. This one has all the photos of our wedding so mum and dad will know I'm happy. Brill, this is not forever, it's just in case. Don't look at me like that mate, we both don't know if we will make it home, but if anyone can, you will, so take care of it. It looks as though our letters won't get back home as the bank was burnt, but this memory card that will be proof enough for the folks.' He shook my hand then gave me a bear hug. 'You will always be on my mind, you and Sam. I'll find him if I can,' he vowed, 'I'll do my very best.' 'Yeah, I know, mate,' I mumbled. 'Go on, get going, I'll see you in a few months.' He turned and walked up the plank, waved once more and went below. I hung around the dock for an hour until the ship left, but they didn't come out again. I could understand; they were feeling lost as much as I was. The boat slowly moved out and I watched it disappear around Devonport Heads. I was still there thirty minutes later when a bloke said, 'We are shutting this gate, sir', and so I headed back up to the hotel for something to eat. Really, I felt like getting pissed; I had no friends at all, everyone had gone. I was feeling like shit.

I popped into the dining room, and sat down at the back table by myself. The place was quite full as lot of workers were helping to rebuild the city, which was creating accommodation problems. I sat and thought over the recent events. I'd never heard of the sacking of Auckland by the Māori in our history books, so am I on a different time line I had no idea. But surely this attack would have been splashed all over papers. I must admit I had seen nothing in any newspaper, well, actually, the day after the attack the news was in a flyer, but now nothing and that seemed unusual. I wondered if the governor and parliament had blocked any news of the attack. I sat there and mulled things over when this young navy bloke asked if he could sit next to me, since there was very little seating. 'Please, take a seat,' I said. He introduced himself as Ensign Reynolds. He just came off the Esk and heading out to join the HMS Avon on the Waikato. He went on to explain that it was a steam ship from Lyttleton, converted for war in 1862. He was going on as the second engineer officer. It had twelve-pounders and rocket launchers and was decked out with steel plates for protection. It was going to be a bit different, he smiled, but interesting. He had a broad Scottish accent; I asked him about the Esk, explaining that my mate was on board recuperating before it up and left for Sydney, then Dunedin, with the governor. 'Yes,' he said, 'the governor succonded it, a spur-of-the-moment thing, but fortuitous for the lads that were wounded. It's not often that we have so many of our Scottish lads together on one ship, and the governor gave the captain leave through General Cameron to take them home. So the Esk will be back here in about four months, give or take a week or so. She can cruise at fifteen knots; took us thirty-one days to come out.' I looked at him, then something clicked in my head. 'Four months?' I asked, 'they are only going down to Dunedin from Sydney, that's not four months.' He looked at me. 'Oh, sorry,' he said. 'Dunedin is Gallic for Edinburgh, we use all the time. The ship is going back to Scotland with the wounded.' My mouth must have dropped open in shock as he said, 'Are you alright?' I just looked at him. Oh Sam, I thought, what the hell is going to happen to you now? I was completely overwhelmed; there was no way Shane, or I could catch up with him. Three months on a sailing boat to get to the UK. I would never survive it. Shane would if he could, but where would he go? Sam would vanish into the population before he got there. I was truly gutted. I had to let Shane know, and it would be up to him to decide what he was going to do. If I could fly I would be gone now, but by boat, I'd never make it. I finished my meal in a daze. The young bloke was talking all the way through it, but I didn't hear a word. I excused myself and went to my room, where I got a quill and paper and wrote down the story the young ensign told me. At the end, I wrote, *'Grunt, I'll have to leave it in your hands, you know I would never make it to the UK myself.'* I dribbled on a bit more, before sealing it and putting Shane's details on the envelope and addressing it to the Thistle Hotel in Dunedin; it was ready to post in the morning. I wandered down to the wharf again, and ran into the harbour master coming out of his office. I asked if there was mail going to Dunedin soon. He answered, 'There are no sailings down there for a couple of weeks, though there might be a chance of one in twelve days, but I'm not sure.' Oh great, I thought, Shane would not get the letter for about a month or so, and by that time he most likely would've worked out what happened to the Esk himself. I thanked the harbour master and thought, it's all out of my hands. I'll post the letter tomorrow at the post office; eventually Shane would get it … well, I hope so.

I went back to my room in the hotel, feeling completely helpless. I had to think now what I was going to do. Well, I couldn't hang around here, that's for sure, I needed to make a decision, something positive, but what? A couple of months in the bush waiting for a reply from Grunt, I could get someone to check the post office for me and if there's no letter then, it will be time to try and get home by myself. Then what? I get home, what then? The folks would have to be told of what happened to Sam and Shane, but do I tell them straight away? Alternatively, leave it until I feel there is no chance they will be coming back. How the hell could I break that sort of news to them? They might think that I have lost my mind, and decide to put me in an institution. What year will I go back to if I do get back, will it be just after we left, or does the time run the same as here? We would have been away for four or five months, even longer, how could I explain that? Bugger me, they might have even had a funeral service for all of us by now; shit, if I keep thinking like this, there will be a reason to put me in the funny farm. Change the subject, my mind was saying. The worst thing about it all was that I had lost my best mates. Oh, Shane was not lost, but I had this feeling in the pit of my stomach that he would do his best to find Sam, but he would be happy staying in the past. He had a wife, and they could have children. I would have no more influence in his life and I felt as if I had lost part of myself. Without those two blokes I was not the same person. I needed to pull myself together and plan what was next.

Without thinking, I started to bundle all my stuff into my pack. I cleaned my rifle, and put Shane's camera card into the bag, wrapped up in a waterproof sheet. I then checked my camera and solar panel, which was still working quite well. Within an hour, I was done. So I went downstairs and signed the chit for our rooms and board, then popped into the bar, had a last pint, and returned upstairs to my room. At last I climbed into bed and slept. Dreaming of Sam, Shane and Tui; boats and far-away places, gold, deer and pigs. Hell, my dream, it was all over the place.

I woke early quite exhausted, but resolved to make a start and get out of town. I will head towards the Hunuas. I was determined to lay low for a few months until I hear from Shane. I walked out onto the balcony. The wind was light and cool, still with that early-morning winter darkness before the sun came up. I could hear people already at work further down Queen Street, banging away on the new buildings. The smell of the sea and the newly-cut timber was thick in the air. I wondered if parliament would ever be rebuilt. I wandered down for breakfast, and overheard some bloke saying the governor had gone to Sydney to raise finance from the New South Wales government to help with the restoration. So that was the reason. It's always about money; it hasn't changed and never will. Time to leave I thought, I would head south to Otahuhu, then turn east towards the Hunuas, from there, I was flexible, and I could change the plan to whatever I wanted as I went. It was still cool when I left. The sun was poking its head through the clouds and there was no threat of rain. I had all of my documentation, just in case I was asked who I was and where I was going. I had to make sure that I also kept out of the way of any Māori as well. The Hunua Ranges were a natural hideout for Māori, and during this period of time, they attacked troops from there before returning into the bush. It was very hard to find them, with a good cover of thick bush, so if it can hide them, it can hide me. I just had to be on my toes.

I headed up Queen Street turned left onto Karangahape Road and headed along the ridge until I got to Symonds Street. An empty wagon came rolling along. The driver didn't stop but called out, saying that if I needed a lift, just jump on board. I accepted and hopped up. The driver explained that he was heading to Onehunga, to collect more timber for the builders. It was about seven or eight miles, which normally should take two hours, but in fact, it took three. The road through Three Kings was terrible, but it was nice just to enjoy the countryside, to think that all of this was now Auckland suburbia and a completely different place. I jumped off as we neared the wharf at Onehunga, thanked the driver and headed out to skirt the Mangere inlet, emerging south of the redoubt at Otahuhu. I wanted to be out of this area pretty quickly, so I made my way south and found cover in a manuka grove until I could see the Great South Road was clear. Beyond that, I aimed toward East Tamaki and crossed into the swamp of Otara. It was here that I came across a cleared area which had been used as a resting place for a hell of a lot of people, cooking fires, bones and feathers everywhere. It went through my mind that this was probably where the warriors, who attacked Auckland, had hidden on their way back to the Hunua Ranges. It certainly looked like it to me. The army didn't venture into the swamp. Clever buggers, I thought, no wonder nobody found hide nor hair of them. I decided I would stay here for a couple of days, not right in their camping area, but further into the swamp, just in case they still might return.

With two days of complete silence, I had gathered my thoughts together and formulated a proper plan. I came to a decision: for two months, I'll wait for news. If there was none from Grunt, then I would try and make a bee-line for Pukekawa where all this started. With a bit of luck, I'd find the track back to the cave, or so I hoped. Shane had marked the tree trunks with his knife. Once back there, I'll wait for the right conditions, and if it took a couple of months, so be it; I would wait. With luck, I'll get home; if not, then I'll have to re-evaluate my options. I felt much better, but I still found myself thinking of my mates and where they would be now. Sam was the biggest worry; I just hope he would be okay. So I had a plan, a driving force to get me home and once home I'd explain to all of our parents what happened. I just hoped it would give some closure for my mates' families. I'm sure Sam would understand that I couldn't follow him by boat, he knew what I was like on the water, and Shane knew; that's why he didn't hesitate to go down to Dunedin instead of me. Listening to the morepork, as the sun set on the second day in the Otara swamp, I had this feeling of peace come over me. It was as though my mates were saying, it's okay Brill, we're fine, and we'll make our lives here. Go home and give the family our love. I dropped off to sleep for the first time in a long time with a smile on my face and dreaming of the good times we all had together. When I woke, it was time to move deeper into the hills.

CHAPTER TWENTY-THREE

I began to lose track of time, it must have been about two months of fart-arsing around in the bush, hiding out from Māori and English alike. Anyway, things started to get on my goat. I didn't mind living off the land, but you usually have some sort of a goal, then you go home. I looked like a hobo to boot, but at least I blended in with the environment. There had been a fair bit of activity around lately; I'd seen troops chasing Māori not far from me and vice versa. I didn't want any involvement so the sound of rifle and musket fire pushed me even deeper into the bush. From snippets of conversations I'd overheard from both soldiers and Māori passing by my hidey-hole, it appeared that the troops had now invaded the Waikato, and it was a full-scale war. I racked my brain to remember the dates and recalled that the English had attacked Rangiriri in November, but that was still a few months off. Before that, they'd gotten bogged down with winter, and the Māori harassed them every step of the way. I must admit, it does rain quite a bit in the North Island in winter, so the tracks are rather muddy. The Māori had made a real nuisance of themselves in guerrilla warfare, tying up thousands of troops who needed to watch their supply lines at the rear. I didn't think it would be too long before the English make a bee-line south. It certainly wasn't going the way they'd hoped. It was best for me to keep well out of the way, to stay hidden, but it was not to be. I knew the English were to attack from the rear of the pa at Meremere, but the date was still elusive to me. They would use steam boats as gun ships, towing barges of troops behind them, and outflanking the pa but when that was, I just couldn't think. But when it did happen, Rewi would pull back to Rangiriri and then of course the slaughter would start. The time must be getting close, though at the moment nothing was happening.

Anyway, I was not having a bar of it, no, not this boy. Then out of nowhere people began to fire all around me. The singing of musket balls whizzed past my head. I hit the deck to see Māori belt out of the bush, nearly trip over me and charge after some English troopers who were desperate to get out of the way. I was stuck in the middle of a fire fight. Ten minutes later, it all went quiet. I thought the scuffle must have moved on. I gingerly stood up, with my rifle ready, creeping slowly through the bush until I came to a clearing to see three troopers lying wounded on the ground in front of me. The phrase came into my head, *welcome to our war*, but at the same time my mind also screamed, don't get involved. I was stuck between a rock and a hard place. Oh shit, I couldn't just leave the poor buggers on the ground. So the hero in me dashed over to render help if it was needed.

As I was bending over one of the soldiers, I was caught in crossfire again. I looked up and saw a couple of Māori coming straight at me. I didn't have enough time to defend myself, a flicker of thought entered my consciousness: this is it. Then there was a deafening yell. 'Taihoa, leave that man alone, that's Captain Kidder.' The lead Māori couldn't stop in time and ran straight into me like a bloody rugby forward, and we ended up, all arms and legs on the ground trying to untangle ourselves. An English voice called out, 'Well-done by jove, wonderful side step, Captain.' I laughed as I got to my feet. 'Bloody hell, Peri, it's good to see you,' I beamed, then offered my hand to the Māori bloke underneath me. 'Thanks for stopping this bloke from crowning me. How are you going, mate?' 'Wonderful, my good man,' he answered, 'well now, I am, since I managed to escape captivity in Auckland; I didn't like being cooped up.' 'Oh, you were with the mob that attacked Auckland?' I asked. 'Yes, I was, Captain, lots of fun, but I was a silly chappie, because I was captured, but I escaped.' I grinned, then turning, I pointed to the soldiers. 'I wonder if you would help me with these English troopers?' 'Thanks for the help my friend, we need to get going now,' I replied, 'I don't think this private, here will survive. The other two should though. Are there any more out there in the bush, Peri?' 'Oh no, old son, they are with Jesus now,' Peri answered. I had forgotten that these blokes where Christians. 'We will say a prayer for the departed when we get back to our pa,' he added. The Māori lifted the stretchers and headed towards the redoubt, with Peri in the lead keeping an eye out in case there were English about. We walked for a couple of hours until Peri came back to let us know we were approaching the edge of the bush line. 'We must be off now; you can see the redoubt not far ahead, Captain.' They placed the stretchers down on the ground, shook hands with the wounded soldiers, hongied me, and disappeared back into the bush. I didn't want to leave the one with the stomach wound behind, but there was no way I could carry him, so I ask the other two wounded blokes to keep an eye on him. 'I won't be too long,' I said. So off I went at a jog. I had a bit of trouble getting into the redoubt, with me looking like a bum, so I had to show them the special orders that Bill had produced for us all those months ago, it sure made them hop. Thirty minutes later I was back with a bunch of troopers to carry the wounded into the redoubt. Now I was caught up with all their goings-on, which pissed me off no end. I explained to the colonel that I had been out in the bush for months undercover for the governor and that it was all hush-hush. But he just said, 'Well, for now you will stay here, you have been compromised.' He wouldn't let me go back out, as it was too dangerous without troops with me. So I latched on to the medical team. I wasn't going to get into a battle for nobody, but I might be able to save a life or two.

The surgeon, William Temple, was about my age and Irish. He asked me, if I had any medical knowledge. 'A bit,' I replied. 'Good, you can help out with the doctors and nurses then,' he replied. As he turned away, I remembered a little about this bloke from history books. He received a

VC at Rangiriri. Bugger, did I want to be around someone who wants to be a hero? After talking to the man though, I felt a bit better about it; he was a really nice bloke, genuine and keen to do the best he could for the wounded men I had brought in. The nurses ran the place quite efficiently. I showed him my papers also, but all he did was raise his eyebrows. 'Secrets, eh. If you can pull musket balls out of people, then you will do fine by me.'

After I had cleaned up and had a clothes change, I had my beard trimmed to a reasonable length. I gave my laundry to the orderly before I made my way to the mess tent. The doctors and nurses were there with everyone talking about medical procedures. They then turned to me and asked if I could add to the conversation. Well, I thought, in for a penny, in for a pound. I said, 'Where I come from, the most important thing in operating theatres and wards is cleanliness. Dirt is the biggest carrier of disease.' I watched the nurses nodding their heads along with some of the newer doctors. 'Secondly,' I went on, 'all instruments need to be spotless; you don't go from patient to patient with the same instruments, they go back into a bin to be sterilised and a new one is given to you. You wash your hands after every patient, regardless. If you have to have an orderly running around behind you with soap and hot water so be it. You never attend a new patient with blood from another on your clothes, a new clean apron each time; if you use a hundred, again, so be it. Face masks must be worn in the operating theatre to stop any disease.' I could have gone on, but stopped as they were all looking at me. 'That's a bit over the top old man,' a bloke said. I replied, 'Ask the nurses and the younger doctors. They will tell you, medical science has moved on. We find more lives will be saved with these procedures I have told you. It's up to you, but when I help, this is the minimal requirement that I want where I'll be stationed. What you do in your situation is up to you. At the end of the day, we will see who has the healthiest patients. It shouldn't even come to this though, since we're talking about men's lives.' 'Where are you from, old man?' one officer asked. 'I can't pick your accent.' I forgot myself for a minute. 'I'm a Kiw– oops, New Zealander,' I said. 'Born in Invercargill. You blokes can go home, but this is my home. The way I speak, my accent is New Zealand, we are pretty causal down there.' I was hoping that no one had been south. It proved to be, as they affirmed that they were all off the ship and only here for the war. I threw in, 'If you stay after all this is over, your descendants will talk like me.' 'I'm not sure I like it,' one lieutenant said. 'It's not English.' 'Well,' I said, 'I'm not English, I'm a New Zealander just like those Māori out there.' Before he could object I added, 'We are still British,' just to appease him, 'your queen is our queen.' 'Well that's something then,' he accepted. 'Just remember,' I said, 'when you work on an English trooper you also do the same for a Māori warrior. He's my countryman, no ifs or buts; if you refuse I'll come over and personally boot your bum.' 'Ladies present, Captain.' 'Sorry, girls,' I grinned. The young nurses just stared at me but the older one smiled. 'I couldn't have said it any better myself, Captain,' she commented.

We sat down for dinner and changed the subject; now everyone was getting on like a house on fire. 'How are those men I brought in I asked? 'Fine, two of them are coming along splendidly,' the lieutenant advised with enthusiasm. 'Although we are quite worried about the third man with the stomach wound.'Later that night he passed away, which I suppose was a blessing, he was in agony and the medicine was quite primitive for this type of wound.

I was given a tent of my own, with an orderly, who would be my batman. His name was Albert Banner. I went over with him what I expected if we were in the ward or with the wounded. He was a switched-on sort of bloke; before I knew it, he had aprons, plenty of soap, surgical instruments and had jacked up a place to sterilise my equipment. He also cut up sheets to use as face masks. So I was set. I spent a lot of time with the wounded blokes and got the feel of the camp. Al followed me everywhere I went, as though he was attached to me. The time just slipped by, so when we were ordered to move out, it came as a big surprise. I still had not heard from Shane, and I was getting worried about him and Tui. What else could go wrong? Well, hundreds of things, come to mind. I was really missing my mates. Sam would be in the UK now, and if his memory returns, I'm sure, he will try to come home, or so I hoped. I asked everyone going through to Auckland to check the post office for me. But no letters had turned up. I was devastated.

In the meantime, we were told we were going down the river with the 12th regiment on the last barge pulled by the steamboat HMS Avon. She pulled half a dozen barges behind her and looked like a duck with ducklings. The medical team cleared the main camp and proceeded to the barge by midday on the thirtieth of October. I spoke to the colonel as we got ourselves settled. 'We'll see more action next month. The attack against the pa at Rangiriri is going to tax us. There'll be lots of wounded, but there's a Māori church just outside the pa; we could use it for your hospital.' 'How do you know so much Robert?' he asked. 'Oh, don't forget I was undercover for months, sir. I have been right through here, and everyone knows that the Pa is formidable. If the general attacks it, there are going to be a lot of casualties. I don't think he realises that this is going to be quite nasty. Rewi will fight, it's not going to be a walk over. So, sir, take it from me, when we do set up, have enough beds for over one hundred patients. No doubt we will have Māori wounded as well, so maybe one hundred and twenty beds would be best.' 'That many? Do you think?' he said. 'Oh, I would bet that bottle of whiskey you have in that bag, sir,' I quipped. 'You found me out,' he answered with a grin. 'I won't say a thing if you don't.' I winked and added, 'Talking about that, have we plenty of chloroform for over a hundred?' 'No,' he frowned, 'not for that many, but I'll see the supply officer now and try to acquire more. If not, Captain, we will have to confiscate all the whiskey here for our purpose.' 'Well that'll be better than nothing sir, we'll just tip it down their throats,' I said with a smile. 'I know we have talked about it before sir, but I'd like to confirm that you're still okay with it, that I'll leave the cutting and dicing to you. You're the expert. If I can't fix any arms and legs, I'll pass them on to you and your team. I'm not competent enough to take a limb.' 'Yes, that's fine,' he answered. 'I like the way you've organised that, Robert; it's first class.' 'Well, it works where I come from so it should work here. Assess, Repair, Operate and Recovery: AROR,' I recalled. 'We always abbreviate things down south.' 'It sounds an interesting place, I must visit it when this is all over,' he said. 'One last thing, sir,' I added. 'We need plenty of water, for the orderlies and for any officer or orderly who have to go out onto the front line to render aid. So can I suggest that we have filled canteens placed at the door of the hospital? We can just grab one if we're needed out in the heat of battle.' 'Good idea,' he approved, 'I'll get Lieutenant Pickard to sort that out now.'

Like all armies, it was hurry up and wait; we never got underway until the next day, the thirty-first of October, under Colonel Austin. I thought of Ensign Reynolds, who gave me the bad news about the Esk going back to Scotland; he would be working on the steamboat ahead. As we came around the bend of the river, Meremere Pa was in full view on the left bank. The Māori fired at us and the tug boat as we cruised past, but the boat and the barges had extra steel protection so there wasn't a single casualty. Though there were some silly buggers who wanted to stick their heads above the gunnels to see what was happening. I shouted, 'Pull your bloody heads in, you stupid bastards.' The nurses looked at me in horror. 'Sorry ladies, but it's better to swear at them than to have them die on you for stupidity.' I was thinking, this is me trying to stay inconspicuous? Yeah right. We steamed about two kilometres south of the pa where the 12th and 14th regiments disembarked, formed up and marched back towards Meremere. We set up our medical station, but I knew that there weren't going to be too many casualties the majority of the Māori, not wanting to be cut off, had left for Rangiriri once they saw us cruising pass. The next day the English broke through the rear and took the Pa with only a few scrapes and bruises. With only light wounds, there wasn't much work for the surgeons which suited me fine. It appeared that the Māori that were left behind were to slow the troops down, so the main Pa at Rangiriri could be completely fortified. They had left a token force behind just to make the English fight for the pa, then they slipped away through the swampy ground at the rear when they could. Even so, it was an expensive mistake for Rewi. He didn't factor in that the army would use the river to their advantage and come in his back door; this meant Rewi lost Meremere completely. I remembered it would be nineteen days before the troops would attack the main pa at Rangiriri.

All this time, I had been asking anyone who intended on travelling back to Auckland to check the post office for a letter for me. It had been over five months since Shane had left, and every time a person I had asked returned, they told me there was no mail. What the hell was going on, surely they would have sent something by now. I felt bloody helpless. I knew that after the attack on the Rangiriri Pa in November, there would be a lull in the fighting until February, when the English attacked the Pa at Paterangi. Well to be honest, they didn't attack it, they outflanked it, but whatever; I was determined that I wouldn't be around for that. The Māori would have been cleared out well south of Pukekawa by then, and that's where I was going to head for. Find that cave, wait for the right conditions and fingers crossed, go home; that was my plan. But, right now I had to survive this little dust-up at Rangiriri. November nineteenth came around quite quickly. The pa looked formidable. The church was not far from the pa but still within range of musket fire; that didn't deter the colonel. He just bullet-proofed it, and the nurses turned it into a working hospital with half of it taken over for all the major operations. We placed quite a few tents behind the building for their protection and used some as our assessment area, with a couple of tents for lesser medical procedures. Though to me, there were never any of these, as every single one was serious.

The next day it started, and I wondered why our bombardment was left so late in the afternoon. For two hours, half a dozen armoured ships, that were anchored in the river not too far from the pa, let fly with everything they had. The noise was deafening. You could see the earth flying in all directions around the pa. It took quite a pounding. After a couple of hours, General Cameron decided the softening-up process was complete. He sent in the 65th with scaling ladders and planks to attack the pa and attempt to get a foothold before evening. With only three hours of daylight available, it was a big task to accomplish. They made progress and took the outer defences, forcing the Māori back into the central pa. Now the defenders were six metres above the assaulting troops, putting them in a perfect position, and it became a turkey shoot. The troops attacked repeatedly, with the 12th and 14th using the 58th regiment as reinforcements and the bodies were now starting to pile up. The Māori had the upper hand so this was where my lot came in. An orderly ran over to inform us that a gunner was shot near the main pa entrance; he was still alive but in a bad way, and also Captain Mercer had been shot in the face. Colonel Temple didn't hesitate; he grabbed a first-aid bag and water bottle and took off to render help to those who needed it. Then Lieutenant Pickard did the same, hollering out for volunteers to give water to the troops that had fallen from the outer earthworks of the pa. There were always brave people around and four orderlies dashed after the lieutenant. In full view and under heavy fire, these men went about their duty to save lives. Later, for their efforts, the officers both received the VC. It was at this stage in the battle when the corporal next to me said, 'Captain, they will never be able to bring all those men in by themselves.' He was right, of course. 'Okay,' I said, 'Al, we need stretcher bearers.' I looked around for help. 'You four up to it? Think of the medal and the stories you will tell your grandchildren.' The corporal moaned, 'Oh bugger, this is scary.' 'Yep. Just keep your heads down,' I said. 'Make for the entrance on the right, we'll pick up the live ones, then return straight back here. If anyone falls, we do the best we can, okay.' So the six of us rushed out, muskets balls singing over our heads. The noise was horrendous, and the smoke of battle was everywhere. With the smell and the screams of the injured, all I could think about was that I'm not from here, what the heck was I doing? Regardless, we scrambled on until we came across a bloke with a leg sticking out at an odd angle. The corporal called, 'You alive?' There was a whimper. We quickly placed him onto a stretcher, and the boys took off back to the hospital. Al and I looked around for more, which was a silly thing to say as we were tripping over bodies everywhere. I was now yelling over the noise, 'If you're injured, call out.' Sounds came from all around me; shit. I grabbed a bloke that looked as though he had shoulder wounds. I shouted, 'This is going to hurt.' I then picked him up under his arms and Al picked up his legs, then we took off back to the hospital. The firing never let up, but we were lucky and so were the other blokes. They had made it back okay and were ready for another run. We dropped our bloke off, and out we went again. The nurses and orderlies with the remaining doctors assessed what needed to be done while we went out and brought back more wounded. I just wanted to be a hero; what a bloody mug. For an hour, we went back and forth to bring in them in. I felt sharp pains in my leg and my hip on the last of my trips to the dark side. It knocked me down along with a patient we were carrying; then another whack came, and the patient went limp. He had taken the hit instead of me. I crawled over to Al who was lying at an unusual angle. He was gone. I didn't have time to mourn a good bloke. I crawled under a flax bush to sort myself out when a voice called out from the pa. 'Go back, Captain, or you'll be shot. My men will not harm you.' Good old Peri, my guardian angel. I could see his big wide grin as he looked down from the lofty height of the Pa. I stood up and hobbled back to safety.

One of the nurses came over. 'You've been hit,' she observed, ripping the legs of my pants to take a look. 'Just a graze,' she added, then got a cloth, cleaned the wound and wrapped a bandage around my leg. 'You'll be fine, but we need you here now, there's work to be done.' So I got up, had a bloody good wash and got stuck in. We worked right through the night and did our best to save the injured. There were a lot of broken bones and musket balls in unusual places, but I was lucky there were no amputations. We cleaned out wounds and set broken bones until the cows came home. The head nurse counted eighty-seven wounded, and we'd found five Māori who'd been shot and had fallen over the earthworks into the hands of our troops. I was shagged; the nurses and orderlies were knackered as well. So when daylight came, I said, 'We'll split the shifts.' I sent half of them away to clean themselves, have something to eat and to sleep until midday. Then when they came back on, it was our turn. We did four hours on, four off for the next day until the fitter patients could be sent up to Auckland. Afterwards, I decided I didn't want to go through that again; working on men with no painkillers was appalling. We had run out of chloroform, so we filled the worse cases with whiskey, and luckily they were pissed when we cut. It worked in most cases.

The next day the pa was taken. It was all a wee bit dubious though, the Māori had raised a white flag to parley, and then they opened the gates and in walked the troops. Everyone was friendly to the English, until the English demanded them to surrender. On their part, most of the Māori chiefs and men had left during the night, but still one hundred and eighty odd were taken into captivity. I was asked to go over to see if any of them were injured. Most were fit as a fiddle, though not happy that the English went against the white flag of truce and took the pa. Amongst the prisoners was my mate Peri. He smiled when he saw me. 'By jingo, Captain. You are alive, splendid, I had hoped you survived.' 'Thanks Peri,' I responded, 'you saved my life again, that's the second time now.' 'What are friends for, old chap,' he replied, 'but this asking us to surrender under a truce is really not British, my good fellow; no, it's not cricket at all.' 'Yeah, you're right,' I mused, 'it seems as long as the ball is in their court it's okay.' 'Oh,' he said, 'tennis, I saw a game once, jolly good.' I could see some of the troopers looking at him. 'Blow me down,' a private said, 'he talks like a toff.' I had to laugh, I was getting used to Peri by now. A plan began to ferment in my mind, and I wondered if I could implement it. 'What is going to happen to us now, Captain?' he asked. 'Well,' I said 'your mates will be marched down to the barges and taken as far as Alexander Redoubt. They will continue marching up the Great South Road into Auckland. There they will be imprisoned on the prison hulk on the Waitamata for a while, and later taken over to Kawau Island.' I carried on without thinking. 'They will eventually escape from there to the mainland and slowly head back to the Waikato, though not in time to help Rewi's next campaign. By the time they get there this part of the war will be over.' He frowned, 'I forgot you seem to have second sight. I'm not going to ask you how you know, but you did say they, not me.' 'Yeah, Peri, I want to ask you a favour. Would you take me back to where you first came across us at the kainga in Pukekawa? I want to get as close to the cave that we found. If you'll do that for me, I'll have a pardon slip for you to return south to your iwi.' 'Ah,' he answered, 'is that where you were hiding? I know of the cave, but to us, it's tapu. Strange things happen in the area, it could even be the home of the Taniwha. If I take you, it'll not be all the way, but I will point you in the right direction. Will that be suitable to your ends?' 'Peri that will be great, it's all I ask,' I claimed with a grin. 'Then,' he replied, 'I'll do what you ask.' We hongied and I took off to see the regimental colonel. I found him in the hospital, and I once again showed him my orders from the governor. I requested that he releases Peri into my care and explained, 'I needed to do some scouting and as Peri knows the area well, and he has agreed to help me.'

He just said, 'Fine, take whoever you want, and thank you again for your help.' He gave me a chit for Peri and had him released into my care. I took Peri back to my tent to feed him and find him suitable clothing. I then went to visit the sergeant who was taking the Māori prisoners to Auckland. I asked him to check the post office for me again, letting him know I would wait for his return. I spoke to the colonel of medicine and gave him the heads up that I was going bush; I didn't want anyone looking for me. He was sorry to see me go as some of the things I had done in the theatre he had never seen before, and he was interested to go over the procedures.

Four days later, after I played doctor with the wounded, the sergeant returned empty handed. 'Sorry, sir, there was nothing for you.' That was it, time to leave. I was genuinely worried about Shane and Tui, but it was well past the time limit; if I hadn't heard from him, he wanted me to go home. I wonder what could have gone wrong. I couldn't wait any longer, I had to leave, and I needed to tell the folks our story.

CHAPTER TWENTY-FOUR

On a wet, miserable day, Peri and I took a hike to the Waikato River from Rangiriri. We were hoping to find a canoe then to paddle towards the opposite bank on our journey north to Pukekawa, and I hope, home. We arrived on the bank of the river appropriately wet and miserable, and were lucky enough to find a canoe pulled up on the bank two kilometres upstream from the pa. The river was flowing deep brown and fast; we couldn't see below the surface, so we didn't have the faintest idea what was flowing beneath. It could be a bloody great kauri for all we knew. We both needed to keep our eyes peeled. I didn't want to end up in the drink and float out to Port Waikato, so it was steady as we go. We really should have waited until the weather was better, as it was a hell of a job trying to cut across the current. Eventually, we ended up back on the same side we had left; it was just too tough. We sat it out for a couple of days on a knoll above the river, making better paddles out of a fallen Matai tree which had come down with the weather.

Was I supposed to get home? Everything seemed against it, and now this bastard river was giving me grief. Quite honestly I was fed up with it all. We sat and yarned the days away until Peri said, 'The current is nowhere near as strong, let's have a jolly good old bash, my good man.' Second time lucky, we got across, though it was a hard slog, at last we were on the side of the river where we needed to be. We pulled the canoe up onto higher ground, leaving it for someone who might want to use it later, then headed inland. I had no idea where we were, but we were south of Pukekawa. As we headed inland, the bush got thicker, I had to rely on Peri to get me to the right spot. He never hesitated; he seemed to know wherever he was at any given time of the day, so my worries on that score faded as we move on through the bush. Resting in the evening on the second night, I asked him how he knew where we were. 'It's all in my head,' he said, 'I've been around this bush since I was a small chap, it's ingrained in my mind. We're not far from the place where I'll leave you; I'm going to miss you my friend. It's a shame we'll not see each other again, but I have this feeling you'll get to your destination. I will think of you and tell my tamariki, my children, of the strange Pakeha who could see the future. I have watched you, Captain; you are definitely from a different place, my good man. You see the future; although actually I think, it's your past and your history. I don't want to know, but I can understand you being out of sorts here: you don't belong.' 'You are a perceptive bloke, Peri: no, I'm not from here, but let me tell you. I will always think of you as a friend. This country, our country, in the future is a good country to live in. We have tried to preserve this ' I waved my arm around in the general direction of the bush, 'and your culture. Of course we've made mistakes, but as a country, we try. Since we're being honest mate, my name is Robert Kydd, or Bob; you're the only one who knows, besides Shane and Sam. I'm not in the army here, I never have been. I won't tell you what armed force I was in as you wouldn't believe me, but I'm a New Zealander like you.' He looked at me and commented simply, 'Yes, you are so different.'

'What is your last name, Peri?' I asked. 'Oh, Nepia,' he replied. 'My whanau is from Waipukurau. I was sent up as a child for schooling with the missionaries here in the Waikato, by my mother's family. Later, I went back home for a while, before I knew there was going to be a battle in the Waikato. I had to help my mother's family; it's what families do, old man, it's our land, and the English are going against the treaty, so here I am. I'm due, I think, to go home very soon. It's time I took a wahine.' I grinned at him. 'Well, with a name like yours, my friend, you will have some bloody good rugby players in your family.' He frowned. 'Rugby? I have heard that word, but I'm not sure what it means.' 'Don't worry, mate, you will know when it arrives; think of me when it does.' 'You're a funny fellow, Bob,' he replied. 'I don't understand half the things you say.'

The next morning we left early, there was no apparent track that I could see, but Peri found it and even though it was slow going, we moved in a northerly direction at a steady pace. We were cutting through pig fern when there was a squeal: I stood on a porker hidden in the fern. I was a bit slow, and before I could get my rifle up, he was gone. Peri laughed. 'Well, my good friend, if that had been my brethren, you would have been tonight's dinner.' 'I'm slipping Peri, I should be more aware,' I claimed with a grin. 'Well,' Peri remarked, 'I have marked his tracks. When I leave you, I think I'll come back and have some pork for dinner.' He didn't have a gun as the English had taken that off him, but he was left with his knife and patu. 'I love chasing the poaka, (pig) it's jolly good fun. The rifle is awkward to move around in the bush. I'd rather hunt with my knife anyway.' I was going to miss this bloke when we split, but split we must. Peri had said a hundred times, he wasn't going anywhere near the cave that I wanted to go to. As far as he was concerned, it was a place of spirits, fairies and possibly Taniwha, certainly not a place for well-brought-up gentlemen. When we get to the drop off-point, we'll have to say our goodbyes.

An hour later, he came to a stop. I looked around and felt the thrill of excitement. I recognised a tree and as I walked around it, I saw the mark that Shane had left. I was now at the place where we'd come out of the bush and onto the track where we had found Bill's footprints all those months ago. It brought back memories of the boys, and I fought back tears. I didn't want Peri to see me with watering eyes, so I used the time to scout around for the next marker that Shane had left. Five minutes later, I found it. Now if I'm able to follow the markers all the way back to the cave, it should take about three hours, if I remembered correctly. I walked back to where Peri was still sitting on a log, carving a piece of wood. He sat there for about an hour while I pulled some food out of my pack and went about making some lunch. Then we ate in silence. Between mouthfuls, Peri continued carving. When he was finished, he got up and came over to me. 'I have made you this,' he said, as he handed me a rough wooden tiki. 'It will bring you good luck.' He took it out of my hand and with the point of his knife, carved a small hole at the top. Next he found a flax leaf, which he'd stripped down to a fine thread, and fed it through the eye. Last of all he tied it around my neck. 'This will protect you, and my mana will be with you.' I had to give him something in return. 'Peri,' I said, as I pulled out my small torch. Flicking on the switch – how the battery had lasted so long I had no idea, but it had – I handed it to him. Peri jumped. 'It won't hurt you my friend, this is yours. One day, the light will fade, but I hope my memory will stay with you.' He flicked it off and on again, marvelling at it. 'Light, but there is no heat; it is fine magic, Bob, it will take pride of place in my whare.' We lingered a while, not wanting to part, but in the end, Peri said, 'Bob, I wish you the very best of British luck. Thank you for not sending me to the prison ship, I'm in your debt.' 'No, Peri,' I said, 'we're even. You returned me here to this place. I'll continue to think of you for the rest of my life. Enjoy your life, I hope you find a wife and have lots of children.' We hongied and without a backward glance, he disappeared into the bush. Once again, I was on my own. I didn't want to be, but, I was. Time to move on: I needed to get to the cave before dark.

I took my time to find each tree that Shane had marked. I thought if I lost his trail, I'd be walking around in circles for ages, so slowly, and methodically I followed the sign. It seemed so long ago, and so many things had happened since the three of us had come down this route, but in my mind's eye, my mates were there, and I didn't want to let them down. It was up to me to let the families know that they were okay – well, to a point. For three hours, I followed the markings which brought me out to under the ledge of the cave mouth. I recognised it immediately, still the same, just above the bush floor. I climbed the bank and stuck my head into the entrance. Immediately I felt there was something different about it, my inner sense picked up something, though what, I didn't know. I popped my rifle against the wall close to me, placed my pack on the floor and proceeded to start a fire. With the light it produced, I could see why I felt something was different. There were footprints on the cave floor and they weren't ours. Towards the back, I noticed a midden of shells and small bones, and tracings of gun powder. Some Māori, or a few Māori, had been here and not that long ago, by the look of it. Bugger, I thought I'd have to watch myself as not all Māori were nice and friendly. My day up to that point had been great, but from now on I'd really have to be on my toes. They mustn't be from around here, as this place, this whole area, was tapu, so they'd probably be from outside the Waikato. I had to have to have eyes in the back of my head from now on. Defence protection was a priority, so I went out and dragged logs up to the entrance, leaving enough space to have a clear view of the bush all around me. I ran flax twine across the rest of the entrance, if anyone tried to come in, they would, I hope, trip over the line, giving me time to have a go at them if needed. I thought I'd be okay; I still had plenty of ammo and enough food for a month or so, and there was water at the back of the cave. I had no idea, how long I'd have to stay there while waiting for the right conditions to appear. For all, I knew, I might have to head down to Ruapehu, but I'd given myself a couple of months. If nothing happened in that time, then that was the next plan. And if Ruapehu didn't work out, I would be stuck here and at that point I'd have to decide where I'd go to settle. Anyway, that was the future; right now, I needed to be aware. I scratched marks on the cave wall every day to keep a track of the time and after about four weeks, I started to get a bit slack. Constant visual awareness was tiring, and I thought it must be getting near to Christmas. I had seen some pigs a week ago, and managed to shoot a little one, so I still had some pork left over for Christmas dinner. I was singing carols in my head, wondering about what everyone was doing and how everyone was coping.

We'd been gone from our time for about ten months. If I made it home, my parents were going to be in for a big shock, and so would Shane's and Sam's folks. How would I explain it to the police, they might suspect foul play? For weeks, all this had been going around in my head, and I was still none the wiser as to what the hell I should do. I gave myself another four weeks there, then I would move down to Ruapehu, but I still didn't want to think about that trip at all. Another couple of weeks went by, and boy,

I was getting delusional from the isolation. I even woke to see Shane and Sam in the cave with me. It was all in my head, of course. I think the rational part of my brain was telling me I was losing it.

Then one day, late in the afternoon, the rain set in. Light at first, then heavy and within a couple of hours, it was pouring down. In the distance, to the south I could hear thunder rolling, and as it crept closer, lighting flashed over the canopy of the bush. This has to be it, I thought, as with the rain came a heavy fog. My heart was pumping as I grabbed all my gear, and crawled out of the cave to the forest floor heading south. I was trying not to trip over anything as the fog was so thick. I came to a clearing when I heard movement behind me, diving behind a tree when a shot rang out. Then a Māori voice yelled out, 'The next one, we'll not miss.' Oh shit, more than one. I jammed a shell into the breach of my weapon and waited for the next move. I could see the fog swirling, then it took on a sort of golden hue. This has to be it, I thought. My hopes were high, but I had to get away from these Māori who were intent on killing me. I took off towards the golden fog, legs pumping like hell. The hairs on my head and arms were standing up with the electricity from this phenomenon; funny how it's the little things you remember. I couldn't even weave as the bush was so thick, then I heard a musket go off and my body fell sideways as the ball punched into my thigh, feeling another hit me in the shoulder at the same time. I didn't feel any pain; I was so full of adrenaline. I turned, and out of the fog this Māori came running and

I shot him in the chest. He made a gurgling sound and fell to my right. His mate was just behind him; I slammed another round into my rifle and just pointed it. He was about to run me through with an English bayonet. I pulled the trigger, and his head blew apart; he landed on top of me, his lifeless fingers having let go the bayonet before he trapped me under his body. I tried to move, but I didn't have the strength. All I could think about was getting out of here and staying in the fog. The glow of gold was all around me, and I lost consciousness.

When I came to I was in a lot of pain, there was blood everywhere, and I was so dizzy I couldn't think straight. I remembered being shot and I began to feel my body, looking for wounds. In the end, I found three: one on my side, one on my shoulder and one in my thigh. The old wound from Rangiriri was sore as well and my hip ached. I tried to sit up, but it was an effort. I grabbed my pack and dragged out what was left of the first-aid kit – mainly bandages now, but at least I could maybe stop the flow of blood leaking out of me. I did the best I could, but then it dawned on me … where were the Māori blokes I shot? I slowly looked all around, but nothing. I was alone. I moved my hands under the canopy of leaves trying to sit up and touched something metal. I dragged it out, and it was the bayonet that the bloke tried to stick me with, all rusty and old looking. Heck, he sure didn't look after this, I thought, but what the hell had happened to them? Had I lost them in the mist? I felt so weak, confused; I felt myself slip into darkness. As I came around, I realised I must have passed out again, and I heard muffled voices way in the distance. It sounded like English, so I forced myself to become aware. I did my best to wake fully, but the voices were still far away. I couldn't let them pass me by otherwise I might die out here; I'd have to take a chance that no Māori were around. I managed to load my rifle, pointed it into the air and fired a round. I did it three times and collapsed with exhaustion.

How long I was out for again I had no idea until I came to briefly. I was on a stretcher being carried by four men. A young lady with a stethoscope around her neck was walking beside me, looking down at me. I said, 'Hi, I didn't know that those were invented yet,' and dropped back into oblivion. Once again, I surfaced, hearing a whirling noise and feeling a flying sensation, but I figured that wasn't possible and dropped back into the blackness. The first real round of awareness came when I woke in a white room by myself, bandaged like a mummy with monitors all around, lines in my arm, and pain in my thigh and shoulder. It dawned on me then: this was modern stuff. I tried to sit up. I was so excited to the point that I exhausted myself with the effort and dropped right back to sleep. I gathered it was the next day when I woke again. This time I noticed a bloke in blue on a chair reading a book. As I attempted to sit, he said, 'Wait!' and pushed a button for the nurse, who came rushing in. 'Well done,' she said, 'you are back in the land of the living.' With the help of the bloke in blue, she helped me sit up straight. 'I could do with a coffee. What's the date?' I queried. 'It's the twenty-eighth of December, 2015,' she answered, then shot off to report my awareness to the doctor and, hopefully, get me a coffee. My God, I was another year out, it should have been December 2014, I thought, as the doctor came in.

'How are you feeling, Mr. Kydd?' he asked. 'Oh, you know my name,' I said. 'Yes,' he replied, 'from your wallet. Although it was hard to get a positive ID as your wallet was a mess.' 'I feel bloody awful, but I'm pleased to be here,' I assured him. 'Good. We operated on you, and took out three bullets; well, not bullets, actually, they were musket balls. We also dealt with an older wound in your hip that showed signs of infection. Now, can you remember how you got those wounds?' 'Yes,' I answered, 'I was shot by some Māori in the bush. Did anyone find them? They fell on me when I blew the brains out of one of them.' I don't think that's what I should have said, because the bloke in the blue had his book out writing furiously. Oh bugger. Too late I realised he was police. 'Hmm,' the doctor said, 'I think we might give you a few painkillers and something to relax you a bit.' Turning to the cop he said, 'I think it will be a while before he's fit to question, Sergeant.' I asked the cop, 'Did you find anyone else where you found me?' 'No,' he replied, 'only you.' 'Did you find the bayonet?' 'Yes. That's evidence,' he added. 'Then would you do me a favour, dig around a bit where I was found, you might come across some bones.' That made his ears pick up. It might help me in the future I thought – or they might put me in a funny farm. I was too tired and sore to worry about such things. But before I dropped off again, I asked them, 'Where am I, and have my parents been informed I'm here?' The cop replied, 'No they haven't, this is a major inquiry, and until we find out just who you are, no information leaves this room. If you say you are this bloke Kydd, then where have you been for nearly two years, and where are your friends? What's happened to them? We've got a lot of questions.' He rose to his feet with the fervour of his speech. 'On top of that, why did you look like a hobo on crack when we found you? It looks as if you lived rough for months. So until this is sorted out, no one will be informed of your whereabouts. Oh, and you're in Whanganui Hospital secure ward.' With that, the doctor left, the policeman sat back down and I went back to sleep at least with the knowledge I was safely in my own time and century.

After two months of being in hospital, my folks still had no idea I had returned, and I was pissed. My strength was getting back to normal, but I think I was going to have a limp for the rest of my life. I was aware that it was getting to the stage where the police were gearing up to interview me, and I thought I'd tell the truth. I could not understand why the delay. I realised that I would most likely end up going into a home for the weird and wonderful, but if I don't tell it how it was, then I might not get to see my family or my mate's family for quite a while. So the police were going to get both barrels. I was allowed outside for walks with two big blokes as escorts. We all got on well, and we talked about the Super Fifteen sports teams. I had missed two years, so they brought me up to date. I had even missed the world cup, but I was over the moon when told New Zealand had won. We avoided what I'd been doing over the last year or so.

On a Monday morning in March, I was picked up in a police car and taken to an office in the city. I found that funny, it not being in a police station. Here I met some government officials, the police team and my own lawyer. I'd spoken to him before, and he didn't believe a word I'd said; he had only nodded and smiled. I thought at least he'd help me by saying I'm a nutter and to be put away for a few years to be analysed. So in I went with my arm still in a sling and limping badly, to a three-man committee along with some black suited blokes sitting in the back of the room. They did, however, have a comfy chair for me, and it was all very amicable. Apparently, they knew that I was who I'd said I was, as a DNA test had been done to prove it. So then it began. For three days, they questioned me. I told them everything from beginning to end; I gave them names and places. At the end of it I asked, 'Is there a historian in this group?' One bloke stuck up his arm. 'Can you tell me why we don't know about Auckland being attacked by Māori in 1863?' I asked. 'They made a hell of a mess, yet we knew nothing about it.' He pulled out some newspapers. 'They mentioned the great fire of Auckland in 1863 but nothing about a Māori attack.' I chuckled. 'Governor Grey was a cunning sod, he must have D-noticed it and then gone around the whole population of Auckland and explained the situation to them, they would never get money to repair and to expand if we say Māori attacked their capital, so new immigrants wouldn't come out. Oh, the cunning bugger, that was clever. However, I was there, I lost a third-great-uncle in the fighting in Queen Street, and my mate Sam was shot and wounded. My other mate Shane and I fought from the balcony of the Union Hotel, we all were there,' I said. 'I know you think I'm in la-la land, but we did our best to help our mate Sam and the rest of the population. I survived Rangiriri and Auckland. We were shot at from an ambush on the Great South Road. If you all think, I'm mad, fine, I can't do a thing about it, but did you find bones where I was found?' They all looked at me, why are government employees always in suits, then one of them replied, 'Yes, we found the bones of two bodies, both shot at from close range about 150 years ago, or so the lab tells us.' 'And?' They hummed and hawed. 'The bullet hole in the head and chest match your rifle.' Oh shit, I felt good. 'We can't explain it and though your story is a bit far-fetched, there are things in it with a ring of truth, this being one. The second was the Auckland raid; it was wiped from history. How Grey did it is beyond us, but those days he was the power. He kept private records and in some of those, he mentions the real reason the fires started. Furthermore, there's a mention of a Lieutenant Sam Mack, who saved the life of a prominent Auckland citizen and a Māori sergeant who lost his life with the lieutenant.' I jumped in, 'William Hohepa, my third–great-uncle that I mentioned. Is there any information on Sam?' 'No, that's all we have. One more thing that came to light was a concert in Auckland with a band that played some very unusual music. A little piece in the local paper, not much, but it does substantiate your story a wee bit.' 'Yeah, that was us. Tui sang, we played, and it got Mr. Wattle out of the office, so we could print off our orders.' 'Yes well, we've seen these orders; we found them in your pack. We'll be keeping them.' I looked at them. 'What happens now?' I asked. 'We'll come back to you next week,' he answered. 'In the meantime you'll stay where you are, and under no circumstances, will you talk to anyone about it.' 'Well, what about my parents and my mates' families? Over the past two years, they'd thought we were all dead. They have to be told.' 'Yes, well, that's what we'll talk about. In the mean time, you will stay put, and we'll be in touch.'

So off they went and I returned to confinement. I was given my pack back so I went through it; my camera survived, and I had Shane's memory card. I wasn't going to let those buggers have those. I took the sim card out of my phone; the card survived but not the phone. My camera was okay, but the solar panel was shagged. I found my clothes from 1860, they would have seen them as well, that's more evidence, and I still had Peri's tiki. I also had about forty pounds in money, still in good order. I wondered if it was worth anything. I was surprised, they returned my gun that had been nicely wrapped in an oil skin, even though they did take the ammo. I wondered if they were going to let me go, and if so, when? Another two weeks passed so much for we will get in touch next week' and I was getting more depressed as the time stretched out. Eventually, they came back to me. They sat me down and placed all this paperwork in front of me, to sign. It was a No Disclosure Notice, about everything that happened to me in the last two years. I also had to sign the Official Secrets Act. Before I did this, I asked, 'Can I tell my parents?' This is when I found out that these buggers had been around to all the families whizzing them up, letting them know that I was home, then making them sign the act as well.

I told them what complete bastards they were. My mates' folks and my mum and dad had thought their boys had died and in comes a government agent to say sign this, your boys are alive but living in the past and have been dead for over one hundred years. 'I wish you'd left me a bullet in the rifle,' I told them. 'I would have stuck it up your bum and pulled the trigger.' They were completely immune to threats. They told me, 'That part of Ruapehu is now out of bounds as there's a lot of thermal activity up there.' So they closed that area of the park, I thought. 'Of course, it will be manned by the army twenty-four hours a day until things settle down.' 'Great,' I answered. I wasn't really interested; I just wanted to go home. 'one more thing, did we get a good funeral?' I said sarcastically. At least, they had brought me all the papers from the beginning when the police and army had scoured the park looking for us. The conclusion was that we had all been swallowed up in a mud pool, which was theoretically possible. The memorial service had been large; I didn't realise that we'd had so many friends who wanted to touch base at the services. So I asked, 'How are we going to get around this?' 'Oh, that's easy, Mr. Kydd, you have had amnesia,' was the reply, 'quite a severe case, and it's only now that you've started to get your memory back. You couldn't remember what happened to your mates. The last thing you can remember is slipping down a shingle fan, until you woke up here in the hospital. You have been cared for impeccably by the health service. It has only come to the authorities' notice after recovering your pack a few months ago that you are Robert Kydd. You were found wandering around Lake Taupo in an awful state. Some way or other, the connection between the missing three men on Ruapehu didn't click with the authorities, and for that we have apologised. This episode will never be discussed outside your immediate families. We cannot have people just wandering in and out of time. So once you sign the Official Secrets Act you can go home.' The cunning buggers, they'd sure put on a show, but understandable I suppose. All I wanted was to just go home and if I had to sign everything in triplicate, I'd do it. So I signed my life away. 'Good,' they said, looking at the signature. 'Very good. The government has decided to grant you fifty thousand dollars for being so cooperative, and to make up for our supposed delay in connecting the dots after we 'found' you. We'll have everything ready for you tomorrow. We also have a new cell phone for you, and tickets to Invercargill. Good luck, Mr. Kydd, we hope you recover and remember: mum's the word.'

They left me and all I could think seeing my family. I was so looking forward to catching up with them. One thing I did know: I was telling the folks the whole truth, not the truth these blokes would want me to say, but the truth about what really happened while I was away.

CHAPTER TWENTY-FIVE

My tickets duly arrived the next day for the flight south. Travelling from a provincial town, and using small aircraft with all the chopping and changing it requires, was going to make it a long day. Whanganui to Wellington, Wellington to Christchurch; and then change again for Invercargill. Even so, at least, I was going home, that was the main thing. I'm not too sure what the reaction would be when I get there, but I'd soon find out. I said a last thank you to the nurses and doctors who fixed me up and to the shrink who worked with me. He said if I had any problems at all, just to ring him. Apparently, there could be a relapse of post-war depression; he made me promise not to be a hero. They understood it more now and were there to help.

It was nice to get away from the hospital, and I enjoyed the flight down the country. Before long, I was in the South Island. I was going home. I never thought I would make it, now I speculated about all the things I was going to say to mum and dad and my mates' families; it was all a bit daunting. I had to be strong, but I wasn't feeling very confident. I might need the shrink after all. After leaving

Christchurch, we hugged the Southern Alps all the way to Invercargill. I was nervous when the city came into view. I looked over the sweeping coastline from Bluff through to Riverton then Colic Bay and lastly, there was Kawakaputa Bay, where my crib is. I could just make out the roof of my place. I had a tear in my eye as the aircraft came around to come in from the south. The plane dropped down and kissed the seal of the runway. I was home.

I sat in the cabin, waiting for everyone to get off. I was beginning to feel that I didn't want to see anyone, I felt like hiding. However, the pilot stuck his head around the door. 'This is it, mate.' 'Yeah,' I replied, 'thanks.' I had no choice now, I had to leave the plane. I stood at the top of the stairs, there were no air bridges in Invers, and looked out towards the passenger terminal, when I heard this cry. Mum was pushing the security guard out of the way and came belting over towards the aircraft, screaming my name at the top of her voice. As I reached the bottom of the stairs, she just flew at me like a front-row forward. Her arms were around me, and she was kissing and hugging me, saying my name over and over. It took a while for her to come back to earth. 'Bobby, your father and Sasha are waiting for you.' We didn't even get inside the terminal before the old man jumped the fence and ran over and hugged me, my sister following him. We all stood there on the tarmac, in a group hug laughing and crying. We were together again. I've never seen Dad cry before today, but then everyone was emotional. 'I'll get the car to the front gate, Bob, won't be a tick,' he insisted as he ran off. The two women in my life ushered me through the building with arms around me and wouldn't let me go. Dad pulled up outside the terminal, and we all jumped in. We headed back to their place. Funny, the first thing that popped into my head to ask when we got going was, 'Did you find my Surf?' 'Yeah, son,' Dad said, 'I went up north and picked it up; I dropped the trailer around at Shane's. So your Surf is still in the garage at your place. We've taken turns to go and start it up. I've kept it serviced and everything is up to date, including rego, and WOF. We couldn't believe that you were not coming home, so by doing the small things, it kept our hopes alive.' Mum came in with, 'Your house is fine. Ron has been there, right up to a month ago, and all your money is still in your account. We paid your rates and insurance over the last couple of years, so no need to worry about anything. You can go home whenever you want.' 'Oh, Mum, Dad, if you don't mind, I'd like to stay with you for a bit. I've been by myself a while now and I'd like to have the company of family around me.' 'You can stay as long as you want, Bob, there's no need for you to leave at all. Just take your time and we can all enjoy being together again,' Mum replied with a smile. 'Well, I have a hell of a lot to tell you. I don't know what the suits from Wellington have said to you, but I've a feeling they missed out quite a bit,' I claimed. 'Yes, I wasn't taken with how they came across, Bob,' Dad replied, 'they were quite abrupt and there was a lot we didn't understand. They said something about history, then they said you went through a time warp. He said you were okay, but a bit disorientated as being out of time had mixed you up a bit. This is why you've been missing for so long. Everyone else has been told you had amnesia. He said a lot of stuff that, honestly, we thought was rubbish. I thought he was on drugs, but he didn't smile. Then he brings out this official form we had to sign.' 'Well, they never told you the whole truth, then,' I remarked, 'but even so, they still got you to sign the Official Secrets Act. When we get home, give me a day to get my head sorted, then I'll tell you what really happened. After that, I will need to get in touch with Shane's and Sam's parents.' I stopped, then murmured, 'I tell you Mum, Dad, I really miss those blokes.' I went quiet. I looked out the window, seeing nothing, my eyes full of tears. Is this the way it will be for me now, crying like a baby whenever I talk of my mates? Maybe I do need to see the shrink again, I won't be able to go on like this. I couldn't stand it, being in this state forever.

We pulled into the drive of my parents' house, a big old rambling place with four bedrooms on a slight rise overlooking Henderson Bay. God, it felt good to be home. The old man grabbed my pack and rifle out of the boot, and both mum and Sasha ushered me into the house. 'Take a seat, Bobby, I'll put the kettle on,' Sasha said. They'd set up a room for me downstairs, one with an ensuite and all the works, and that's where dad dropped off my gear. We talked about everything, bringing me up to date about the town, the people we know, and my house, but nothing about my story. Then Sasha's boyfriend came up in the conversation, who I was told was a fisherman from Northland, who thought he might try something a bit different in the South.

He had brought his boat down, met Sasha and the way the talk was going, it looked like there might be wedding bells. 'I'll introduce you Bob, when you feel up to it,' she told me. We had an early dinner, then I excused myself and went to bed. I was exhausted, well no wonder, it was my first full day out of hospital and an emotional day to boot. I just died that night, and slept in late.

By the time I was up, dad and Sasha had gone off to check another boat over, with the hope of adding it to their fishing fleet; it would be their third, they were becoming a nice little company. I think if and when Sasha gets married to Neil, his boat might be incorporated into the business as well, splitting the partnership three ways. I was happy for them all. I waited until they eventually arrived home at two pm. They had had lunch in Invers, so we sat down and I began my story. 'This is going to take a while, it might sound far-fetched, but you have to believe it's the truth. How it happened, I have no idea, but it did. So here goes; you can ask questions later.' I started at the beginning and by six pm, and I was still going. I had them spell bound. By seven pm it was finished, and I stood up. 'These are my wounds.' I took off my shirt to reveal the scar on my shoulder where the ball had entered and a bigger hole in my back. I took off my shorts. 'Sorry, Sasha.' I exposed two big scars on my thigh and calf, and a beauty on my hip. 'They only found that when they were operating on me. These are all musket wounds, and I will always have a bad limp.' I dressed again. 'I think some food is called for, a takeaway?' Dad asked. 'The local shop is open till eight pm.' So we ended up with fish and chips, with mussels and oysters and big slices of homemade bread lathered with butter. I felt better now that I'd told them, but I was still waiting for a reaction.

After the meal, Sasha looked at me and said, 'You were lucky to come home Bob, but now you're here we don't want you going anywhere for a while.' Poor old Mum and Dad kept shaking their heads. I don't really think my parents were convinced, but that will come when I have all the parents together to retell the story with pictures. That was my next project.My biggest regret was Sam. I'd lost him. I didn't know how to apologise to his parents. Shane, I thought he'd be okay, he had his wife. If they couldn't find their way back to our time, they would've been dead for one hundred years or so by now. Yet I was with them only a few months ago. I still couldn't come to terms with it all, as it's now 2016. The next day, I borrowed mum's car and went over to my place. I apprehensively open the door; but I was pleasantly surprised. It was just as I had left it, even though Ron had been renting it. I loved this place, with its cosy warmth, and I could see Foveaux Strait from my lounge window. To the left was a nice little knoll where I'd go and sit to clear my head. It was quiet and peaceful. My computer was there so I booted it up, oh, it wanted to install updates forever, but I didn't want a bar of that at the moment so I clicked the updates off. I took Shane's memory card and put it into the port and held my breath. A new window popped up on the screen: it worked. I was over the moon, the pictures came up perfectly. I went through over three hundred of them. Then there were more on my camera. It was a shame I had nothing from Sam's phone; it was in his pack when we took him out to the HMS Esk, so those photos will most likely be lost forever. First of all I went through my photos, putting them in order in a file and then dragged Shane's photo's over, making a total of some 600-odd photos. I then reordered them to fit in sequence. I found a handful of empty USB sticks and copied all the photos onto seven of them: one each for Shane's parents and his sisters, and three for Sam's family. I can give the copies to my family later. Looking through the photos from the beginning they covered, the pigs we shot, the mist in the trees, even the Huia. Images of Bill and the kainga with Rita and her tribe; the time Stu and Bill had a go with the camera; and of course Shane and Tui's wedding, it was all there recorded for them to see. I didn't realise we'd taken so many; they would have to believe me now. It's not as though they didn't believe it as such, it had been just a far-fetched story to this point. Even I wouldn't think it was very plausible if I was told it cold turkey. However, I did have the wounds to show and Peri's tiki was carbon-dated at one hundred and fifty years, and you don't just find that stuff lying in the bush. Now I have the pictures to prove it all.

I had another bawl when I finished going through the them, then I got the shakes. Something wasn't right with me; body-wise I was okay, but mentally I was a no-hoper. So there I was, blubbing into my coffee, when there was a knock at the door.I threw water on my face, opened the door and a young bloke was standing there. 'G'day, are you Robert Kydd?' he asked. 'Yes,' I replied, 'that's me.' 'Good, right bloke then. My name is Jeff Barns, I'm from the Southland Times, is it possible for you to give me an interview?' Instantly I thought, oh no, you can bugger off, but before I said anything he continued, 'I know you had amnesia, but we just want to do a welcome-home story, a sort of a warm fuzzy, that after all this time you are okay and home safe.' Well, I thought that wouldn't hurt, so I said, 'Okay mate, come in, do you want a coffee or a tea?' 'No thanks, just a few lines for the paper is all I want, and when you are in town next,' he grinned, 'I'll buy you a beer.' 'Okay so what do you want?' I said. 'Oh, just where you were, and your feelings on what it is like to "come back from the dead," as such. Would that be okay?' 'Yeah, fine.' So I talked about our trip and my mates who didn't come home, until I came to the official government version of me falling and hitting my head, and not knowing who I was until my memory came back a couple of years later. I explained I was shocked, I'd been away for so long and the sad part was that no one had twigged who I was. He walked out the door a happy bloke, with 'I owe you a beer'. I thought, I hope the Wellington suits think that's okay, but if they didn't, what the hell. It was in the newspaper a couple of days later, on the second page, under the heading, 'Back from the Dead.' A good piece of journalism, I'd say. In the meantime, with the okay from my parents, I'd been in contact with Shane and Sam's folks, and invited them all down to stay with us. They were over the moon to talk to me and of course wanted to know the full story about their boys. They were in tears on the phone, but promised to be down within a week and would be happy to stay with us all. So we'd put Shane's family with mum and dad, and Sam's parents, including his sister, at Sasha's. Since I'd been away, Sasha had brought a big old house in Bluff, which had plenty of room. I think she and Neil were talking about living together there sometime soon. Anyway, it had four bedrooms, so there would be plenty of room for seven friends to stay. I went over everything in my mind: I'll talk the story though, but this time I had all the photos on my laptop to show. There were a lot of images of all of us blokes, enough to make it more credible for them to see that the story was real. I'll connect my computer to the large TV in mum's lounge so it'll be like a power point presentation. Trouble was, every time I looked at the photos I got the shakes, and I'd bawl, so I wasn't really looking forward to the evening when I had to do it in front of everyone.

I moved back into my place about three days before the visit as I felt I'd rather be by myself again. I was starting to become a bit of a recluse. I spent my time out on my knoll and walked the beach, not looking for company and in general retreated into myself. I had no thoughts of the future, nothing. Sometimes I felt a bit numb from the neck up. So there I was again, looking at the photos, shaking like I was chilled to the bone with tears rolling down my face, when there was another knock on the door. Poop, I thought, I didn't want to see anyone, but the knocking was insistent. I got up, wiped my face with a towel and opened the door. My mouth dropped open, for there in all her beauty, was none other than Tui. I let out a yell, grabbed her and hugged her then cried into her hair. She didn't fight me, she just accepted it and hugged me back, as I kept saying, 'Tui, Tui.' I pulled back, my eyes unfocused through my tears. 'Where's Shane?' 'You are Robert Kydd, then?' she said with a worried frown. 'Of course I am, you know me; come on, Tui, stop kidding me.' Her reaction forced me to take step back, though it wasn't until I took a second look that I thought, oh heck! She looked just like Tui, even to the point of the small indenture in the lobe of her ear which I had just been slobbering over. Though she was much lighter in colouring, and I began to notice other small differences. Wow I had just made a complete arse of myself. I composed myself. 'You'd better come in,' I offered. She entered, and I shut the door and apologised, saying, 'You look so much like a really good friend I've lost, I'm so sorry. I haven't been well, and your looks took me by surprise.' She smiled, 'Yes, I'd read you haven't been well, no need to apologise.' She looked around my room, then her eyes came to the photo on the mantelpiece of Shane, Sam and me on a tramp, taken a year before we went up to Ruapehu. 'Who's that?' she asked. 'That's my mate Shane Langford, and the other bloke is my mate Sam McInnes,' I answered. 'He looks so like my dad. And my distant relation, Shane Lang,' she said. 'I'm Tui Lang, by the way.' I bloody near choked. 'What do you mean your relation?' I stammered. 'Look,' she said, 'this is weird for me, so let's get a coffee or something and I'll tell you my story.' So I got up and made her a coffee while she wandered about the room. She seemed completely at ease, but I sure as hell wasn't. She came and sat down at the table as I passed her a cup. Taking a couple of sips, she reached into her bag and took out a very old thick envelope... She looked at it before handing it to me and said, 'In my bag I also have a book wrapped in canvas. This letter and book have been handed down from my third-great-grandfather until now. He gave us this task through every generation with the oldest child having to pass this letter and book onto each new generation, until it could be handed to a Robert Kydd in Southland in 2014 or thereafter. You're the first we've found. It took longer than we expected, obviously, as it's now 2016. No one has ever opened either of them, it's been our family's duty for over one hundred and fifty years. My family has always scanned the newspapers daily and your name recently popped up in the Southland Times. I'm quite lucky as I live in Dunedin, so I was able to drive down, and here I am. Today our duty has come full circle. I have to admit I'm quite curious, it's been one hundred and fifty years of intrigue, so I hope you are going to put me out of my misery.'She continued after taking a breath. 'So how do you come into the picture, all these years later, and how did you know my name?' I looked at her and smiled. 'Because you are the spitting image of your third-great-grandmother, even to the dimple on your earlobe.' 'How the heck do you know that?' she gasped. 'Because Tui and Shane were my mates.' She looked at me as if I was mad. 'You've been quite sick, Mr. Kydd, amnesia and such, so I don't want to tax you. Just tell me the basics, and I'll be okay with that. I'm a charge nurse at Dunedin

Hospital, so I understand your situation. Just take your time. Relax.' I opened the envelope very gingerly, and read the first words.

Dunedin 1923
Dear Brill,
By the time you get this letter, I will have been gone close to a hundred years.

After reading those words I just blubbered, shaking like an old steam train. I dropped the letter on the table and stammered, 'I have to go for a walk, I don't mind you reading it.' I shot out the door and headed to my spot on the knoll, where I hugged my knees and swayed like a drunk, repeating Shane's name over in my head repeatedly. I must have been there for ages until Tui came out and joined me. She took my hands and said, 'Just take it easy, Mr. Kydd.' 'Robert,' I said, 'or Bob.' 'Okay, Bob, take big breaths and relax. I read the letter, and I don't really understand what it's saying. However, if you can read it yourself, you might find it to be a real healing path for you. Let's walk back and put the kettle on for a cuppa, and when you are ready, you can have another go.' Hell, she was so nice, and softly spoken to. She squeezed my hand and added, 'Come on, we both could do with another drink.' So I plodded reluctantly back inside, sat down and picked up the letter again, while Tui got the kettle going and found some bickies.
The letter continued.

Brill, mate, I'm so sorry I didn't get back to you. Things were against us right from the beginning. I didn't receive any mail from you until two years later. Everything went to the wrong address. Instead of the Thistle Hotel, it went to Thistle Street, and ended up at the Otago Club. How it happened, no one knows. I sent letters to you, but I found out four months later that the ship ran aground in the Wellington Heads with the loss of all the mail.

Then I had a letter returned to me, saying 'moved on, no forwarding address'. It was later that I thought you must be having a go at getting home. I tell you mate, I was devastated. What must you have been thinking of us?

While all this was going on, Tui had become pregnant with our first child and was quite sick for the first four months. I was very worried, but she came right. So all this made it difficult to stay focused on you; I'm so sorry. Eventually, mate, we went on to have eight children, eight kids, I love them all. Our first was Robert (guess who he was named after), our second boy was Samuel, then David, Tui, Mona, Carolyn, Elizabeth and Rita. All our kids did so well, I'm so proud of them, and I hope that whatever descendent who's showing you this letter has kept the tradition alive with a good education. All through our lives, the names have been handed down: the first boy always Robert or Sam, the first girl Tui. My Tui died a couple of years ago, and even though my family really look after me, mate, I'm tired, and I miss her so much. I'm ninety-three now, and I've had enough, I want to see Tui again.

We've been fortunate in our lives. We made contact with Stu's family and helped him get the shop on the gold fields up and running. I put all my wages from the army in and become a silent partner. I staked a claim. There was this bit of history that I remembered from school: after Gabriels Gully, a small find was found just past Lawrence. I staked it out and you would have been proud of me, I made enough to set us up for life. I worked the claim for a year and took nearly fifty thousand ounces from it, which made us millionaires. Luck, hard work and a bit of inside knowledge paid off. Eventually, I sold the claim and never went back digging again. We started up Lang's Engineering and made sure all our children had a good education, including the girls. That was a hard job, women were not encouraged to be educated, but our money fixed that. They become nurses, lawyers and Rita is a doctor. The boys became engineers and a geologist. Mate, I am so proud.

I buried my rifle at Larnach Castle. Our firm constructed the stables and under the cobblestone floor, six feet deep, that's where she lays. I was always frightened that someone would come across it.

The sim card just disappeared. I tried to find it, I looked everywhere, but as with my phone it died a natural death. So I'm pleased I gave you my camera's memory card with all the photos; I hope they came out okay. Once I relised that the ESK ended up in the UK, we were devastated.

I tell you, Brill, I never gave up looking for Sam. Tui and I went to the UK in 1900. We scoured the country but had no luck. The Esk arrived in Edinburgh about the end of June or July 1863. There was a mention from the army hospital that he was discharged into the care of his nurse, Bella Wrightson. According to the records, he was not fit to serve again, and also the documents mentioned he used to say some awfully strange things. One of the doctors reckoned he should have been put away in a lunatic asylum. A colonel, I found his notes later, vetoed this as he put it down to amnesia; his nurse suggested to the authorities that she would take him home to her family and help bring him back to full health. That is the last thing we heard on them. He was discharged with gratuities of one hundred pounds, which was still a tidy sum, and Sam and Bella just disappeared in a puff of smoke. I went to the town where she was supposed to have come from, but no one knew the name Wrightson. We tried for months, Brill. In the end, we had to admit defeat. All my life I have regretted it and no doubt you have too. I just hope he had a good life. I placed his army pay in a deposit box with the ANZ in Dunedin under your name; it should still be there in your time. I have a feeling those pound notes might be worth a bit in the future. The box number is 17664. I kept in touch with the bank right up to 1920, with a letter to say that you would be in sometime in the future to check it. Would you be able to send it on to his parents or his sister Mary?

We came back to New Zealand and spent the rest of our time in Dunedin. I was always worried about going north just in case I got too close or involved with my family up there. Tui and I did get back there at one point, to Te Awamutu, in the early stages of our marriage with a couple of the boys. I wanted to check up on Watene and his whanau; I tell you mate, the hospitality was embarrassing, and they wanted to make you a king; well, Watene did. By the way, he sported a limp for the rest of his life. His boys turned out to be great kids and fine men. Well, one was my second-great-grandfather; I had trouble believing in that. One went into politics after all the problems Māori had with the land. He was successful with the land courts. So mum's story did have an ending. I didn't think about it until we went back to catch up with Watene and his family, well, my family, really. Sometime later, over the years, I've thought about it and had to smile. We made history, us three. Both of you have been in my heart and on my mind all my life. I hope your life works out for you, my friend. Give my love to mum and dad, let them read this letter. Please pass on my love to Sam's folks and tell them we tried. Love to my sisters; always they were with me in my heart and their names lived on with my family. Love also to your parents and Sasha.

One last thing my friend, the bearer of this letter will be a direct descendant. To me I send my love and hope for their future. If it's a man, the name Robert or Sam, always a strong name to me; and if it is a woman, Tui, the blood of my wife will flow through her, making her a strong and dependable person to love. The book which goes with this letter is a diary. Please read it, make copies, but give it back to the deliverer, so they can read for themselves the story of their family. For you, it's months, for me a lifetime, but it feels like yesterday that we were pig hunting up north. You've been on my mind, mate, all of my life and I'll be waiting for you with my pack on and rifle in hand, just waiting for you to join up with Sam and me for the big tramp of our lives.

Your mate,
Shane.

Tears were rolling down my face. I read it again, then again. I had to go outside. I was completely buggered, and drained. How do I cope with this? It was final. Tui left me to sit on my knoll until the sun was setting. Then she came out once again, took my hand and said, 'Come on, Bobby, let's go inside. I made us dinner.' I followed her like a wee puppy; I needed someone to tell me what to do. Tui stayed with me that evening. I couldn't bear to be alone or to look at the book-come-diary. So I just went to bed thankful that I didn't have to think for the rest of the evening. I dropped off to sleep with Tui singing quietly as she cleaned up the kitchen.

CHAPTER TWENTY-SIX

I woke the next morning with the sun in my eyes. Tui came into my room and thrown open the curtains; it was a beautiful autumn morning. 'Come on Bob,' she said, 'time to get up, I'm making you brunch. It's eleven am, and you've slept for fourteen hours straight. Jump into the shower and I'll finish up the last part of the meal.' I was a bit bewildered, but I did as I was told. As I was coming out of the bathroom, she called, 'It's ready, come and get it.' I went into the kitchen. She had made a feast for a king, and I realised I was really hungry. I'd been neglecting myself food-wise, and she did her best to fill me to the gunnels. I looked at her, between shovelling bacon and eggs into my mouth, and thought she was a good-looking woman. She seemed to have a lot of Shane and Tui's traits, with Tui's good looks and the body strength of Shane. But of course, she also had a lot of other people's genes running through her body. As we ate we chatted about ourselves, I explained a little bit about my recent adventures, but didn't sound convincing, however, were amazed at how much we clicked. We both liked the bush and music; she played the piano and liked to sing. She also enjoyed history, and was looking forward to opening the diary; I didn't flinch at that, which was a good sign. She loved medicine too, that's why she became a nurse. I was interested in medicine myself, but wouldn't do it as a job; Rangiriri had been enough for me. She played netball, and was even good enough to have tried out for the Southern Sting netball team. She had applied for a job as a senior nurse at the hospital here in Invercargill and was waiting for a reply. If she got it, she would move down to Invers in a month and play goal attack for the Sting. She told me she was twenty-eight, born in Hamilton, went to university at Victoria in Wellington and at the moment lived in Dunedin. She had two siblings, Carol and Lizzy, both younger. She wasn't up with the play about her third-great-grandparents as her family had moved north years ago. She had a lot of cousins in the South Island though, so she felt right at home down here. She did know that her third-great-grandfather was a man of vision and wealth, making his money on the gold fields of Otago. His legacy had come through the generations, but what I had spoken about, and the letter, was all new to her, and it gave her a real insight into his life. 'I can only thank you, Bob, for letting me share it with you. You don't have to do it on your own, you know, I'm here and can help you, we can give each other support.' She asked if I had thought about what I was going to do, and I looked at her with a vague expression. 'Oh, don't you worry,' she murmured, 'early days yet, as you get better, you will decide. I'm sure you can put your mind to anything.'

Finally, we sat on the couch together, and I picked up the diary. Tui put her arm in mine, nestled into my shoulder. 'This is nice, how are you feeling?' I turned to her and looked into those big dark eyes smiling at me. 'I'm fine,' I said, 'as long as you're here.' I opened the diary, and some photos fell out. They were old glass-framed ones taken in the late-nineteenth century of Shane and Tui, with various combinations of their first four children. Tui remarked, 'This looks like the oldest photo, it's looks as though it was taken while Tui was still quite young and very pregnant. My god, it's like looking at a mirror of when I was eighteen.' 'Well, that's how old she was,' I said looking at the picture. 'God, she was lovely, just like you,' I murmured. Tui looked at me and said, 'Thank you for that. That's the nicest thing anyone has ever said to me outside of my family, I really mean it,' then she kissed me. Oh hell I couldn't believe it, it was bliss; I didn't want her to stop. When we parted, I admitted, 'I had a real soft spot for Tui.' I smiled. 'I sure envied Shane, she was a lovely lady, and it seems to run through the family.' We took our time reading the diary together, and by the time we looked up, the day had gone. I announced, 'I better give my parents the heads-up that I'm feeling okay.' I really did feel better at last, not a tear or a shake all day. I rang mum to tell her I was fine, and that I'd be there to meet and greet my mates' parents when they arrive on Friday. I told her I just wanted these last couple of days to myself, and that I was feeling really good. 'Oh, that's wonderful Bobby,' she sighed, 'we were getting quite worried about you.' 'I'll see you at the airport at three pm on Friday then.' I never mentioned Tui.

We both got up and started to prepare dinner. I found a bottle of wine and said with a grin, 'We have to celebrate today. For the first time in a while, I didn't break down.

I believe you are my guardian angel.' After dinner we did the dishes and sat together again on the couch. We listened to some easy music, it has been a long time since I was so relaxed and content. Tui had said she had a week off, so it was cool that she didn't have to rush away. It seemed natural to ask her to come along on Saturday evening to mum's place. 'When everyone's there, after I've told the story and shown the pictures, you would be the icing on the cake since you look so much like your ancestor. Furthermore, you'll get to meet your third-great-grandfather's parents; I know that sounds really weird. I think you could call them your grandparents, but it fact they are your fourth-great-grandparents and no one has ever had that privilege before. I don't think that'll upset Mona; you'll be her link to Shane, you and your family. You'll be put on a pedestal I'm sure, but also you'll get to meet Shane's sisters, and they're really nice.' She answered, 'You don't think it'll be a bit much for them to meet me, at the same time as finding out what really happened to Shane?' 'No,' I replied, 'I believe it'll be shock for them, but to see you, his descendant, their blood, they will be ecstatic. You must remember that they've thought he was dead for the last few years, which I suppose he technically is, anyway, but to hear he has family, they'll be thrilled.' 'It's a bit unnerving Bob,' she said, 'but to have another set of grandparents would be wonderful, and I'd love to meet them.' 'You won't be able to hold Mona back, Tui. She'll make a beeline to Hamilton on her way home, so she can meet your mum and dad as long-lost children, so be prepared,' I laughed. 'The only people I'm anxious about are Sam's parents and Mary. They've nothing to hope for now. I feel gutted. Reading between the lines with that army report, Sam must have come out with all sorts of modern words and such like, and they thought he was nuts because of it. I hope the nurse was good to him; we can only hope. I went off to bed feeling really quite good, more content than in a long time, maybe even happy. Just as I was dropping off to sleep, the bedroom door opened and Tui snuck into my room to slip into bed beside me. She nestled into me like a glove. 'I think, Bobby, that it's time for you to be loved. I think it's been missing in your life, and it's has been a long time for both of us.' The next morning when I woke, we lay looking at each other. She smiled and said, 'Bob, you're a very lucky man to have me. You know I wouldn't mind making this my base if the job is offered to me. Let's face it, I'm a one-woman man, and I think you're that man.' 'Oh hell, Tui,' I blurted out. 'We've only known each other for a few days, but I feel as though it's been forever.' 'Well,' she grinned, 'it took Shane one day, you're a bit slow.' We laughed and giggled like teenagers, but boy did I feel good.

The week slipped by quickly. Tui and I arranged that she would turn up late on Saturday, giving me enough time to tell the story, to show the photos and let them read Shane's letter and diary. Friday arrived, and I went to the airport to join the folks; we took all of our cars as we had to pick up seven passengers. Mum and Dad recognised the change in me from the last few days and commented, 'You're looking like your old self, Bob, and we think being back in your own home has really helped.' 'Yeah, Mum, I'm feeling really good now and much stronger.' When my mates' families came through into the arrival's area and saw me, there were hugs and tears from them all. It was exactly the same as when I had arrived home myself last week. We drove them all over to mum and dad's place, settled them down and gave them a cuppa. 'The story I have to tell you is going to take a long time,' I explained. 'After that, I have photos to show you. Something special happened to me this week, which I'll be able to tell you all about as well. It'll take me a couple of hours to set everything up, but tomorrow we'll meet up here for lunch, and I'll spend the afternoon telling you the story of what happen back in 2014. The story that you have from the suit-police from Wellington is lacking in substance and not really correct. So will you bear with me tonight, and wait until tomorrow, if that okay with you all? I want you all to hear it together, not piecemeal.' Everyone agreed. There were a few comments on my limp. 'Yeah,' I said, 'no more rugby for me.' So after an early tea, and lots of 'you're looking well's and 'two years is a long time to be lost to us all', I said goodnight. With a 'see you all midday tomorrow', I was off. I wanted to be near Tui, who was home waiting for me, worrying about how it all went. I burst in the door, and she looked up with a smile. 'I feel great.' I grinned, 'Oh, there were a few tears of pleasure to see them all, but no breaking down and no shakes.' She came over and kissed me. 'I'm incredibly proud of you,' she said, smiling softly at me as she took my hand, and we settled in for the night.

The next morning I was up singing as I got dressed. 'Don't forget Tui, about nine pm, you have the folks' address, and I'll see you then.' 'Are we going to tell your parents, Bobby?' 'Yeah, we should, I don't want to muck around. You okay with that?' 'Oh yes, but we'll have to head north afterwards, to my place.' 'Not a problem, any family of Shane's is my family, or soon will be,' I grinned. Jumping into the Surf, I drove slowly to my parents' home. I had this silly grin on my face, my heart soared; man I was happy, life was sure worth living. Everything had changed in such a short time, and I had Tui to thank for that. I arrived at the folks' place and got to work setting up the computer, making sure that everything would work okay. I had the letter and the diary close to me, in a bag out of sight. There was a ring on the door at midday, and everyone entered with expectation written all over their faces. I kissed all the girls and shook hands with the blokes. Mum brought out a snack lunch, and everyone sat down, with food on their laps, in anticipation. I pulled the curtains so the TV was at its best for seeing photos, and started my story of three mates on a pig shooting trip up north.

Firstly, I asked them if they refrained from questions until the end, so I could keep the story flowing. I told it, warts and all; it took quite a while and at the end, I said, 'I know that you might think that this is far-fetched, but I have proof to show you.' I turned on the computer and started showing the photos. When we got to the pictures of us emerging in 1863, the first of the tears started to roll. In these photos, we saw Sam standing over Bill after Shane had knocked him out, before our first stop in Pukekawa. Then there was another of Watene and his whanau; all the time I was pointing out the relations. It was the same with my folks when we came to Bill, then also Sam's folks with Stu. Looking at them, you could see the resemblance to our families. When they saw the wedding photos, Mona, David and Shane's sisters just cried. It was all there: the funeral at Otahuhu, the fighting at Rangiriri; how the hell I took them I can't even remember, but I was always sneaking off so I must have; as they were there on the sim card. I even took snaps during the fires. There were also photos of Shane walking onto the boat as they left for Dunedin. I told his family that this was the last time I saw him. The last one was a selfie from when I was in the cave, looking like, as the cop said, a hobo on crack. After I finished, I passed out the USB sticks to everyone, including my parents. Of course, there were questions, they went on for ages, but in the end we all sat quietly, thinking about the boys. There was another thing I needed to talk about. I turned to Sam's parents. 'There is one thing I want to say. If it is in my power, I'll not give up looking for Sam. I know now that he's gone. But as a mate, I need to try to find him, for myself and especially you. I promise you I will do my best.' Mary came over and hugged me. 'Bob, you've been a good mate to both our boys. I would love to know what happened to our son, but I don't want you messing up your life with guilt because you can't fulfil a promise. Try by all means, but if you fail, we can only pray that our Sam had a wonderful life.' She kissed me and turned to sit down. 'There are a couple of things I need to show you now,' I said. I took out the letter, 'It arrived this week. I think I should let Mona read it aloud, or shall I just pass it around? There were nods that yes, Mona should do it. She picked up the letter and started to read it to everyone, until her lip started to tremble. David gently took it from her and carried on until he passed it on to Elizabeth, and then to Carolyn, who finished it. 'I can't believe it, I've heard of the Lang's,' David was saying, 'who didn't. My god, it was Shane's family, our family. They have a big plot in the main cemetery, that's where he'll be.' More tears flowed. 'Then lastly, there's this.' I handed the diary to Mona. 'There are photos in there of the family, and this is his diary up until 1922. I'll copy that for you before you go home.' It also did the rounds, with everyone having a quick squizz then the doorbell rang. 'I'll get it, Mum,' I called as I rushed to the door. Tui was there with her lovely smile. 'How did it go, Bobby?' she asked. 'Good. Tears, of course, and I think there will be even more now with you here.' We walked back into the lounge holding hands and everyone looked up as I said, 'Mona, David, this is Tui. She's a descendant of Shane and Tui.' Bugger me, Mona came off the couch as if someone had thrown a cracker at her. She swooped onto Tui like a maniac, and Tui hugged her right back. Both women were crying, then David joined in, then the sisters and everyone was crying and laughing and crying again. After the bedlam settled, Tui said, 'You're my new grandparents.' 'The resemblance to your third-great-grandmother in the photos is uncanny,' Mona observed, stepping back from

Tui. 'I can vouch for that,' I said. Of course, they wanted to know how she happened to be here, so that story did the rounds until I announced the bombshell. 'Oh, Mum and Dad, Sasha. Tui and I are getting married.' 'Well, that's another revelation, when did that happen?' Mum was astounded. She thought about it for another moment. 'But you've only known each other a little while.' 'Yeah, I know, Mum, but it only took Shane a day, and I fell for this woman one hundred and fifty years ago; I'm not going to let her go again. Shane was my mate and Tui was his wife, but I think deep down I loved her like Shane loved her. Now I have another chance. The only difference is, though,' I quipped, looking at Tui, 'is that my Tui wears shoes.' That drew a few laughs from everyone there.

From then on my life changed. We all went up to Dunedin to Shane's family plot. That brought back the tears, but it helped with closure. Then we headed on up to the North Island, to Hamilton, to meet Tui's folks. My god, her father had Shane's looks; maybe not his size, but his features were pretty close. He was the second son: his name was Sam and his wife's name was Barbara. Mona was just over the moon. She had lost a son, but gained so many family members from all around New Zealand, and would have years of catching up ahead of her. My folks were amazing; they fell right into the big family thing, considering our family was quite small, we will have a really large extended family after our wedding. Tui and I were married in March. My mate Sam's wee sister Mary was our flower girl, Tui's sisters were bridesmaids, and I had a real job of trying to think who would be my best man. My mates were gone. In the end, I asked my brother-in-law-to-be, Sasha' fiancé Neil, to do the honours. We'd got on well after Sasha had introduced us and it kept everything in the family. We married in the Waikato, in the small church at Pukekawa where it all started. All the families of Shane's and Tui descendants turned up, and for the small church it was a big wedding. We had a hangi for the wedding breakfast; it was quite a day to remember.

Tui and I settled back in Invercargill, and she was appointed charge nurse at the hospital. I used the money the government gave me to go into a silent partnership, with Dad, Mum, Sasha and Neil on the fishing fleet. Then I went to SIT – Southern Institute of Technology – where I finished my degree in history. As they have zero fees, there was no cost to us, and it was much easier for us to live off Tui's income than if I had gone elsewhere. After three years, including a year at teacher's college, I graduated, and secured a job with Southland Boys High as a history teacher and rugby coach. During the years of study, we had two children, and Tui was given maternity leave. Things were a bit tight, but we got through. Regardless of everything else going on though, I kept coming back to Sam. What the heck happened to him? It was always in the back of my mind niggling away.

It was four years later, when I was cleaning out my old wooden junk box, and I came across all that old 1863 money that the army had paid me. It amounted to forty pounds in one-pound notes and sovereigns; there was about half of each. I wondered if they were worth anything. I had a friend who knew a coin collector in Dunedin, so one fine day in the school holidays, I took the family up there to have the money appraised. We walked into a surprisingly large shop with show cases on every wall. The owner was waiting for us, as I had rung him about my collection. Well, when I brought out the notes and coins, he just about wet himself. He had his magnifying glass out, I could even see his hand shaking a bit, and a line of sweat formed on his top lip. My god, he kept saying. He rushed away to grab some books. It eventuated that each note we had was worth about twenty thousand dollars or more; the better ones were worth about fifty thousand each. The sovereigns were eight hundred to a thousand dollars each. So the collection we had could be worth about half a million dollars. Tui and I had to sit down for a minute to digest what he told us. Then I remembered. Shane had given me the code for a deposit box with the ANZ in Dunedin. There would be more of this money there, and I'm sure it would have the same sort of value. I mentioned it to the owner, and he was so excited. So before we went back home, we took a trip to the bank. Sure enough, the notes, which were in much better condition than ours, were valued at a couple of hundred thousand more than what we got. I was more than happy with the outcome. When we called in on the way home to tell Sam's parents, they couldn't believe it. We decided to leave the money with the bloke in the shop; he had collectors all over the world and would get a better price for them that way. Eventually, we received six hundred thousand dollars after his commission. Sam's parents received eight hundred thousand. It wasn't much compensation for losing a son, but it gave his sister a good start in her life. We invested some of the money into an account for our children's education. Then it dawned on me: I now had the money to try to find Sam. Oh, of course it wasn't going to cost that sum, but it was enough to let me take a year off work and devote time to the task. I talked it over with Tui, and finally she said, 'Bobby, it's something you need to do. You need closure on this.' So I rang Sam's parents and told them what I was on my mind, and that I was going to have a go to see if I could track him down. 'I don't know if I will find him, but I will give it my best shot. I'll not leave a stone unturned.' I looked at a photo I had of Sam with his big smile, and it brought back all those memories. 'I'm coming Sam,' I muttered, 'I'll find you if I can. Hang in there mate, your story's not finished yet.'

EPILOGUE

The digger scraped deep into the hole that was created for the foundations of the new forty- story hotel. It was being built on the original site of the first ANZ bank in Queen Street, Auckland. As it scraped away a scoop of dirt, the bucket rasped against something solid: some broken bricks, that had partially come away with the last scoop were piled in the bucket. The digger driver jumped out and peered into the hole, he could making out a vault-like construction embedded in the brickwork. So he called his boss over to take a look, who then rang the museum and an archaeologist arrived to remove the remains of the vault. It took all day, but eventually they came away with the contents.

Back in a safe environment, in the Department of Archaeology at the Auckland University, they revealed the time capsule. It had varied papers and coins plus the name of all the staff who had worked at the ANZ bank in 1863. The most unusual thing though was a container that, when opened, had a note asking for the three letters in the box to be sent to various addresses in 2014. Included was a current fifty-dollar note, which was to be used to pay for

the postage. All the addresses were correct, and the people
on the envelopes were very much alive and well. The paper
and the envelopes had all been dated back to the early
1860s. It had the department scratching their heads.

As it tends to happen with these things, the press got on
to it, and it was soon all over the papers and TV before the
government could put a stop to it. Finally, however, the
envelopes were each delivered to a Mr. and Mrs. Langford
of Kaitaia, a Mr. and Mrs. McInnes of Dunedin, and a
Mr. and Mrs. Kydd of Invercargill.

I found out when mum rang me to say she had received my
letter and will from 1863. I was delighted it had worked;
it was a bit late, but better late than never. We decided to
go on holiday to get out of the limelight. Eventually, the
press got fed up with not getting any answers and accepted
that they were private letters to the writers' descendants.
But that fifty-dollar note was the talking point for years to
come, and how did they know the future addresses of their
descendants? So another page of the story had turned and
this also gave me more of an incentive to try to find Sam.
I'm not sure how long it will take, or where it will take me,
but I'm going to give it my best shot.

www.ingramcontent.com/pod-product-compliance
Lightning Source LLC
Chambersburg PA
CBHW030813110726
47900CB00006B/1603